WHEN KINGS CLASH

WHEN KINGS CLASH

The War of Whispers
Volume III

J.E. Lowder

WordCrafts

Dedicated to my wife and children,
my grandson who inspired a character,
Ben H. for bringing my map to life,
and to all the readers who have cheered me onward.
I couldn't have finished without you.

04-12-15

Troubling Tale

Mothers, guard babes; *Fathers, draw steel,*
Thunder approaches, soon blood on the fields.
Tempest of war, so black and so vile,
Spreads o'er Allsbruth; lament suckling child.

Orphaned stories, treasures from Claire,
Like buried embers, burst forth and flare.
Hear not a whisper, sweet lark on the wing?
Tales shall crush steel when gors have a king.

Whisps of white, forever snow swirl,
Rays of crimson protect pallid girl,
Waltz of Claire lilting like lace,
Breathe delight o'er sweet child's face.

What was is now past, what loss no more,
As phantom rides winds that morn for the gor.
Tulips shall bloom despite ice so deep,
Fair daughter do dance, for we no longer weep.

ISLE OF
Claire
NETNIATH
VORAK
CAVE OF FREERS
KISE
THORNNBLEN
Ebon
Cliffs of Claire
Forrest of Ebon
NORRBURN
MARRH
DIOBATH
BLOMSETH
Field of Reeds
GILDEN
Th
The Ebon Plains
HALL OF THE GOR KING
The River Arrgier
Mountains of Kline
River Effrim
WAELRYTH
River
Allsbruthian
ONDERLING
Valley of Clouds
TELLENDALE
Mountains
Le
Allsbruth
MERRINOON
HETHERLINN
T
N
W
E
S

RHYTHE
Gilden Sea
BAL-MALIN
DRAIGLORE
Addoli Ridge
Pillar at Addoli
HOLMAN
Tristan
HAPSTON
The Gilden Plains
MIN BROCK
Ingloid
LELLE
DALLIN
River Dill
le
Ferra
GILNISH
HOITT
ORREN'S BAY
MOLDEEN
SOUTHSBROOK
THE ISLE OF LILLS
Sea of Illsbruth

Chapter 1

Blue Skin

Three Wurmlins darted through the forest, shadows of stealth hunting their prey. The trio ran on tiptoes, as was customary to avoid snapping twigs or rustling too many leaves, and were dressed in typical Wurmlin garb: mottled colors of olive, gray and brown to blend with the foliage, layered to provide protection from heat, rain and wind.

Even their labored breaths were muffled, a trick all three learned at an early age. Their tribe used games of hide-and-go-seek to sharpen their abilities to hunt without making a sound. Thick, restrictive cloaks were worn while running to train lungs to breathe short, quiet gulps, and after the event, the child who was able to best control his breathing was rewarded with a trinket.

The leader of the Wurmlin trio, a man of forty summers, reached the top of the incline and held up a clinched fist. The other two, boys of sixteen and thirteen summers, froze in place several steps behind. Without turning to address them, the elder shot his index finger up and tapped his head three times.

Stay. I'll scout, he signaled.

He unsheathed his dagger and disappeared down the hill.

The two boys exchanged glances. Faces, masked with grime from living outdoors, surrounded large, round eyes. Long, black hair, disheveled and filthy, fell to their shoulders, a few strands matted to their foreheads by sweat and grease.

"I don't like this," the youngest whispered.

"Don't matter whatcha like, Mälque," the elder hissed back. "We gotta live."

"I know," Mälque sighed with a slow nod as he watched their leader head into the shadows. "Still don't mean I gotta like it."

He paused then asked, "Vonn, do you like what we're doin'?"

"Olke is the best there is, little brother. Soon, we'll be the best thieves ever known. *That's* what I like."

Mälque flashed a smile. White teeth, surrounded by leathery flesh, glistened. "Yeah, I like that part. But sure miss our folks. Olke treats us like dogs."

Vonn's eyes narrowed and he nodded. "Life's never been the same since that night."

"Hard to believe it was four summers ago. Feels more like ten."

They stared in the direction Olke disappeared and reflected on that fateful night...

"Vonn, Mälque, wake up," their mother whispered as she jostled them from their sleep.

The boys, recognizing her voice, rolled over and opened sleepy eyes. Their mother stared at them with a wild look, her face aglow with bluish light from a MerriNoon firestick clutched in her hand. Despite its brightness, it was cool to the touch until heaved onto a stack of wood where it would spark with fire.

Mälque opened his mouth to ask a question and she clapped it shut with her free hand.

"Hush up. Listen. It's your father. Somethin's happened to him. Somethin' bad. Now get up. I need your help, but be quiet. Don't need anyone followin' us."

As the boys rose, she fired off more instructions. "Vonn, grab a shovel. Mälque, bring an extra firestick. Hurry."

She spun on her heel and disappeared into the gloom.

They snickered.

"Here we go again," Vonn mumbled as he searched for a shovel.

"Yeah," Mälque huffed as he reached for their stash of firesticks. Like everything they possessed, these were acquired from thievery. "When is she gonna quit?"

When they were little, she took them on walks in the woods and pointed out what she ascribed were omens: A fresh pile of gor dung was a sign that death would visit their tribe; a white stag - rare indeed - prophesized that a chieftain would be born; a hawk feather was a portent that great fortune would come their way.

As they matured, they noted that more times than not, the grand events the omens foretold never occurred. Vonn found a hawk feather but riches never followed. Death often visited their tribe, with or without dung sightings. When Vonn and Mälque pressed her for an explanation, she reinterpreted the portents in light of a new day. They accepted her explanations faithfully until the day she heard whispers, voices from the dead. From that moment on, they dismissed her beliefs as Superstitious nonsense.

They grabbed their tools and caught up with her.

The bluish light from the two firesticks burned a hole in the dark. Despite Vonn and Mälque's skepticism in their mother's beliefs, the shadows still sent shivers through them. They pressed close to her side.

"Your father came to me...in a dream." She shoved the firestick this way and that. "All I could see was his face."

The boys snickered. Tonight, like all the others, was just another exercise in craziness.

"He was ghostly pale. Said we was to bury him so he wouldn't wander these woods forever."

She led them up a hill and they continued to laugh.

"Then the vision opened up, like someone takin' a sheet off a corpse, and I could see everythin'."

At the summit, she stopped and held her firestick overhead. Mälque copied her.

Two dead bodies lay in the ravine.

The boys gasped. Mälque fumbled his firestick and Vonn dropped his shovel. As Wurmlins, they'd seen their share of dead bodies, but nothing prepared them for this. Arms jutted skyward, frozen in place; fingers hooked as if digging to escape, but from what they could only wonder.

"Ain't laughin' now, are you?"

They took in her expression. The bluish light from the firesticks made her already wild eyes pulse. A faint smile twitched at the corners of her mouth as if discovering morbid bodies at night was commonplace.

"Still think your mom's crazy?"

Young heads wagged as they focused once again on the corpses.

"Now pick up that shovel and come on."

She led them downhill with long strides and stopped beside the bodies.

"Look," Vonn half-whispered from around her side. "Their skin's blue!"

Mälque stuck out his firestick for a better look. Despite the men's grimy faces and hands, a bluish tint could be seen. But it was their twisted arms jutting straight up, their gnarled fingers reaching for the unknown, and their legs lying every which a way that made his skin crawl.

"Why are they all twisted up like that?"

"Hush up!" She lowered her light to the bodies to identify them. "I recognize these two. They were part of your father's pack. But where's he?"

She swept her firestick searching for any sign of her husband's body. "He aint' here," she mumbled to herself. "But I already knew that, 'cause I had the dream." And then to the boys: "I sense he's close by. He's already walkin' the woods as a spirit...whisperin'. Ya hear him?"

She pushed her face close to Vonn and Mälque. The glow from the firestick cut deep shadows into her face making her feral eyes all the more terrifying. They leaned away from her. "Can you boys feel him; hear him," she asked, eager for them to join her on her supernatural journey. "Gotta believe. Gotta listen."

Unable or unwilling to connect with their father's ghost, they shook their heads, spooked by the night's portents as well as her expression.

"Don't ya worry," she offered with a half-smile. "One day, you'll hear whispers too. I promise. Now come on."

She spun away and resumed her quick gait deeper into the woods. When they skirted around a huge tree, Vonn and Mälque froze in place.

They found another body.

His lower portion - from his waistline down to his boots - stood erect, as if awaiting their arrival, while his upper half lay nearby.

Their mother approached the upper torso lying in the leaves, not the least bit distraught by the macabre scene.

"It's just like I dreamed," she mumbled, more to herself than to her sons. "But what sorta monster kills like this?"

She knelt for a better look and thrust her firestick close to identify the face. A death mask of blue skin surrounded glossed over eyes; mouth - agape with leaves stuck to pale lips - locked in what undoubtedly was his last scream. "Yep, that's him."

Vonn dropped his shovel and turned to throw up.

Mälque buckled to the ground and also puked. When their convulsions ended, they wiped mouths with their sleeves. Vonn retrieved his shovel and offered Mälque his hand.

"Look at her," Mälque whispered as he was pulled to his feet. "Not a tear or even a scream."

"I know. This ain't right."

She rose and made her way to the erect half and sized it up like they'd seen her do a slab of meat at the market. She ran her hand back and forth over the torso's top as if to make sure it wasn't a mirage.

"Cut clean in two," she half-marveled as she continued sweeping her hand back and forth, "and ain't a drop of blood no where. But how?"

She jerked her hand away as if stung by a wasp and hopped away from the corpse.

"Boys, come here!" Fear was in her voice as she waved them over. "Hurry."

Her tone told them they were in danger, so they ran to her side.

Mälque eyed his father's corpse but when the bile returned, focused instead on his mother's face. Her twitching smile was gone, replaced by taut lips stretched across yellowed teeth; her eyes were narrow slits that searched for danger.

"What's wrong," he asked.

"Shh!" She backed them away, her firestick darting this way and that, probing the darkness - for what, the boys could only wonder.

When she felt they were far enough away from the grisly scene, she knelt and took in their confused looks. "You boys listen, and listen good."

They could hear the fear in her voice; smell it on her sweat.

"You don't tell no one what you just saw, you hear?" She shook them to make sure they understood.

Vonn nodded.

Mälque squinted at her in confusion.

She zeroed in on her youngest son. "No one, Mälque. No one."

"But who cut him in..."

She covered his mouth with her hand.

"Ain't seen this kinda thing since the Dark War." She paused to make sure he would be quiet.

"Boys, listen to me." She released her hold on Malque. "An Awakenin' has occurred. Dangerous creatures you've never seen before prowl about, or make their dens in dead trees. Those are called fea dracas - tiny dragons that'll swarm and eat ya alive. Never go near trees like that, I don't care how brave ya feel. Understand me?"

They nodded. She continued.

"Stay sharp. Whatever killed your dad is still out there." She eyed the darkness surrounding them. "These woods are cursed. *Cursed.*"

She turned her attention back to her sons. "You'll hear whispers, and I ain't talkin' about voices from the grave, neither. They might come from Claire or Ebon. Sweet as songbirds. Might even sound the same, promisin' this or that. Ignore them. Stay true to the whispers in your head."

She tapped their foreheads to make her point.

"You're gonna see things ya never seen before, too. Crazy things. Don't pay them no mind neither."

Her eyes narrowed, she pressed closer, her nose touching theirs, hot breath vaporizing before their eyes. "'Cause chances are...' Her eyes darted left then right to make sure they were still alone. Zeroing in on their wide-eyed expressions again, she finished. "Storytellers from Claire are on the prowl."

The boys gasped, well versed by their mother on the horrors she ascribed to the tellers of tales.

"Conniving men and women." Yellowed teeth were gritted now, words sharpened by painful memories cut open the night's stillness. "Magic herbs that can ease pain and heal, or kill. Stories that can open the ground like a grave or," she wet her lips, "make ya wish ya was dead."

She wiped the snot running from her nose as if to clear the memories of the past. "No matter what happens to me, you two stay together. Don't trust *no one*. Not even other Wurmlins." Softer still. "Especially other Wurmlins."

She snapped her head away, either spooked by something nearby or merely checking their surroundings. Convinced they were still safe and alone, she looked back into their frightened faces.

"Now help me bury 'em. Don't need our tribe knowin' about the Awakenin'. Not yet, anyways."

She marched to her husband's body but the boys didn't follow.

Vonn and Mälque exchanged worried glances.

"Boys!" She flashed them a hot look and waved them on.

They swallowed the bile rising into their throats and crept forward, the only sound coming from Vonn's shovel that he dragged through the dead leaves.

✠

Olke caught the scent of burnt wood. It was faint, barely noticeable, and most people - whether Allsbruthian or even Ebonite - would have missed such a clue. But he was a Wurmlin, a nomadic thief who read the woods, the winds and the streams for the slightest of signs and clues leading to their victims' whereabouts. Like wolves, Wurmlins could follow a scent for days.

Energized that he was closing in on their target - the village of Tellendale - he increased his pace. When the trees thinned, he hid behind a fat hickory tree and surveyed what lay ahead.

Beyond a grove of saplings sat Tellendale, or what was left of it.

Mounds of white and gray ash sat where cottages, shanties and barns had been. Littering the ground were dead bodies that he assumed were the villagers. Aside from a large bird pecking a corpse, the village was void of life.

Without taking his eyes off the grisly scene, he cupped his hands together, brought them to his mouth and blew through the opening. He fluttered several fingers to create an owl-like sound. In a flash, the boys were by his side.

"Look at 'em," Olke half-whispered as he slapped Vonn's shoulder. "Ripe for the pickin'. Time to go to work, boys."

With a final glance about the clearing, and a sniff of the wind to make sure that whoever destroyed Tellendale was gone, Olke rose and strutted out into the clearing. Long, dark hair swayed in time to his bold stride, and when a strand fell across his face, he whipped his head to set it free. Broad, determined steps brought him to the closest body where he knelt with dagger in hand and prepared to go to work. He glanced back at the brothers who were lollygagging toward the bodies. Olke snarled his lips and squinted at them.

"Get a move on," he barked. "Who knows how much time we got."

Mälque reached him first. As instructed from previous undertakings, he assumed his position near the body. Disgusted by the mutilated flesh, the tunic stained black with blood and death's sick scent permeating the air, he turned away. "I hate this work. Too much dyin' everywhere," he blurted over his shoulder. "I wanna do honest Wurmlin work, like stealin' or robbin' or cheatin'." Bile rose into his throat. It was all he could do not to throw up.

"Sure ya do," Olke countered with a snort as he patted the dead man's pockets with the flat side of his dagger. "But that's 'cause you're young, and like most *yung-ers,* you're just plain stupid."

Mälque glared at Olke. He hated the word. Although it was what Wurmlins used to describe boys of his age, Olke used it like a cuss word.

Vonn, unfazed by the gore, plopped down beside Olke who backhanded the boy. "Next time, don't be late. Now help me find the treasure this dead fool's tryin' to take to the grave."

As he tapped the man's last pocket, the blade struck something hard. He hit again, producing a muted thud. "You know what that sound means, don'tcha?"

Vonn knew the only answer that would spare him from being whacked again was to do his job. With tongue poking out of the side of his mouth, he slid his fingers into the blood-soaked garment.

"Well," Olke asked, impatient with his progress.

"Hold on," Vonn answered while swishing his tongue from side to side as fingers probed the sticky pocket. "There's too much blood."

Olke was about to punch him when the boy yanked his hand free and held up the prize for all to see.

A collective gasp rose from all three. Clutched between Vonn's bloody fingers was a coin, stained with crimson.

"There you are," Olke sang to the coin, his voice sultry and smooth, as if addressing a lover. "Come to me." He stretched his hand toward the money. Vonn dropped it into his palm.

"A golden giln," Olke gushed as he held it up to the light of day between thumb and forefinger.

Stained with blood, it was a shocking reminder of the manner in which they found it as well as its owner's horrible demise. Yet all three were oblivious to such calamity and instead, gawked in awe at the coin. It promised better days ahead.

"Here, yung-er." Olke flipped it into the air. "Make 'er shine."

Mälque, who had anticipated such an action, had already removed a cloth from his pocket. With eyes riveted on the end-over-end flight of the giln, he caught the coin in the cloth and started wiping the blood off. In no time, the gold glistened; sunlight danced across its surface.

"So, boy," Olke asked as he pushed himself up from the ground, "what were you sayin' about an honest trade?"

Mälque shrugged off the question and stared at the coin he twirled between his fingers. Maybe Olke was right. The giln meant hot meals and warm beds in a tavern, a far better life than chewing on rabbit gristle and sleeping in the open, using leaves as a blanket.

Olke held out his palm.

Mälque smirked, and for a brief moment, thought about pocketing the giln and dashing off for the woods. After all, thievery was in his blood, even if it meant robbing another Wurmlin. But when he felt the prick of a dagger through his tunic, and caught Olke's evil expression, he thought better of his idea. With a heavy sigh and a parting glance at the giln, he surrendered the coin.

"Thata boy," Olke said as he withdrew his dagger. He flashed the boy a wry smile. "Never rob a robber, I always say."

He pocketed the coin and led them to the next corpse. They dropped the banter and went back to work robbing the dead.

Mälque, while awaiting more loot to clean, scanned the surrounding woods. "So you're certain that crazy man and his gors won't come back to eat us," he asked, his voice cracking ever so slightly as his imagination conjured gors devouring people…alive.

As a Wurmlin, he had been trained to the traits of every animal in the woods. Gors were scavengers who feared men and prowled in small packs. That description changed three summers ago when men from their tribe witnessed a village being mauled by the beasts. A baldheaded man mounted atop a massive bull led the slaughter. His assembled gors - a mystery unto itself - were an army of ravaging predators. Jaws snapped arms or legs clean off while paws swatted bodies this way and that with ease. When Mälque asked what had caused the shift in the gors' disposition, the Wurmlins hushed him with a swat to the head, or wagged their heads and mumbled to themselves.

But he knew the answer. His mother had forewarned about such sightings the summer before.

The Awakenin'.

"Yep, that crazy fool is long gone," Olke answered, snapping Mälque from his reflection. Olke continued to swat the corpse up and down, listening for the *thud* or *clink* of loot or jewelry. "We been followin' them now for…" he stopped tapping and scrunched up his lips to calculate the amount of time. Unable to do simple mathematics, and not about to let the boys belittle him for such ignorance, he dismissed the problem with a loud huff and blurted, "…a long time…a very long time."

"Do we always have to steal like this," Vonn asked in a dull voice. "It ain't excitin'."

Olke stopped, leaned back and gave them both a stern look. "You want *excitement.*"

"Yeah," Vonn answered with a glint in his eye. "We're Wurmlins, ain't we? This ain't stealin'."

Olke folded his arms across his large chest and cocked his head. A greasy lock fell over his face, which he cleared with a violent shake of his head. "Well, these kind folk ain't exactly handin' their loot to us, now is they?"

Mälque pulled away from his gaze and took in the ash, the blood, the severed limbs, the mangled bodies. "But this…this is…" He once more became overwhelmed by the sights and smells, and could feel his stomach rumbling. He covered his mouth and nose with his sleeved arm.

"Look," Olke fired, irritated by their tirade about how to make a living as a Wurmlin. "I don't like it much neither, but what choice do we have? When this Gor King and his army started attackin' villages, most folk sought refuge at Min Brock. The ones that didn't," he used his dagger as a pointer to highlight the death and destruction all around them. "Well, that crazy fool destroyed 'em all. Even our own kind have scattered or been killed."

His last words pressed down hard on Vonn and Mälque as they recounted the day their father died, followed soon after by their mother's demise. From that day forth, per Wurmlin custom, they lived with Olke since he was their only living relative, even if he was a distant cousin. And unfortunately for them, Olke held to the custom that the boys were property - not adopted sons.

Wild dogs lived better lives.

Their mother's warning echoed in their minds; *"Don't trust no one. Not even other Wurmlins."*

"So now," Olke continued, "we follow his army of gors, wait 'til they're gone and rob the dead. Still thievery. Accordin' to my codes, anyways."

"We could go to Min Brock," Mälque offered, eyes fixated on a child's mutilated body and longing to see life beyond thirteen summers. "Ain't nothin' but dyin' everywhere."

Olke's eyes narrowed; slits of anger burned at Mälque. "I'll tell ya why not, *yung-er.*" He held his answer until he had their full attention. "Because we're Wurmlins!" He thrust his blade at them and spittle flew off his lips. "We're nomads," his dagger darted from boy to boy as his tone became more impassioned. "Thieves. Highwaymen. And this here," he waved his dagger at the woods, "is your home. Always has been. Always will be. You don't need no castle."

Olke's eyes flared with anger as he whipped his hair to intimidate and remind them of his power over them. "Besides," he added with a smile that was as greasy as his hair, "I'm the only family ya got."

His last words struck the boys like jabs to the gut and Olke savored the misery that coursed their faces and the despair that weighed down thin shoulders. "Have you no respect for Wurmlin traditions," he asked as the veins on his forehead pumped with passion. "You should be ashamed. I didn't have ta take ya in and feed ya, or teach ya how to survive, but I did. You know why? 'Cause I'm a Wurmlin!" He pounded his chest with pride. "I take care of my own. So *never* ask such a thing again. Ya hear me? Be proud of your heritage...your bloodline...your...."

Too flustered and perturbed to continue the lecture, he waved them off with his dagger and returned to his task. As he knelt over the body, he mumbled to himself about *yung-ers* not appreciating the sacrifice of kin.

An odd sound made all three freeze in place.

Training took over and they snapped their heads toward the woods. Without a word, Olke rose and the boys took up positions on either side, daggers drawn, ready to kill or be killed.

Chapter 2

Gor Kings

"Someone's whistlin'," Vonn noted.

"Yeah," Olke answered as he spat onto the ground. "Stay sharp. Ya know what to do."

Vonn and Mälque nodded. Knuckles flexed white around dagger hilts.

From the foliage came the crunch and crack of twigs as the whistler neared.

"He sure is makin' a racket," Mälque added, a tinge of disgust in his voice for the stranger's ineptitude at being stealthy.

"Ain't a Wurmlin, that's for sure," Vonn chimed in. "Too dang noisy."

"He's either a fool," Olke concluded, and then in a more subdued voice added, "or he's a trickster."

They could see the whistler's shadow lumbering toward them. The man made no effort to conceal himself.

"He's alone," Mälque noted.

Olke looked this way and that, making sure there were no others lurking in the shadows, or creeping up behind them. He breathed a sigh of relief and focused back on the merry traveler.

"That song," he said to himself as his brow furrowed. "Where have I heard it before?"

The stranger marched out of the woods and the Wurmlins set their feet and thrust daggers forward.

The man of fifty summers stopped and let his whistled song fade. If he was shocked to have walked into a trap, his face did not show it. He raised his arms and turned empty palms toward the Wurmlins. "See, I'm unarmed." His voice was raspy, like dried leaves crumpled in one's palm.

"Shut up," Olke spat with the thrust of the blade. "Could be a trick. Ya just stay right there while we figure out what to do with ya."

The stranger lowered his arms, careful to not alarm the Wurmlins, and flashed them a smile. Age lines gave his face the appearance of old leather. Beard stubble, peppered gray, covered his face, while short, curly black hair with splotches of gray here and there crowned his head.

"Why's he smilin' like that," Mälque whispered to the others, a bit unnerved by the man's jovial spirit.

"Simple," Vonn quipped. "'Cause he's a fool. Look at 'im. No sword or dagger…walkin' alone through the woods. Dang fool's as loud as a gor in heat."

"Hush up," Olke fired between clinched teeth. He kept his eyes glued to the stranger. "There's more to him than meets the eye."

Olke sized up the man. His riding boots were black as were his breeches, but these could be worn by anyone - assassin or even a smith. They had not caught the scent of a horse nearby, so why wear such boots when hiking the woods? They would make walking more difficult and were less comfortable, too. His form-fitting tunic was secured with a belt, and as the boys had surmised, he was weaponless.

But what is it that makes you so familiar, Olke pondered.

"Turn around," he ordered the stranger with a twirling motion of his dagger. "Don't need ya whippin' out a sword strapped on your back."

The stranger snickered, as if amused by their paranoia, and turned in place. When he had completed his circle, he continued to flash them his smile. Mälque fretted about his sneer and wondered what tricks the man knew that they did not.

"See," Vonn chirped. "Nothin' strapped to his back, neither. He's just a fool."

It was at that moment that Olke's eyes widened with insight to the man's identity. "No, he ain't no fool. He's an Ebonite," he announced.

The stranger flinched, as if the accusation had stung him. "An Ebonite," he echoed with a snort. "But I'm beardless." He fingered his stubbled chin.

"You musta hacked it off," Olke fired.

The stranger's smile widened. "Have you ever known an Ebonite to shave off his cherished beard?"

Olke stepped forward and tightened his grip on the dagger. "I do now."

The stranger's smile continued to glow and he seemed unfazed by Olke's approach and claim. "Friend, that's quite a story you've concocted."

"Ain't no story," Olke replied with another cautious step. "Your hair is shorter too, and although it's grayed, it's definitely Ebonite. Look how curly it is. But that ain't what gave ya away. It was that dang song you was whistlin'. Couldn't remember where I'd heard it before. Then it came to me. The Dark War. You Ebonites sang it whenever you marched."

The stranger's smile dimmed but his features remained unchanged, a rock cliff able to withstand the fiercest of storms. Black eyes sized up the Wurmlins in a flash. Although he was not the stoutest of men, he carried himself with the confidence of a mercenary. Or an Ebonite warrior.

Neither man said another word. The silence between them grew. Tension hung thick in the air.

It was the stranger who broke the spell and he did so by singing the tune he had whistled.

"Rise, whisper hailing the Dark Flame,
Fly! Conquer tales that rival your name.
Scourge all who dare to muster their will,
Steel will flash, blood will spill,
Usher in the days of deception."

Before the stranger had finished singing the first line, the Wurmlins - spooked by the minor melody and dark lyrics - backed up. The song confirmed Olke's suspicions that this fellow was an Ebonite, but why he was alone, unarmed and on foot remained a quandary.

The Wurmlins regrouped, huddled shoulder-to-shoulder and listened spellbound to the next verse.

"Winds, cast the glory of Ebon before us,
Fall to the dust city and buttress.
Drone, like the sea pounding the shore,
Carry death to those Claire adores,
Usher in the days of deception."

The Wurmlins searched the woods one more time for reinforcements, specifically Ebonite cavalry, but just as before, the thickets were empty. Olke gripped his dagger tighter and waved it before the Ebonite, a reminder that they were armed and he was not, yet the Ebonite could tell by their expressions that the tables had turned. Despite being outnumbered, he now held the upper hand.

"It don't matter," Olke fired. "Ebonite or not, we found 'em first." He flicked his head toward the bodies littering the ground. "They're ours. Once we're done takin' our share, ya can do what ya want with 'em."

"But I don't want them," the Ebonite replied in his raspy tone, his smile now more defined than before.

Three Wurmlin brows furrowed. Daggers quivered from fear.

The stranger stepped closer. His smile twitched and Mälque had a flashback to his mother's creepy smile. "We want you," he rasped.

"*We?* You're alone."

"Are you willing to bet your life on that?"

The Wurmlins swept the woods for any signs of an ambush, and as before, spotted no one, nor caught the scent of warhorses hiding in the coppice. Olke snorted and puffed out his chest. "I ain't fallin' for that ol' trick."

The stranger jerked a thumb over his shoulder.

The Wurmlins leaned as a group to peer around him. Deep in the shadows of the woods they saw a bulging darkness. From the shade came the snort of a warhorse, and if the shadowy form mounted on top was any indication, whoever commanded the beast was formidable indeed.

Wurmlin eyes bulged and all three took a step backward.

"Where'd *he* come from," Olke asked, angered that they had missed catching the scent or discovering the warrior's shadow.

"No one knows for sure." The Ebonite picked at a bothersome fingernail as if bartering for food with a dimwitted merchant. "But he is obviously cunning enough to sneak up on three Wurmlins."

Olke spat on the ground and used his dagger to accent his next words. "Ya expect me to believe *that's* an Ebonite warhorse and warrior, and that both ya deserted the army to be scavengin' thieves?"

The stranger snickered at Olke's inability to embrace the reality of the moment. "Now who's the fool," he asked as he continued cleaning his nails. "I may be Ebonite by birth, but he," another thumb jerk to the mysterious rider, "is *not* from Ebon."

As if on cue, the dark warrior made his way through the woods toward the gathered men.

"To be honest," the Ebonite added as the soft sound of metal against leather grew louder, "I don't know where he's from." He dropped his arms to his side and glared into their faces. "And I dare not ask," he half whispered. "If you want to live, I advise you do the same."

Mälque gasped as the rider emerged from the woods. He was a massive warrior in black attire, and wore a helmet not forged of metal but fashioned from a gor's skull. Bleached white from the sun, it covered his head and face; only his mouth was exposed.

The skull's eye sockets looked like caves of eternal blackness. Mälque blinked and saw them flare red like a stoked fire.

Or was that a trick?

A gor-like howl echoed out from the skull, but it sounded far off, as if coming from a deep ravine, or a forgotten tomb.

Black armor, void of an insignia, covered his barrel chest. Arms were exposed and his muscles bulged like the Addoli Ridge upon the Gilden Plains. His warhorse was a fiery steed, as dark as the grave. Hooves dug into the soft ground like shovels while he tossed his head this way and that as if to free the bit and bridle that controlled him.

Mälque eyed the warrior's right arm that dangled by his side. He raised it to reveal a massive sword clutched in his gloved hand.

Vonn and Olke retreated back a step while Mälque stared spellbound at the weapon. *It's blue!*

But it wasn't the hue he associated with summer skies or tranquil waters. It resembled ice, and Mälque sensed the warrior wielded the weapon with unrelenting power and without mercy. Snapping out of the sword's enchantment, Mälque joined his brother's side.

Olke wagged his dagger at the ghoulish warrior. "We ain't afraid of ya," he shouted, which made the brothers look at each other in dismay, for all three sets of knees were wobbling like those of a newborn colt.

Mälque gathered his courage and whispered to the others: "Now do ya believe me? I told ya them stories I heard was real."

"Ah," the Ebonite sang as he overheard Mälque's claim, "so you know the stories of the Gor King."

"He ain't the Gor King," Olke spat, making sure he kept shaking his dagger, although even he knew such countermeasures would prove useless against so powerful a foe. "We been followin' the *real* Gor King for some time."

"You mean that baldheaded madman and his flesh eating gors," the Ebonite chortled.

Olke and Vonn nodded while Mälque stared at the tomb-like sockets of the Gor King's helmet.

Will they burn red like I'd seen before?

Nothing happened and Mälque breathed a sigh of relief.

"So, boy," the Ebonite rasped as he neared. "You're familiar with his tale. Why don't you share them? I think it's time to remind your friends about the *true* Gor King."

Mälque looked to the others for help but they ignored him and instead, kept their gaze fixed on the Gor King.

Mälque swallowed down his fear and faced the Ebonite, alone.

"Accordin' to the tales," Mälque tossed a quick glance up at the Gor King, "he appeared three summers ago. He stormed unsuspectin' villages with a blue sword and robbed 'em of everythin' of worth. No one knew his name. No one knew his homeland. And as time passed, tavern stories about him grew in fantasy until no one knew what was true and what was myth. Some claimed he was a ghoul, others that he was a rogue storyteller, still others that he was the incarnation of the Cauldron.

"These tales were passed with pipes and drink from town to town, province to province, and despite the variations, this much everyone agreed on: he served neither Ebon nor Claire. His allegiance was to himself and his blade of blue."

The Ebonite arched an eyebrow. "Rather eloquent." He pressed closer and flashed a sinister smile. "Especially from a Wurmlin *yung-er*."

Mälque ground his teeth at the insult but a quick glance at the Gor King quelled any thoughts of being defiant.

"Please continue."

Mälque swallowed the queasy feeling rising from his gut, and repositioned his feet so his legs wouldn't cramp. The last thing he wanted was to collapse before so formidable a warrior. He swallowed a gulp of air and delivered the rest of his tale. "As the warrior's reputation grew, so did his followers. Outcasts, criminals and madmen served him with steel-like resolve."

"That's partially true," the Ebonite interrupted. "As your friend here has surmised," he gestured at Olke, "I'm an Ebonite and fought for Ebon in the Dark War, but I'm anything but a madman or a criminal." He leaned close. Mälque caught a whiff of his foul-smelling breath. "Would you not agree?"

Mälque thought otherwise but was shrewd enough to keep his mouth shut. Instead, he offered a subtle nod. His eyes hopped from the Ebonite's twitching smile to the Gor King. He sat statuesque, and as far as he could tell from his body language, seemed unfazed by his story.

But is this good or bad?

Mälque decided to continue the tale in hope that it would spare their lives. "In honor of their devotion, this warrior let 'em taste the spoils of their campaigns. As their appetite for bounty increased, so did their numbers, and yet, even his army didn't know his identity, and fearin' his wrath, they dared not ask."

The Ebonite leaned back on his heels and nodded to confirm as much.

Mälque felt rivulets of cold sweat roll down his spine. His mouth became dry; his tongue felt too large for his mouth. He flicked it about, lizard-like, in an effort to find enough spittle to finish the tale. Satisfied he had wetted his mouth, he let the conclusion fly.

"By the end of the fourth summer, the sound of his army's thunderin' hooves sent fear into the remotest villages, and a name was given the mystic warrior. Unbeknownst to 'em all, they crowned him with a title already given to another - the Gor King."

The Ebonite clapped his hands together. Then he clapped again, and then again, each time faster than the former, until he was clapping with wild abandon. And then he stopped, as if given a silent order, and ruffled Mälque's greasy hair. "Not bad. Not a bad rendition at all, even for a yung-er."

Mälque bit his lower lip to keep his anger checked.

Olke regained his senses and fired a hot look at the Ebonite. "So? What's that gotta do with us?" Olke's brash tone had returned but was as useless as his dagger against the Gor King's blue sword.

"As the boy's story claimed, we are seeking men to join our ranks."

Olke snorted and wiped his nose with a sleeved arm. "We're Wurmlins. We join no army; not even *his*." He pointed his dagger at the Gor King.

Mälque held his breath, expecting the sockets of the Gor King's helmet to glow crimson, but they remained as black as night.

Vonn elbowed Olke. "Shut up," he half-whispered. "Maybe you wanna die, but we don't."

The Ebonite positioned himself in front of Olke. "You know as well as I do that there are less and less villages to plunder. That fiend *you* call the Gor King," he accentuated the word with an index finger into Olke's chest, "has butchered most hamlets this side of the Gilden Plains. Others, sensing war on the wind, have fled to Min Brock."

"Yeah, so," Olke spat.

Spittle landed on the Ebonite's face and his smile disappeared. Jaw muscles flexed and dark eyes narrowed. But instead of retaliating, he regained control over his emotions. Like the sun emerging from a storm cloud, his smile returned.

"War looms." He wiped the spit off his cheek. "Gone are the days when Wurmlins can live nomadic lives and plunder whenever they please. Today, we offer you a choice, and it is far better than what Min Brock, Claire or even Ebon can offer."

"An offer," Olke asked, his interest piqued at the thought of gaining easy treasures in such harsh times. The boys were equally intrigued.

"This choice," the Ebonite continued, "comes with a price."

"Name it."

"You three will have to vow allegiance to the Gor King." The Ebonite swept an arm up to his lord. "In return, you will retain your anonymity as Wurmlins as well as receive your share of the plunder."

"And what of Ebon and Claire? What will you do when war breaks out?"

"Our plan is simple: skirt the battles and skirmishes until we see who will be champion. At that point, we will either align ourselves with them or..."

He paused to take in their faces and was pleased to see them hungry for more than just survival. His smile arched wide. "We destroy that army - whether it be Claire's or Ebon's - and seize all the lands as rulers and kings." He pressed his face closer. "How does that sound? Even a Wurmlin like yourself would appreciate a noble title with land to govern and people to tax."

The Ebonite winked and the reality of the proposal - at this point nothing more than a risky dream - made Olke nod. Lips twisted about as he imagined himself a monarch capable of stealing at will - or taxing, which he defined as legal thievery - and he snorted with zeal. As his lust for power and wealth grew, so did his jovial laughs.

"Very well," Olke boomed. "We'll join your army. But remember:

Wurmlins sleep light and are fleet of foot, so no trickery or tryin' to slice our throats while we sleep."

"I'll keep that in mind." He snickered and made his way toward the Gor King.

"Why don't he talk," Mälque shouted.

Vonn elbowed him in the ribs. "Shut up! You wanna get us killed?"

"Well, he ain't said nothin'. He just sits there. Maybe he can't talk."

Olke backhanded him. "Hush, yung-er! Just *hush*."

The Gor King shuffled in his saddle. Leather groaned and his warhorse whinnied in anticipation of combat.

Olke and Vonn distanced themselves from Mälque who rubbed his sore cheek.

The Gor King drove his spurs into his horse's flanks. The beast lumbered toward Mälque. The Gor King pulled back on the reins and the animal stopped short of plowing Mälque into the ground. The animal's spirited mannerisms were no more. Now, as if under a spell, the warhorse became unusually still, as if it knew the role it would play in the Gor King's heinous scheme.

Mälque stared at the Gor King, his eyes wide with fright as chilly sweat soaked his tight clothing.

The Gor King brought his blade forward but not lighting fast like Mälque had expected. Instead, the movement was shadow-like. Mälque sucked in staggered breaths and prepared for the worst.

The Gor King turned the blade sideways and Mälque felt its steel touch his chin.

Icy cold; colder than I expected.

Sweat beaded on Mälque's forehead. His eyes wandered up the blade, past the warhorse's snout, to rest upon the black tombs of the gor skull helmet.

Did I see 'em flare red? Am I gonna die?

The Gor King raised Mälque's chin with the tip of his sword and cocked his head this way and that as he sized him up.

Mälque stared at the Gor King's thin lips, willing them to open with speech.

And offer mercy.

They parted, and a voice that crackled like thunder and echoed dark as if from death's crypt, answered his foolish question: "I speak only when necessary."

The blue blade retracted with the same sluggish speed and returned to hang once more by the Gor King's side. Without another word, the Gor King jerked the reins and turned back toward the woods.

Mälque, overcome by his ordeal, dropped to his knees gasping for air and rubbing his chin, although not even a crease could be found as evidence of the blade's presence.

Olke gave Mälque a grunt of disapproval and followed after the Gor King. "Dang yung-er," he fired over his shoulder at Mälque.

Vonn stood traumatized, eyes darting from the Ebonite to the Gor King then down to his brother.

The Ebonite offered Mälque his hand who studied it with suspicion, still not certain he could trust him. "Believe it or not, the Gor King has taken a liking to you."

"Well," Mälque quipped as their palms clasped and he was yanked to his feet, "as long as it keeps me alive, I guess he can take a likin' to me as much as he wants."

Mälque watched the Gor King slide into the shadowed woods, his horse's gait silent despite leaves and twigs being turned or snapped. Olke followed close behind like a stray calf being led back to the herd.

Or a butcher.

"What's puzzlin'," Mälque offered Vonn, "is how come we didn't hear him approach or catch his scent? Even now, he doesn't make a sound."

The Ebonite answered by pushing them along.

"And where's the rest of your army," Vonn asked the Ebonite as the shock of their nightmare started to wane.

"If you three pass your test, you'll soon find out."

The boys flashed bewildered expressions to one another. Like Olke, they assumed that they were already accepted into the fold.

Will we have to fight each other?

Mälque searched Vonn's face for a clue to the answer or to find strength to face whatever would come their way.

All he found were eyes that stared bug-eyed at the Gor King.

And what does someone like the Gor King want with thieves like us?

The Ebonite started to whistle his dark marching song, and Mälque felt a numbness creep through him as they trudged deeper into the woods. Instinct, like a slap across his face, told him that their lives would never be the same.

Chapter 3

One Step

Crack!

The sound jolted Previn out of a deep sleep. Perched in his nest, he had the perfect vantage point to guard Il-Lilliad's cave.

Four summers, he reflected. *And not once has Ela Claire ventured out.*

He used his keen senses and searched the woods for whoever, or whatever, was prowling below. Sunbeams sliced the early morning haze, dotting the forest floor with golden light. Aside from the hoot of a distant owl, nothing stirred, not even the wind.

The sound came again - the crisp report of twigs breaking - only now it was closer.

He rustled his feathers; wings flexed, ready to attack. Black eyes swept the shadows for the telltale signs of yellow demolith eyes or the purple plumage of vul jens.

Nothing. He sniffed to catch the scent of the threat, but without even a breeze stirring was unable to detect anything unusual.

He tossed a quick glance up through the thick canopy.

Branches - charcoal fingers in stark contrast to the morning sky - obstructed much of his view, but aside from thin clouds slicing the salmon-colored heavens, he saw nothing threatening.

Snap!

Previn directed his gaze toward the sound. It came from the thicket guarding the passage into Il-Lilliad's cave. He unfolded his wings and glided to the ground without a sound. Cocking his head to the side, he listened for the slightest movement or even the thumping of the assailant's heartbeat. A quick sniff revealed nothing, but once more he assumed this was a result of the motionless air. He was about to dismiss the footfalls as being from a wandering doe when he spotted a silhouette crouched behind a tree.

Human, he noted. *Wurmlin? Ebonite?*

His next steps were cautious should a blade flash or a crossbow bolt zip his way. When he was close enough to attack, the stranger stepped into the light.

"Ela Claire," he stammered, stunned that after four summers of isolation she was out in the open. During his tenure as her protector he had only gotten glimpses of her, and these were few and far between. He gazed into her face that was as pale as snow. Her hair - still cinnamon-hued - was longer, full-bodied and pulled back and secured with a sash. But it was her figure, cloaked within her white dress, that made him realize just how long it had been since he'd seen her last. The soft curves of her hips and breasts graced her with splendor.

Ela Claire was a woman now.

"You're finally out of your cave," he exclaimed as he fluttered forward. "Let me pull you close with my wings and..."

She jumped back and hid behind the tree.

Previn stopped. Cocking his head, he savored her scent while he stared into her wild eyes. Relieved that this was indeed Ela Claire and not an apparition or trick of the Cauldron, he also detected something else. Her decision to reclaim her Clairian name and mission to the Isle of Rhythe still hung in the balance.

Not wanting to frighten her back into the cavern, he willed his emotions into submission, although his chest continued to billow in and out with excitement, and he nestled to the ground like a hen covering her nest. He was still a good distance from her, which he hoped she would take as non-threatening, and took in her image as his years of service rolled past his memory.

The summers protecting and serving her had been like the seasons themselves, each one having a unique disposition, wonder and darkness. Some days blurred together, spilling and tumbling into the next like rapids of a thunderous river. Most, however, moaned and groaned along like a wagon laden with too much weight; axles bending, mule braying, the driver listless. And yet, through them all ran a common thread that stitched time together: she never spoke to him nor let him see her.

Initially, in his effort to protect her as best he could, he tried to push into the passageway to reach the cave where she hid, but he was too large and could not get beyond the opening. Undeterred by this setback, he resigned himself to the thickets and his nest to make certain Il-Lilliad's cave remained her sanctuary.

The four summers would test his resolve.

No sooner had she disappeared into the cave than the Cauldron attacked. Demoliths dove to assassinate her by heat and claw, but Previn anticipated as much and with each attack, he proved to be too cunning and too ferocious a foe. Although he was always outnumbered, he met the attacks head on. Singed by their fiery eyes, his white plumage became mottled with grays and blacks, evidence of his vow to always protect her no matter the cost.

Vul jen patrols were another matter. Smaller and capable of quicker maneuverability during aerial combat, Previn worried one would eventually slip past and enter her cave. Once inside, he knew it could hide in the shadows and wait for the perfect opportunity for her dreambreath to come, knowing full well Previn could not intervene.

When the first vul jen patrol dove for the canopy below, Previn was about to lose hope when an ally appeared in the sky beside him. Clear blue and mounted on a steed of similar appearance, Manno Vox unsheathed his sword to defend Ela Claire.

His face fluttered like rainbow light on a wintery horizon and his blade slashed vul jen after vul jen. Previn picked off those lucky enough to escape Manno Vox's sword.

None passed. None escaped.

The skeletal remains of their enemy littered the woods, warnings to future assassins or mercenaries that a similar fate awaited them as well.

By the end of the second summer, the Cauldron called off its attacks, which Previn reasoned was because it assumed Ela Claire had resigned herself to her fate: a useless life of pain, misery and mistrust of the tales from Claire. Previn, on the other hand, hoped that with each passing moment her convictions were growing stronger, ready to leap out and believe once more.

Every morning, he fluttered to the opening of her cave to deliver grape leaves laded with fish to cook, wildeberries and nuts to nibble, as well as gourds filled with cool water. Setting them on the ground, he cawed into the passage, urging her to venture out and join him for a meal. During the first and second summer, she ignored him, daring to dart into the light only to snatch a quick bite or swig down some water. Before he could see her face, she ran back inside.

The third summer was more of the same routine: provisions were set at the foot of the passage, he hailed her name but she waited until he flew off before venturing out.

Despite her aloofness, he did not give up on her, and when her eating habits changed, he became encouraged. Instead of merely nibbling or taking a sip, she snatched all of the food and drink and scurried back into her dark cavern.

A good sign, he concluded, *an optimistic turn of a dark tale.*

And on the day she returned the empty gourd and grape leaf soon after eating, Previn interpreted this to mean that she wanted seconds. Excited, he darted to the stream to snare a fish and fill the gourd with the sweetest of waters. In no time, he was back to deliver his bounty, and for the first time in over three summers, he got a better look at her, even if she hid in the shadows.

He called her name.

She retreated further into the dark.

Not wanting to spook her, and fighting his urge to grab her and pull her out, he bowed his head and flew back to his nest. From such vantage, he saw her arm protrude to grab the grape leaf and gourd. So frail, so white was her flesh, and yet Previn's heart warmed to catch a glimpse, even if it was comparable to witnessing a phantom hover over a grave.

Unable to contain his excitement at her marked improvement, he cocked his head back and let loose the most glorious song.

Previn returned his thoughts to the moment and eyed her, peering from around the tree.

She's so afraid. Even of me.

Time passed, and when she did not venture from her hiding place or engage in conversation, his impatience got the better of him. Rising off the ground, he beat his wings with such frenzy that a cloud of dust and leaves swirled her way.

Overcome by the windstorm, Ela Claire coughed and covered her nose and mouth with her arm.

"Forgive me," Previn stated as he pulled his wings close to stop the zephyr, "but I'm so excited to see you! I can only assume that your appearance is a sign that you've made a decision about your future."

As the dust and debris settled, she lowered her arm and stepped out into the open. She offered him a dull smile.

Previn drank it in as he eyed her dark blue cape and backpack draped over one shoulder.

Are these signs she has chosen to be Ela Claire and continue her mission to the Isle of Rhythe?

His excitement grew and he yearned to press her for an answer but sensed she would race back into her cave. With great restraint, he nestled to the ground and waited.

She took in the surrounding woods. Springtime - like the breath from a lover - hung in the air; buds sat poised to bloom, awaiting the brush from a warm breeze. Despite the advent of a new season, she shivered, as if in the midst of a frigid winter.

"Yes, Previn, I've made a decision, but I must warn you that I'm not the same girl I was four summers ago. The cave has changed me."

"That I can see. Gone is the Hetherlinn girl of fourteen summers. Before me now is a beautiful young woman."

She dared a look at him before withdrawing her gaze. "My story may not be what you're expecting to hear, either."

Previn steeled himself for the worst. "Nonetheless, I would be honored to hear it."

She stared off into the deepest part of the coppice as if looking back into time. "The first summer…"

She let her voice trail as she remembered the season when pain was the deepest cut: raw and vulnerable. Drawing in her courage, as well as a big gulp of air, she recounted her story.

"Il-Lilliad's cave became my cocoon, isolating me from witnessing sunrises and sunsets, beholding the first frost or budding flower. Time blurred. Days folded into nights while my pain sat ever-present, crushing my hope, my passion…my will to live.

"I heard your voice, pleading for me to join you on a walk in the woods, trying to lure me beyond my despair with the wonders you'd discovered: a nest of chirping birds or a thicket concealing a fawn. As you know, I didn't answer; I couldn't answer. You must have wondered why I didn't cry or scream or moan from the pain of all I'd lost: Romlin, my oak, the abandonment from the Only… But in order to weep, I'd have to accept my pain, feel it - and to such a dictator I dared not bow. So I chose to live in my timeless cave, embracing the darkness of life with gloomy numbness."

She stole a glance at Previn to catch his reaction. He sat still, yet attentive, eyes held open, as if blinking would break the spell of her tale. Within his gaze she felt his strength, his passion for her that brimmed with mercy and hope. Unable to take anymore, she pulled away.

"Is there no end to your devotion," she asked, her voice quivering.

"No," he replied. "Never."

"But I took my anger, my hurt out on you, and yet you were so good to me. Why?"

"Why," he repeated, allowing himself to blink, shocked she would ask such a thing. "Because I gave you my word. Because…I care for you, deeply."

"You had every right to give up on me and return to Claire for another storyteller."

Previn stood up and fluttered his wings. "*You* are my storyteller!"

She spun around to face him. "I would have understood."

"Not I!"

She reached for him, but upon second thought, let her arm fall and turned on her heel.

"After all I've done to you, do you still want to hear my story?"

"Yes!" He restrained from beating his wings with excitement and cawing with joy. "Hearing your tale was the hope that kept me going all these summers."

He nestled back to the ground and waited.

She stepped to a sapling and fingered a branch.

"If I had any hope that first summer, it was as vulnerable as this little tree. Sometimes I dared to dream of better days, but most of the time I imagined crushing it with the heel of my boot. You must have sensed as much. It would explain your faithfulness to me through such dark times."

"Yes," he answered, wishing she'd turn so he could take in her face. "But I was powerless to assist."

"That must have frustrated you."

Previn didn't answer. They both knew it was the truth.

She knelt to the forest floor, picked up a twig and began flicking leaves this way and that. "The King of Claire whispered my name daily, but my anger at him drowned out his calls. After all, he chose not to rescue Romlin or defend Hetherlinn. Silence became my hedgerow of protection. And yet, his whisper didn't abandon me. Even when my rage boiled like molten steel, he whispered, his tone as gentle as the day I first heard him...back when I yanked that invitation from my door."

She jabbed the twig deep into the dirt as if looking for nuts or roots - or to destroy that fateful day, once and for all. Her efforts lessened and she returned to scattering leaves about.

"On many an occasion, I smelled the warm sea breeze of Claire. Despite my dour mood, it filled my cave with a spring-like newness. One day, I discerned something hidden within. A familiar melody pulsed in the wind, fluttering just far enough away that I had to strain my ears to hear it.

"Sensing my interest, the melody became louder and I recognized the tune. It was my waltz! It showered me with passionate music, but I covered my ears and turned my back to the breeze. I wasn't ready for such reunion."

She threw the twig into the woods and stood back up. Crossing her arms over her chest, she continued her story, all the while keeping her back to Previn.

"Thus I lived: void of feelings, void of life and void of purpose. It wasn't until the end of the first summer that anything changed, and even then it was subtle. At first I didn't notice it. But when my sight became blurred, and I wiped my eyes, I discovered on my fingertips the evidence of a stirring within."

She took in Previn's face. "My first tear."

Previn blinked as he fathomed the depth of her suffering. It was deep. Very deep.

She bit her lower lip and looked away. Walking to a nearby tree, she leaned against the trunk and stared at her feet as if they held the answer to the riddle of her pain. With a heavy sigh, she said, "And then there was my second summer."

She raised her eyes to Previn's and began to unpack the memories.

"My first tear was like a key. It unlocked the feelings I'd imprisoned and they exploded like thunder over the Gilden Plains. Tears fell like a monsoon. I cried so much that I wondered if I would spend the rest of my life lamenting. The whisper and waltz continued to reverberate about the cave, but I wasn't willing to entertain them. Instead, I poured out my story:

> *'Oh, harbored pain, your dark waves crash my shore.*
> *Hope is but ash, death prowls my moor.*
> *Anguish so bitter, its budding fruit abounds,*
> *Dreams lie in dust; they make not a sound.'"*

She paused to check Previn's reaction. Would he shake his head in disgust at her abandonment of Claire? Would he charge forward to try and convince her that her pain-filled journey was part of a wonderful plan to make her a stronger storyteller? Instead of either reaction, Previn met her gaze with compassionate eyes. She spun away from the tree and paced.

"Soon, story upon story flew from my mouth. Some were tales of pain while others were brash and bitter. And yet, the waltz and whisper remained nearby, unaffected by my ranting. On and on I raged, sometimes pacing like a caged animal or pounding my fist against the cold stone as if to cut a passage into a new world."

She stopped, shook her head and ground her teeth; the memories still throbbed with pain.

"I don't recall the exact day," she delivered over her shoulder, "but I eventually allowed the whisper and waltz to come closer. I still didn't trust. After all, wasn't it their leading that brought me heartache?"

Once more, she checked on Previn, relieved he nodded in agreement.

"You continued bringing me food and water and my appetite improved, which I'm sure brought you great joy. Do you remember?"

"As if it were today. I could see you hiding in the shadows. It was the first time you'd allowed me to get close to you in...in well over two summers."

A faint smile crossed her face. "I know. I saw you as well. Even from a distance, I could see the concern in your eyes. I sensed you longed to whisk me back to Claire."

"Yes, but such force wouldn't have healed your spirit." Passion swirled within his blinking eyes. "Instead, I vowed to protect you all the more, even if that meant you'd never speak to me again."

"I never meant to hurt you."

"I know," he offered. "That I most certainly know."

She swallowed down her emotions and continued.

"I pretended to converse with the Only, my mother, or father, or…Romlin. I could go for days without thinking about him until a sudden crackle from the fire brought him to life. I could see him in my cave, leaning against the hearth, and then I'd catch his scent, hear his laugh…"

She stared off into the distance, her eyes glossed over with memories. Fingers combed her hair. "Such visions pierced me like an arrow. I crumbled to the floor and wailed."

"You cried for days. I longed to help."

"But you couldn't. I wasn't ready for your service."

"Nevertheless, I'd much rather forget those days than remember."

She nodded and sighed. "Me too. But the reason I'm sharing it again is to tell you this: During such mourning, I shouted to Claire the one word that haunted me; that plagued me. Do you know what it was?"

"Yes." Previn stared into her dark eyes. "*Why?*"

She closed her eyes and confirmed with a gentle nod. "But there was no answer."

With a deep sigh, the next chapter of her story rose like a tulip petal caught in an updraft. She returned to the sapling and stroked the buds on a low branch. Glints of white and green were proof that spring was close.

"Then came the third summer…"

Her finger trailed off the branch.

"Like a turbulent storm moving out to sea, my tears subsided. This didn't happen overnight, nor were my tragedies forgotten nightmares. The pain and the memories lingered, rising like ghosts when I least expected them. To this day they prowl.

"And yet, despite the uncertainty of my tomorrows, despite the calamity of my life, I began to remember Claire. I reminisced about my journey with Romlin and longed for the sweet respites in Marsien Vur's gardens."

She fingered another bud as if her caress would make it bloom that much sooner. "I wanted to sit and gaze at the vistas; they were so grand, invigorating…peaceful. It was in this state of mind that the whisper spoke a fresh word to me."

She spun around to take in Previn. "Care to venture a guess?"

"Delight."

She gasped, stunned at how quick and accurate his answer was.

Previn ventured closer. "Did you reply?"

She focused on the budding branch clutched in her hand. "Yes, but not as you would have wished."

"What do you mean?"

She released the branch and it snapped back and forth.

"I turned the word over in my mind, studying it from every

conceivable angle. 'Delight,' I challenged. 'Delight in what? My misery? Claire?' I was confused and angry."

"Yes, but…"

"In reply, the whisper said: *You, Ela Claire, are my delight.*"

She paced with arms flailing to accent her words. "I shouted: 'I'm not *ready* to be Ela Claire nor may ever be. Although you delight in me, I don't feel the same way.'"

Her animated motions subsided and she sauntered over to a massive log. She sat and leaned back to study Previn's face. "You don't look surprised at my confession of unbelief."

"No, I'm not. Don't think I didn't wrestle with similar issues."

She studied him for a long time, realizing that she was not the only one who had experienced pains and doubts. She let the silence grow between them, but instead of it separating them more, it became a bridge into both their stories, one in which they both could offer respect, empathy and compassion.

She twisted her mouth about and reflected back to that summer. "I expected the whisper from Claire to abandon me to my own misery. Much like my father did after Min Brock. But the whisper stayed and never spoke in a harsh manner. Looking back on it now, I can honestly say he delivered…delight."

She stood, brushed off her hands and approached Previn.

"Honesty and passion exploded from me. My words, like blisters, were filled with anger, doubt and fear. The whisper listened and never voiced displeasure or irritation, and although the answer to *why* such tragedies occurred hovered unanswered, I sensed that justice, perhaps even a greater purpose, would grow out of such ash."

She stopped in front of him and resisted the urge to stroke his plumage.

"As I poured out my deepest despair, a mysterious stirring awakened where the pain had been. Like a tulip pushing up through the deepest snows to start life anew, I hungered more and more for Claire.

"Then came the day that marked the biggest change. I found myself standing before Il-Lilliad's books." Her eyes narrowed. "Oh, how they haunted me during the first two summers in the cave. I blamed them for the pain I'd suffered. I even thought about burning them in the fireplace."

She let her emotions settle before continuing. "And yet here I was in the third summer, standing close to them. Would they still be as invigorating as I remembered, or was my heart too crushed to experience new wonders? I took a step closer. I touched a binding. Not sure what to expect, I let my finger lay there for the longest time. With what courage I had, I grabbed it and headed for the fireplace, holding it away from me as if carrying something dangerous or loathsome."

Previn cocked his head to the side. "Did you burn it?"

She grinned and shook her head. "I sat on the hearth and let the book rest unopened on my lap. Orange and yellow firelight gave it a mysterious, perhaps even dangerous appearance. I read its title: 'Deepest of Tales.'

"I read it many summers ago, shortly before Romlin's death, but now it appeared different. Was it hailing me like a friend, calling out to one that had been absent far too long? Or would it be like Mithe and others in Hetherlinn, heaping abuse and chastisement on me?

"As if in a dream, I watched my hand stretch toward the cover. I wondered if the book was magical and had cast a spell over me, making me reach for it. But I knew that wasn't the case. I *did* want to read it, while at the same time, part of me wanted to hurl it into the flames."

She glanced up into his eyes and caught his concern. "My fingertip brushed the leather cover and I jerked my hand away, as if it would lunge like a beast and tear open my flesh. Of course, nothing happened, except that I became more curious. I braved another touch, and this time I felt a warming sensation shoot into my arm and through my body. It reminded me of the times Mother warmed buckets of water for a bath - a rare luxury - and I'd step into the halved barrel of water and sink until it came up to my chin. Had the waters not cooled, I'm sure I would have remained in that bath to this day."

She relished the memory, serenity traversing her troubled face.

"I opened the cover. After a moment of hesitation, not sure what to expect from the book, or the whisper, or even from my own reaction, I began to read. The words tumbled into my thoughts, then fell into my emotions like stars from a darkened sky. I discovered a satisfaction that defied explanation. It was as if I was reading the tales for the very first time, each word unfolding with what seemed to be eternal proportions. Wondrous they were, delivering me through the horrors of my life.

"I turned the page. I nibbled at more words, cautious, like a fish upon bread floating on a pond. The last thing I needed, or wanted, was to be hooked by Claire and tricked into service again. When nothing like that happened, I turned yet another page.

"Again I read the words, only now with more zeal. Another page turned. I devoured the words with an unabated hunger: savoring and cherishing the richness of flavor like sun ripened grapes. I read as if my life depended upon every nuance from the stories."

She paused and an eyebrow arched. "Maybe it did."

She brushed back a strand of hair and continued.

"Before I knew it, I was at the end. I snapped the cover shut, stood and hurried to the bookcase. I slid it back into place and grabbed another. Returning to the fire, I repeated the process over and over. I don't recall how long it took, but one thing is certain: I didn't stop until I read them all.

"The stories flowed like a river into my emotions - sometimes placid, other times white water - and I felt a deep joy growing within, wild and free, a meadow of flowers amidst the tarnished debris of my sufferings, their sweet fragrance filling me with contentment, tranquility and intention."

She brushed both sides of Previn's face with her fingers. Previn leaned into her touch.

"At the dawn of my fourth summer, I began to prune my hedgerow of silence. In so doing, I invited my waltz and the whisper to draw near. They pulled me close, as if in an embrace, and for the first time since those disasters, I felt safe."

She looked into his face as she buried her fingers into his feathers. They tickled her wrist and she enjoyed the warmth radiating outward from him.

"I asked the whisper: 'You say I'm your delight. But deep within me, I wonder how such a thing is possible. Me? A delight? It was my curiosity, my desire to leave Hetherlinn to be someone else that ushered in destruction and war. I should have left Manno Vox's bolt stuck in our door as all the others had. Then the Cauldron would have never heard, and the warriors would have never come, and all would be well. My family would still be in Hetherlinn, my oak tree would still grace the knoll...'"

Her hands plopped to her side. "... and Romlin would still be alive."

Previn rested his head upon her forehead.

"My heart aches for his loss, too," he whispered.

She nodded and glanced into his black eyes. With a sniffle, she continued.

"The whisper answered: 'Such destruction was not your doing, nor is it yours to undo. You simply answered my whisper, a child yearning to hear my tales. I haven't forgotten such innocence, such hunger for truth and daring for wonderment. Your pain and your loss are very dear to me. For every tear you've shed, I too have shed a tear. For every wrong that has come upon you, I also have felt sorrow. I won't reverse the seasons and eliminate your loss, but I vow this: Ela Claire, you are my delight, and in such delight I will fight for justice.'"

Silence.

Previn did not press her to continue. Instead, he let her words settle like seeds in his heart where they would root into deeper passion for her.

She steeled herself to offer the conclusion to her story. "My reply was this: 'I don't think I'm capable of such belief. What I mean is, I doubt life will be the same.'"

"'True. What has happened is forever a part of your tale, but beyond your ashen dreams, beyond your darkest fears lie adventures and stories awaiting a teller of tales. I wish you could see them as I do, for they are wondrous indeed. So dare to dream again, Ela Claire. Dare to let your heart dance with your waltz. Dare to love and live as never before, carried by the words of my stories. For in such choosing, death begets life.'"

Previn searched her face. It glowed like a jewel caught in the sunlight, yet there was a strand of apprehension - like a chip or a crack - that caused such reflection to wane and bend with uncertainty. As much as he longed to hear her answer pertaining to which name she would embrace, his plumage ruffled with fear.

She stepped back from him. "And so it is that today, as I near the fifth summer, I chose to leave my mire of darkness and race to freedom like I did across my meadow, many summers ago.

"But in many ways," she said as she pulled away from his gaze, "I'm wounded and crippled and incapable of such daring. All I can do is take small steps, indeed, tiny ones. In so doing, the whisper and waltz have led me to a richer, deeper fellowship as if a secret chamber..." She placed a hand over her heart, "has been unlocked and flung open."

Previn fluttered his wings with excitement. "Does this mean..."

"It only means I desire to leave the cave, nothing more."

"And your name? Have you chosen which you'll live by?"

Their eyes locked.

"Ela Claire," she half-whispered.

Previn brushed his head against her, like a mare would its master, and cawed, his voice echoing through the woods.

He stepped back to take her in. "This calls for a celebration! I'll prepare a feast the likes..."

"No feast. At least not yet."

"I don't understand."

She stroked the side of his head. "You've been so faithful a friend, so I hesitate to ask anything more of you, yet now is when I need you the most."

"Knowing you feel that way brings me great joy." He lowered himself to look her square in the face. "What do you need?"

She was about to answer when she noticed his wings.

"Previn!" She eyed the singed and battered plumage that she knew was a result of battling demoliths and vul jens. "You're wounded."

"I'm fine," he answered as he rose and spread his wings to not only prove his point but to get her mind off his injuries. "Such tarnishes are my badge of honor."

A tear rolled off her cheek.

"There, there. No need to cry. You've shed enough tears already."

She nodded and dotted her eyes with her sleeve.

"So tell me," he asked as he eyed her backpack, "what do you need my services for?"

"I need you to carry me to DioBaith."

Previn blinked in rapid succession. Her request was the furthest thing he had expected. "Is it wise to return to the place where your greatest pain…"

"It's too difficult, complex, to explain. I simply must go and see - one last time."

Previn sniffed her, looking for any sign that she would lapse back into her hermit life, or something worse. Sensing nothing alarming, he questioned her more. "I don't mean to alarm you, but during my tenure as your guard, the Cauldron attacked me with its whisper."

Ela Claire flicked her dark eyes up to his. "What did it say?"

"Usually it taunted and threatened my resolve, but there were several occasions when it spoke of a *Gor King*. This was followed with the oracle: *Tales shall crush steel when gors have a king.*"

Ela Claire clasped a hand over her mouth to conceal her shock. "I read something similar in one of Il-Lilliad's books, *The Whispers of Claire*.

> *Mothers, guard babes; Fathers, draw steel,*
> *Thunder approaches, soon blood on the fields.*
> *Tempest of war, so black and so vile,*
> *Spreads o'er Allsbruth; lament suckling child.*
>
> *Orphaned stories, treasures from Claire,*
> *Like buried embers, burst forth and flare.*
> *Hear not a whisper, sweet lark on the wing?*
> *Tales shall crush steel when gors have a king.*

She took in his face. "Could this story pertain to the Gor King?"

"I have no idea. That was all that was offered. My point is this: the past four summers have brought a lot of change to the lands. DioBaith may be even more dangerous than before."

She stroked his face. "Gor King or not, this is something I must do before we fly to the Isle of Rhythe."

"So you *do* want to fulfill your mission!"

"Not so fast," she chuckled. "One step at a time."

"Yes," he replied as he lowered himself to the ground. "I remember, but such a pace will be difficult for me to maintain."

She hopped on and he relished the moment.

"I've waited four summers to feel your weight upon my back!"
She gripped his feathers in both hands and leaned close to his head.
"Ready?"
Previn answered with a great caw and then launched into the air.

Chapter 4

Death to a Dream

Ela Claire, who'd forgotten how fast Previn flew, squealed and nearly toppled off. Regaining her balance and grip, she leaned out over his neck.

Wind whisked past as they zipped around trees, dodged low-lying branches and climbed for the sky. With three quick strokes, Previn cleared the woods and leveled off at treetop level.

"Are you sure about this," he asked over his shoulder, hoping she'd changed her mind about returning to Romlin's watery tomb.

"Positive."

Previn gave a nod and followed the River Arrgient toward DioBaith.

Ela Claire sat upright and took in her surroundings. The sun looked like a tarnished ball of copper on the eastern horizon.

"I don't remember the morning sun looking so dull."

"Your memory is correct. Much has changed in the last four summers."

"Like what?"

Previn ignored her question and focused on staying on course.

"Did you hear me, what else?"

Silence.

Flustered at his obstinance, she looked for any new signs of change. The northwest horizon made her perk up. "There!" She pointed to Ebon's sky. "Why is it so bright?"

Previn didn't even turn to look.

Ela Claire, undeterred by his lack of interest, continued with her observation. "In the past, Ebon's sky would be dark this time in the morning, but now, it looks as if a new sun is rising in the northwest."

"It's not a sun."

"Then what is it?"

"While I was fighting off our enemy, they taunted me about Ebon's growing military strength. I pieced together their boasts to form one concise story.

"The furnaces of Ebon burn day and night to melt ores for weapons. Throughout the land, bonfires are lit for Ebonites to pay homage to the Cauldron's Dark Flame. That's why their sky glows like a sunrise: Ebon is preparing for war."

He paused to see how she would react. She didn't shuffle about or pepper him with questions - signs that she was worried - so he continued.

"The night sky is another matter. The light from the moon and stars began to fade as if being drained. And now the sun is undergoing the same transformation. My hunch is that the Cauldron is responsible for these anomalies."

Ela Claire focused on Claire's horizon ahead of them.

"Claire looks black, like night." She glanced at the dull sun then back at Claire's sky. "How is this possible?"

"Claire is also preparing for war."

"Like this? Shadowed? Cowering against Ebon's brightness?"

"That's what your eyes tell you. What do your senses tell you?"

She closed her eyes and concentrated. Within the wind was her waltz being sung by a choir and accompanied by majestic horns. The scent of tulips and the sea engulfed the musty aroma rising from the River Arrgient. She imagined being in Marsien Vur and beholding the King of Claire walking toward her; eyes blazing like stars and footfalls reverberating like thunderclaps. He touched her cheek.

"Ela Claire-My delight!"

His whisper boomed like a waterfall. She opened her eyes and the sensations vanished.

"I sense that Claire is stronger than ever."

She noted Ebon's sky and another concern popped into her thoughts. "In the past four summers, has Claire's sky become brighter or darker?"

"I was too busy protecting you to notice."

She snickered. "I know you, Previn. You would have spotted the tiniest change. You're avoiding the question."

"And you're forgetting that there are certain aspects of the Only that we'll never comprehend."

"I'm waiting."

Previn stalled, wishing he could change the topic. But she was no longer Elabea, the naive girl from Hetherlinn. She was Ela Claire, a young woman seasoned by pain's fire; wiser and more persistent than before.

"Darker," he answered.

"So Ebon has become stronger while Claire has become weaker."

"You don't know that. Our eyes can trick us into trading a truth for a lie."

"So you don't have any doubts?"

"I never said that either."

She redirected her gaze back at Claire. "Is it wrong to be afraid, to doubt, to wish life were different?"

"If it is, than I'm just as guilty."

The River Arrgient looked like a ribbon of brown satin in the dull sunlight.

"Even the river looks different."

"Having second thoughts about visiting DioBaith?"

She bit her lower lip.

"I can take you somewhere else."

"No. I'll be fine." She nestled down on his feathers. "I'll be fine," she hummed.

She tried not to worry about the reversing skies or dwell on the last four summers, but the recollections and feelings became stronger, impervious to her will. She tried to sleep. She tried to hum her song. She even tried to think of happier times but nothing helped.

She wasn't sure how long she daydreamed, but when she heard rapids, she welcomed their roar, eager to abandon her inner war.

She sat up and peered over Previn's side. Brown water gushed around mossy boulders creating torrents of white foam.

"We're getting close," Previn advised.

They glided past a massive waterfall whose thundering waters created mists that billowed like smoke. When they soared around a bend of tall pines, DioBaith came into view.

She recoiled at its sight. "I thought I was ready for this."

"I can fly to somewhere else."

"No. I'm just surprised that something I haven't seen in four summers can stir up old feelings so fast."

She set her jaw and leaned into the wind as waves of bereavement washed over her. "I have to do this."

He landed on the tower and Ela Claire slid off.

"I need to be alone."

Previn blinked his eyes in rapid succession and sized her up.

"Don't worry." She flashed him a half-smile. "I won't jump."

Previn pressed his head close to her. "I know, but now that you're out and about, well, I don't want to lose you again."

She patted his face. "You won't. Honest."

Previn stepped back and ruffled his feathers. "I'll be close by." With that, he flew off and circled overhead.

Ela Claire knelt and slid off her backpack. She flipped open the flap and stared into the shadows. There, sitting on her flask of water, was what she was looking for, and like DioBaith, it was able to invoke powerful memories of Romlin: climbing the oak in the meadow; dreaming incredible dreams; listening to his hunting stories; soaring beside him on the Draiggs of Cor len Bluun...

For the longest time she stared at it, trying to master her emotions, trying to find the courage to fish it out. And when she did find the nerve to act, she did so as if a scorpion would sting her if she dawdled.

She was already familiar with its every angle, every blemish, every hue, for there wasn't a day in Il-Lilliad's cave she didn't hold it…cherish it. Cradling it in her palms, she spoke to it as if, by magic, it could deliver her words to Romlin.

"When I think about the times you made me laugh or listened to my endless stories or protected me, I realize how much you loved me." She rotated the object; sunlight danced over its edges. "I only wish I'd told you how I felt."

Her stomach was in knots despite her best efforts to control her feelings. "I hope I was as much comfort to you…" Her voice broke; eyes misted. "As you were to me."

She clutched it to her breast and rocked back and forth, and when her emotions settled, extended it outward to continue her epitaph.

"You changed my story…my life. Without you, I wouldn't have become a storyteller." And then to herself, "So why doesn't such achievement ease my torment?"

She threw back her head in an effort to suppress her pain. Through blurred vision, she watched Previn circling high overhead. "In fact, I'd gladly trade being a storyteller…to find you…alive."

She rose, regained her nerve, and while cupping the object in her hands, made her way to the precipice. The rapids roared and her knees buckled as she remembered Romlin fighting for his life, sinking into deep brown water, disappearing forever. The recollections were as fresh and painful as they were four summers ago.

"How can I be a storyteller without you by my side?"

She wiped her runny nose with a sleeve and checked on Previn. Had he heard her? His steady flight indicated he had not. She dangled her toes over the edge and focused on what she held.

"And yet, I must press on, somehow, someway. If I don't, then your death will be meaningless. That's why I've come to DioBaith, your grave, to tell you that I'm going on our mission to rescue the treasure from the Isle of Rhythe. It's my way of paying tribute; no, of saying that I love you and…" Her lower lip quivered. "You were my best friend."

She sat in the moment and rocked on her heels as the tears fell.

"And so, my love, it's time for me to say farewell. You'll always be in my heart where we'll dance to my waltz. And in the summers to come, and in the stories I'll tell, you'll be a part of all that I do; all that the Only does."

She extended her arms and let the object slip from her fingers.

"Death begets life."

The balmwood teapot, the one Romlin had crafted and brewed mint tea in, floated like a feather on the wind. It spiraled through the air until an updraft caught it and it hovered, bounced, tipped as if palmed by a ghost.

Was it questioning her decision to part ways? Mimicking her? Offering her another chance? She shook off the superstitious notions and backed away from the vessel laden with memories.

The wind shifted and the teapot corkscrewed down where it landed on the tan water without a splash, and like a ship on a great adventure, careened atop the rapids. It rushed over rocks, floated around bends, and when it reached a small waterfall, soared over the edge. Righting itself in the frothing water, it bobbed and spun around and around in an eddy.

For a moment, she thought it would spin forever, but it filled with water and sank where Romlin had perished.

Chapter 5

The Ruse

Three men sat in a dark corner of *The Slaughtered Sow* and observed the activity of the small tavern. Crammed to the brim with men and women, most clapped along to the bard's song or hefted pewter mugs to herald the start of a new chorus. Voices, infused with too much drink, sang loud and out of tune. Gray pipe smoke drifted like clouds through the rafters and mingled with the scent of the blazing fireplace, spilled drink, cheap perfume and body odor.

The trio avoided conversation, did not sing and aside from an occasional sip from their mugs, did not move.

The largest of the three studied the drunken men like a hunter would his prey. He sized up each man's potential, studied their movements in an attempt to anticipate their next move, and calculated how successful the ruse he was hatching would be.

The second, a wiry man, had his hands wrapped around his mug and was more interested in swirling his ale than in anything, or anyone, in the tavern.

The youngest of the trio was fixated on the maidens that sang, flirted and danced in time with the music. One in particular captured his attention.

He elbowed his skinny friend swirling his drink. "Look at her," Lassiter whispered. "Isn't she beautiful?"

DeMorley lifted his eyes to take in the girl. "Her," he asked in a dull voice, "You mean the barmaid behind the counter washing the plates?"

"Yes. And look," Lassiter said in an excited but hushed voice. "She's staring at me. I bet I know what she's thinking."

"That you're sitting beside a very attractive fellow." DeMorley raised his mug to the girl and winked to which she snickered and shook her head.

"See," Lassiter chided, "she's not interested in your flings. She wants someone like me. Someone intriguing, mysterious and handsome."

DeMorley sized up the barmaid. "Naa, she may be cute, but she's too quiet. *Those* are the ones to stay clear of, my boy. Deep trouble. *Deep* trouble indeed." He sipped his ale as if to accent his sage advice.

"Nonsense," Lassiter countered as he admired how she handled a drunken man who tried to steal a kiss: a kind smile before shoving him away. "She'd make a perfect wife."

DeMorley choked on his ale. "Wife," he blurted as he cleared his throat and wiped his mouth with his sleeve. "You're too young to get married."

"We all know that war is imminent," he offered, eyes glowing with passion. "Death will soon prowl about like a wild cat. It makes me long for the things of life I may never taste, hold or experience."

"Agreed," DeMorley answered with a confirming nod. "But a wife? Here? In *The Slaughtered Sow?*"

Draemel, who had been listening in on their conversation, leaned close. "Pipe down," he ordered. "You'll give away our plan." He followed Lassiter's line of sight. "Besides, she's a snake."

DeMorley snickered and shook his head at Draemel. "Spoken from one who knows nothing of love."

Draemel tossed the minstrel a disconcerting look. "I know more about true love than you." His eyes wandered to Lassiter who continued to stare at the barmaid. "In any event, the future king of Allsbruth will *not* find his queen in *The Slaughtered Sow.*"

Lassiter snapped a stern look at Draemel. "That sounded just like something Newcomb would've said."

Draemel caught Lassiter's expression, and despite the boy's frustration at being chastised, cocked his eyebrow and seized the teachable moment. "As you can see, your own feelings and convictions speak the truth about her."

DeMorley threw back the dregs of his mug and slammed it down onto the table. "Maybe Lassiter won't find a queen within this *fine*, upscale establishment," his words were cynical at best, "but why can't he taste love's fruit before matrimony?"

Draemel grabbed DeMorley's shirt and pulled him close. "Because he's the future King of Allsbruth, not some whimsical minstrel. Unlike you, he desires a love that lasts, one that honors the stories of Claire. You know nothing of love, and the lady in question is nothing short of being a viper."

He shoved him back into his seat. DeMorley raised his chin and readjusted his shirt. "Perhaps, but I'm a master at reading a woman's heart by simply gazing into her eyes or studying her from afar. I know for a fact that Lassiter's little lady," he tossed a thumb over his shoulder at the barmaid, "is *not* a viper but an innocent dove."

"Very well," Draemel said matter-of-factly as he once again scanned the rowdy patrons. "It's time I prove you wrong."

DeMorley's chin dropped. "How?" he squeaked.

"You of all people know that a person's true nature emerges when they're trapped."

"Possibly, but..."

"So the question is this: when cornered, whether in principle or in ideologies, will our lovely lady become the innocent, love-sick dove you claim she is - or will she attack like the scorned viper?"

Before DeMorley could answer, Draemel fired his next words to Lassiter. "Is your sword at the ready?"

Lassiter's eyes bulged as he realized what Draemel was up to. It was the same hoax they had used in countless other taverns across the lands. The origin of the ruse was Draemel's and required each of them playing a key role like actors in a well-scripted play. Although they had always been successful, and could perform the con blindfolded, today Lassiter was more interested in love than in Draemel's ploy.

Lassiter's eyes narrowed and he ground his teeth.

"I'll take your silence as a *yes*," Draemel concluded.

DeMorley, who also realized what was about to transpire, wagged his head back and forth like a defiant child. "No," he whined, "not again. Not *here*. There are too many and they're *all* dangerous."

"For once, minstrel, you've spoken the truth," Draemel snarled as he once more sized up the patrons.

The Slaughtered Sow was nestled in the forest of Ferra on the outskirts of the village of Gilnish. The townsfolk, who relished the simple life of tilling the land or fishing the River Dill, were stuck with being in the most unfortunate of locations: Gilnish was the halfway point for those traveling south to the seaport of Southsbrook, or those heading southwest to Torrens Bay.

Trappers, thieves and mercenaries passing through the region found the sleepy hamlet of Gilnish too dull for their tastes. *The Slaughtered Sow* provided an outlet for their urges, while the inhabitants of Gilnish wanted nothing to do with the riff raff and stayed clear of the tavern. *The Slaughtered Sow* was not a place to venture if one needed peace and quiet - or feared being cheated, beaten or killed.

Draemel met DeMorley's pensive expression with a cold, calculating look. "You started this." He pushed back from the table. "I'm simply ending it."

Draemel rose from the shadows. "My lords and ladies," he bellowed. The horde ignored him and continued their songs and conversations. Unfazed, Draemel waved his arms to get their attention and raised his voice. "Ladies and gentlemen of *The Slaughtered Sow*."

The noise died somewhat and a few heads turned to see who was making all the fuss. "My young friend," Draemel rested a hand on Lassiter's shoulder, "has just informed me that he thinks you men have the brains of a donkey and smell like a fly infested dung pile."

Draemel's last few words snuffed out the din like a gust of wind to a candle's flame. All eyes turned and glared at the trio. The tavern became still. Tension hung thick in the air. The only sound came from the lapping flames in the fireplace.

Lassiter dropped his forehead to the table and bounced it up and down, frustrated that he would soon be forced to join the trick. DeMorley, snapped his head about like a trapped animal looking for an escape route. Draemel, the mastermind behind the hoax, arched his back and drank in the tension of the room. A wry smile coursed across his face as he fingered the scar on his cheek.

He continued his ploy. "He also told me why this tavern is called *The Slaughtered Sow*." Draemel eyed Lassiter's love interest and delivered his next volley to her. "It's because your maidens look...

Lassiter stopped his head bashing and looked to see her reaction. Bright green eyes, wide and full of expectation, were sizing him up.

"...and smell..."

She clutched the metal plate to her chest, her full lips parting as if longing for his kiss.

"...like butchered pigs."

She scowled, set her jaw and drilled her emerald eyes into Lassiter. "Kill him!" She hurled the metal plate like a discus at Lassiter's head. He ducked and it clanged off the wall behind them.

"Why'd you say that?" Lassiter snapped at Dreamel.

"To show you that the viper has emerged from her lair. Now get ready."

Lassister huffed as if bored, and rose like an aged actor about to perform his tired role. He drummed fingertips on his sword, still hidden from view, and even yawned as he awaited Draemel's signal.

"No blood in my tavern," shouted the aged owner from behind the counter, knowing a fight was about to break out. "Take them outside and let the dirt of Ferra drink their blood!"

The crowd erupted with shouts and charged.

In defense, the trio hopped onto their table. Draemel tossed DeMorley and Lassiter a smirk.

"Time to go to work, boys."

DeMorley cowered and clutched his lute - a Bellini - to his chest. Draemel and Lassiter drew their swords in one swift motion and brought them into the light of the room.

The crowd stopped and stared spellbound at the steel glinting from the glow of the fireplace.

"How'd you renegades get swords," one dagger-wielding patron challenged. "The Oracles forbid them."

Draemel fingered his scar. "We don't adhere to the teachings of the Oracles."

The crowd murmured and continued to eye the swords.

Draemel took charge. "Gentlemen," he boomed with bravado, "we'll accompany you outside without resistance on one condition." He raised his index finger and swept it about so every eye could see. "Only one of you fights my young friend," he nudged Lassiter in the side. "Defeat him, and you may do what you wish with us. However," he pressed his finger forward to accent his next point, "if my young friend is the victor, then you *all* must fulfill one of our wishes."

"So let me get this straight," a man blurted as he pushed his way to the front of the mob. Draemel had spotted him earlier and figured him to be a hunter. Burly and appearing to be of forty summers, he had thinning, greasy hair that cascaded down to his shoulders. Draemel knew he would be a formidable fighter, and if the scar above his eyebrow was any indication, he had perhaps even fought in the Dark War.

"If I kill the boy," the contender said with a flick of his head at Lassiter, "then we can kill you both. No resistance, no questions."

Draemel's wry smile returned as he nodded.

The hunter rubbed his chin as he considered the deal. "As you can see," he said with mock seriousness, "we're men and women who respect the Oracles." A collective chuckle rose from the surly rabble. "None of us possess a sword. Either your young friend uses a dagger, his fists or..." the hunter eyed Draemel's weapon.

"Once outside," Draemel offered, "you may use my blade."

A wicked smile revealed several missing teeth. "Then let's step outside and settle this once and for all."

The crowd roared with approval and pressed forward.

"But," Draemel shouted with a thrust of his sword to get their attention and halt their advance. "Should he defeat you..."

"Yes, yes, *yes*," the challenger interrupted as he waved his hands to hurry up the process. "We must grant you one wish. But seeing that he's just a boy, and seeing that I killed many a man in the Dark War, I'm not concerned about such conditions to our contract. Now come on! Time to step outside."

The trio hopped off the table and the crowd herded them toward the door.

Draemel whispered into Lassiter's ear. "Remember your training. Discover his weakness and strike hard. Don't attack his strengths. Fight on your terms."

"Yes, of course," Lassiter whispered back. "But when I defeat him, will you promise me something?"

"What?"

"That we stop doing *this!*"

Chapter 6

Strike of the Viper

Once outside, the mob pushed Draemel, Lassiter and DeMorley to the edge of the woods and formed a large circle around them.

The challenger forced his way into the middle. As promised, Draemel handed him his weapon, hilt first. The challenger examined the sword. His eyes glistened as he turned the sword over and marveled at its perfect balance and lethal edge. "So tell me," he asked while swishing the blade through the air. "What's stopping me from killing all three of you right now?"

"Two things," Draemel replied in a calm voice. "I believe you are men of your word."

"Us," the hunter chuckled as he took in the mob's faces who snarled or snickered or spat on the ground in response to Draemel's glowing praise. "Here in Gilnish? In *The Slaughtered Sow?*" The challenger burst out laughing which ignited the pack into cackles.

When the chuckles subsided, the challenger eyed Draemel once more. "Either you're a wise man or a fool. Time will soon reveal which one; but you said there were two things. What's the other?"

"Simple," Draemel answered as his eyes swept about the circle and took in each man's face, wanting to be certain every ear heard his next explanation. "Now that we're outside, we have the advantage. You would be killed before you made a move."

The contender wagged his head, which made his long greasy hair whip about. "You're one arrogant fool! Look around you. There are over fifty of us and only *two* of you!"

"Three," Draemel added with a thumb jerk toward DeMorley.

"Him?" The combatant sniffed as he took in the minstrel. "He'll soil himself and die of fright before one blade falls."

"Perhaps, but his power is in a song."

DeMorley clutched his lute tighter, his brow lined with confusion. This part of the ruse was new, and DeMorley wasn't sure what his role would be. He caught Draemel's raised eyebrow and his subtle head-flick at Lassiter.

"Show your worth," Draemel ordered without taking his eyes off the combatant. "Play us a song, one that reveals our might."

DeMorley raked his brain for a tune, specifically one that Draemel had in mind for the occasion. While sorting through his repertoire, he plucked the strings and tapped a nervous toe, desperate to find the song.

The competitor met Draemel's gaze, noting that his features were poised, as if Draemel knew something he did not, and that such knowledge would sway the outcome in their favor. But as hard as he tried to fathom what it was, he was unable to come to any logical conclusions.

"Suit yourself," the challenger replied with a snarl. "Time is on my side." Without taking his eyes off Draemel, he shouted over his shoulder: "Go ahead, minstrel, sing us your tune, but it will be your death dirge."

DeMorley was about to give up his search when a song came to mind. He stopped plucking and gave Draemel a nod. He tuned his Bellini and strummed the first chord. The lute rang in glorious wonder and DeMorley found his courage and enough spittle to sing.

> *"Gallant men, do draw near,*
> *I sing of one who faced dark fear.*
> *A storyteller with noble intent,*
> *I honor him now with sweet lament.*
>
> *"O'er the Isle of Lills he went,*
> *To mentor a boy of royal descent.*
> *Stories, dreams and whispers from Claire,*
> *Guarded the prince from vapor's despair.*
>
> *"Newcomb, your sacrifice,*
> *Shall crush the drone, shall crush the drone.*
> *Allsbruth, your king awaits,*
> *To claim his throne, to claim his throne."*

After the chorus, Draemel signaled DeMorley to stop singing.

"The song pertains to *this* young man." Draemel placed a reassuring hand on Lassiter's shoulder. "Lassiter is the rightful heir to the throne of Allsbruth."

The throng from *The Slaughtered Sow* burst out laughing.

"Imagine that," the challenger blurted with a thumb jerk at Lassiter. "I'm about to kill his royal highness!"

Cackles, taunts and spittle were hurled at the trio.

Draemel smiled at the challenger, not out of mockery, but as a teacher who knew what his protégé, Lassiter, was capable of doing.

"Remember," Draemel shouted above the hoopla, "when my young friend wins, you *all* owe us one wish."

The challenger ground his teeth like a miller's wheel on grain. "Enough talk," he fired at Lassiter between clinched teeth. "It's time to fight, your *majesty!*"

Lassiter had been studying the man since meeting him inside the tavern. He noted his confident gait but caught the slight limp - an injury from the Dark War? - as well as the man's age and round belly. To deceive him, Lassiter positioned his stance in what would appear to him as a weak position: legs spread apart; sword tip buried in the ground; shoulders slumped; eyes wandering about the mob.

Taking the bait, the challenger whirled his blade overhead and brought it hurtling for Lassiter's head. Lassiter whipped up his weapon, snapped his legs into a battle stance and caught the blow with the forte of his sword, near his guard. The metallic report echoed over the cheering crowd.

Steel to steel and face to face, the challenger put all his weight into the fight, hoping to overpower Lassiter's parry. Lassiter surprised the larger foe with his strength and not only held his position but flashed him a cocky smile.

The challenger, infuriated by Lassiter's strength and brashness, jumped away, and in a feinting maneuver, swung for the gut, but Lassiter had expected as much. With a counter-parry, he spun, leapt and struck from the opposite direction. Caught off guard, the combatant gasped as the sword tip just missed his bulging stomach.

Lassiter, gaining the upper hand, took the offensive. Combining the classical sword training he received from Newcomb with the power and cunning he learned from Draemel, Lassiter attacked with might, finesse and trickery.

He beat the challenger's thrust to the side and using broken-time technique, made the man waste energy swinging in desperation. The combatant backpedaled with Lassiter in pursuit, sword at the ready, eyes focused and muscles taut.

The challenger, convinced his size and past experience would win the day, whipped his sword overhead to cut Lassiter down.

Lassiter parried and their blades locked at the guard. Sweat rolled as they grimaced and pushed to gain the edge. The challenger shifted his weight and heaved Lassiter backwards toward the crowd. Stumbling into the arms of a bearded mercenary, the crowd became energized by their champion's ploy, and ignited with cheers, jeers and catcalls.

"I don't wantcha," the mercenary sneered with a great heave. "Go fight, your majesty!"

Lassiter, propelled toward the challenger, was greeted by his toothless grin and sword cocked over his right shoulder. Lassiter's training with Draemel became instinctual. He dove to the ground, and when the challenger's sword swooshed harmlessly overhead, sprung to his feet. He delivered the flat side of his blade to the man's rear-end.

Smack!

Vulgarities spewed from the challenger's mouth. "Where did you learn to fight like *that*," he spat while massaging his throbbing buttocks.

Lassiter cocked an eyebrow and gestured at Draemel.

"I see," the challenger muttered, gaze darting from Draemel to Lassiter. "Maybe I underestimated your skills." He tightened his grip on his sword. "I won't make the same mistake. Let's see how you handle *this*."

He shouted a battle cry and charged with sword poised overhead. Lassiter steeled himself with his weapon set to parry. The combatant closed the gap and swung his sword ax-like for Lassiter's head. Lassiter ducked as the sword whistled overhead and the combatant stumbled sideways, his momentum making him lose his footing.

Lassiter seized the opportunity and jabbed him in the side. The crowd gasped as their hero staggered about like a wounded beast. He toppled to the ground and the crowd fell silent.

The challenger rolled over in the dirt and fingering his ripped clothing. Surprised he wasn't wounded, he sneered at Lassiter. "You missed!"

Lassiter, who had repositioned himself for a counterattack, chuckled. "I never miss. That was a gift."

Incensed, the challenger pushed himself up and whipped his hair in an effort to intimidate Lassiter. The combatant stomped forward, sword at his side, and stopped far enough away not to be struck.

He shot Lassiter a hot look and ground his teeth. "Wipe that grin off your face."

"No."

"Then I'll *teach* you to respect me." He spat in Lassiter's face.

Lassiter lunged, but instead of running him through with his sword, kicked the man's injured leg.

The challenger howled and hobbled around in pain. "You kicked me! Like a girl!"

"And *you* spat in the face of your king like a coward," Lassiter wiped the spittle off with his sleeve.

"You're no *king!*"

Swords were repositioned and they charged forward emitting battle cries. The mob roared their approval. Steel collided with a loud *clang*. Toe-to-toe they pushed and grunted, neither willing to give ground. Faces reddened from exertion, sweat streaked shirts and tunics.

As they struggled, the challenger met Lassiter's piercing eyes. Staring back at him was a focused warrior: taut jawline replaced his playful smile; determination filled his once dancing eyes.

"Had enough," Lassiter barked.

"Never!"

With a loud grunt, the challenger leaned all of his weight into the fight. Lassiter grit his teeth and pushed back. They staggered about, neither man giving ground until Lassiter leapt away like a cat. The challenger stumbled forward, staggering to catch his balance. Lassiter spun and delivered a swift thrust. The combatant, out of desperation, raised his sword and with a stroke of luck, deflected the jab.

Lassiter sidestepped and delivered a thrust to the combatant's shoulder. The man yelped and gave a wild swing for Lassiter's stomach but he slapped it away. Lassiter, sensing victory was near, pressed forward, both hands around the hilt, sword in front of him, eyes glued on his opponent's every move.

The man, wounded and only able to use one arm, swung his sword. The effort was weak and Lassiter hammered the slow moving blade to the ground. The combatant retrieved his weapon and kept a safe distance away from Lassiter.

The crowd, witnessing Lassiter gain the upper hand, shouted louder encouragements to their champion in hope of turning the tide. The combatant, weakened from the effort and the loss of blood, stumbled about like a drunk, dragging his blade through the dirt, gasping for air.

Lassiter looked as strong as when the fight first started. "Bow to me and I'll grant you mercy."

The mercenary raced to the challenger who was doubled over sucking in air. "He's just a boy. Kill him! If not, we'll lose the bet." He shoved the champion toward Lassiter and exited the arena.

The challenger made his way for Lassiter, dragging his blade through the dirt. With all of his effort, he swung the blade up for Lassiter's chin. Lassiter dodged the lethargic attack and with a quick thrust, sliced the man's cheek. The challenger yelped and stumbled backwards; free hand covering the bloody wound.

"Lucky blow!" Crimson spittle flew off his lips.

"I don't believe in luck," Lassiter countered with shoulders righted and weapon at the ready.

The challenger, reenergized by adrenaline and rage, raised his weapon with his good arm. He screamed like a mad man and the mob cheered him on. With confidence soaring and renewed strength, he charged.

This was the moment Lassiter had been waiting for. As he had surmised before the fight, the challenger's pride would be his downfall. Lassiter set his trap. He relaxed his stance and lowered his sword, feigning fatigue and fear. The combatant took the bait and increased his speed, sword ready to split open Lassiter's skull.

Lassiter, who had the perfect opportunity to kill him, opted for another tactic. He dove head first into his attacker's shins and sent him crashing to the ground. The crowd fell silent as a cloud of dust rose where their champion lay.

Lassiter sprang to his feet and sauntered over to his challenger. Dust matted his sweaty, bloodied clothes. The man pushed himself up and Lassiter kicked him in the side, sending him sprawling to the ground. In a last ditch effort, the combatant rolled over and raised his sword but he was too weak to be of any real threat.

Lassiter kicked the weapon and sent it sailing through the air where it landed at Draemel's feet. With one eye on the crowd, Draemel retrieved it and flashed Lassiter an approving smile. Lassiter gave a subtle nod and turned his attention to the man lying at his feet.

"Surrender." Lassiter positioned his sword tip at the man's throat.

"Never!" He coughed and spat blood and dirt from his mouth.

"I spared your life. I could have killed you."

"Then do it! I'd rather die than surrender to a waif like you."

"I'm not a waif." Lassiter pressed the tip into his flesh. "I'm the future King of Allsbruth."

"You have no such claim," the man countered as he once more tried to free his mouth of dirt and blood. "I'd rather die like a dog in the dust." The challenger rolled his head toward the throng. "What are you waiting for? Kill them!"

Draemel, who had anticipated as much, raised the sword. "I'd think twice about doing that."

"We outnumber them," someone quipped. "Let's run 'em through!"

The circle rallied their courage, and with a loud shout, squeezed toward them.

"Your majesty," Draemel shouted loud enough for the horde to hear, "order in the reinforcements."

The circle stopped and looked all about them for an ambush. Seeing there was no one else, and that this was just another ruse, they resumed their attack.

Lassiter, with his eyes on the challenger, shouted a command. "Right flank, advance! Left flank, stand ready!"

One hundred armed men, most on war-stallions, charged from the shadow of the woods and surrounded the mob. The horde stopped their advance, and realizing they were outnumbered, dropped their weapons.

Lassiter's army was a mish-mash of Tristanites, Allsbruthians, and Ingloids. Some wore captured Ebonite armor while others wore only simple peasant attire. But each carried an Ebonite weapon - sword, lance or longbow - no doubt captured during one of their prior campaigns. More importantly, they bore expressions that told the men of *The Slaughtered Sow* that they would fight to the death for Lassiter.

Draemel sheathed his sword and sauntered about the circle, his steely gaze drilling into the horde. He pulled out his gor weapon and tapped it in his palm. "I'm very disappointed," he chastised with a head wag and a steady tap, tap, tap of his weapon. "*Very* disappointed, indeed.

When men no longer honor their words, their hearts dishonor them as well. In fact..."

He stopped before one unsuspecting man and took in his ghost-white expression. "Are they even men," he asked with a chilled whisper.

The man's eyes bugged out in horror.

Draemel, with lightning fast reflexes, grabbed him and pressed his gor blade to his throat. "I should *gut* you like a pig," Draemel muttered between clinched teeth. "I should let your blood stain the dirt of Ferra. Isn't that what the tavern owner said?"

The accused winced in pain and nodded, but panic set in when he realized that he had possibly answered the wrong question and had just given Draemel permission to slice his throat.

Draemel pressed his weight into the man and whispered, "But I won't. Do you know why?"

The man's eyes bulged like grapes being squeezed too hard. "No," he squeaked.

"Because," Draemel bellowed over his shoulder so all the men could hear. "Unlike you, I *am* a man of my word."

Draemel yanked the weapon free and spun away. The man grabbed a frantic breath and massaged his neck.

"Prior to this fight," Draemel announced as he paced about once more, "you all agreed to honor our wish should Lassiter win. It's time to ante up. Prove to us that you can be men of your word. Honor us with such a deal."

"What do you wish," the challenger asked from his precarious position.

"Join my army," Lassiter answered as he repositioned his sword tip over the man's heart.

The challenger, along with the crowd, did not snicker or make snide comments as before. Lassiter had impressed them not only with his swordsmanship but with his leadership and tactical abilities as well.

"How do we know you're the rightful king," one man inquired. "There are tales of two others who claim to be rulers. Perhaps one of them is the future king of Allsbruth."

Draemel nodded. "Yes, we too have heard such stories. One I have met and he's a madman whose allegiance is to Ebon and the Cauldron. Surely you wouldn't want him to be king? And the other, a rogue warrior, commands an army of criminals who plunder the helpless for their own gain. Aside from being a campfire tale at best, would you vow allegiance to such a tyrant?"

Murmurs and mumbles emanated from the mob as they discussed the validity of Draemel's claim.

"Could be, but either way, you don't frighten us with such dribble," another interjected. "Gilnish is far from Ebon and we can defend ourselves should a fight arise. Besides, Gilnish was never bothered during the Dark War and this time will be no different."

Draemel snickered. "You have faith in these Gor Kings…and *his* platitude," he gestured at the man who made the last challenge, "yet want proof of Lassiter's lineage?" He shook his head and cast them a look of disgust.

"I can offer some proof," Lassiter fired as he kept his sword pressed against the combatant's chest. "It's found in my story."

"Tell it," came an earnest cry from an old man in the mob.

"My mother, the Princess Annestesia, was the daughter of King Culdean. I'm his grandson. I lived on the Isle of Lills to escape the Cauldron's influence. A great storyteller from Claire, Newcomb, mentored me during those many summers. He later sacrificed his life in order that I could fulfill my destiny as king. I'm sure you saw the Martyr's Moon."

A murmur arose along with several confirming nods.

"Now," Lassiter continued, "I gather loyal men who are willing to fight with me to reclaim Allsbruth and defeat the Ebonites."

The mercenary, the one Lassiter stumbled into during the fight, crossed his arms. "That's a nice bedtime tale, boy. Anyone could claim such a thing. Do you think we're that *stupid?*"

"No, which is why I have this. DeMorley, show them."

The minstrel, who during the fight had cowered behind Draemel, reached inside his tunic. He fished around in a pocket and pulled out Lassiter's invitation, and as he had done many times before during this phase of their ploy, raised it overhead like a victor's wreath. Turning around, he let the mob check its authenticity. Necks strained and eyes scanned the golden letters that shimmered in the sunlight. Most could not read, but the ones that could verified its genuineness with a whisper.

"Your invitation proves nothing."

The voice came from a maiden beyond the circle. The crowd parted as she marched inward. "We've never cared about Allsbruth or Claire for that matter," she added, the top of her head now in sight. "We simply want to live our lives as we see fit."

She stepped inside the circle and Lassiter's eyes bulged with recognition.

The viper.

She put her hands on her hips, cocked her head to one side and stared at him with her liquid green eyes. "We don't need a king. We don't need your stories or invitation. Besides," she ran her eyes up and down him. "You're not a man. You're just a boy."

Lassiter flinched at her accusation and stood speechless. Newcomb had prepared him to battle with logic and wit. Draemel had trained him to fight with brawn and shrewdness. He had even learned a thing or two from DeMorley, but nothing in all his training had prepared him for this skirmish.

"I'm *not* a boy," he argued while keeping an eye on the pinned combatant. "I'm a man of twenty summers."

"Your majesty," DeMorley chided as he smothered a smile with his hand, noting the dire predicament Lassiter was in, "do you still desire her to be your queen? Her words are so eloquent, and her spirit is - dare I say - compliant."

The viper cast a hot look at DeMorley who raised his hands in defense.

She snapped her gaze back to Lassiter. Her eyes softened.

"So," she cooed in a soft voice, "you want me to be your queen."

She slid across the open expanse toward Lassiter as if floating on air.

Lassiter flashed her a nervous smile then stared down at the challenger, preferring to reengage in combat than to answer her question.

"Don't look at me," the man pleaded as if reading Lassiter's mind. "She's as stubborn as her mother and doesn't listen to me much, either."

"She's your daughter," Lassiter asked as his eyes hopped from girl back to the father lying beneath his sword.

The man flashed his toothless grin and arched his eyebrows.

"Be careful, Lassiter," DeMorley shouted with a mischievous chuckle. "Nothing stings like a woman scorned."

She was close now and Lassiter could smell her perfume. His muscles relaxed and he felt light-headed. Warmth pulsed his veins and his face reddened when her seductive eyes sized up his athletic frame. With a long finger, she twirled one of his long locks. Lassiter drank in her perfume, her smile, her figure…

"Am I worthy to be your queen," she asked, her voice sultry and silky smooth.

Although an attractive woman, her true personality was emerging as Draemel had predicted, and Lassiter could not picture himself by her side. Not for a day. Not for a summer. And especially not forever.

"Well…umm," he mumbled as he stalled for time.

"My name is Matralene," she whispered. Her eyes, warm pools of green light, danced across his face with desire.

"Yes, Matralene," Lassiter stammered as he tried to maintain control not only of his sword that pinned her father, but his emotions as well. "I did say those things in the tavern, but…"

Her eyes narrowed and she let go of his hair. "So I *do* look and smell like a butchered pig?"

"No, not *those* things," he blurted. Then, in a calm voice full of confidence, he added, "You see, Draemel says things like that all the time. It's how we draw men into a fight to join my army and…"

She pressed her index finger against his lips to silence him. Emerald eyes flickered as she met his gaze. "Did you or did you *not* say I would make a great queen?"

Matralene lowered her finger and her eyes were no longer sensual. Instead, they looked lethal. Almost like those…

…of a viper?

Lassiter looked to Draemel and DeMorley for wisdom as to how he should proceed with her. Convinced he was in no real danger, and enjoying the comedic situation the young lover had created for himself, they smiled and shrugged their shoulders.

Lassiter huffed and turned his attention back to the woman. "Dear maiden…"

"Matralene," she corrected, her voice as cool as Ebon's breeze, long fingers fondling his hair.

"Yes, Matralene…of course. You see, I'd had several ales, the tavern was dark, and well, you know how men can be."

Fingers tightened about his lock and yanked. He winced from the pain. Her eyes blazed. Did he see her tongue flick?

"No, King Lassiter, I'm afraid I *don't* know how men can be. I'm *not* a whore, so do explain."

"Umm…" he stammered as he tilted his head to relieve the pressure from having his hair pulled. "Sometimes…sometimes men talk just for the sake of talking and…"

She jerked his hair.

"Just…*talk*," she repeated. Releasing her grip, she stepped back and planted her hands on her hips. Lassiter glanced at her waist to see if she wore a sword or a dagger. She was unarmed, which made him moan. He would have preferred a sword fight instead of fending off her barbed tongue.

"Yes, Matralene, just talk," Lassiter answered as a surge of confidence coursed his veins, convinced a logical explanation would repel her attacks. "You see, men like telling stories - usually of wild proportion, about hunting or conquests…"

"*Conquests,*" she hissed.

Lassiter gulped.

"Be careful," Draemel offered through cupped hands. "The viper has exposed her fangs."

Matralene threw Draemel a hate-filled look. He held up his hands in mock surrender and she whipped her gaze back to Lassiter.

"Now I understand," she fired. "To *you,* I'm simply a deer to hunt. To your friends, I'm but a snake to torment."

"No, no, no, Matralene," Lassiter countered with quick shakes of his head. "You're more like a boar than a deer. You see, boars are…"

Smack!

Matralene turned on her heel and pushed back through the crowd to *The Slaughtered Sow* while Lassiter rubbed his cheek.

Matralene's father, still pinned beneath Lassiter's sword, chuckled.

"Lassiter," he chuckled, "I doubted your story about your royal lineage, but by the stories of Claire, I believe you now. Only a sheltered boy, living with a storyteller on the Isle of Lills, would be *that* ignorant in the ways of conversing with a woman."

The men of *The Slaughtered Sow* burst into laughter.

Matralene's father continued. "Release me, Lassiter, grandson of King Culdean. You have defeated me, and as we agreed, we shall honor your wish."

Lassiter removed his blade.

The challenger labored to his feet. "It seems that today," he said while brushing himself off and favoring his wounded shoulder, "that your army has grown. Let's celebrate. Call out your left flank so they can join us."

"There is no left flank," Lassiter answered in a flat voice as he rubbed his throbbing cheek.

"You mean to tell me you were bluffing?"

Lassiter nodded.

The challenger flashed a toothless grin.

"Handsome, strong *and* cunning," he praised with a slap across Lassiter's back. He turned to address the tavern owner. "Bring ale for everyone. Today we toast the future King of Allsbruth!"

The once unruly mob let out a unanimous shout and milled about with Lassiter's soldiers.

Draemel came alongside Lassiter. "And so," he said while inspecting Matralene's glowing handprint. "With the strike of the viper, King Lassiter's army grows."

"What did I say to make her so angry," Lassiter asked, as hundreds of questions about the opposite sex swirled through his thoughts.

"A word of advice, your majesty," DeMorley offered as he swung his Bellini over his shoulder and draped an arm across Lassiter's back. "When we go back inside, don't say another word to Matralene. For that matter, don't say a word to *any* woman. We have a *lot* to teach you!"

Chapter 7

Visitors to Min Brock

Gundin strolled along Min Brock's western walkway with hands clasped behind his back, the wind whipping his hair. The sun, a mandarin orb, sat low on the Gilden Plains. Sunbeams brushed the grasslands with ginger hues while the Addoli Ridge took on a purplish tinge, the sparse trees standing out in stark contrast.

As wondrous as the spectacle was to behold, Gundin knew that such beauty was deceptive. Soon, a distant roar would signal that the lions prowled for food. To date, no refugee had been attacked, but Gundin knew they were lucky. During the Dark War, he had seen his share of corpses - or what was left of them - while traveling the plains.

Aside from the lions, there was a more nagging reason he dreaded the night. Based upon his experience in the Dark War, this was when the Ebonites attacked. The only sign of their enemy had been demolith patrols, but thanks to Linwith and his worms, these never ventured close to Min Brock.

Gundin tossed aside his worries and took in the tapestry of colors. Since his arrival to Min Brock, he walked the western wall alone, a warrior on a spiritual journey, seeking answers beyond the keep. Gundin's sojourn was as calculable as the sun's course.

It was during these respites that he set aside his responsibilities as a leader and focused, as a father, on one name - Galadin, his son.

Sometimes he daydreamed of holding him as a toddler. Other times he pictured him in the present, a warrior galloping toward the keep, muscles defined, chin held high and commanding a legion of men.

But most of the time, he simply hoped he was alive.

"Sir."

The call came from a young sentry approaching from his right. Gundin huffed, irritated that his daydream was interrupted. He looked the sentry over. In the dim light, the young man reminded him of Galadin. He stared into the young sentry's eyes and drifted back in time.

"My son," Gundin half-whispered as he reached for the sentry's shoulder to pull him close.

"Sir?" The sentry took a cautionary step back.

Gundin, shook off his musing, dropped his arms and his gruff demeanor returned. He spun away from the guard and stared at the horizon. "Nothing happened."

The sentry swallowed hard.

Gundin turned to take in the boy's face. "Is that clear, soldier?"

He nodded, eyes wide with fright.

Gundin let his gaze drift back to the western horizon. "Now, what's so important that you had to interrupt my reverie?"

"Sir, we were just wondering…"

"We?" Gundin zeroed in on the young man's face.

The sentry jerked a thumb over his shoulder to a group of soldiers huddled by the turret door.

Gundin rubbed his chin. "I see. Not your lucky night, is it?"

"No, Sir."

"So what do *we* want to know?"

"Well, when the Ebonites come, will…will…"

Gundin planted his hands on his hips and scowled. "Spit it out, soldier!"

"When the Ebonites come, will we be ready?"

Gundin took in the young man's expression. He was pale and although he kept his chin raised and his back stiff, his lip quivered.

Gundin turned his attention to the walls and towering turrets of Min Brock. The rebuilding of the citadel began five summers ago. Linwith, as he had vowed, took the worms to the coast where they retrieved boulders from the cliffs of the Gilden Sea and set them in place where men chiseled and mortared them into position. With the worms expediting the process, the rebuilding of Min Brock was completed by the second summer.

"Look at her," Gundin offered with a sweep of his hand at Min Brock. "Isn't she grand?"

"Yes, sir," the sentry answered in a dull tone.

"She's perched atop this knoll and reigns over the Gilden Plains like she did before the Dark War!"

"That's what I've been told, sir."

"From our height, you can even get a glimpse of the Gilden Sea."

He pointed out the landmark but the sentry was unimpressed. Gundin flashed him a disapproving look.

"How old are you?"

The sentry clicked his heels together in salute. "I'll be eighteen this summer, sir."

Gundin rubbed his chin. "You've never seen her before the war. You don't know the power she possesses."

"I only know what you've taught me, sir."

Gundin pressed in. "To *know* takes this." He tapped his skull with his index finger. "To believe takes *this*." He thumped the sentry's chest.

The sentry tried to hold Gundin's gaze, but blinked.

Gundin stepped away and turned his attention to the courtyards. Refugees milled about and campfires were lit in preparation for the cool evening. The number of refugees had grown with the turn of every season, some coming from as far away as Tristan. Despite the influx of men, most were not battle-hardened warriors. Instead, Min Brock was a conglomeration of farmers and artisans who had never seen combat.

From Day One, Gundin trained them on tactics, weaponry and military decorum. The men, eager to learn how to fight to defend their families, rose to the challenge. Gundin was impressed by their hard work and level of improvement. Over time, they transformed into an army, but Gundin wondered if they'd have the stomach for war. It was one thing to spar in the safety of a keep. Combat against an Ebonite warrior was another matter.

Gundin's gaze drifted past the central tower rising from the Grand Hall and came to rest upon the keep's arsenal. It was stockpiled with weapons, thanks again to the worms who had flown to Tristan to purchase them. Yet despite such preparations, Gundin knew they were out-numbered.

"War is coming," Gundin answered as his gaze swept the Gilden Sea, now a sliver of black beyond the Addoli Ridge. "I can feel it, almost like a typhoon blowing in from the Gilden Sea. Even though the sky is clear, the winds have shifted and a storm is racing across the waves. It's just a matter of time before it slams into us."

The sun slid past the horizon and the sea disappeared in the dusk as if to further emphasize Gundin's prophecy. Gundin drank in the moment while the young sentry shivered at the thought.

"No matter," Gundin concluded as he patted the parapet. "We'll be ready." This he said to encourage himself more than the sentry. Gundin spun and rested his hands on the guard's shoulders. "*You'll* be ready."

The soldier gave a quick nod and bit his lower lip.

Commotion from the guards milling near the turret drew their attention.

"What's wrong," Gundin shouted.

"Someone's approaching!"

Gundin snapped his gaze to the Gilden Plain. "Where?"

"Beyond the dry creek bed." The men pointed to the spot.

Gundin followed their line of sight. "I don't see them. Are your eyes playing tricks on you?"

"No, sir. They're barely visible in the tall grass."

Gundin leaned on the parapet and stared out into the dusk. Suddenly, his back stiffened. "Yes. There they are." And then to the sentry who had sounded the alarm, "Good spotting."

The soldier beamed and the alarm was passed down the line.

"Sir," the guard near Gundin asked, "who are they?"

"I'm not sure. They're short and are dressed in white. Doubtful they're children. Who'd send forty or so children gallivanting through lion-infested grasslands?"

"Gundin!"

The familiar voice rose from the courtyard. Gundin spun around to find Quinn amidst the refugees. No one moved or said a word. They knew that accurate communication could be the difference between life and death.

Quinn cupped his hands over his mouth and shouted into the wind. "Who is it?"

Gundin, who still wasn't sure who the travelers were, turned for another look.

"Hurry," Quinn fired, anxious to know whether to order men to arms or open the gates for more refugees.

Gundin gestured to Quinn that he needed more time. When he recognized their identity, he spun on his heel to deliver the news.

"MerriNoons," he shouted.

The distance and the winds altered his words. Instead of hearing, "MerriNoons", Quinn discerned, "Very soon."

"No," he countered, "Not *when* will they arrive but *who* will arrive."

"MerriNoons."

"Yes, I understand - *very soon*. But *who* will be here very soon?"

The sentry snickered and turned away.

Gundin cupped his hands, and at the top of his lungs shouted: "Like I've already told you, *Mer-i-noons*."

"Yes, yes, *yes*. But *who*?"

Gundin groaned and let his head drop.

"Sir," the sentry chimed, doing his best to contain his laughter, "it appears we need a better means of communication."

"Tell me something I *don't* know," he huffed as he gestured for Quinn to come see for himself.

Quinn raced to the closest tower and sprinted up the circular stairs.

"Didn't you hear me," Quinn fired as he pushed past sentries.

Gundin met his gaze with hands planted on his hips. "We *all* heard you, Quinn. You, on the other hand, have the ears of an old man. I said, *MerriNoons*. Look."

Quinn stared to where Gundin pointed. Baldheads, short stature and white attire confirmed their identity. He started to relax until a new worry came to mind.

"The lions," he muttered to no one in particular.

All eyes focused on the grove of trees near the base of the Addoli

Ridge. Even from far away, the men could see the pride rise to their feet and saunter into the taller grasses. The lions blended in with the color of the plains, but due to their incredible size, their heads could be seen cutting through the stalks like the bows of warships.

Their pace was slow, measured, toward the unsuspecting refugees.

"The wind," Quinn noted as his eyes jumped from the lions back to the MerriNoons. "The lions have caught their scent."

Gundin took in the MerriNoons' position and calculated the distance to Min Brock. "They're too far away. They'll never make it here in time."

"The worms," Quinn exclaimed as he spun around. "Linwith," he shouted below.

His brother, who had just returned from a reconnaissance mission, stood in the courtyard.

"MerriNoons," Quinn shouted down to him.

This time it was Quinn's words that the winds shifted.

Linwith's face twisted with confusion. "Very soon?"

Quinn, as well as the others on the walkway, gasped in horror. What had been a comical exchange was now a matter of life and death. Quinn and Gundin flicked concerned looks to one another.

"*Merr-i-noons*," they shouted in unison while gesturing to the plains.

Linwith, still unable to hear, discerned the urgency in the matter. He spun on his heels and ran to mount the Worm King. With strong, powerful strokes the sapphire worm soared over the western wall, but still not certain what to be looking for, Linwith overlooked the MerriNoons directly below, focusing instead on the sky and horizon.

Alarmed, the men on the wall jumped, shouted and waved to get his attention. Unable to hear them, Linwith climbed higher, flying away from the very people he was sent to rescue.

"Archers," Gundin shouted, desperation tinging his voice.

The command was passed down the line to the nearby towers. Inside the towers, archers pulled arrows from quivers while reserves raced out onto the western wall.

"Prepare to fire," Gundin ordered, "but await my command."

Arrows were nocked.

Quinn leaned on the parapet and gauged the distance to the lions. "They're too far away," he shouted to Gundin.

"I know, but I can't stand here and do *nothing!*"

Quinn turned and grabbed the nearest sentry. "Send out a patrol. Now!" He pushed the guard on his way.

The pride was closer and had split into two groups, one to attack the MerriNoons' right flank and the other their left. The MerriNoons continued their trek, oblivious to the hungry jaws moving their way. The doors of the keep opened and ten riders galloped down the knoll's winding road.

Gundin sized up their progress. "They won't get there in time." And in a voice that boomed, "Archers, take aim!"

Bowstrings were drawn back and their collective groan echoed along the wall. Nocks rested beside cheeks.

"Steady..."

Archers calculated the distance to the lions. Tips were aimed higher.

"Fire!"

Shafts whizzed out and disappeared from sight. They fell short of their mark.

"Surely they can defend themselves," the young sentry offered.

"They're MerriNoons - cooks," Gundin barked. "They don't know *how* to fight. Their only weapon is a firestick."

The men leaned against the parapet, aghast at the horror unfolding below.

The MerriNoons stopped and huddled back-to-back pushing their children into the middle for protection.

"What are they doing," the sentry asked.

"Isn't it obvious? They're preparing to die."

Sunburned grass parted. Manes fluttered like brown smoke. Dark roars rolled.

Quinn, unwilling to watch the massacre, turned away. The collective gasp from his men made him flinch.

"Look," Gundin shouted with an elbow into Quinn's ribs.

"How can you watch such..."

"No, it's not what you think. *Look.*"

Quinn braved a look. Instead of bloodstained grass, he saw the miraculous. The MerriNoons were unscathed and were continuing their journey. This alone would have been remarkable, but it was the lions that made him question his vision. They strolled beside the MerriNoons like hunting dogs with their masters.

"How is this possible," Quinn asked.

"All I know is when the lions charged, the MerriNoons held up their hands and the lions...*stopped.*"

The patrol from Min Brock reached the entourage, but as they neared, the pride caught their scent and growled. Horses bucked and whinnied. Riders regained control of their steeds, and convinced they were now in greater danger than the MerriNoons, galloped back to Min Brock.

When the MerriNoons reached the road leading up the knoll, the lions stopped. Yellow, primal eyes watched until the last MerriNoon was safe within the keep. As the gate closed, they turned and disappeared, like brown smoke, into the sea of grass.

Chapter 8

Walk of Hope

Areall stood alone atop the south wall of Min Brock. It was late in the day, and the breeze whistled over the parapet. With each passing day, with every changing season, she walked the walls, a mother longing for her daughter's return like a pilgrim awaiting an epiphany.

She endured the scorching sun, battled howling zephyrs, weathered torrential rains, and suffered winters that chilled the bone.

As a seasoned observer of the Gilden Plains, she learned the difference between the winds parting the grass from that of roaming lions. But initially, she wasn't as discerning and her mistakes brought false hope.

Areall reflected on her most painful lesson. Grass atop a far knoll swished aside in a different direction from that of the wind. Her heart skipped a beat.

Is it Elabea and Galadin, or more refugees?

She leaned out over the parapet for a better look, refusing to blink, the wind burning, causing tears to streak her cheeks.

The parting grass rolled toward her like…

Children running through a meadow!

Her passion swelled and she called their names. When no reply came, she cupped her hands and shouted even louder, but as the moving blades roamed closer, she realized her mistake. A rogue breeze, distinct from the wind, had brushed aside the stalks like a phantom running a hand over the tops. Areall slumped behind the parapet as if struck by an arrow, wailing at the top of her lungs as a whisper snickered in her ear.

Areall threw off the memory and pulled her shawl close. Daryess made her way to her side, eyeing Areall's slouching shoulders and forlorn expression.

"Rough day?" Daryess took her hands.

Areall stole a glance into her face. "Isn't every day rough?"

"Yes, but today seems darker than usual." Daryess massaged her scarred fingertips.

Areall jerk them away and hid them beneath her armpits.

Daryess rested a consoling hand on her shoulder. "I'm not trying to shame you."

Areall flicked a cold look her way before staring back at her feet. "That day was the darkest."

Daryess nodded. "Yes, but I've made my share of mistakes, too."

"Perhaps." Areall's voice quivered. "But you didn't rake the stone wall with your fingers like a mad fiend." Dark eyes took in Daryess. "I remember doing it, but didn't feel a thing, as if I was in a nightmare. These prove otherwise." She pulled her hands out and wiggled her fingers.

Daryess squeezed warmth into them. Their eyes locked. "You are *not* insane, do you hear me?" She shook Areall's hands for emphasis. "I know madness. I lived with it for many summers. You are anything *but* mad."

Daryess released her grip.

Areall worked up a weak smile. "You're such a good a friend."

"Today, I helped you. Tomorrow, you'll help me, just like we've been doing now for many summers. And we won't stop, will we?"

Areall wiped her eyes. "No, we won't." And with more passion: "We won't."

They clasped hands and started their walk around the keep, keen eyes searching the plains for any sign of their children's return.

Rounding a corner, Areall turned her attention to a large group of women down in the courtyard. Huddled in a pack, some glowered with arms crossed, others whispered and pointed out Daryess and Areall. "Do you know what one of them told me the other day?"

Daryess followed her line of sight and gave a disapproving huff. "No, but I can imagine."

"She had the gall to quote an Oracle. *'Plant bitter seeds, drink sour wine.'* I informed her, in a polite manner of course, that we follow the stories of Claire, *not* the Oracles."

"You're too nice, Areall. I had a few confront me awhile back; said they needed to speak to me in private of 'a matter of grave importance.'" She met Areall's gaze. "They said it was time we ended our walks, that after four summers of no news about our children, it was obvious that they were dead. *And,*" Daryess raised a finger for emphasis, "to top that off, they said that the Only had whispered this 'vision' to them."

"What did you do?"

"See the fat one wearing the red scarf?"

Areall scanned the women below. "Is it covering an eye?"

"That's the one," Daryess chimed as a smile arced her face.

Areall gasped and flicked a concerned look at Daryess. "You hit her...*in the eye?*"

Daryess met her gaze and shrugged off the accusation. "I prefer to think of it as realigning her 'vision.'"

A commotion in the courtyard made them spin around to investigate. People were running and pointing in the direction of Min Brock's western wall. Even the nagging women had joined the surge.

Areall and Daryess had seen this type of activity before and it always filled them with hope. Without a word or even a gesture, they sprinted for the staircase. Racing out into the courtyard, they joined the crowd surging toward the main gate.

"More refugees," Areall asked a nearby woman.

"Yes, possibly children!"

Areall and Daryess, hoping it was Elabea and Galadin, darted ahead and reached the gate where the crowd had congregated. They pushed and clawed their way to the front. Reaching the newcomers, they sighed and let their shoulders slump.

"MerriNoons," Areall noted, dejection in her voice.

She squeezed Daryess' hand and swallowed back the tears.

The crowd parted and Quinn made his way to Areall and Daryess. Together, they took in the MerriNoons.

Short and plumb, they all wore matching white attire and huddled together like frightened animals. One MerriNoon stood apart from the group and had his arms wrapped around two children who buried their faces in his tunic. He smiled and was looking into Quinn's face.

Quinn, who towered over him, knelt to appear less intimidating.

"My name's Quinn."

"And I'm Digri."

"Welcome to Min Brock, Digri, but tell me something. MerriNoons have never needed our help before, even during the Dark War, so what brings you here today?"

Digri's smile fell. "War comes."

"Yes, but war has come to these lands before. How is this war different?"

Digri's head dropped and he pulled the children at his side close.

Areall, sensing something horrible had happened, knelt and put a comforting hand on his trembling shoulder. Digri was weeping.

She flashed Quinn a flabbergasted look, hoping he understood what had caused such heartache but he only shrugged.

Digri patted the children's baldheads and lifted moist eyes. "Because this war has the Gor King."

A collective gasp went up from the crowd.

"With all due respect, Digri, the Gor King is a tavern myth."

Digri's face reddened and he stepped forward with clinched fists. "Myth," he spat, his dark mood alarming Quinn who had never seen such rage before in a MerriNoon. "He's like a mad dragon and commands a frightening army. They came and we fed them and they liked. But all was not good. They laughed at us and then…"

Digri closed his eyes and the memory he held cut lines of pain across his forehead. Lips twisted and teeth ground to squelch the agony welling up inside. When his face finally relaxed, he opened his eyes, drew in a deep breath and continued.

"We pled…screamed. They laughed all the more. I searched the Gor King's eyes to see if there was any kindness within. Madness! Evil! Nothing good dwells in this one. Then he shouted to his army, *Feast upon their flesh! First blood!*"

The MerriNoons shivered and cringed at hearing the command again. Daryess, moved by his story, knelt beside Areall.

"My wife," Digri continued, "my children…" His voice broke; eyes became moist. "So many butchered by this Gor King. These children," he stepped back to the two that were at his side and rested palms atop their heads, "are now orphans."

Digri gave them several consoling pats. "Then, for no reason, he left. We knew we were no longer safe. So now, here we are."

The crowd murmured to themselves.

"So," Gundin said as he made his way through the crowd, "the Gor King exists after all, and preys upon the peaceful MerriNoons like a jackal upon the hare. Such are the days before us. Gone are the battles of honor."

Quinn met Digri's teary eyes. "We'll protect your people. In exchange," Quinn offered, knowing full well that MerriNoons never received a gift without giving one in exchange, "you may cook for Min Brock."

Digri wiped his eyes and a smile reappeared. "This would be a great honor. We have brought our spices and firesticks; necessary tools of our trade. But we ask one favor."

"Anything," Quinn replied.

"When it is time for battle, you summon us."

Quinn was thunderstruck. He looked to Gundin for insight. He wagged his head. Quinn sized up the MerriNoons. They were master chefs, not warriors. To send them into combat would be a sentence of death.

"I understand how you feel," Quinn began, "but with all due respect, MerriNoons are short chefs and not…"

"Warriors," Digri finished with jaw set and fist knuckles turning white.

"Well, yes, but…"

"Who were not afraid of the lions."

Quinn blinked and nodded. "Yes, that was amazing…"

"And were not attacked."

"True, but…"

"Escorted by the great lions of the Gilden Plains to Min Brock."

Digri stepped forward and put his nose close to Quinn's. "Can your *tall warriors* do that?"

"No," Quinn replied with a sigh as he realized Digri was making a good case. "I suppose," Quinn continued, "that to deny you the opportunity to battle the foe that murdered your families, would perhaps be the greater crime."

Digri stepped back and a faint smile traversed his face.

Gundin, shocked that Quinn made the MerriNoons an auxiliary unit of their army, stormed forward. "Well, as a commander, I need more information. Tell us why the lions didn't eat you."

"Simple. MerriNoons do not eat lions. Therefore, lions do not eat us."

Gundin snickered. "Foolish gibberish. We don't eat lions either, but they *would* eat us!"

"Naturally, because you are not MerriNoon."

Dumbfounded, Gundin scowled and scratched his head. "What does that have to do with anything?"

"To lions, you smell and taste...delicious. To lions, MerriNoons smell and taste...nasty."

Quinn and Gundin exchanged confused looks. Even Areall and Daryess raised eyebrows.

"I shall prove." Digri stuck his arm out. "Smell."

Quinn and Gundin sniffed and immediately gagged. Curious, Areall and Daryess leaned close, but catching his aroma, covered their mouths and jerked away.

"See? Nasty! Now I smell you."

All four rolled up their sleeves and presented exposed arms to Digri. He sniffed and backpedaled away.

"What's wrong," Gundin snickered. "Do we smell nasty?"

Digri's eyes were wide. He shook his head and addressed another MerriNoon in their native tongue. The MerriNoon nodded and took tentative steps toward the two couples. He lowered his head, keeping his eyes on them as if expecting them to attack, and sniffed dog-like. He too backed away and nodded to confirm Digri's suspicions.

Digri turned his attention back to the couples. "Forgive us if our behavior seemed rude, but I needed to be certain." Digri's eyes sparkled. "I've smelled your scents before."

"That's impossible," Gundin huffed. "This is the first time we've met."

"Not you, but a young girl, a young boy, bearing the same scents."

Areall gasped as she put two and two together. "Our children..."

Daryess took Areall's hand and directed her question to Digri. "You met our children? Elabea and Galadin?"

"Yes, but I never knew their names."

"Where did they go," Areall asked.

"Claire. I helped...gave them a map, but please, you ask questions like you Allsbruthians cook: too much fire and not enough spice. Show me to the cooking area and I'll answer, one at a time, as best I can."

Areall and Daryess nodded and faced the crowd. The gathered refugees, stunned not only to learn of the bloodlust of the Gor King but that Digri's tale of Elabea and Galadin offered hope, parted without a word.

A woman with a scarf covering her eye caught their attention. Daryess met her glare and leaned close to her ear. "How's your vision now?" she whispered.

Before the woman could respond, either by word or gesture, Daryess and Areall marched off with chins lifted and smiles radiating.

Chapter 9

A Dangerous Test

Mälque and Vonn kept in step with the Ebonite while Olke - who was far ahead of them - followed the Gor King through the woods like a faithful dog.

The brothers walked in silence, afraid even a whisper would be misconstrued by the Gor King and stir his wrath. During their journey, he had not once turned to check on them, nor did he glance to his left or right in search of foe. Instead, he rode with shoulders broad and gaze centered, which sparked their curiosity, and fears, to new heights.

The woods thinned and a clearing lay ahead. The Ebonite broke the silence. "What are your names?"

"I'm Mälque."

Vonn held his answer and flashed Mälque a look of reprimand.

"My name's Woren," the Ebonite offered. "I know it's none of my business, but your father," Woren flicked his head at Olke, "seems more interested in the Gor King than you two."

"He ain't our father." There was a sharp edge to Mälque's tone. He coughed up a ball of phlegm and hurled it from his mouth like a dagger into a nearby tree.

"I see," Woren acknowledged as he rubbed his chin and arched an eyebrow. He tossed his head toward Vonn who continued to scowl at Mälque. "And is he your brother?"

Mälque opened his mouth to answer but Vonn interrupted. "Quit talkin' to him."

"I can talk if I want to!"

Woren's creepy smile widened. "I'll take that as a *yes*," he rasped.

Vonn grabbed his brother and yanked him close. "Don'tcha remember momma's warnings? We can't trust him. If anything, we're the ones that should be askin' questions."

Woren pushed them along. "In time," he encouraged. "In time."

"No," Vonn fired as he dug his heels into the ground. "Why should we? For all we know, this test could kill us."

Woren met Vonn's gaze and his unflinching smile brightened.

Vonn and Mälque noted the change and exchanged quick glances. Did his smile mean they had stumbled onto the truth or did it mean they were completely off target? Neither knew the answer.

Vonn, agitated by Woren's silence and odd smile, spun toward the Gor King. Cupping hands to his mouth, he shouted: "We ain't goin' further until you tell us what this test is."

The Gor King pulled back hard on his reins. His warhorse whinnied and snorted.

Vonn and Mälque cowered together while Olke - who had never heard Woren explain that there would be a test - scrunched his lips together in confusion and stared at Woren. "Test? What test?"

The Gor King did not answer either question. Instead, his head turned as if it were too great a weight to bear. His tomb-like eyes settled on Vonn and the boy's knees wobbled. Vonn puffed out his chest to appear brave, but he was a poor actor.

Woren leaned close and whispered into their ears: "Lesson number one: Never ask the Gor King a question. Direct it to me. If I deem it relevant, I'll relay the question to the Gor King. Got it?"

They nodded their heads.

Woren waved his hands at the Gor King as if to turn away a charging animal. "I explained our protocol to them. It won't happen again."

Satisfied Woren had the boys under control, the Gor King turned his stallion away and proceeded out into the clearing.

Woren pushed the brothers along.

Olke didn't budge. He crossed his arms and burned his eyes into Woren. "Enough trickery. Tell me what's goin' on. What test?"

Woren stopped in front of Olke, and with the corners of his smile twitching like the tail of a snake, pressed his nose close to Olke's. "Lesson number two: joining our ranks isn't free. It must be earned. You three have a test before you. And I must confess, it's quite dangerous, quite dangerous indeed."

The boys gulped and flashed nervous looks at Olke. He too was perplexed. His face contorted with varying emotions as he tried to untangle the puzzling information.

Woren gave Olke a shove toward the clearing and the brothers followed after him.

Once they were out in the open, Woren made his way to the Gor King and turned to address the Wurmlins. A demented smile rolled across his face like a shadow over a meadow. He bellowed out instructions in a raspy, nonchalant voice. "To join our ranks, new combatants must fight each other to prove who is the strongest and bravest."

Olke's expression changed from worry to delight. Before Woren's words had faded away, he jettisoned his tribal oath to protect the brothers and instead, opted to save his own skin, no matter what. He snarled at the boys, knowing even unarmed, he could kill them both in hand-to-hand combat.

"However, this time," Woren added, "the Gor King has a special mission for you three. Since Wurmlins are skilled at stealth, as well as the lay of the lands and the ways of the beasts, you three must retrieve a weapon of great destruction."

Olke let his snarl fade and planted his hands on his hips. He whipped his head to free some hair from his face and stared at Woren. "Weapon? Out here, in the middle of nowhere?"

Woren's smile became more sinister. "Yes, oh yes indeed."

"Then show me," Olke countered as he swept his arms about in a mocking fashion. "Ain't nothin' but bunny burrows in this field."

The Gor King spurred his steed toward Olke whose brash expression fell, as did his dramatic arms. The Gor King unsheathed his sword and all three Wurmlins jumped back, but instead of placing it under Olke's chin as he had previously done to Mälque, or raising it to hack them to death, he used it as a pointer to mark a spot on the clearing's far perimeter.

Woren interpreted the motion for the Wurmlins. "Behold the dead tree. Within is the weapon of choice. Retrieve it, and you may join our forces."

The brothers, who were relieved they were not going to have to fight each other or Olke, made their way to his side. All three stared at the tree.

The top half was gone, shattered no doubt by a lightning strike or great windstorm. Spike-like splinters rose from what remained like a wicked crown. Stripped of its bark, the white trunk stood in stark contrast to the greens, yellows and grays of the surrounding forest. Most of the lower limbs were gone or were ragged stumps, as if gnawed off by an irate beast. But it was the black hole within the crown of spikes that filled them with an eerie dread: The tree was hollow and all three knew what lay inside.

"No way!" Olke shook his head so hard that his long hair flung about like black whips. "We ain't doin' that. That's suicide. No treasure is worth *that* risk."

"Suit yourself," Woren answered matter-of-factly. "But you must understand that we can't release you simply because you no longer wish to join our army. You would disclose our whereabouts to anyone willing to pay a giln. Therefore, you forfeit your lives."

"We won't snitch," Vonn offered, his tone wavering between a whine and a plea. "We promise."

"You promise," Woren snickered. "When has the word of a Wurmlin ever been trusted?"

With their fate being non-negotiable, the boys turned their attention to the dead tree. Despite the danger lying asleep inside, it offered them their only hope of survival.

Olke, on the other hand, spied an opportunity that would work to his favor. With the boys' backs to him, and their attention focused on the tree, he reached for their sheathed daggers. When his fingers were close, he yanked the blades free.

The boys spun around and came face-to-face with their own daggers.

Olke snarled. "Never trust a thief, I always say."

"But we gotta work together," Mälque whined as he stared at the blades.

"Spoken just like a *yung-er.*" Olke injected all his anger into the word.

Mälque narrowed his eyes in contempt.

"Ain't figured it out yet, have ya," Olke asked as his eyes darted from the boys to the Gor King and Woren. "It's simple. I'm makin' you two steal that den of death while I stand far off, nice and safe."

"But we're Wurmlins...family," Vonn pleaded, bewildered that Olke would betray his own kind, his own blood.

"Ain't no family in times like these," Olke snapped as his eyes drilled into them. "Now *git!*"

He jabbed at them with the blades and the boys hopped out of the way. They flashed a concerned look at Woren in hope that he would intervene, but his smile merely twitched.

They were on their own.

Olke's steely eyes cut them to the quick; he meant business. Pink tongue swiped fat lips and he flicked his head to cast hairs from his line of sight.

Mälque shook his head in anger at Olke's betrayal and marched toward the tree. Vonn regained his senses, turned on his heel and raced to join his younger brother. "Whatcha thinkin' of doin'?"

"Ain't nothin' to think, Vonn. We just gotta do."

Vonn checked on Olke. He lingered far enough behind to stay out of harm's way, but was too close for them to run away. Olke whipped his hair and thrust the two daggers to intimidate him.

Vonn turned his attention to his younger brother. He sensed that their roles had switched and Mälque was somehow wiser and more mature.

Is he braver, too, Vonn wondered.

He shook off the thought and eyed the lifeless tree. A memory from four summers ago flashed within his mind. He could still hear their mother's voice.

"Boys, listen to me. An Awakening has occurred. Dangerous creatures you've never seen before prowl about...or make their dens in dead trees. Those are called fea dracas - tiny dragons that'll swarm and eat ya alive. Never go near trees like that, I don't care how brave ya feel. You understand me?"

Vonn left the memory and stared at the den. They were marching straight for it like children on a dare to not only verify fea dracas lived inside, but to corral them for the Gor King…to be used as a weapon, if such things were even possible.

Cold fear, like glacial water, coursed his veins.

Vonn stopped.

"Mälque, this is suicide!"

Mälque continued onward as if he hadn't heard, or worse, didn't care.

Vonn raced to catch up. He grabbed Mälque's shoulder and spun him around. "Crazy *yung-er!*" Vonn's eyes were wild with fright. "Ya know what lives inside that tree just like I do."

Mälque glared back. "Don't call me that." His dark eyes drifted to his brother's hand clutching his tunic. "And let go of me."

Vonn, shocked by his brother's bravery - or death wish - released his grip. Mälque pushed past him and continued his trek, alone.

"You're gonna die," Vonn shouted after him.

"Yeah, probably so." He didn't take his eyes off the tree. "But there's a chance I won't. That's more than Woren offered."

"Well I ain't doin' it!"

"Suit yourself." He crept closer to the den. "You stay with Olke. I'll do it."

Olke stormed up to Vonn. "You coward. Get goin' to that tree or I'll gut ya here and now."

"Mälque said he'd do it."

"He's too little. It'll take both ya to fetch 'em. Now go!"

Something within Vonn snapped. Maybe it was the countless mauled bodies they had scavenged in order to survive. Maybe it was this new Gor King and the mysterious spell he seemed to cast over everyone. Maybe it was the fact that Mälque was brave and he was afraid. Whatever the reason, he looked around for any means of escape; eyes wild with fright.

"I ain't gonna die. I ain't!"

He took off running.

Mälque, alarmed by his brother's shout, spun around to see Vonn dashing for the other end of the glen. "*No,*" he shouted, horrified at his brother's mad sprint. Out of the corner of his eye, he saw the Gor King unsheathe his blue sword, ready to charge after Vonn if Olke couldn't catch him. "Stop," Mälque ordered. "He'll kill ya!"

Vonn ignored Mälque's pleas and headed for the woods. He glanced over his shoulder to check on the Gor King. His blade glistened in the sunlight but he remained stationary, as did Woren. Olke, on the other hand, was in hot pursuit.

"Come back here," Olke ordered. "Now!"

Vonn snapped his gaze forward. His legs plowed through tall grass. Lungs burned for want of air. Arms pumped to increase his speed. He willed himself onward to the safety of the woods and the chance to escape.

Sweat rolled into his eyes and stung, his vision blurred. He swiped a hand across his eyes to free his sight. He was almost there. Life, freedom and hope lay only a few steps away in the thicket.

He was about to check on Olke when he felt a sharp, burning pain in the center of his back. His legs suddenly went limp; he staggered and fell face first to the ground. The burning sensation fanned outward, a fire of pain that swept across his back and down through his legs. His breathing became labored; vision dimmed; pulse thumped an ominous cadence in his eardrums. Panic and fear swallowed him whole.

He felt himself relax and breathing came easier, less urgent. His blood no longer thumped its dark rhythm but instead, peeled like distant drums urging him home. A lark-like whisper flitted through his thoughts, dancing atop the drumbeats, wooing him to a land of tranquil summers and tepid waters and hot meals and warm beds. "I just wanna go home," he mumbled, his lips pressed hard against the ground. "That's all…"

"Vonn!" Mälque shouted. Despite the tall grass concealing much of Vonn's body, he could see the Wurmlin dagger sticking out of his brother's back.

Vonn heard Mälque's cry as if he were asleep or listing off into a dream. "Don't ya worry, little brother." He tasted blood and dirt and tried to clear his mouth, but the ground blocked his weak efforts. "I'll be fine. But ya need to be strong. Oh so strong…"

"*Vonn!*" Mälque shouted once more, hoping his impassioned voice would stir his brother to rise and flee.

Vonn felt as light as a feather, as if the pain, filth and worry of his life had been washed away. Mälque's pleas dissolved into a musical note that meshed with a beautiful waltz; and swirling amidst such music was the whisper that was sweet and pure, good and noble.

Mälque stared at his brother's motionless body.

Reality smacked him hard.

Vonn was dead.

Mälque snapped his gaze to Olke who stood nearby and unsheathed his dagger to replace the one he had thrown into Vonn's back.

Mälque's blood boiled with anger. Tears chiseled streaks of white on his grimy cheeks.

"Whatcha starin' at," Olke fired. "Ya better get goin' or you'll get the same."

Mälque grit his teeth. "Traitor," he spat from clinched jaws. "You're gonna pay."

Olke spat on the ground and flicked his hair. "Shut up, *yung-er*, and get a move on to that tree."

Instead of complying, Mälque set a path back toward the Gor King.

Olke stared, bamboozled at Mälque's brazen move. Regaining his senses, he ran over to block his way. "No you don't. You ain't goin' back to *him.*"

Mälque stared at the dagger and then up at Olke's curled, greasy lips.

He sniffled back the tears. "Ya ain't gonna stop me, and ya ain't gonna kill me neither." He dragged a sleeve across his nose to wipe off the snot. "If ya do, then you're stuck gettin' those fea dracas outta that tree yourself. And we both know you ain't man enough to do *that.*"

Mälque pushed past, making sure he bumped into him.

Olke stared after him with mouth agape.

"Ya think you're so smart," he taunted. "Ya think you're *so* brave. *Yung-er!*"

Mälque ignored him and kept walking.

Olke glanced back at the fea draca tree. The spiked crown and dark hollow sent a chill down his spine. He whipped his hair in an attempt to toss aside his fears. It was a wasted effort.

"Dang *yung-er.*"

He spat on the ground and hurried to catch up with Mälque.

Chapter 10

Den of Death

Mälque stopped in front of Woren, and although he directed his words to the Ebonite, he fixed his gaze on the Gor King's dark eye sockets.

"Is this a real test or just somethin' to get us all killed, 'cause if you mean to kill me, I'd rather have *him* do it," he motioned at the Gor King, "than have fea dracas eat me alive."

Woren's smile never flickered. "No, it's a genuine test and a real mission."

Olke made his way to Mälque's side.

Mälque let his eyes wander from the Gor King over to Olke. "Now that Vonn's dead, you've gotta help."

Olke gazed into Mälque's unflinching eyes and then up at the Gor King. The rogue warrior positioned his blue sword over Olke's head to help him make up his mind. "Fine," Olke conceded with a gulp. "But you're doin' most of the work."

Mälque, satisfied that Olke would at least be available to assist, albeit more like a mule, addressed Woren. "If we're gonna do this, then we need some supplies or else it's a suicide mission."

"Smart boy," Woren answered with a consenting nod. "But we're out in the middle of nowhere, so what do you have in mind?"

"I gotta look inside the tree to make sure it's full of fea dracas but it's too tall. I can't shinny up it, 'cause I'll alert them and they'll swarm. I need somethin' to stand on so I don't have to climb as much. Plus I'll need somethin' or someone to haul it back."

"Haul what back?"

Mälque ignored his question and continued listing his needs.

"Aside from that, you got any tools or supplies I can rummage through? Not sure what I need until I see whatcha got."

"We're alone and in the middle of nowhere, remember?"

Mälque locked eyes with the Ebonite. "We ain't alone."

Woren's smile flickered like a flame. "Whatever do you mean?"

"I caught the scent of horses; lots of 'em. My guess is your cavalry is hiding in the woods. I figure you've gotta have supplies with you, too."

Woren turned his attention to the Gor King. "He's sharp," Woren commended. "A true Wurmlin."

The Gor King eyed Mälque. This time, the boy did not fear his gaze.

"So be it, young Mälque," Woren said. "We'll answer your request."

Woren stuck his fingers in his mouth and gave a loud whistle. From within the woods they heard a man shout, "Giddy up, now," followed by chains rattling together and wood creaking. A rickety wagon emerged from the shadows. The driver managed the reins of loping horses.

Mälque studied the wagon while Woren explained his intentions. "You can use the wagon to help you see within or to scale the tree. All the tools you'll need are there as well."

Mälque nodded. "I'm also gonna need fresh meat for bait." But as his mind began to hash out his plan, another thought came to mind. "Never mind. I got a better idea."

He kept this part of his scheme to himself.

The wagon driver pulled back on the reins and the animals stopped nearby.

Woren gestured at the wagon.

Mälque followed his lead and climbed up over the wooden side and stared at the amassed supplies.

"This is just a pile of junk."

"I can have the wagon removed, if you wish."

Mälque huffed and shook his head. "Didn't mean no harm. I'll make do."

He foraged through the scrap that ranged from pewter plates to garden tools to old daggers. When he found some ropes of various lengths, daggers that weren't too rusty, and an ax that still held an edge, he became excited as ideas of how to catch the creatures materialized in his imagination. He clutched his finds to his chest and made his way across the junk to the front of the wagon. Reaching the tall, wooden wall that separated the driver from the load, he heaved his stash with a grunt over the top. They landed with a clatter in the floorboard.

"Careful," the driver chastised with a stern look. "You almost hit me."

Mälque ignored him and turned to survey the scrap heap. Unable to find what he was looking for, he wagged his head. "Need some metal," he said to Woren.

"You're standing in a wagon *full* of metal."

"I know, but I need somethin' flat, about this wide." He stretched out his hands to show the length needed.

"You'd better not be stalling the inevitable, *yung-er.*"

Mälque shook his head. "Ain't no trick. I need 'em to trap those fea dracas. Nothin' in this scrap heap will do."

Woren sized up the boy and then looked to the Gor King for his answer. Although slight - almost imperceptible - the white skull nodded.

Woren faced the woods and whistled. Several lines of cavalry charged out of the shadowed thicket.

Mälque took in the cavalry lines charging toward them. Their armor was an assortment of gear ranging from Ebonite breastplates to Tristan swords, while their steeds - powerful animals - stirred up sod and dust. The warriors pulled back on the reins and the wave of warhorses came to a halt behind the Gor King. Mälque eyed the cavalrymen's faces and was met with gruff, stern and cold expressions. A verse from the Gor King's tale popped into Mälque's thoughts.

Outcasts, criminals and madmen served him with steel-like resolve.

One warrior made his way to Woren. In his free hand were the reins to a saddled, but riderless, warhorse.

That explains a lot, Mälque noted with a glance at Woren. *Figured you didn't walk all this way in those boots.*

Woren took the reins and began untying something from his saddle. When he had finished, he spun around and held up his shield for Mälque to inspect. "Will this suffice?"

Mälque glanced back at the white tree, did some quick calculations, and then nodded to confirm. Woren made his way to the wagon and handed up the shield that was no wider than Mälque's shoulders.

Mälque flipped it over. Two, parallel leather straps were attached on the back. He pulled to test their strength: firm and tight. He raised his eyes to meet Woren. "Need one more."

Woren sneered. "You'd better not be stalling, *yung-er.*"

"Ain't. I just need one more, that's all."

Woren motioned to a nearby warrior who untied a similar shield and tossed it over.

"Lesson number three," Woren said as he held it up to Mälque.

Mälque grabbed it but Woren didn't let go. He caught Woren's serious expression. "Always return a warrior's tools or weapons after borrowing them." Then for emphasis: "*Always.*"

"I will."

Woren released his grip. Mälque pulled it close and tested the straps on the shield's backside. "This'll do. And I promise to return them. It just may be awhile."

Mälque made his way across the jumble to the front of the wagon and climbed over the partition to sit beside the driver. The warrior glowered at him with cold eyes.

"What are you doing up here, *yung-er,*" the driver huffed.

Mälque returned the scowl. "I need ya to drive the wagon over there." He pointed to the lone tree. "I'll stand on the back to get as close to the top as I can. I gotta climb up the rest and look inside."

The driver followed his line of sight, and spying the fea dracas den, shook his head. "Not my test, nor my day to die. She's all yours." He handed the reins to Mälque and hopped down.

Woren turned his attention to Olke. "That would be your cue."

Oblivious to the new role he was being asked to play, Olke stared dumbfounded at Woren.

"Let me simplify." Woren's smile twitched. "*You're* the new driver. Now get going."

Olke huffed and stomped over to the wagon. He climbed up and snatched the reins from Mälque's hands.

He slapped them like whips on the horses' flanks. "*Ha*," he ordered with a hot glance at Mälque. The wagon jerked forward, and the payload clattered and chimed as they rolled along.

When they were far enough away that Woren or the Gor King couldn't overhear them, Olke asked, "What's your plan, *yung-er*."

Mälque flinched at *yung-er* but kept his eyes zeroed in on the fea dracas den.

"*Yung-er*, you hear me?" Olke cracked the reins down hard on the animals.

"I heard," Mälque answered with a quick glance to his right as they rolled past the corpse of his brother. "Ain't nothin' but dyin' out here today."

In a softer voice, as if offering a prayer or reciting a prophecy of his own demise, he added: "Nothin' but dyin'."

Olke elbowed him in the ribs. "Tell me your plan," he muttered through clinched teeth.

Mälque's eyes drifted back to the tree and the death lurking inside. "No plan. Makin' it up as I go along."

Olke thought about stopping the wagon to chastise the boy, but as he imagined the Gor King charging after him, he thought better of the idea. Instead, he tried another angle. "Look, we gotta work together on this or we're both dead."

Mälque, still lost in grief over Vonn's death, replied, "Yep, nothin' but dyin'…everywhere you look. Gor Kings out killin'. Fea dracas ready to eat ya alive." He tossed a quick glance at Olke. "Wurmlins murderin' their own."

Olke's eyes narrowed. He whipped his hair and leaned into Mälque. "He ran," he whispered, his breath as foul smelling as his body odor. "He had it comin'. What was I supposed to do?"

Mälque locked eyes with him and replied in a voice as cold as the Ebonite wind, "Nothin' but dyin' everywhere…everywhere ya look."

Olke pulled away from Mälque's spooky expression and brought the reins down hard on the flanks.

The tree loomed. Although it was not as big around as Mälque had imagined, it was still tall and the black hole at the top made his skin crawl.

Mälque gave Olke some final instructions. "Get the wagon as close to the tree as you can without makin' noise or hittin' it. Last thing we need is for them to swarm before we set the trap."

"What trap," Olke asked, but Mälque didn't answer.

When they were as close as they could get, Olke pulled back on the reins and the wagon stopped. Olke hopped down and made his way to the horses' bridles. Grabbing hold, he gave a firm pull and led the animals toward the tree, trying to be as quiet as possible.

Mälque rode along, eyes glued on the opening.

Are fea dracas inside?

Without taking his eyes off the tree, he listened to the soft tings and pings coming from the junk in the wagon. *Can the fea dracas hear us? Maybe they're just waitin' until we're close to swarm.*

He swallowed down his apprehensions and drew in a deep breath to settle his nerves.

When the wagon was as close to the trunk as possible, Mälque leaned out from where he sat and pressed his palm against the white meat of the tree. It was warm, whether from the sunlight or from the hundreds of tiny dragons on the other side, he didn't know. He was about to remove his hand when he felt the tree shiver, as if cold, but he knew that trees did not behave in such a manner.

Fea dracas, he fretted. *They're awake!*

He had seen the tiny dragons on only one other occasion, and even then he was too far away to discern their features entirely. He'd caught a glimpse of their mystical eyes and yearned to touch the glowing blue orbs, but he also saw the buck thrashing about, blanketed with the ferocious dragons that dined on its flesh.

Mälque shook the memory off and focused back on the situation at hand.

Are you about to swarm, he wondered as his eyes ran up the trunk to the opening. He tuned his ears in anticipation of the boom that came when they exploded from their den, or so he had been taught as a boy. It took all of his will power to keep his breathing in check. Sweat beaded on his forehead and his lips became dry.

Nothing happened. It was only after the tree became still again that he realized he had been holding his breath. He let the breath escape with a soft puff and knew the time had come.

He stood up, careful not to make a sound, and stretched his hands up toward the shards of wood guarding the opening.

Olke, aghast at Mälque's plan to shinny up the tree, retreated to what he considered was a safe distance.

Mälque's fingertips caught hold of the shattered wood, and although they dug into his flesh, he gritted through the pain and pulled himself upward, careful that his boots did not kick the trunk and spook the fea dracas.

He wrapped his legs around the trunk for support and pushed himself up toward the opening. His cheek pressed against the tree, noted its warmth, and when he reached the shards marking the apex, peered into the abyss with one eye.

Total blackness.

He was about to stick his whole face over the side for a better look when blue lights, like glistening facets from countless gems, sparked to life.

He felt a warmth rush through him, much like he did when he snuck a swig of his father's brew - a brownish concoction made from sweet roots, that burned the throat and packed a punch stronger than wine. His heart beat with longing and desire for the blue lights. It was the same feeling he experienced long ago when he witnessed the fea dracas devouring the buck. Only now, the sensation was stronger, more powerful.

Despite the horrid memory of the deer's demise, his muscles pried and pushed him higher to take in the wondrous eyes. He found himself thinking about dropping down into the hole so he could hold them, pet them, claim them.

Fortunately, his will gained the upper hand and he recentered his thoughts and his muscles on reality and his own mortality.

Shaking off the spell, and with his legs still wrapped around the trunk, he slithered down toward the wagon, keeping his eyes glued on the trunk's top should they swarm. When he was close enough, and with eyes still staring upward, he stretched his boot out but only caught air. A quick glance down at the wagon made him gasp.

It's moved, he fretted. *The horses must have smelled the fea dracas.*

Mälque's gaze darted to where Olke was supposed to be holding the bridle.

Gone!

He looked this way and that for Olke, and discovered him a good distance away, cowereing near a bush. He whipped his hair from his face to reveal a sinister smirk.

Before Mälque could signal for help, the tree shivered. Instead of dissipating as it had before, it grew in strength to that of a growl. He thought about dropping to the ground and running for his life when an unexpected whisper cut through the din.

Hold fast, was all it said.

Mälque did not have time to argue, nor did he have time to wonder who or what had uttered such a decree, even though his mother's warning about such whispers came to mind. Instinct confirmed that running away was a bad idea. All he could do was trust the whisper's order and hope for the best.

He pressed his cheek to the trunk and held on with all his might. The tree vibrated and shook. With his ear pressed close, he heard the sound of hundreds of wings buzzing and fluttering inside. The drone grew into a high-pitched whine that rumbled through his bones. The whine roared like an angry beast and the tree shook with such violence that his grip slipped.

They're gonna swarm. I just know it!

Mälque steeled himself against the horrors that awaited him, but despite his brave efforts, he couldn't contain a scream rising from his gut and he let it fly.

The fea dracas exploded from the tree, drowning his gut-wrenching shriek.

The trunk became still once more and Mälque, still clinging to the trunk with white knuckles, studied the fea dracas overhead that pulsated like a storm cloud.

Mälque then turned his gaze to Olke, who stared up at the hovering death, mesmerized by the dazzling blue eyes and buzzing wings. Olke must have realized he was easy prey out in the open, so he pulled away from their alluring eyes and found himself staring at Mälque. As their eyes met, another truth popped into Olke's mind. He understood why Mälque had changed his mind about needing fresh meat for bait.

He was the bait.

Olke's face turned white with fear and then crimson with rage. He hurled curses at Mälque, but his voice was drowned out by the raucous noise made by the fea dracas. He abandoned his tirade, turned on his heel and darted for the woods.

The fea dracas spotted him and dropped from the sky with incredible speed. Olke swatted at them as he ran. Claws ripped at clothing and hair. Wings fluttered all over his face. Bright, blue eyes stared into his as the dragon cloud darted, buzzed and swooped all about him.

Olke tried to outrun them but they engulfed him from head to toe. Talons tore away clothing while razor-sharp teeth ravaged his flesh. Olke's blood curdling screams meshed with the tiny dragons' high-pitched screeches. His arms - layered with fea dracas - flailed like windmills in a windstorm as he ran in circles, blind to his whereabouts, pain seizing reason and logic.

Mälque was horror-struck at the savageness of the attack. As much as he hated Olke and wanted revenge, watching him being eaten alive was more gruesome than he had imagined. He pulled away from the grisly scene and focused instead on the rest of his plan.

He slid to the ground and raced to the horses. They pranced and whinnied against the wagon that wouldn't budge. Mälque eyed the wagon's brake handle.

Olke must have set it. Lucky me.

Mälque yanked off a top layer of clothing and draped it over the horses' heads. Unable to see the fea dracas, and upwind from the scent of the swarm, the animals settled down.

I ain't got much time. Sure hope this works.

The mysterious whisper returned.

You do and it will.

Mälque looked for the source of the mysterious voice but found no one. With no time to ponder such wonderment, he darted to the wagon and grabbed the ax.

He ran to the tree and drove the blade into the base while keeping an eye on the feeding frenzy nearby. Olke, covered with fea dracas, lay motionless on the ground. He was either dead or soon would be.

Based upon his previous experience with the buck, Mälque knew that once their prey was dead, fea dracas took their time eating. When finished, they'd return to their den, at least he hoped so. He had left the buck long before that time had come.

I can only hope.

He gritted his teeth and swung the ax again and again. Wood chips flew into the field as sweat streamed from his brow.

Above the chattering of the fea dracas, he heard the trunk splinter. The tree listed to the side and with one loud crack, toppled to the ground with a thud.

Mälque, certain the ruckus had alerted the fea dracas to his presence, spun to check on the tiny dragons. Several stared at him, sapphire eyes blazing like fire. Mälque froze and prepared for the worst, the lure of their gaze making his legs feel weak. Instead of attacking him, they resumed eating.

Mälque breathed a sigh of relief and straddled the end of the tree. Using the blunt end of the ax head like a hammer, he smashed the splinters and shards to form as smooth an edge as possible. He darted to the smaller end and repeated the process.

He ran back to the wagon and hopped up into the driver's seat to grab the shields, ropes, and daggers lying on the floorboard.

Running back to the trunk, he dropped to his knees and placed one shield over the opening to make sure it was large enough. Satisfied it was a snug fit, he flipped the shield over, tied a rope to each leather handle and refitted it back onto the trunk. Next, he drove two daggers deep into opposite sides of the trunk and wrapped the ropes tight around each hilt and guard. He pulled hard until the shield pressed down tight over the tree's opening.

He checked on the fea dracas. They continued to peck and pluck Olke's corpse.

Wish I knew how much time I had. Can't worry now.

He focused on the job at hand and knotted the ropes about the dagger. Grabbing the ax, he stood and once more used it like a hammer to drive the blades deep into the trunk, yanking the shield down even more over the trunk. He tested his work by trying to pull the shield off. It didn't budge. He knelt and eyed it from the side. Despite his best efforts to flatten the edge, there were still a few gaps.

Hope they can't squeeze out. Gonna have to risk it.

He threw another glance at the feeding frenzy. Between the fluttering bodies of the fea dracas he caught sight of Olke's body or what was left of it: strands of red meat dangled from white bone. He felt nauseous and turned away. They were almost done. Time was running out.

With the ax in one hand, he tossed the daggers and rope into the other shield, and using his free arm, cradled it to his side as he raced to the opposite end of the tree.

This time his work was faster, but instead of completely sealing off the entrance, he only secured one side and set the shield and ax on the ground beside the trunk.

Without even a glance at the fea dracas, Mälque darted for the horses and unhitched them from the wagon. After unyoking them, he yanked his shirt off their heads, grabbed the reins of one and swatted the flank of the other.

"If this don't work," he told them, "at least you'll be alive."

He watched the animal gallop for the safety of the woods as he pulled himself onto the back of the other horse and rode toward the Gor King.

When he reached the army, he pulled back on the reins and positioned himself beside Woren who had remounted his own warhorse. He met Woren's gaze with wild-looking eyes.

"That's quite a scheme you concocted," Woren acknowledged. "Too bad about your friend."

Woren motioned at Olke's body littered with the tiny dragons.

"He ain't my friend," Mälque muttered between clinched teeth.

"Very well," Woren answered, unfazed by the boy's cold-hearted nature, "but your assignment was to retrieve the fea dracas as a weapon. So far, all you've managed to do is tumble their den and stir them into an eating frenzy."

"I ain't done yet," Mälque snapped without taking his eyes off the fea dracas. Several had flitted off the body and fluttered nearby like butterflies. He had seen this behavior before, after they had eaten the buck, and concluded it meant they were done eating. But on that particular day, he did not stay around long enough to know for sure. The remaining part of his scheme was a gamble.

Woren turned his attention back to the fea dracas. "What makes you think they won't attack us next?"

Mälque shrugged. "I don't."

Woren's smile faded and his eyes burned into the boy. "So your plan is that they'll return to their den where you'll trap them, is that it?"

Mälque nodded. "Hope so. It's all I got."

As if on cue, the remaining fea dracas flew off one-by-one and coursed overhead in what appeared to be a leisurely manner. With Olke's body free of the tiny dragons, the Gor King's army could ascertain the damage done. Even the most hardened and cold-blooded amongst them gasped.

White ribcages jutted up out of the grass, and when the wind blew just right, and the grasses parted, they could catch a glimpse of his skull stripped clean of flesh.

While the army whispered about the gruesome scene, Mälque kept his eyes focused on the fea dracas. With their bellies full, they swooped down and entered the fallen tree, just as he had hoped.

Woren breathed a sigh of relief. "You're lucky, but you still have to trap them inside. You better hurry, *yung-er*."

Mälque whipped his head around to look Woren square in the face.

"I ain't a *yung-er* no more."

With that, he dug his heels into his horse and galloped for the den. When he was close enough, he slowed the animal and slid off before it had come to a complete stop.

He tiptoed to the fallen tree, careful to make sure his shadow and scent did not cross the opening and alert the swarm. He grabbed the shield he had left unattached and stared at the opening, steeling himself to stretch out his arms - knowing he would have to expose himself briefly to their attack - and seal them inside the log.

With his thigh nestled beside the trunk, he felt it vibrate. His heart boomed inside his eardrums and his lungs drank in quick gulps of air.

Ain't nothin' but dyin' out here today, he mused. *But today ain't my day*.

With lightning fast reflexes, he battened down the opening with the shield and wrapped the ropes tight around the dagger he'd already stabbed into place.

The trunk shook and rocked as the fea dracas awoke to the trap.

Before they could press against the shield, Mälque grabbed the ax and sprung to his feet. Swift, sharp blows sunk the daggers deep into the trunk just as the horde pressed against the shield.

Mälque dropped the ax and stepped back in fear. High-pitched squeals and squeaks echoed from the tree. Frantic scraping sounds, like hundreds of miniscule blades upon metal, resounded from where the shield covered the opening. As with the first shield he had set, there were small gaps between the armor and trunk. Fea dracas pressed against the openings. Dagger-like claws raked the air and sapphire eyes burned outward at him. He took another step back, hoping his trap would hold.

He pulled away from their mystical eyes and focused instead on the ropes battening the shield down. Despite the fea dracas' best efforts, they could not reach the ropes to chew or cut, nor were they strong enough to collectively push the shield off.

Relieved the trap would hold, he wiped the sweat off his brow and waved the all clear to Woren. Woren motioned for a patrol in to assist Mälque with loading the log onto the wagon.

As the soldiers galloped across the meadow, Mälque walked back to the wagon. He reached over the side, grabbed an old shovel and headed for Olke and Vonn's bodies.

Reaching Olke's bones, he stared down at the remains. Despite the maulings he had witnessed at the hand of the other Gor King, this sight made him shiver. Olke's clothes lay ripped, stripped and scattered all about the area. Lying atop the biggest pile was his skeleton cleaned of flesh, muscle and tissue. Aside from his bloodied clothes, not a crimson drop could be found on the bones. In fact, the white carcass seemed to pulse—or so Mälque thought—in the sunlight, but it was Olke's open mouth and dark eye sockets that spooked him through and through.

"Ya tryin' to say somethin'," Mälque jested as his courage returned. "Like maybe tryin' to curse this here *yung-er?*"

He flicked his head and greasy hair whipped about. "I ain't a *yung-er* no more."

With that, he turned and let his eyes sweep the killing field. Something sparkled in the sunlight and piqued his curiosity. He made his way over to it, and using his shovel to flick off the strips of bloodied cloth and matted grass, he uncovered a giln. Without a second thought, Mälque snatched it from the ground.

He flipped the blood-covered coin up into the air and sneered back at Olke's skull. "Never trust a thief, I always say."

He wiped the blood off and pocketed the gold piece. Then he flung the shovel over his shoulder and trudged through the grass toward his brother.

When he reached Vonn's side, he stared down at his lifeless body. Memories of growing up together flashed in his mind's eye. His stomach muscles tightened and tears swelled in his eyes. He shook his head, willing himself to overpower such grief, and pressed his emotions back down into the hollow of his soul. There would come a time for him to weep for Vonn, to mourn the summers lost and to savor the ones lived. But now was not the time, and what unnerved Mälque most was that the knot growing inside his gut signaled that such a time was many summers away.

He sniffled and wiped his nose with his sleeve.

"'Ya shouldn't have run, Vonn," he mumbled to himself as he drove the shovel's blade deep into the soil.

"But I ain't angry at ya. I just hope that wherever you are…"

He dropped the dirt into a pile and dug up more earth for the grave.

"…that you're safe, warm and have lots to eat."

His pile began to grow in size.

"'Cause around here, there ain't nothin' but dyin'…"

Another plop of dirt followed by a glance across the way at the Gor King, whose gaze was centered on his work.

Mälque threw off the look and thrust the blade hard into the ground.

"But it aint' me. Not yet, anyways."

Chapter 11

Fear Bridled Tongue

Quinn made his way out of the Great Hall to walk off his breakfast. He patted his belly. Food at Min Brock had been plentiful and he enjoyed sampling dishes from the different nations. Tristanites were noted for their hearty stews, rich chowders and flavorful cheeses. Ferranites contributed tasty treats - chocolates, sweet breads and puddings - along with wines of varying tastes and colors. Ingloids proved to be masters at smoking game and fish as well as concocting a savory beverage from mashed wildeberries, mint and broth.

But when the MerriNoons arrived, the cuisine at Min Brock soared to a new level of excellence. Skewered meats - seasoned with herbs, hot spices and oils - were so tender that they melted on the tongue like candy. Breads were drizzled with flavored oils or butters and had a richer flavor than those from Allsbruth. Vegetables were sautéed in broth seasoned with wine and served with breadcrumbs sprinkled on top. A favorite dish amongst the refugees was the pre-meal bowls of melted cheeses seasoned with wildeberry sauce and herbs they called *lling*. The MerriNoons urged their diners to use chunks of bread to swab up the gooey sauce, but those with ravenous appetites, like Gundin, were too impatient, so they raised the bowl to their mouth and raked the creamy *lling* in with their fingers.

Quinn made his way toward the southwest tower and marveled at how their numbers at Min Brock had grown. He skirted around children playing a game of hide-and-seek. He acknowledged a group of women gathered near a doorway with nod of his head. Making his way across the courtyard, he smiled at the families huddled close to open fires, saluted soldiers milling about and waved to the craftsmen - blacksmiths, tinkers and bakers – who were opening shop.

Quinn reached the turret and exchanged salutes with the guards manning their posts. He jogged up the tower's circular route to the walkway. No sooner had he emerged than the alarm was sounded.

Quinn raced to the parapet wall and stared in the direction the sentries were pointing. A tiny, dark spot sat above the Addoli Ridge.

The commander in charge of the men, a towering Ingloid, saluted Quinn. He returned the salute.

"Sir, it looks like Linwith and the Worms are returning from their reconnaissance mission."

Quinn nodded but continued to study the flying anomaly. Over the course of four summers, he had acquired a good eye for discerning the various silhouettes in the sky. Demoliths came in droves, and from afar looked like a dark rain cloud. Vul jens, although much smaller flew in small packs, and from a distance appeared like mist or falling rain. This, however, was a small dot, which is what the worms looked like when flying back to Min Brock.

"So it appears. But it could also be a trick of the Cauldron. We'd better play it safe. Alert the archers."

The officer snapped his boots together as a salute and shouted the directives down the line.

Archers, who had been standing at ease, snapped into action. With bow in hand and arrow nocked, they took their positions along the parapet wall.

"Await my command," Quinn instructed the officer who confirmed he understood with a nod.

Gundin made his way to Quinn's side and followed Quinn's line of sight. The black spot was closer now, the size of a walnut. He gave a disapproving huff. "*Sir Linwith* loves to put on a show."

Quinn flashed him a hot look. "Keep your opinions to yourself."

Gundin ground his teeth and thought about making a condescending comment about worms looking like dragons. Quinn's fiery gaze, as well as the officer watching his every move, made him reconsider.

Quinn, satisfied Gundin would mind his tongue, turned his attention back to the flying formation.

The worms - who had been flying single file to help disguise their numbers - fanned out; three worms on either side of the Worm King. Linwith's silhouette was visible atop the Worm King. He waved and the sapphire worm's tale glowed with light.

"He's given the all clear signal," Quinn said to the Ingloid commander. "Have the archers stand down."

The order was passed along and the archers returned to their positions as the worms descended for Min Brock.

Gundin crossed his arms. "Worms," he mumbled to himself. "They look like dragons, if you ask me. Simple sky mules."

The seven worms swooped over and were so low that everyone on the wall instinctively ducked. As was customary, the worms circled Min Brock at their low altitude in tight formation, wings tilted as they banked for a final inspection of the castle. Soldiers and refugees cheered, thankful that the worms had not only returned safely, but that from what they could ascertain, they had not encountered any of their enemy.

The worms, after completing their loop, broke formation and glided to their assigned turrets: the emerald and ruby perched on the two western turrets, the amber and the pearl took the two eastern towers, while the gold landed upon the north tower and the mandarin roosted on the southern most tower.

The Worm King glided to the ground near the Great Hall. Once his saddle and bridle were removed, the worm would claim his spot on the central tower above the Great Hall.

Quinn, eager to hear Linwith's report, ran to the emerald worm's tower and descended the circular stairs. He exited and made his way to Linwith. Curious bystanders flocked around Linwith, which was typical whenever he returned, as he labored to carry the worm's saddle back to the armory. Quinn pushed and shoved his way through the pack to reach his brother.

"Anything?"

"Nothing," Linwith answered, his voice pinging off his metal helmet.

Quinn opened the armory door for Linwith who entered and headed for a table. Quinn shut the door to keep the mob outside.

Linwith removed his helmet and ran fingers through sweat-matted hair. "The worms smell the scent of war; it's thick on the wind." He set his helmet on the table. "My fear is that when Ebon does strike, we won't be strong enough."

"We're ready, or as ready as we will be. Besides, we have a weapon the Ebonites do not."

"I know: the Worms."

"True, but I was referring to him."

Quinn gestured at something outside the window.

Linwith made his way closer for a better look. "Do you mean him, the skinny boy playing in the dirt with a stick?"

Quinn smiled and nodded. "His name's Phinnton. He's a storyteller. I saw his birthmark four summers ago on our way from Hetherlinn to Min Brock. He even carried our tulip. Brave boy."

"That's all well and good, but look at him!"

Phinnton, who must have been envisioning the ground to be some ferocious beast, drove his stick sword-like into the dirt.

Linwith smirked and faced his brother. "Quinn, I've watched him. He's a loner. A dreamer. He's picked on by the other children...all the time."

"Yes, but his knowledge of the stories is vast. I've often had tea with Phinnton and his father, Bruun, in my chambers. His mother taught him well."

Phinnton made a wild gesture with his arms to match the adventure in his imagination. Linwith wagged his head. "Please tell me you're *not* wagering our success upon this boy's storytelling skills."

"No. But we do need a storyteller. The Martyr's Moon four summers ago told of Il-Lilliad's death. He was the last storyteller."

"You don't know that for sure. The moon could have been for…"

Linwith cut off his sentence before he said too much, but Quinn, who ached for Elabea's return every waking moment, took it as an attack. His smile faded and his face clouded over in pain.

"So you think the moon may have been for Elabea," Quinn asked as he clinched his jaws tight.

Linwith pulled away from his brother's pain-filled eyes.

Quinn spun Linwith back around. "Listen, as much as it pains me to think that Il-Lilliad is dead, I choose to believe the Martyr's Moon was for him and *not* Elabea."

Quinn gave him a shove and glowered at him.

Linwith bit his lower lip and did not answer. Instead, he pictured the mandarin and gold worms perched on their turrets, wings outstretched to warm in the sun. Unbeknownst to his brother, Linwith knew more about Elabea than he was letting on.

Over the past summers, he used every waking moment to learn all he could about his worms' skills, gifts and abilities. The mandarin's ability to see into the future had proven to be invaluable, and he had amassed a wealth of information pertaining to Ebon, Claire and the refugees. The gold worm's gift of reading another's passions and thoughts had given him insight into who in Min Brock could be trusted.

Despite the close bond Linwith had with his brother, he had kept his worms' abilities a secret. It wasn't that he did not trust Quinn, he simply wanted control over who knew what and when. If not, Linwith was convinced that word would get out, and that every refugee would hound him to ascertain someone's future, or enquire if a sick child would live, or learn what number to bet when gambling around the fires.

When he discovered something pertaining to Min Brock's security, Linwith selectively released bits and pieces of foreknowledge to Quinn. But this he did only after a scouting mission to throw him off the trail of discovering the source of his information - his worms.

But now, hearing the anguish in his brother's voice, he longed to pull Quinn close and reveal what the visions had showed him in regards to Elabea. He knew she was alive. He even knew she bore a new name, but the visions were incomplete and clouded with mystery. Instead, he had chosen to keep it secret until he knew for certain. Besides, it was Galadin's future - or Romlin, if he opted for his new name - that chilled him through and through.

Linwith let his gaze drift back to Quinn. "You're right. I'm sorry. It won't happen again."

Quinn nodded and accepted the apology.

Linwith, not wanting Quinn to ask any probing questions, redirected the conversation back to Phinnton.

"So what do you have in mind," Linwith asked with a head nod at Phinnton.

"Phinnton needs a mentor to fan his father's wisdom and his mother's instructions into the passions of a young man. Also, as a storyteller, Phinnton is vulnerable to the Cauldron's Dark Flame even within Min Brock."

"And let me guess who you have in mind."

Quinn's smile returned. "You're the logical choice. You're without family, and as the Worm Master, you're the envy of every man and child..."

It was now Linwith's turn to be offended. He held up a hand to interrupt. "I didn't seek this glory; such glory sought me."

"I agree. I'm not saying this because I'm jealous or angry at your popularity. I'm simply asking you to consider helping Phinnton. We both know that he'll be the first to be attacked by the Cauldron. Although knowledgeable in the stories of Claire, he is innocent to the ways of the Dark Flame."

Another thought came to mind and Quinn spun around to take in the saddle. "In fact," he added as he tapped his chin with a finger, "you need help with the worms. Especially getting the saddle on and off your Worm King. Phinnton would make a perfect page."

Linwith, startled by Quinn's proposal, nearly dropped his helmet. "Page? Look at him. He can barely lift his arms let alone my helmet and saddle. My life will be *cursed.*"

Quinn chuckled, noted Phinnton dancing in place, and patted his brother on the back. "I disagree. I think you will be blessed."

With a final pat, Quinn opened the door and walked out.

"Oh, sure," Linwith fired after him as he made his way to the threshold. "Let me wipe his snotty little nose and wipe his stinky little bottom. I won't mind! After all, you're the great leader of Min Brock and don't have *time* for such trivialities!"

"You'll do fine," Quinn shouted back. "Besides, Phinnton reminds me of a boy from my youth."

Linwith scrunched up his face in sarcasm. "Who?"

Quinn spun to catch Linwith's scowl.

"You."

"Me? I'm *nothing* like him!"

Quinn waved him off and disappeared through the crowd.

Phinnton, who realized he was at the center of the heated exchange, stared at Linwith with his stick dangling by his side.

Linwith caught his look and rolled his eyes. Why hadn't the worms revealed a vision about Phinnton? Had they been evasive or did they know the boy would never measure up to such an undertaking?

Linwith retrieved his helmet off the table, determined to prove his brother wrong. He made a bee line for the boy.

"Are you Phinnton?"

Phinnton, stunned that the Worm Master had personally addressed him, dropped his stick. His tongue felt too thick for speech, and his head too heavy to nod, so he all he could muster was to stare bug-eyed at Linwith.

"Are you *deaf?*" Linwith fired with a hand on his hip. "Are you or are you not Phinnton?"

Despite Linwith's less than compassionate tone, the boy's face beamed. Able to find enough spittle, he licked his lips and answered.

"Yes, sir, I heard you, and yes, I'm Phinnton."

Linwith sized him up and tried to picture him as his page. Hidden beneath Phinnton's loose tunic was undoubtedly a scrawny, weak frame. How many times would the boy drop his helmet into the dust or worse, in a dung pile? How many times would he whine because the hour was late or too early? How many times would he nag to ride a worm, as if it were a tame pony? And when war came and battles were hot, would he have the courage to fight or would he cower in a corner of the keep and weep for his mother?

"How strong are you," Linwith asked as he tossed his helmet up and down in both hands.

Phinnton sucked on his lower lip as he thought. "My arms aren't as strong as the other boys, but my legs can carry me for days."

"War is coming. You'll need strong arms before you'll need strong legs."

Unless, Linwith thought, *you decide to run away.*

Linwith caught his helmet and noted Phinnton's eyes. Dark like the deepest of wells, they had a vibrancy lacking in the other children's eyes. Surrounding these black pools was his handsome face. Despite lacking a Mother and being picked on for being weak, his countenance radiated like the River Arrgient: strong, purposeful and wild.

He's nothing like me, Linwith mused, outraged and yet…curious.

"When war comes," Linwith asked, "will you be ready to fight?"

Dark eyes blinked. It was a question Phinnton had wrestled with on countless occasions, especially at night…when the whispers came. One tormented with dark questions while the other offered drinks of cool delight.

"Yes." Phinnton stepped forward. "But not as you might think."

"Very well, tell me how *you'll* fight?"

"I know I'm not like the other boys: I'm not very good with the bow and my arms may never be strong enough for the sword. But within my heart I feel…no, I sense…"

Linwith unleashed a dramatic sigh, agitated not only by the

prospect of mentoring him but with his drawn out replies as well. "Boy, just answer before I die of old age."

"I'm trying," Phinnton replied, more frustrated with himself than with Linwith's cold response. "But it's like trying to explain what Claire looks like, or how one whisper can fill you with dread while another offers joy…"

Linwith had had enough. He scanned the courtyard in search of Quinn, hoping he had reappeared so he could chastise him for such a foolish idea. How could this waif possibly be his page? And what, if anything, made Quinn think he was just like Phinnton? Linwith's anger began to boil.

"Sir," Phinnton asked, "do you believe in the stories?"

"What stories," Linwith quipped as he stood up on his toes searching over the crowd for his brother, mumbling to himself.

"The tales of Claire."

"I suppose." Unable to find Quinn, he huffed and dropped down from his elevated search. As he collected his thoughts, he gave Phinnton's question a better look over. "Yes," he answered. "I believe them."

"Well, what am I to do with them," Phinnton asked with arms up in the air as he shrugged in dismay. "They swirl within my thoughts like your worms upon the wind."

Linwith wanted to walk away. He found himself getting angrier every time Phinnton looked at him with admiration. But something within Linwith, something distantly familiar, made him stay.

But what is it?

Giving up his inner search, and still resolved to be rid of the boy, he came upon a better solution: he'd test him.

"Hold out your arms."

Phinnton complied.

Linwith raised his helmet high and dropped it. Phinnton caught it, and after a few bobbles, gained control over the helmet and beamed Linwith a victorious smile.

Linwith remained stoic. *He's stronger than he looks. But I'll find his weakness and fear…*

"Are you afraid of heights," Linwith asked while retrieving his helmet.

"Heights," Phinnton asked with a scrunched up face.

"Yes," Linwith fired, irritated at the boy's inability to grasp the deeper meaning to his question. "Are you able to climb, let's say," Linwith searched around the courtyard for the perfect platform in which to test him. His eyes lit up when he found what he was looking for. "*That* wall over there. And once at the top, can you jump up and down without falling off?"

Phinnton followed Linwith's line of sight and studied the wall in question. It guarded one of the tall, stone staircases that ascended to the walkways and parapets. The wall was three times as tall as his cottage in Hetherlinn, and the zenith was no wider than a tree limb. He gave Linwith a casual shrug.

Linwith snickered. *I doubt he is capable of such daring.*

Phinnton cocked his head and squinted his coal-like eyes up at Linwith.

"Why are you staring at me?" Linwith spat.

"Why do you think such things about me?"

"Think what things?"

"That I'm not capable of such daring? And that you want to find my weakness...and fear?"

Linwith's face became white. *Can he read my story like the great storytellers of old?*

"Yes! Phinnton replied within his mind. *"And I won't run away from battle, either!"*

Linwith's eyes bulged as Phinnton's voice echoed within his head. Regaining his composure, Linwith focused his thoughts and redirected them to the boy.

"Very well then, prove your worth. Climb the wall."

Without a word, Phinnton turned on his heel and strode to the towering partition. With hands on his hips, he studied the wall like an explorer would a map, searching for the best path through a labyrinth of woods, deserts and rivers.

His hands felt along the wall until he found something to grab. Without a moment of hesitation, he launched his ascent. Feet found the tiniest of cracks for footholds while fingers grasped the thinnest of fissures.

Linwith was impressed. *"Look at him go. He climbs with cat-like speed as if the wall was..."*

He finished the sentence aloud. "The great oak tree of Hetherlinn."

Memories from Linwith's childhood flashed in his mind. Like Phinnton, he could scamper to the top of the meadow's tree faster than anyone in Hetherlinn, even Quinn.

Phinnton reached the top and pulled himself up with ease. He took his time rising to his full-height and stuck his arms out for balance.

Phinnton wobbled. Arms flapped like a bird to keep from falling off.

"I've sent him to an early death," Linwith feared.

Phinnton lost his balance.

Linwith gasped.

Phinnton, who had been reading Linwith's thoughts the entire time, laughed and regained immediate control.

"Ha! I had you scared."

"Never do that again!" Linwith scowled.

Phinnton jumped up and down, and then showed off by switching from one leg to the other, back and forth, back and forth.

"Agile. Athletic. Brave. Quinn might be right, he will make a good…"

Linwith contained his next word, hoping the boy had not been listening.

But Phinnton stopped jumping. "What were you about to say?" His question echoed over the din of the keep. "What will I be good at?"

Linwith smirked; he knew the battle was over. He would give in to Quinn's request, albeit with great reluctance. He cupped his hands to his mouth and shouted the word.

"Page."

Phinnton's eyes widened. Stunned by the good news, he nearly fell. Regaining his balance, he turned and jumped to the nearby stairs and raced back to Linwith.

"A page? For your worms," he asked in quick bursts of energetic banter.

"No, a page for me," Linwith corrected. The last thing he needed was for Phinnton to think that he was not under his tutelage.

Phinnton was so excited at the prospect of being a page that his words stumbled out of his mouth. "Yes, of course, not the worms! I will serve, no, what I mean is that I would be honored, no, delighted…"

Another thought filled his mind then tumbled out. "Shall I get my father's permission? I suppose not. After all…"

More tumbles. "Food! How foolish of me. Your worms must be famished. I'll feed them…"

His eyes bulged with wonder at the many tasks flying through his mind. "But what of your saddle? Do I remove it, or is that something you do?" Followed by: "Naturally, I'll sleep by your side. That way I can…"

Linwith raised his hand to interrupt. Phinnton covered his mouth in order to contain the words that were about to explode from his mouth.

"First off, you will *not* sleep in my chambers or live with me. I'm *not* your father."

Phinnton's eyes glistened with joy above the hand clamped over his mouth. He nodded with zeal to the arrangement.

Linwith continued. "Second, I can only recommend you as my page. The worms have the final say."

Phinnton's brow furrowed with questions, but he kept his mouth covered and he dared not talk in the silent tongue for fear that one more word would cancel the deal.

Linwith, sensing his confusion, explained. "You must meet the

Worm King. He'll decide if you're worthy to be my page. Follow me."

Linwith turned on his heel and headed for the Worm King. Phinnton, however, stood frozen in place and eyed the Worm King. He was all too familiar with the story about the worm.

When Linwith first arrived to Min Brock, he alerted the refugees to the danger the worms posed, that he was the only one that could approach, converse and touch them. Several boys, convinced Linwith was just telling scary tales, decided to find out for themselves.

Late one night, they snuck into the Grand Hall's turret and crept up the circular stairs. When they reached the top, they peered around the corner. Torches flickered beside two open windows, and aside from a ladder stretching up to the ceiling, the room was empty.

Excited to find the tower unoccupied, they headed for the ladder, tossing an occasional glance back at the stairs to make sure they weren't being followed. Reaching the ladder, they stared up at the shadowed ceiling and spied the access door to the roof. They elbowed each other, giddy to climb out onto the tiled roof where they knew the sapphire worm slept.

The strongest of the boys climbed first. When he reached the door, he unlatched it and flung it open. The door landed with a loud *thud* on the tiles, but instead of coming face to face with the light blue underbelly of the worm, all they saw was the starry night.

Curious to the worm's whereabouts, they climbed onto the tiled roof for a better view.

What they saw took their breath away.

Hovering off the roof was the blackened shape of the worm, his wings beating a quiet cadence, gaze centered on them. The dim fires within his black eyes flashed red. The boys, frozen in place by fear, watched as the worm raised his tail, and for the first time they could see its eerie glow, and blue light fell over faces wrought with horror.

Before they could scream, jump down or cry for help, the tail flung the blue light like a fisherman casting a net to snare fish. Engulfed in sapphire light, the boys were encased in a cocoon of translucent blue. The bubble rose into the air and the boys pressed against its interior wall, hitting it to break free or at least alert a watchman of their predicament. But the surface of the clear blue ball merely shivered from their hits and muffled their anguished cries, and carried them over the wall of Min Brock. Had a sentry not spotted them and alerted Linwith, their blue tomb would have floated upon the winds, forever.

Linwith noticed Phinnton was not by his side so he spun around to check on him. "You coming?"

Phinnton peered around Linwith at the Worm King. Black orbs glared back.

Phinnton felt air leave his lungs as tingly sensations raced over his skin. He was about to have a close encounter with the sapphire worm, something he had always dreamed of doing, but also feared, especially after hearing the boys' experience in the blue ball.

But deep within him, he also sensed that there was more at stake than just the opportunity to examine the creature's shimmering tail or peer into the flames of his black eyes. This was for the honor of being a page, and perhaps a whole lot more.

With a gulp to douse his fears, Phinnton ran to Linwith's side. Together, they continued until Linwith once more stopped to address Phinnton.

"This is as far as I'll escort you. The rest of the journey is for you alone. When you approach the Worm King, do so with determined steps. If you run up to him, the Worm King will misconstrue your zeal to serve as being an act of aggression. Don't proceed too slow or on tiptoe, either. These mannerisms he will assess as proof that you're timid or weak, or that you lack passion for the position. The only way to make sure he won't strike you is to approach with a smooth, steady and confident gait. Got it?"

Phinnton nodded his head as he eyed the colossus sitting nearby. This was the closest he had ever been to one of the worms and he was in awe of the creature's size, flicking blue tail and mysterious powers. Although he had daydreamed about such an opportunity, he had pictured himself walking toward the beast without any fear and that the creature would smile at him, even though he knew worms were incapable of such a thing. Reality crushed his fantasies when the black orbs flashed with bright flames and an orange tongue whipped out to taste the wind and no doubt his fear-filled scent.

Phinnton shot Linwith a frightened look. "Will you be close by?"

Linwith nodded and added: "You don't have to do this. You can turn and walk away if you want."

Phinnton swallowed hard and stepped toward the beast.

He made sure his pace was not too fast or too slow, and just to make certain, glanced back at Linwith who gave him an enthusiastic thumbs-up. Phinnton smiled and focused on the worm should he fling a ball of light at him, although if that happened, there was really nothing he could do to escape or retaliate. Phinnton was close; he caught his scent: a mixture of fish, sea and wind.

The Worm King lowered his head and Phinnton stopped. Orange tongue flicked at his chest, whether to check his scent or intimidate, Phinnton could only guess. Sapphire tail twitched in the dirt, and as much as Phinnton wanted to hop away, he steeled himself for whatever would come next.

He peered up into the worm's eyes. Bright fires glowed within.

Phinnton felt the worm wandering through his thoughts and emotions, just as he could as a storyteller, examining every aspect of his character. Would the Worm King allow him to be a page, or would he find a flaw and send him scampering away, or worse, snap him in half with his massive jaws?

From afar, Linwith addressed the Worm King.

"Before you stands Phinnton. I have asked him to be my page. Do you find him worthy of this position?"

The worm raised his head and directed his gaze toward Linwith.

"He possesses a brave heart," the worm noted as Phinnton gasped in awe to learn that worms could talk. The Worm King's voice was deep, like a pounding waterfall, yet was delivered at a calculated pace like an aged, wise king full of unquenchable strength.

The Worm King continued his report. "But does he have the will to match? I found the tales of Claire within him. Strong as tempest winds they are, but it is one thing to know them and another to live by them."

The worm turned his head back toward Phinnton who, fearing the worst, drew in a deep breath as if he were about to dive into the Sea of Illsbruth.

Several children, drawn by the worm's voice, peered around a far wall to watch. Intrigued and at the same time horrified to see Phinnton so close to the Worm King, they waved others to join them.

The Worm King brought his reptilian snout close to Phinnton's face.

"Very well, Phinnton," the Worm King whispered, his fishy-breath overpowering the boy. "Prove your worth: tell me a tale."

Phinnton let his thoughts run wild to find a suitable story. While he searched, he checked on the worm's black orbs to ascertain the mood he was in. They pulsed with a brighter fire.

That's what happened before the boys were trapped in a blue ball. Am I doomed?

He eyed the tail. It flicked across the ground and sounded like a giant broom sweeping a dirt floor. He swallowed hard; nothing came to mind.

Come on, come on, he urged himself. *Remember a story!*

The Worm King pressed his head closer. "Where has your courage gone, young one?" he whispered. "What use are stories when fear bridles your tongue?"

Phinnton's heart pounded within his chest and he was so nervous that he forgot to exhale. He became dizzy and wobbled in place.

Get a grip, he encouraged himself. *Don't pass out. Breathe!*

He drank in volumes of air and the dizzy spells diminished but he was still unable to find a story to share. He eyed the bright blue tail.

Will I float the heavens…forever…in a blue prison?

The worm opened his mouth. Fish breath enveloped Phinnton. Rows of sword-like teeth towered before him. Still unable to find a tale to share, he closed his eyes and accepted his fate.

When nothing happened, he dared a peek, half expecting to find himself within a blue ball floating on the winds high above Min Brock. Instead, he was relieved to find that he was alive and still on the ground.

The Worm King retracted his head and once again towered over the boy.

"He's not ready," the worm informed Linwith.

Phinnton started to open his mouth and argue his case, but reason came to mind and he clamped his jaw shut. The Worm King was correct: he had failed. He knew he should be thankful that the Worm King had spared his life, but he was too depressed by his failure to celebrate.

The gawking children, realizing Phinnton was no longer in danger, seized the opportunity to belittle him. Taunts and snickers jabbed Phinnton like punches to the gut. He dropped his head and sulked away.

Linwith breathed a sigh of relief, not only because Phinnton's life had been spared, but that he would not be allowed to be his page. He could at least tell Quinn that it was the Worm King, and not he, that ultimately rejected the boy. And yet, he was perplexed to find himself sympathizing with Phinnton's rejection.

Did I secretly want the boy to pass the test, to become my page, even though I was - or so I'd told myself - so opposed to the undertaking?

Linwith glared at the mob of children. Their bullying dredged up pain-filled memories from his childhood, memories he had buried many summers ago. Now they pressed up like ghouls from the grave.

He too had been picked on in his village, and until now, had forgotten just how painful the experience had been. Linwith absorbed the words hurled at Phinnton, felt his fists tighten, wanted to grab the bullies, shake them and give them a good lashing with his tongue and belt.

Why do they pick on him so, he wondered as his memories intertwined with the present. *Is it because he's thin and not as strong as the others? Does it have to do with how he looks, or walks or talks? Or is it because Phinnton prefers solitude instead of being a part of the gang?*

Linwith turned his attention to Phinnton. Shoulders slumped. Feet shuffled through dust. He remembered a similar journey home. *Quinn was right. We're very much alike.*

Linwith readjusted his critique of Phinnton, and instead, found himself connected to the boy in a new way. He was about to shout a word of encouragement when Phinnton stopped. His back righted, shoulders straightened, and he turned back around. His look of failure and shame were gone. In their place was a faint smile. But what was most impressive was what he did next.

Long strides propelled him back toward the Worm King.

Linwith's mouth dropped open, awestruck by Phinnton's sudden bravery. Even the bullying children stopped chanting to see what would happen next, even if it meant Phinnton's death.

When Phinnton reached the spot he had previously vacated, he addressed the Worm King. "If it's not too late, I do have a tale. I think it will show that I'm worthy to serve Linwith as his page."

The Worm King arched his long neck higher and emitted a horrific bark. In answer to the call, large shadows fell from six turrets and swept across the courtyard. Phinnton stared overhead, alarmed to see the other six worms descending to the courtyard.

He was surrounded.

The worms' collective breath smothered him with the scent of fish and sea and wind. Wings were spread and filtered sunlight encased him in gray-green shadows. Deep and ominous howls - like peals of thunder - hailed from the seven worms. The ground shook from their howls and everyone, including Linwith, covered their ears.

Everyone, that is, except Phinnton.

He turned about in a slow, carefree manner as if gazing up at a beautiful sky and not seven worms that could end his life.

Linwith noted the change. Not much time had transpired since the worm rejected him as page, yet Phinnton's countenance radiated confidence, as if the tale he had nocked to his imagination like an arrow, gave him great courage, strength and delight.

A radiant smile - bright as the day - lit up his face.

Much like the worm's tails at dusk.

The worms stopped bellowing and retracted their wings to their scaled sides. The Worm King pressed his enormous head against Phinnton's forehead.

"Very well, tell us your tale, but this is not a game, young Phinnton. Fail this time, and you will forfeit your life, here and now, to my brothers."

Phinnton's smile did not fade.

In fact, Linwith thought he saw it widen.

Chapter 12

All for Bal-Malin

The news of Phinnton being surrounded by the worms spread like a prairie fire through Min Brock. Men, women and children flocked to watch what would happen next.

Linwith looked them over with disdain. *Boredom breeds curiosity, even if it means the loss of life. What a wretched lot we are.*

He turned his attention to the worms and Phinnton.

Outstretched wings formed a membrane tent over the boy. Loud barks shook the citadel's stones, and then, as if cued by some silent command, all seven retracted their wings simultaneously with the precision of palace guards changing shifts.

The Worm King lowered his head like a serpent about to strike: slow, methodical, threatening. The onlookers gasped, but instead of snapping Phinnton in two, the sapphire worm stopped just short of touching the boy.

Phinnton kept his chin raised and stared at the worm.

No one uttered a word.

No one moved a muscle.

No one except Linwith.

He slid over to his armory and snuck inside without being noticed. He scampered to the table beside the window where his saddle lay. He positioned his palm over the saddle horn and kept an eye on Phinnton and the worms. Linwith's fingers flexed, ready to grab the jewels in a moment's notice should Phinnton fail his test and the worms attack. Phinnton, on the other hand, appeared oblivious to the danger he was in or the mob watching his fate. Phinnton's countenance reflected a heart swelling with wonder, not fear or trepidation.

Linwith's thumb graced the top of the sapphire gem.

Phinnton looks confident, as if he indeed has a tale that will please you.

Yes, the Worm King replied in the silent tongue of the worms that Phinnton, even as a storyteller, was unable to hear, *but if he does not, you know the consequences.*

Linwith gulped down his fears. *Surely you can overlook such shortcoming this time?*

The Worm King raised his eyes to find Linwith's shadow in the armory. *And surely you know such a request, even from our master, cannot be honored.*

Linwith jerked his thumb off the gem and leaned toward Phinnton, willing him to pass the test.

The Worm King took in Phinnton. "Time is up. Recite your tale."

Phinnton noted the beast's black orbs as they pulsed with firelight, shifting from yellow to orange to red and back to yellow. Despite the worm's intimidating persona, Phinnton's resolve remained intact, and in fact grew stronger, all of which was a result of flashbacks to his childhood.

Cool nights far from Hetherlinn...

A white marker, aglow in the moonlight, bearing a lion seal...

His father, Bruun, keeping watch on the road...

Korvik, his mother, whispering sweet tales of wonder that whisked him to a land of indescribable beauty...

One night in particular stood out. He could still hear his mother's voice: silky smooth, strong as granite.

"Phinnton, a day awaits you when you'll be asked to do great things by amazing creatures. If you attempt to fulfill these requests with your own ability and strength, these beasts will consume you. But if you offer them the tales I've taught you, like an emissary bearing gifts to a foreign king, they will usher you into their fellowship."

Phinnton's thoughts leapt back to the present. He focused on the story she had taught him many summers ago, out beside the marker where the moonlight bathed her face with argent light. Now the story stood sharp and true, ready to be released like a cavalry to charge forward in his defense. His mother's face - silvery fire - flashed in his mind. She beamed Phinnton a proud smile, and with a reassuring nod, whispered:

"Begin your journey, my son."

Without further hesitation, Phinnton released the story with a rush of gusto, and his tale charged into the fray.

> *"Far from Gilden's sandy shore, o'er its frothy sea,*
> *Lies the Isle of Bal-Malin, with valleys, crags and leas.*
> *Majestic oaks on crested butte bend against the wind,*
> *With bark as white as forever snow they guard Bal-Malin.*
>
> *Towering cliffs reside beside, sweet oaks oh so grand,*
> *And seven lairs, shaped like eyes, gaze out o'er the land.*
> *Great beasts - I'm told - lie within, their legend n'er to resend,*
> *For every nation knows the tale of the Worms of Bal-Malin.*

> *With tails that glow like gems afire, and talons strong as steel,*
> *The Brothers Seven bellow a bark, that sounds like thunder peals.*
> *Mighty wings beat a path o'er celestial sky,*
> *And vibrant colors - arcs of light - flash from tails on high.*
>
> *Countless summers they lay asleep, awaiting champion true,*
> *A master that would earn the right to lead them forth anew.*
> *Many journeyed into the lairs to command the worms to fly,*
> *But e'er the path of foolishness, and thus each had to die.*
>
> *'Til the day when scent revealed, a man from Hetherlinn,*
> *Who neared the lairs of the Seven, the Worms of Bal-Malin.*
> *Forgotten song from his youth, this man did humbly speak,*
> *The worms gave homage to the one, others had deemed weak.*
>
> *Thus began their Master's reign, o'er the worms so bold,*
> *Talons of steel and stories from Claire, and caches filled with gold.*
> *United as one to fight dark foe, the victors rise again,*
> *To end the Cauldron's rule of night, all for Bal-Malin."*

The Worm King lowered his head for Phinnton. Gasps arose from the onlookers who were convinced this marked his end.

The only person who saw what was truly transpiring stood within the shadows of the armory. *The Worm King doesn't glare at you with disgust, anger or revenge,* Linwith marveled, knowing Phinnton could hear his thoughts. *He's staring at you with the utmost of respect!*

"Brothers," the Worm King bellowed as his forehead grazed Phinnton's with affection like that of a stallion. "Behold our page!"

Loud cheers erupted from the spectators.

Linwith was so preoccupied with the ordeal that he did not realize someone was beside him.

"I see Phinnton has proven himself well," Quinn interjected as he followed Linwith's line of sight out the window.

Startled, Linwith turned to take in his brother's smiling face. "So it seems," he replied as he turned back to watch the worms stir clouds of dust that spiraled across the courtyard. They then ascended into the air and glided back to their towers.

"You were right about the boy," Linwith added as he shot Phinnton a proud smile. "He's very much like me."

Quinn draped his arm over Linwith's shoulder as the children - who only moments before had mocked Phinnton - raced to their champion and showered him with praise. "I'm glad you see that, big brother."

Boys and men slapped Phinnton's back to congratulate him, while girls and women pooled together and cooed over him. "Do you think the Dark Flame is aware of his powers?"

Quinn's smile fell. "I'm sure the tale he just delivered to your worms is floating back to Ebon. It's only a matter of time before the Cauldron discovers it. And Phinnton."

Linwith shuddered at the thought of Phinnton being hounded by the drone or worse, hunted by vul jens. Strong feelings toward the boy, which Linwith concluded must be similar to those a parent felt, coursed his veins. "Then I must make haste to train him. Who knows when the Cauldron will attack?"

Quinn shook his head. "Not today, Linwith. Not today."

"But time isn't our ally."

"We both know war is imminent, so let him enjoy being a boy, if only for today. Let him laugh and play and dream of sweet summers in Hetherlinn's meadow. In fact..."

Quinn let his sentence fade while his eyes brightened with a wonderful idea.

Linwith, who had seen this look before whenever Quinn launched into a wild adventure or cockamamie scheme, flashed him a stern look.

"Do *not* share whatever is flying around in that head of yours. I've had enough of your *ideas* today to last a lifetime."

Quinn's smile widened as his notion came to life. "Perhaps a ride to the beach is in order."

"What?" Linwith asked, befuddled at the thought.

"According to your recent scouting report, the sky, sea and plain are void of our enemy. It's a perfect time for a respite by the Gilden Sea. If his father approves, of course."

Linwith scowled and folded his arms across his chest. "Let me get this straight: You want me to take him flying...on a worm...to the beach...to play in the surf?"

"Yes," Quinn answered as if such a notion was commonplace during wartime.

Linwith's jaw fell open. "You're mad."

Quinn chuckled. "That would certainly explain a few things about me." Quinn's smile softened. "When war does come, who knows how many summers are left for him." Softer still, "...or for us."

He regained his composure and delivered his final thought with the passion he was noted for. "So for today, let Phinnton play in the waves and dance on the sands."

Quinn swatted Linwith on the back. "But you must hurry. The day is quickly disappearing."

Linwith took in Phinnton and the animated children. "Unfortunately for me, not fast enough."

Chapter 13

Dark Mission

The Gor King led his army deeper into the woods, and every now and then Woren turned in his saddle to check on Mälque. True to his Wurmlin training, the boy kept to the shadows as if trying to remain undetected from Woren and his men.

Lucky for you, Woren pondered, *that the Gor King has not ordered us to a cantor or gallop; you would not be able to keep pace.*

As night fell, Woren shouted out a command and the army fanned out to make camp. Fires were lit, tents or lean-tos were set up, and leisurely conversation was exchanged amongst the patrols.

After Woren had tethered his steed, he searched the area for Mälque. Unable to find him amidst the shadows, Woren opted to wait until morning when his boot caught something firm yet soft, and he stumbled to catch his balance.

"Why'd 'ya step on me," Mälque snapped.

"Because I didn't see you, that's why." Woren stared down at the ground, searching for the boy amidst the darkness. "It's going to be a cold night," he noted, still unable to see Mälque. "Why not sleep near one of the fires?"

"Don't need to. Been through colder."

"That I don't doubt, but this time's different."

"How so?"

"Because you serve the Gor King."

Mälque fell silent as he pondered Woren's charge. "I ain't gonna run away, if that's whatcha mean. I coulda done that already and you'd never known."

"True," Woren confessed.

"And I ain't gonna try and kill no one neither. Not with him around."

Although Woren was still unable to see Mälque, he nonetheless knew he was referring to the Gor King. Woren turned his gaze to the Gor King's fire that, as usual, was nowhere near the other men's camps. The Gor King, still wearing his skull helmet, sat near the flames eating what appeared to be venison jerky. Yellow and orange light danced over him making the skull look all that more ominous. Woren, who had witnessed this night after night, still felt a shiver arc his back when his eyes wandered across the blackened eye sockets.

Woren focused on Mälque. "Wise choice," he rasped to the shadows. "But you are a Wurmlin, and thievery is in your blood."

"Ain't nothin' I can do about that."

"True, but there's something I can do about it."

Woren held his idea and was pleased to hear leaves rustle, either caused by the boy's curiosity or because he was frightened to learn of the plan.

"What?" Mälque braved.

"You'll camp beside my fire."

More rustling, and then in a voice that Woren noted was closer: "Don't want to."

Good, Woren thought. *I have your interest and now you're standing.*

"Doesn't matter what you want or don't want to do, Mälque. You're in the army now."

"Ya gonna try and make me?"

The soft sound of a blade being slid from a leather scabbard made Woren flex.

"Sheath your weapon," Woren commanded in a firm voice.

"How'd ya know…"

"I'm an Ebonite, not some fool you can rob on the highway. You don't want to test your fighting skills with me, boy."

Woren crossed his arms to emphasize his point, knowing that although he could not see Mälque, the boy could see his every move.

"Alright," Mälque huffed. The blade slid back between oiled leather. "I'll camp near you. But I still need the shadows. Ain't used to sleepin' so close to a fire. It'll keep me up all night. Lead on."

Woren gave a nod, turned and headed for his campfire. He never looked over his shoulder to check on Mälque. Woren needed to demonstrate trust; it was the first step in getting Mälque to accept the mission the Gor King had for him.

Woren squatted by the fire and dragged his saddlebag close.

"Hungry," he asked as he fished through his belongings.

"Yeah," Mälque said, ashamed he had to rely on another for food. He plopped to the ground and leaned his back up against a tree.

Woren found what he was looking for and tossed a hunk of dried meat to Mälque.

"What is it," the boy asked as he caught the food.

"Smoked boar. I have water and some berries, too."

Mälque ripped off a bite and did his best to contain his famished state. But as he chewed the meat, and the sweet scent of smoke filled his senses, he threw caution to the wind and devoured the jerky.

Woren didn't wait for him to ask for more food. Instead, he tossed him more meat along with a few branches littered with berries.

Mälque ravaged them all.

"Sorry about your brother," Woren said as he poked the fire with a stick.

Mälque stopped chewing and sized up Woren. Aside from Vonn and his parents when they were alive, no other person had ever consoled him. Mälque still wasn't ready to trust Woren, so he decided not to reply and focused on his meal instead.

Woren snuck a glance at the boy.

Strong. Tough. Wise, he surmised. *You're just a boy, and you've seen things no one, not even a Wurmlin, should witness.*

Woren let his gaze wander to the Gor King's campfire. The enigmatic warrior, per the routine established over four summers, had stretched out on his back to sleep with helmet on and sword clutched to his chest as if dead.

Your mission for Mälque is an odd one, especially in dark times like these. Nonetheless, I'm your commanding officer and I'll obey.

He turned his attention back to Mälque.

"So what happened to your parents," he asked the boy.

Mälque stripped berries off a twig and popped them into his mouth. "They died."

"That much I figured. I'm familiar with Wurmlin customs: Olke was a relative and when your parents died, he became your caretaker."

Mälque flashed Woren a hot look. "Caretaker? He treated us like slaves!"

Woren let his gaze fall to the embers and turned his back to the boy. He smiled, delighted that Mälque was opening up to him. "Tell me more."

"I ain't talkin' about him no more." Venom filled his words. "Never wanna say or hear his name again."

Woren nodded and tossed another log onto the fire. "I don't blame you, but I'd be honored if you shared the story about your folks."

Woren could almost feel Mälque's eyes burn into his back, sizing him up, wondering if he could trust the Ebonite. It took all his will power, but Woren remained fixated on his fire despite the urge to turn and grab the boy and shake the news from him.

"My dad," Mälque offered, his voice now soft and reserved, "died a Wurmlin death."

"How's that," Woren asked as he continued to fuss with the fire.

"Died stealin.' At least that's what we figured. Hard to know exactly. The entire patrol was killed so there were no witnesses."

Woren stiffened. He knew Wurmlins were stealthy and fierce combatants and that for a patrol of three to be wiped out would take military skills most villagers lacked.

The fire crackled and popped. "Did Ebonites do this," Woren asked with his back still to the boy.

"Not likely. Never seen nothin' like it."

Mälque flashed back to that fateful night. Shaking off the memory, he took in Woren who continued messing with the fire and decided to trust him.

"Happened about four summers ago. Our mom woke us. Said she had a dream that dad had called to her from the grave. At the time, we didn't believe her 'cause she used to believe in so many superstitions. But that night was different. It was as if everything she'd been tellin' us or teachin' us came true.

"We found the two men that had gone stealin' with him. They were blue, stiff, with arms and legs twisted all about. Mom later told us it looked like they'd been poisoned. Said she saw it only once before, during the Dark War, when she watched a rusk - this flying creature that storytellers from Claire had - strike an Ebonite with its tail.

"Whatever the cause, Vonn and I had never seen anything like it before. Then we found Dad…"

Mälque's iron resolve softened as the memory from that night rolled through him, the emotions as strong as when he had experienced them long ago. "He'd been cut in half, but that's not what was so strange. The bottom part stood erect, while the upper half lay in the leaves not too far away. I'll never forget his face - eyes wide open as if he'd seen somethin' horrible."

Mälque shook off the feelings that made him shiver and squinted at Woren. "Ya believe my story," he asked.

Woren poked the fire, and with his back still to the boy, simply gave a firm nod to confirm. "I've seen my share of the bizarre during the Awakening. So what happened to your mother?"

"Caught the plague or somethin' like it the next winter. Died that summer."

Woren gave a sympathetic nod and tossed his stick into the growing flames. "And now you're here with me," he offered as he turned to take in Mälque. "And with him." He tossed his head toward the Gor King.

Mälque twisted his face in confusion. "Yeah. So?"

"Do you think it was merely coincidence that we found you three in the woods, or that you're the survivor?"

"Only reason I'm alive is 'cause Vonn ran and Olke was a coward."

"No, the reason is *you* chose not to run and *you* killed Olke."

"Did not. Them fea dracas did."

Woren chuckled. "Do you think I'm stupid enough to believe that you didn't plan or hope that swarm would kill him?"

Mälque blinked but remained silent.

Woren continued. "And I know you're not stupid enough to believe you have been welcomed into the Gor King's ranks merely because you captured a trunk full of fea dracas."

"No, I ain't. Figured there was more for me to do."

Woren's eerie smile flickered. "There is."

Instead of telling the boy what the plan was or what his role would be, Woren turned away and curled up near the fire to sleep.

Mälque fidgeted, trying to contain his curiosity that flashed and danced within. He watched Woren settle near the fire, hoping he'd share such information before he drifted off to sleep. But when Woren found a comfortable spot and settled in for a good night's sleep, Mälque could not bear the wait any longer.

"You ain't fallin' asleep before ya tell me what I'm supposed to do."

"It can wait until morning," Woren said mocking a sleepy voice, excited the boy was eager to learn of his role.

Mälque squirmed. "No. No it can't!"

"Suit yourself." Woren's smile widened. "You're to find someone."

"Who?"

"A girl."

Chapter 14

Between the Pages

Mälque tossed about on his bed of pine needles, unable to sleep. Flashing in his mind like lightning were the grisly events that had led him to the Gor King's camp: his mother's superstitions; his dad's macabre corpse; looting dead bodies; Vonn being murdered; fea dracas devouring Olke.

He looked in the direction of the Gor King's fire. Argent moonbeams crisscrossed the woods and a line of smoke snaked through the tree limbs marking his fire. Many nights had passed since Woren disclosed his purpose, to find a powerful girl, but time passed without him being pressed into service.

Mälque pushed himself up to his elbows for a better look. The Gor King was staring at him, orange hues from the firelight lancing across his skull helmet, the eye sockets deep and dark like caves. Mälque swallowed hard and dropped face-first to the ground, motionless, listening for the slightest sound signaling that the Gor King approached.

Nothin' but an owl hoot, he noted.

With a sigh of relief, he rolled onto his back only to discover the Gor King straddling him.

Mälque gasped, stunned that he had snuck up on him undetected. The skull flashed in the silvery moonlight, and Mälque was unable to take his eyes off the gaping sockets where eyes - if they even existed - were hidden from view.

Mälque squirmed and wiggled to get away. "I know whatcha want me to find," he muttered with a glance at Woren's sleeping frame.

The Gor King cocked his head to the side in curiosity.

"A girl," Mälque said in a half-whisper. "He told me so." Mälque flicked his head to where Woren slept.

The Gor King gave a subtle nod, whether to confirm or simply to patronize, Mälque was unable to discern. "But listen," Mälque added as he pushed himself up on his elbows. "I ain't *never* hunted a girl before. May be easy. Might be impossible. Besides," he surveyed the dark woods, "ain't no girls in these woods. They're all dead or gone to Min Brock."

The Gor King stepped closer, boots pressing down leaves and twigs without making them crack or snap. Mälque backed away on hands, butt and heels. "Did you hear me," he fired between clinched teeth. "I can't find you no girl!"

The Gor King extended him a gloved hand. Mälque eyed it with suspicion. After much thought, and realizing he didn't have any other options, he grabbed it.

Yanked to his feet, Mälque found himself being pushed through the woods toward the army's tethered horses. He flicked his oily hair, like he'd seen Olke do, in an effort to show the Gor King he wasn't intimidated. A gruff laugh made him glance over his shoulder.

"I've seen that head flick before," Woren said, greasy smile glowing in the moonlight. "A certain - *relative* - if I'm not mistaken before fea dracas raked his flesh."

Mälque acted as if Woren's sudden appearance wasn't a shock, but the commander spied the twitch of his mouth. "I'm a light sleeper," he offered with a snarl. "Now mount up. We have a long ride ahead of us."

Mälque made his way to his steed and was surprised to find it saddled. "Yes," Woren answered as if reading his thoughts, "we've been planning this night for some time."

The Gor King and Woren mounted while Mälque held the reins to his horse and pondered his choices. If he took off on foot, he stood a chance of outsmarting them both, even if they were on horseback. But what sort of life would it be? Where would he go?

On the other hand, if he rode off with them to hunt for a girl, he could stall the inevitable by taking them down numerous paths of his own making. Maybe, with a little luck, he could make a break for it on horseback, which would afford him a better livelihood not to mention a faster means of escape.

"Choose wisely," Woren fired from his saddle.

Mälque sucked on his lip, once again shocked at how it seemed Woren could read his mind.

"Ain't got much choices, now do I," Mälque countered as he swung his leg up and over the saddle.

He followed their lead through the woods, all the while wondering when they would turn and ask him to find the scent of some girl. As he hashed out his plan - finding an animal trail and leading them all night on a wild goose chase - the Gor King signaled for him to approach.

Mälque spurred his animal and lumbered up beside the dark warrior. He knew better than to expect him to speak, but considering the challenging task he'd been given, he hoped for a clue as to where he might begin his search.

The Gor King pulled back on his reins and the entourage stopped. Fishing something from his rear saddlebag, he handed it to Mälque.

A white feather. It's as long as my arm.

Mälque ran a finger along the edge and watched the feather fan apart. "What's this from," he asked.

"Isn't it obvious," Woren offered with a condescending huff. "A bird."

Mälque stopped fingering the feather and snickered. "I aint' *that* dumb. I know it's from a bird, but it ain't from nothin' livin' in these parts. Besides, what's this gotta do with findin' a girl?"

"Pertaining to the latter part of your question," Woren answered. "When you find the bird, you'll find the girl. In regards to where this bird is from, well, our hunch is that he - or she - is from Claire."

"Claire?" Mälque studied the feather, twisting it in the silvery light of the moon. His mother's warnings about the nation, especially storytellers, came to mind. He brushed them aside. "Heard it don't exist."

"Well, you've heard wrong. How else do you explain so large a feather?"

"Easy." He flapped the feather to simulate flight, amazed at the amount of air it moved. "The Cauldron. Seen some crazy, spooky things in the woods." He recalled the night he discovered his dad's corpse standing erect in the woods, upper half lying on the ground, eyes wide with shock and awe. "Magic, or spells, or some other mumbo-jumbo could have made this giant bird."

Woren waved off his analysis. "It really doesn't matter, now does it? Your job is to find the girl, not to identify this creature's origins."

Mälque nodded and stuck the quill down into the side of his boot, careful not to damage its shape. "Fair enough. So we're ridin' to Claire?"

"No. We're following you as you track this bird."

"Track him," Mälque snapped. "How? I can't fly and I don't know where this feather came from. That bird could be anywhere."

Woren turned his attention to the Gor King who sat motionless during the entire exchange staring at the feather sticking out of Mälque's boot. The Gor King pulled away from his gaze and shifted about in his saddle. His horse snorted, blasts of mist firing from his nostrils, and trudged forward up the incline.

Woren motioned for Mälque to follow and they rode single-file to the crest.

At the summit, the Gor King stopped and pointed down below.

Mälque stared into the vale but it was thick with gnarly trees that blocked the moonbeams. All he saw were shadows and darkness.

"At the bottom," Woren instructed, "you'll find a thick grove of saplings. The feather was found nearby. On the other side of the coppice is a cave. I believe you'll find everything you'll need inside to begin your hunt."

Mälque eyed them both, suspicious that this was a trap or simply another test like he and Vonn had experienced with the fea dracas tree.

Woren sneered, and as if reading his mind, grabbed his tunic and pulled him close, almost yanking him out of the saddle. "We'll be watching," Woren half-whispered. "Don't be a fool."

Woren pushed him away with a huff.

Mälque adjusted his tunic, unflustered by Woren's threat, and clucked his tongue. His horse whinnied and started down the hill.

At the bottom, he not only found the vale eerily dark, but so thick with growth that his pace was slow at best. He pulled back on the reins and fished out something from his saddlebag. Hopping to the ground, he held up the MerriNoon firestick and tapped it twice like he'd seen his mother do to ignite it.

Bluish-white light fanned out all around him.

He swept his makeshift torch about and gasped when it fell across a skeleton lying face down. He held the firestick high, the light making the remains look all the more creepy, and tiptoed toward it for a closer inspection.

It's a man...a big man...but what's that?

He stared at the long bones arching outward from the spine like twisted fingers and curling to a point far over the skull.

Wings! And his skull...looks like a lizard head.

Comprehension knocked breath from his lungs. *He's part man, part dragon!*

He recalled his mother's warnings the night they found his father's body.

"*You're gonna see things ya never seen before, too, crazy things.*"

He backed away from the skeletal remains.

Don't matter none what you are, he reasoned yet shaking his head to clear his eyes from the anomaly as well as to regain his nerve. *You're dead. And I ain't, and I plan on stayin' that way, too. Now let's see if there are more of ya out there..."*

He braved a step back to the skeleton, sniffed, and caught the beast's remnant scent. He searched the surrounding woods for signs of the creatures. Off to his right, he caught the familiar whiff of a man-dragon, but swirling with it was the stench of death, so he paid it no mind. He detected another deep in the woods, but it too was dead.

Not finding any other traces, he was convinced he was safe, at least from the man-dragons. Sweeping the firestick in a new direction, he spied something of interest on the ground. He made his way to the spot and knelt to inspect.

Droppings, he noted as he fingered the large, dried balls. *And smaller feathers. And animal bones.*

His gaze wandered up through the tree limbs, and with the firestick hoisted as high as he could get it, spied what he assumed was the bird's lair: a massive nest of twigs, leaves and moss. *This ain't some songbird I'm huntin'...*

Something white, and barely visible in the nest, fluttered in the night breeze.

A feather, stuck in the nest.

Without taking his eyes off it, he pulled the feather from his boot. Holding it up, he compared the two feathers, and although the distance was too great for an accurate measurement, he was convinced they were identical.

His gaze fell on the tiny bones littering the ground. *This thing eats meat. It's a bird of prey.*

Mälque, using the nest as a reference point, deduced just how large a predator it was that he was hunting. The answer made him swallow hard and a shiver coursed down his back, making the firestick quiver.

He's as big as a small horse. Followed by another realization.

What if he's still in the nest?

"Don't worry," Woren shouted as he and the Gor King made their way to Mälque. "He's been gone for some time now."

Mälque slid the feather back into his boot and focused on the saplings blocking the cavern. "Okay, but what's inside that cave?"

"All sorts of things," Woren fired, and although it was too dark to see his face, Mälque knew that his greasy smile was twitching.

"Well," Mälque challenged, "I ain't goin' in without a weapon."

"Not necessary. The cave doesn't contain *those* type of things. You'll be fine as is. Now hurry."

"I ain't got a good feelin' about this."

"It doesn't matter how you feel. You were given an order."

"But if you've already been in there, why do I need to?"

"Because you're a Wurmlin. You'll be able to find her scent or discover a clue. Now quit stalling and *go*."

Mälque gulped down some night air, pretending it was his dad's brew to settle his nerves, and set off for the mysterious cave.

This better not be a trick, he fretted as he ducked under some low vines. *Don't need to come face-to-face with that giant bird or a man-dragon.*

He was about to give up his search when he cleared the last bit of undergrowth and stumbled into a small clearing. Directly in front of him was the cave, its mouth as dark and foreboding as the eye sockets of the Gor King's helmet.

With the firestick held high, and another swig of air for courage, he entered the cave. It was narrow, the cold stone pressing in on him; streams of water trickled down the sides, the scent of wet earth and musk thick in the air. He tiptoed deeper into the cave, senses alert for any sign of ambush, blue-white light from the firestick leading the way. Up ahead, he noted a black opening. He stopped to study it.

Looks like this empties into a larger cave or...

He crept forward, eyeing the ground near the dark hole.

...falls into a black hole.

Once he was by the opening, and his light flooded inside, he was awestruck by what he witnessed.

Or someone's home!

He thrust the firestick into the room and moved it about in search of anything or anyone dangerous.

Empty, he noted as he took in the ornate fireplace carved into the cave wall. Candles stood in nooks while pots and pans - charred from cooking on the flames - were stacked with precision on the hearth.

Making his way to the center of the room, he stopped to take it all in. Dried herbs, bundled with leather strands, hung on one wall. Pewter plates and mugs lined an alcove chiseled in the stone. Dried grape leaves stained with berry juice and fish oil were tossed in a pile near the entrance. Spiced scents and smoke from the fireplace filled the room with its bouquet.

He swept the firestick to another area. A bed - constructed of tree limbs - sat in a corner. Linens were folded and stacked at the foot of the bed. A dark wool blanket, tucked tight, covered the mattress.

So tidy; as if someone could return at any moment.

Making his way to the bed, he noted an outline pressed into the wool blanket. He lowered his light and eyed it with his experience as a Wurmlin. He traced the indentation with his hand. *Cold. Ain't been used in some time, but looks like the shape of a girl.*

A pillow, goose-down quills sticking out here and there, caught his attention. A long strand of cinnamon-colored hair lay on one edge. Retrieving it between finger and thumb, he twisted it about, studying the curly lock that shimmered in the light of his firestick. He ran it under his nose to catch the scent before pocketing it.

Turning from the bed, his light fell across stacks of oddly bound items. He made his way to them, noting that they were crafted of leather and held - what he perceived from his limited education as a Wurmlin - great amounts of parchment paper.

A table sat nearby and held one of the leather bound objects. He turned his head to catch the inscription on the cover. He was unable to read, but his mother had taught him two words - *Ebon* and *Claire* - in hopes he would steer clear of anything associated with such words. He traced the gold inscriptions with his finger. The first words he didn't recognize, but the latter made his skin crawl.

Claire!

Superstitions that he could trace back to his mother overcame him.

He jerked his finger away in fear that the book was charmed.

"Ela Claire. Delight!"

The whisper resonated about the cave.

Mälque backpedaled away from the book, arms and legs flailing about.

"Who's there?" he blurted after catching his balance. He thrust the lightstick about the room. "I ain't afraid of ya! I'll burn ya *alive.*"

He whipped the firestick about like a dagger to intimidate whoever was there, but the cave was empty. A terrifying thought came to mind, and he eyed the book. Cold sweat pooled between his shoulder blades and trickled down his back as his mother's warning came to life...

"You'll hear whispers, and I ain't talkin' about voices from the grave, neither. These come from Claire or Ebon...sweet as songbirds...promisin' this or that. Ignore them...stay true to the whispers in your head."

A burst of warm air, scented with flower and sea, flipped the cover open. Mälque bit his lip to contain a scream, lightstick shaking in his hand. The wind rustled the parchments, invisible fingers in search of a tale to impart to the Wurmlin. The gush of wind died and the book lay open.

Despite the sweat beading on his brow, and his pounding heartbeat at realizing the Cauldron or Claire had whispered, Mälque tiptoed to the table, his curiosity overruling his mother's warnings. After all, hadn't a similar whisper spoken to him near the fea dracas tree, urging him on with his plan, as if eager to see him succeed?

"And I ain't dead...yet," he concluded as he hovered over the open parchments.

Etched in black ink across both pages of the yellowed parchment was a map. He leaned close, lightstick even closer, to study it.

The only titles he could identify were those labeling the nations of Ebon and Claire. At the center of the map was an island off the coast of Claire, and judging by the artwork, there was a castle perched on its highest crags.

He eyed the citadel's name, burning the letters into his memory to be deciphered at a later time...

R-H-Y-T-H-E

"The Isle of Rhythe. Ela Claire," the whisper repeated as a stiff breeze struck the feather in his boot and launched it into the air. *"My Delight!"*

Mälque stared spellbound at its flight, not sure whether to run screaming out of the haunted cave or to stay to see what happened next. The wind chose for him. It died and the feather floated down in graceful arcs to the open book where it settled atop the drawing.

Intrigue and curiosity tamed his fears. Without knowing why he was doing it, he pulled the strand of hair out of his pocket.

"Ela Claire. My delight!"

This time, instead of jumping away, he listened with rapt attention.

"Who's Ela Claire," he asked, staring up at the ceiling, expecting to see a spirit or some other vision from Ebon or Claire to dialogue with. All he saw were streaks of soot and spots of moisture.

"This is hers, ain't it?" He held the strand overhead and turned around, assuming that whatever was in the cave with him was unable to see it otherwise.

Frustrated that the whisper didn't answer, he laid the strand beside the feather and stared at the drawing of the castle, biting his lower lip as he tried to put two and two together.

"Are ya tryin' to tell me," he shouted in an effort to be heard or to get the ghoul's attention, or so his superstitious mind reasoned, "that this girl, Ela Claire, was flown to this island by that giant bird?"

He waited for an answer, doing his best to appear patient in case such a character trait was more appealing to the sprite than impatience. When no one spoke and the wind no longer rustled, his true temperament emerged. Grinding his teeth, Mälque gave a flick of his head and whipped his hair.

"My mother was right. Shoulda never paid you no mind in the first place. You're just a ghost."

Mälque felt a rush of warm wind brush his cheek. Wurmlin instinct kicked in and he backed away from the table just as the blast lifted the book covers and smacked them with fury on the tabletop.

"I am no ghost."

"Okay," he replied with a nod of his head. "Ya ain't no ghost, but that don't mean…"

"And your mother was wrong about Claire."

"Possibly, but then again…"

"How could a whisper from Ebon be the same as one from Claire?"

"Don't know and it don't matter 'cause…"

"Identical in tone yet opposite in nature?"

Mälque made fists. "I don't know."

"Where one taunts 'Death begets death' and another 'death begets life?'"

"Circle talk," Mälque fired. "Makin' no sense, no sense at all. Ain't important if ya gotta stay alive."

"Like Vonn tried to do?"

"Leave my brother outa this. He died a brave death."

"Yes, yes he did, and I greeted him that day on the killing field, offering the very same gift I now offer you."

"What…what are you talkin' about?" Mälque turned about, equally perplexed by the offer as well as the fact that he was dialoging with a whisper.

"My stories offer life."

"Are you the Cauldron?"

"The Cauldron wouldn't meet you in the cave of a storyteller."

Mälque felt his blood freeze at the thought. He took in the leather bound parchments and the herbs hanging on the wall before staring at the book on the table. And as his imagination recreated his mother's face in perfect detail, he heard her whisper...

"Conniving men and women...Magic herbs that can ease pain and heal...or kill. Stories that can open the ground like a grave or...make ya wish ya was dead."

Aware he was in the heart of a storyteller's lair, and fearing the worst, Mälque grit his teeth.

"I ain't scared!"

"You should be."

The answer cut Mälque to the quick.

He jabbed the lightstick through the air like a blade, hoping to slice the whisper in half.

"Woren and the Gor King knew better than to enter a storyteller's cave, so they sent you instead."

Mälque swiped the lightstick in an arc. "How do you know about them?"

"Nothing is hidden from me."

Mälque, afraid he'd be jumped by the whisper, pressed his back against a wall of the cave.

"So you're gonna kill me."

"No. I offer you life, just as I did Vonn."

"Maybe." He waved the lightstick around. "But then again, you could be tryin' to trick me."

"Like I did when you were with the fea dracas?"

Mälque stopped waving his firestick.

"If I wanted you dead, don't you think I could have done so in the meadow...or when you stepped into this cave?"

Mälque bit his lower lip as reason returned to him. He lowered his guard but remembered he was in the lair of a storyteller. Muscles tightened and he whipped the lightstick through the air. "Tricks of the tale! My mother warned me about ya! You're a trickster!"

"Your mother's stories were misguided, a trick of the Cauldron, maneuvering her passions into superstitions that she handed down to you."

The warm breeze caressed the open book, rustling more parchment to a new page.

"Behold."

Mälque stopped his theatrics and tossed a curious glance at the book. "What's that?"

The whisper didn't answer. Mälque crept closer for a better look.

The sea breeze rustled a page, the edge folding and bending with the grace of a bird's wings in flight. Mesmerized by the motion, Mälque marveled at the black etchings, words he could not comprehend, that shivered like wheat in a field. They rose off the page, rows of letters that glimmered in the light of his firestick.

The wind picked up, and the towering words swayed all the more, and as their tempo increased, dissolved into a glossy surface, uniform, that spread out like molten silver onto the page, filling it with luster. Within the pool of liquid, a vision formed, and like clouds parting to let sunbeams past, the vision took shape. A beautiful young woman, attired in white with a dark robe, clung to the feathers of a massive harrier soaring across a blue sky.

Mälque swallowed down the emotions rising up from his gut, not only captivated by her stunning splendor, but at the realization that she was a girl, no, a woman of great power.

"Does she look like someone wielding death or life?"

"Life, but could be a trick or a disguise."

The vision faded and the wind died.

"Be careful, Mälque. She has a purpose, but not as you are hoping."

Mälque sucked in air, spooked that the whisper was on to his plan. And with a move that surprised even himself, he lunged for the book and slammed it shut, wedging the feather and hair between the pages.

He scooped it up and dashed for the exit, tossing a glance over his shoulder to make sure the whisper wasn't taking form and chasing him. Relieved the room was still empty, he sprinted into the narrow passageway, his lightstick shimmering off the wet walls and ground.

Primal instinct warned him he was being pursued. A look back told him otherwise but goose bumps rallied him to faster speeds.

He cleared the passage, thankful to be free of the haunted cave, and was about to dismiss the whole thing as some sort of bewitching, when the book pulsed and light shot out of it like spears.

He stared at the pages, wondering if they would flame and burn him alive. Instead, the light waned and the whisper called...

"Mälque, my delight!"

Chapter 15

Sojourn to the Sea

Linwith put his helmet back on and retrieved his saddle. He trudged out of the armory and made his way to the Worm King. As much as Linwith disliked Quinn's request to fly Phinnton to the beach, he was at a loss to find a valid excuse not to go. Besides, he was under his command and would respect the order. He hoped the boy's father, Bruun, would squash the notion, citing the dangers of flying as well that of playing in the Gilden Sea.

The sapphire worm caught Linwith's scent and turned to check on him.

"Another mission," the Worm King asked as he lowered himself beside the mounting stairs.

"Not quite," Linwith answered as he climbed the steps. He heaved the saddle onto the worm's back. "Quinn has requested that we carry Phinnton to the beach." He took off his helmet and rested it over the saddle horn and then finished his message. "To play."

The Worm King's eyes flared and he rose to his full height.

Linwith retreated down the stairs to tighten the cinch straps. "I know, it's an embarrassing request." He grabbed the leather harnesses and fastened them together. "After all, the Worms of Bal-Malin were created for much greater missions than being nursemaids for a child." He yanked the buckle tight and stepped back to take in the sapphire worm's face.

The mystic flame within the worm's eyes danced about. "We would be honored."

"Honored? But…"

"Do you perceive us only to be creatures that hunger for war? That we do not delight in the frolicking of the innocent ones?"

"No, I simply meant that you are creatures above such trivialities."

"With all due respect, Worm Master, it is *you* who believes he is above such humility."

Linwith's shoulders slumped. "Wonderful, chastened by my own worms."

The Worm King took in the children who were now busy playing a game of tag. "They are the reason my brothers and I have waited patiently for so many summers for your arrival, for our strength and greatness is not to wage war for the sake of spilling blood, or to make one man's name great. Our passion is to be the spearhead, the battle ax, for the tales of Claire when war will be forgotten and death extinguished; when children can dream sweet dreams without fearing the lions of the Gilden Plain; when the true whisper sings like a lark from the glen; when the dread of the drone and the threat of the Cauldron are forgotten nightmares. These desires, my great Worm Master, are why we exist. These are at the heart of why we will fight for you. So today, let us relish Quinn's request for a respite by the sea. The best way to celebrate the tales of Claire is by watching Phinnton, our page, dance upon the sands."

"You're right." Linwith took in the children congratulating Phinnton. "I've become too proud. I've forgotten what I was fighting for."

Linwith put two fingers in his mouth and whistled. Phinnton, as well as a few of the children, spun to see who had whistled.

Linwith waved the page over and Phinnton ran to his side.

"Phinnton, it's time for your first lesson as my page."

Phinnton's eyes widened and countless thoughts filled his mind. Linwith quelled the boy's desire to spew his questions with a wag of his head.

Linwith pointed to the sapphire worm's saddle. "Climb on up."

"Me," he asked, his liquid eyes wide with anticipation.

"Yes, you."

Phinnton let his gaze hop from Linwith to the worm and then back to Linwith. Phinnton's brow furrowed with wonder and worry.

Linwith rolled his eyes "Must you always be plagued with questions?"

Phinnton smiled and let his concerns fly away.

Linwith continued.

"You've shown me you can climb a wall, but can you climb into the worm's saddle?"

Phinnton, eager to prove his worth, ran up the mounting steps and jumped for the leather grip but it was too high. The Worm King, who was watching his every move, lowered himself to the ground. Phinnton sprung like a cat and with one outstretched hand, caught hold of the strap. He grunted and strained to slip his left foot into the stirrup. Stretching up from the stirrup, he grabbed the saddle and pulled himself into position. His feet dangled over the sides, many summers away from reaching the stirrups, and he eyed the helmet resting on the saddle horn.

"Put it on," Linwith commanded as the worm rose to his full height.

Phinnton picked it up and lowered it over his head. It was much too large and rested upon his shoulders. Fortunately, the alabaster lenses were long enough that he could still peer out. But as he turned his head, the helmet stayed in place like an overgrown tortoise shell. Linwith chuckled at the sight.

"Everything looks golden," Phinnton shouted, his voice tinny as it reverberated in the metallic helmet.

"Do you see the saddle horn?"

"Yes."

"And the colored gems?"

Phinnton studied the jewels. Even with the alabaster lenses colorizing everything, the jewels glistened and sparkled with brilliance.

"Sapphire, crimson, pearl, mandarin, emerald, gold and amber," he noted.

"Each gem represents a worm. The color corresponds with their tail tips. Do you understand?"

"Yes," he shouted as he eyed the worms crouched on the ground.

"Notice that each worm has a tower in Min Brock that corresponds with where his jewel is positioned on the saddle horn. So the emerald, gold and amber descend down the horn's right side, while ruby, mandarin and pearl track around the left."

"And the sapphire gem is in the middle, just like Min Brock's central tower."

"Correct. Now hover your thumb over the ruby."

"What will happen," he asked, a tinge of fear on his words as his thumb lingered above the crimson jewel.

"Don't worry. You'll simply be able to talk and listen to that particular worm."

He pressed his thumb down onto the ruby. An invisible presence-full of intelligence and wisdom engulfed him, as did a great heat, like that of a noonday sun.

"*Now what do I do,*" he thought to himself.

A new voice entered his mind. "*Young Phinnton, page to Linwith, you may converse with me as you please.*"

Phinnton took in the worm with the crimson tail.

"*Yes, I am talking to you, within your mind.*"

"*Your heat. Is it for good or evil?*"

"*For good, but a worm may never use its gifts for selfish gain, and can only use them when called upon by the Worm Master… or his page.*"

Phinnton's mind wandered with the possibilities. Suddenly, as if coming across something he had lost, blurted out his discovery:

"Fire!"

What happened next was chaotic and swift. Phinnton just happened to glance at the north tower; the worm followed his gaze and emitted a deep bark. A ball of fire sailed out of his mouth toward a sentry in the tower. He ducked and the fireball zipped out over the Gilden Plains where it exploded with a flash. The onlookers screamed, horrified that Phinnton was able to utilize the worm's powers just like the Worm Master. People scattered like mice for the safety of their homes. The only person remaining was an old man in the shadows, leaning on his cane and rubbing his chin.

Linwith charged up the mounting steps. "What'd you do?"

"I simply said…"

"No! Don't utter another word, and get your thumb away from those jewels!"

"But I only…"

"*Now.*"

Phinnton's shoulders sagged as his arm fell to his side. With a heavy sigh, he removed the helmet as obscenities from the man in the tower fell like burning pitch.

Quinn, who was on the walkway and witnessed the ordeal, glowered at them with hands on his hips. "What was *that* all about?"

"Sorry," Linwith hailed with a sloppy smile and wave, "Just a lesson that got a bit out of control."

Quinn shook his head and resumed his patrol.

Linwith's smile gave way to his anger at Phinnton. With long, deep breaths he regained control of his emotions, and in as soothing a voice as he could muster, met Phinnton's dejected face. "So, tell me *exactly* what happened."

Phinnton pulled away from Linwith's look. "As soon as I touched the ruby, I felt the crimson worm's presence and at the same time a great heat." He dared a glance at Linwith and continued. "Just like…fire. I didn't realize it was a command to shoot out fire. I was simply saying that he, the worm that is, must be associated with fire and that…"

Linwith silenced him with a raised hand and cleared his throat.

"This time, I'll take the blame for not explaining the worm's capabilities to you; I forgot how curious you are. As you have discovered, not only can you converse with each worm by the jewel on the horn, but each worm has a gift, a power, that I can wield."

"So you knew the worm could belch fireballs?"

"Yes, but I didn't know *you* could order him, too."

Phinnton's inquisitiveness mounted new heights of discovery. "And what of the others?"

"Well," Linwith took in his worms. "Pearl has the gift of invisibility; emerald emits poisonous gas clouds; sapphire - capable of freezing time and motion."

Phinnton counted the worms and flashed Linwith a puzzled look. "You left out the mandarin, gold and amber worm."

"Oh yes, amber. I suppose I forget him because, well to be honest, I don't see how he can be helpful."

"Tell me."

"He shrinks."

"Shrinks?"

"Yes. I experimented once and had him shrink to the size of a cat. He may even be able to get smaller. I really don't know."

Phinnton flicked an eager look at the amber worm. "If you don't need him, may I make him my pet?"

Linwith rolled his eyes. "Phinnton, these are the Worms of Bal-Malin. Even though his gift doesn't *seem* useful, that does *not* mean he's to become a plaything."

Phinnton nodded and tossed a glance at the mandarin and gold worm. "And what about them?"

"Stirring up mischief again, Phinnton?"

The question came from the old man hiding in the shadows. He hobbled into the light and Linwith recognized him as Bruun, Phinnton's father.

Bruun, whose gaze was focused on Phinnton, was tall, and a loose, gray tunic hid his thin torso. Strands of silver hair framed his gaunt face like lace. He stopped at a safe distance from the worms and rested his full weight upon his balmwood cane.

"I didn't mean to," Phinnton answered. "But I'm his page, and you see, I touched the ruby jewel and then..."

Bruun wagged his head to cut Phinnton off.

"This is my fault," Linwith said as he hopped off the steps and made his way to Bruun, relieved he was spared answering Phinnton's question. He wanted to keep the information about the other worms a secret for as long as possible. "I didn't realize he was capable of launching an attack from the worms."

Bruun's features relaxed and a faint smile made his wrinkled face all the more defined. "Page." His smile became more pronounced. "Just as his mother predicted."

Linwith checked on Phinnton. He was fidgeting and tapping the helmet, no doubt adrift in a fantasy centered on the Worms of Bal-Malin. "So you aren't surprised by this news."

"No."

Linwith turned his attention to Bruun. His smile was gone and there was an urgency radiating outward from his piercing gaze. "He's more than a page," Bruun half whispered. "He'll be a great resource."

"I know. He's a storyteller."

Bruun shuffled closer and rested a hand on Linwith's shoulder. "I'm old. My days are numbered. When war comes to Min Brock, Phinnton will need you."

Bruun squeezed Linwith's shoulder to emphasize his message.

The gravity of the moment fell upon Linwith and he swallowed to regain his composure. "You underestimate yourself, sir. I'm certain you'll play an important role in the battles to come."

Bruun released his hold and his eyes hardened. "Yes, the battle that lies before me will be unique indeed." He paused to contemplate his future and fate. Whatever he saw, whether an actual vision or something dredged up from his own imagination, made him suck in a deep breath. "Come what may, I won't fail you, or Phinnton, that I promise."

Linwith nodded and was at a loss for words. Remembering Quinn's request, he cleared his throat to ask Bruun the question.

"Quinn has instructed me to fly Phinnton to the Sea of Gilden."

Bruun's brow furrowed. "Whatever for?"

Linwith smiled. "To play by the sea."

Bruun shifted his weight and rubbed his chin. "I see..."

"I'll understand if you feel the flight is too dangerous or that playing in the Gilden sea too risky."

Bruun took in Linwith's expression. "Do you promise to guard him with your life?"

The question struck Linwith hard. In the back of his mind, he had reasoned that as the page's mentor, he would be called upon to protect him in times of battle or peril. Now that the question was out in the open, and presented by the boy's father, it made him question his own mettle. Linwith thought it over and gave Bruun a confirming nod.

"Then you have my blessings."

Linwith, stunned by the answer, coughed. "You realize that he'll be flying without a safety belt...just holding on to me?"

"You are the Worm Master, aren't you?"

"Yes."

"Then I'm confident that no harm will come to him. The King of Claire has great things in store for Phinnton. I doubt part of that plan was for him to fall off your worm."

"But you don't know that."

Bruun turned his attention to Phinnton and waved. "Oh, but I do."

Phinnton paused playing make-believe long enough to wave back.

Linwith, irritated by Bruun's confident retort, wanted to argue but knew the matter was settled. He was flying Phinnton to the beach. Linwith spun on his heels and stormed back to the page.

"Are you strong enough to hold on to me during our flight?" His tone was biting.

Phinnton looked to his father for approval. Bruun smiled and gestured for him to go.

Linwith huffed and continued. "Slide back so I can get on."

Phinnton scooted off the back of the saddle and Linwith climbed up the side of the Worm. He swung up into the saddle and looked over his shoulder at Phinnton. "Now get as close to me as you can. You'll have to hold onto my leather jacket with *all* your might." Linwith put his helmet on. "Just don't fall off. Ready?"

Phinnton hugged Linwith with all his might. "Ready!"

Linwith smothered the jeweled saddle horn with his palm and in the silent tongue, ordered the worms to flight. Large wings opened and flapped, creating dust clouds that swirled around Bruun. He coughed and shielded his face from the storm.

The Worms of Bal-Malin rose into the air at a slow speed so the page wouldn't loose his balance and fall. Phinnton took one last look at his father. Bruun waved and beamed a proud smile. Phinnton braved a wave back, and as the worms soared over the wall, grabbed hold of Linwith.

Phinnton pressed the side of his face against Linwith's back and watched Min Brock fall away. The height was dizzying and he gasped, afraid he would fall to his death.

A bedtime melody popped into his head, sung by his mother, and his fears diminished. The song comforted him and he hummed along to the melody. One refrain repeated over and over, the tempo matching the cadence of the worm's wings.

> *"For the Singing Stones of Addoli*
> *hum songs from distant throne…"*

Chapter 16

Stones of Addoli

When the sapphire worm reached its cruising altitude, Phinnton checked on the other worms following single-file.

They're in a perfect formation. Even their wings beat in unison, as if dancing to the same music I'm humming.

Phinnton steeled himself for a look around Linwith's side, knowing he would experience the wind's full force. With a gulp of air for courage, he stuck his head into the wind. His eyes burned and watered, but he fought through the irritation and wiped his face on Linwith's jacket to free the tears without letting go of his grip. With sight adjusted to the wind shear, he marveled at the view.

From way up here, the Addoli Ridge is even more amazing. The bushes look like dots and the trees like twigs. He ducked back behind Linwith to avoid the wind and stared over the side.

And look at the Gilden Plains. It's so big.

Linwith, who felt him shift about, tapped Phinnton's thigh to get his attention and pointed to his head. Phinnton, who took the motion to mean Linwith wanted to speak to him in the silent tongue, zeroed in on Linwith's thoughts.

"Up ahead is the Gilden Sea," Linwith informed him.

Phinnton braved another look into the biting winds. Beyond the Addoli Ridge was a vast expanse of deep blue that glistened and twinkled like countless coins and jewels.

Despite his eyes burning and watering from the wind, he stared in wonder. It was the first time he had seen the sea, and its beauty and size overwhelmed his comprehension.

When they soared over the ridge, the sea became a tapestry of blues and greens.

"Hold on," Linwith warned. *"Time for some fun."*

Linwith leaned forward and pulled Phinnton down with him. The sapphire worm pulled his wings to his side and dove head first for the sea.

Phinnton gasped, fingers digging into Linwith's leather jacket as his stomach did somersaults. The wind roared past and he caught the scent of salt. Curious, he peered around Linwith, but the wind was stronger than he anticipated. It smacked his face and he started to slip off the saddle. His heart raced. He strained and grunted to not slip off but the wind was stronger than his best efforts.

Linwith, realizing the problem, reached a hand around and grabbed his belt and tunic. With a firm yank, he pulled him close and Phinnton held on like a drowning man to driftwood.

Phinnton pressed his cheek against Linwith's jacket and stared at the sea. White-capped waves rushed upward.

We're going to dive into the sea!

Phinnton sucked in a big breath and held it.

Linwith leaned back, which pushed Phinnton upright, as the worm pulled out of the dive and zoomed over the sea.

Phinnton, relieved they weren't underwater, released his held breath and took in the sea's majesty. Their flight had slowed considerably and they were low enough that the worm's talons smashed through rogue waves, spraying them with cold surf. Salt was strong on the wind and the waves curled and crashed, the sound reminding Phinnton of rain or the wind.

"I never grow tired of this," Linwith shouted back to Phinnton.

"Let's do it again," Phinnton exclaimed as he wiped the salty water from his face.

Linwith chuckled. "This coming from someone who almost fell off."

He tugged on the reins and the worm banked on his left wingtip. Phinnton stared down at the swirl of blues whose depths could consume him. Spooked, he tightened his grip and was relieved when the worm righted himself. Gulls flew along side, cawing as if to announce their arrival to the creatures of the sea.

Phinnton snuck a peek around Linwith.

Up ahead was a white beach that sat at the base of the Addoli Ridge. Cliffs and caves marked the ridge's face and birds of various size and color flitted about what he presumed were nests.

The worm banked, although this time in a more leisurely arc, and flew along the shoreline. The worm tilted his wings downward like sails to catch the wind, and their flight slowed all the more. With a soft *bump*, they landed on the beach.

Linwith unstrapped his helmet.

"Welcome to the Gilden Sea," he offered Phinnton with a smile. Linwith slid off and helped Phinnton to the ground. He darted for the surf.

Linwith removed his helmet and eyed the remaining worms circling overhead. He turned his attention to the sapphire worm. "We're safe. Go join your brothers and hunt the sea. Stay close; I'll signal when it's time to leave."

The worm nodded and flew off.

Linwith eyed Phinnton. He was darting back and forth between the watery swells to avoid getting wet. Linwith set his helmet down and made his way to the page.

"You're not like the other children of Min Brock, are you," Linwith asked.

"It's not that I don't like them," he said as he jumped out of the way of a surging wave. "I just don't want to play games all the time."

"I know. Such were my thoughts as a boy: deeper than hunting the woods or eating fresh stews, longing for more than what my friends hungered for."

Phinnton turned his attention to Linwith and a wave doused his feet.

"So, I'm not - different - in a bad way?"

Linwith met his gaze. "No, not in a bad way. Looking back, what I thought was odd or different about me are now jewels in my crown. But such gems are only suitable for me; I cannot foretell what qualities will be your treasures. Such is your journey as a page."

"But you have the gold and mandarin worms. They could tell you."

Linwith gave him a serious look. "How do you know that?"

"You told me."

Linwith crossed his arms. "No I didn't. You asked me but I never told you. Remember?"

"Oh, yeah" Phinnton half-mumbled as he kicked some sand.

"Were you searching my thoughts?"

Phinnton shuffled his weight from one foot to the other.

Linwith spun him around and glared at him. "*Never* read my thoughts or my story without my permission. Got it?"

Phinnton saw the seriousness in Linwith's eyes and swallowed down his guilt. He bit his lower lip and nodded.

Linwith released his hold and his face softened. "You can't tell anyone about this, not even your father. If you do…" he made sure he had Phinnton's attention. "You'll no longer be a page."

Phinnton gave a solemn nod and turned his attention down the beach.

"Then tell me what that is."

Linwith followed his line of sight to a rock tower that stood on the beach like a castle turret. Shorter than the cliffs, it was tucked beneath a high overhang whose waterfall splashed its flat top. Excess, trickled and drooled over the sides, making it shimmer in the sunlight. Despite the distance, they both could see that it was smooth as if honed by a blade or polished by a sculptor's touch.

"Oh, *that,*" Linwith teased. "That's just the Pillar of Addoli."

Phinnton shot a bamboozled look at Linwith. "*Just* the Pillar of Addoli? Haven't you heard the stories about it?"

Linwith feigned ignorance. "Um, no."

"Well, it's an amazing story." He shielded his eyes to get a better look at the pillar. "Has anyone climbed it?"

"Climb those slick, smooth walls? No, only the gulls can reach its summit."

"Or one possessing a worm."

"Really? I never thought of that."

Phinnton spun around to take in Linwith's expression. He was chuckling.

"Yes you have," he fired with hands on his hips, "and I can tell by your smile that you've been to the top!"

"So I have."

Phinnton's eyes bulged and his mind formed questions that his tongue could not keep up with.

"What's up there? Is it big enough to land on? Can I go? Who else has been? Did…"

Linwith held up a hand. Phinnton slapped a hand over his mouth to silence his tongue.

"I discovered it on one of my first scouting missions. I circled it several times to investigate, and yes, it's large enough for a worm to land upon."

"So, what's up there?"

"A pool of water that is so deep it's black in shade, but the rocky banks are shallow and filled with smooth stones the size of your palm."

Phinnton turned his hand over and imagined one of the stones in his grasp. "Anything else," he asked, looking back at the Pillar of Addoli.

"Visibly, no. But there was something: a sound."

Once more, Phinnton's excitement got the best of him and his questions tumbled out of his mouth. "A sound? What type? Was it loud? Were you frightened? Did you…"

Linwith arched an eyebrow and Phinnton once more slapped his hand over his mouth.

"On that particular day," Linwith continued, "it was difficult to hear amidst the the surf, gulls and drone. So we circled closer."

Linwith paused, not so much to remember as to tease the boy.

Phinnton's eyes bulged. His hand dropped. "Well? *Well?* What did you hear?"

"Music."

"Music?"

Linwith nodded. "Rich, pure tones that sounded like children's voices singing - or humming - eternal notes; they were harmonious, soothing, inviting and yet..." he paused to take in Phinnton's jubilant expression. *"Strong."*

The page's mouth dropped open. "So my mother's song and tale *were* true."

"There is a story and song about this music?"

"Yes! The Singing Stones of Addoli. Haven't you heard it?"

Although the worms had not given Linwith a vision about Phinnton, they had showed him the Pillar of Addoli with the silhouette of a boy standing on top. Clutched in his hands were the singing stones that hummed their tune. *Was the boy Phinnton, or someone else from Min Brock? Were the stones key in defeating Ebon and the Cauldron?* He could only guess. Nevertheless, he continued his ruse and shrugged in response to Phinnton's question.

"Then I'll tell you." Phinnton closed his eyes and in a reverent voice, he spoke.

"Pillar of rock so grand you stand,
with flattened top and shore of blue,
Beneath your water's glistening depths,
are stones with voices true.
No man may hold these precious rocks;
pure tones no man may own,
For the Singing Stones of Addoli
hum songs from distant throne."

"Imagine that," Linwith said as he tapped his chin with a finger. "Singing stones, resting in a pool on an enormous rock tower. If only someone could reach them. Perhaps they'd serve us well in the war to come."

Phinnton rolled his eyes. "Weren't you listening? *No man may hold these precious rocks...*"

"Yes, it appears we have a serious dilemma." Linwith rubbed his chin. "But the story says nothing of a boy - or a page - or one that has the mark of a storyteller. If only I knew of someone possessing such qualities..."

Phinnton's expression brightened. Without another word he raced to the sea, waving at the worms who were skimming the surface for fish.

"Worms, return! I must ascend the Pillar of Addoli and get the Singing Stones."

He continued gesturing and calling but the Worms ignored him. Linwith walked up to his side.

"In time, my good page, in time," Linwith said with a reassuring pat on his shoulder. "Today is not the day."

"Why not?"

"Quinn ordered me to escort you to the beach to play, not to go on a quest."

"But to me, a quest is playing!"

Linwith smiled but didn't answer. He turned and walked away from the beach.

"You can stay here," Phinnton shouted after him, "and I could go alone...on a worm."

Linwith plopped down on a mound of sand and gave the page a firm wag of his head.

Phinnton thought about arguing, but realized it might jeopardize his position as page. He turned his attention to the pillar and cocked his head to the side to study it.

Linwith eyed him and knew by his body language, as well as how wild his imagination was, that he was busy devising a plan.

"Stop scheming and go play!" Linwith shouted to Phinnton.

Phinnton huffed and squatted to inspect the seashells littering the beach. He fingered them until he found one of interest and held it up for a better look. He wiped off the sand and pocketed it. He continued his search and picked up another but it was broken so he threw it into the sea. With every shell he studied, he tossed several glances at the Pillar of Addoli.

Linwith let time pass but when Phinnton became more interested in staring at the tower than playing on the beach, he knew it was time to leave. He stood up and brushed the sand off. He whistled, and although not very loud, the worms heard his call and returned to shore.

Linwith scooped his helmet up off the sand and mounted the Worm King. He leaned over the side and helped Phinnton up to the rear of the saddle.

"My story about the Pillar of Addoli," Phinnton asked as he grabbed hold of Linwith. "It wasn't a surprise to you, was it?"

Linwith tightened his helmet and rested his palm on the gems.

"No, it wasn't," he answered as he ordered the worms in the silent tongue to fly. "The visions from the gold and mandarin worms showed me the tower and I heard the song your mother sang."

"So you knew I'd become your page?"

He snickered as they gained altitude. "No, that tiny detail they didn't show me."

"Why didn't you tell me about the tower before we came?"

"I wanted to see if you would discover it on your own, and if you indeed knew of the story, the music and their mystique."

Phinnton buried his head on Linwith's back and tried not to think about the tower, but the more he tried the more intense his thoughts became.

"Is it my destiny to retrieve the Singing Stones?"

"That, my dear page, is an answer I too would love to know. They are indeed a mystery and as far as I can discern, you're the one best suited for such a mission. For now, let's give you a better look."

Phinnton peered around Linwith at the monolith ahead of them. They circled the summit and Phinnton gasped. The tower and waterfall were larger than he expected. In the middle of the rock was the pool that stared up like a black eye. Blue shallows encircled the foreboding well and were filled with black, white, and tan stones.

The Singing Stones of Addoli.

He leaned out and strained to hear them sing, hoping to catch but a fragment of their song. Nothing. Desperate, he sorted through the sound of the wind, surf, gulls and drone for a mere note. He was about to lose hope when, hidden within the noise, he discovered the music.

It's more beautiful than I imagined!

The worms changed course and headed for Min Brock, climbing higher to clear the cliffs. As the Pillar of Addoli faded from view, so did the song, but the music continued to chime and reverberate like bells in his heart. Their harmonies reminded him of his mother's voice - pure and gentle – singing about Claire, the lyrics a stone path into forever.

Phinnton nestled against Linwith's back and hummed along to the melody. He thought about the Pillar of Addoli, the Singing Stones, and if it was his mission to retrieve them. But most of all, he thought about his mother and realized just how much he missed her.

Chapter 17

Stories & Myths

Lassiter and Draemel stood outside *The Slaughtered Sow* and watched their men celebrating; mugs were lifted and cheers were raised.

"Today was a good day," Lassiter offered Draemel with a smile.

The bounty hunter remained stoic. "Yes, but we mustn't lose our edge with too much drink and merriment."

Four inebriated soldiers stumbled out of the tavern.

"You need to relax and go join the fun."

Lassiter gave him a playful shove toward the door. Draemel stiffened and arched an eyebrow. Lassiter waved him off and turned his attention to the four soldiers. They had come to attention, as best they could under their condition. They stood with interlocked arms, but whether as a sign of unity or a means of maintaining their balance, Lassiter was at a loss to determine. They started singing and other soldiers who were already outside turned to listen. When they recognized the marching song, "Homelands, Hearths and Heroes," they joined the foursome.

"What's your plan," Draemel shouted over the song being belted with gusto.

"I think the safest route," Lassiter said as he clapped along, "is to head east into Ingloid."

"No; not a good idea. As an Ingloid, I can attest to the fact that aside from the coast, there are no resources or towns worth visiting."

"Well, I'm open to suggestions."

"We follow the River Arrgient north to Dallin on the southern border of the Gilden Plains."

"Dallin?" The swaying choir lost their balance and nearly toppled over. Lassiter chuckled. "The men of Gilnish tell me it's nothing but a few shacks with thatched roofs. A handful of trappers, hunters and mercenaries live there. Talk about not worth seeing."

"True, but it does act as a gateway to the Gilden Plains or..." He stalled his answer until Lassiter, who was more interested in humming the music than talking war strategy, looked his way. Lassiter finally met his gaze and Draemel delivered his destination of choice.

"Claire."

Lassiter stopped clapping.

"Claire?"

Draemel pulled away from Lassiter's wide-eyed look and took in the chorale. From out of the corner of his eye, Draemel caught Lassiter's stunned expression. Draemel smiled, satisfied Lassiter was focused back on tactics and not marching songs. He tapped his boot in time with the music and offered Lassiter an explanation to the destination. "We're doomed unless we get a larger force. Claire offers that and much more."

"Agreed, but you don't believe the Only exists, let alone Claire."

"While you of faith are afraid to journey there."

"Because we'd travel past Ebon!"

Draemel spun away from the merriment and drilled his steely gaze into Lassiter. "Which is why I suggested Dallin! It's a gateway to the Gilden Plains or any other point of destination you could choose. As a shantytown, it won't draw much attention from Ebon, which will give us time to put a plan together."

Lassiter didn't flinch or even blink. Draemel continued. "Your next move will determine our fate; and the outcome of the coming war."

Lassiter swallowed hard and turned his attention to the chorale of men. They gestured for him to join them, but Lassiter was so deep in thought that he was oblivious to their waves and shouts. They went back to their song and Lassiter continued to mull over Draemel's counsel. It took several choruses before Lassister faced Draemel.

"Very well. Pass the order along to the commanders."

"And what about tonight's celebration?"

Lassiter let his gaze drift back to the men celebrating at *The Slaughtered Sow*. He set his jaw. "Tell them it's over. We leave at dawn."

Daylight came too early for most of the men who moaned from the lack of sleep and pounding headaches. Campfires were snuffed and horses were loaded with provisions and gear. The men from Gilnish kissed loved ones goodbye and fell into formation behind Lassiter's men. The army marched in silence and by midday the dense pines, thick underbrush and flat topography gave way to rolling hills and thinning vegetation. They were leaving Ferra's coastal region and nearing the Gilden Plains. When they were still a good distance away from Dallin, Draemel ordered them to halt.

"What is it," Lassiter asked.

"Tracks."

Draemel pointed to a stretch of sandy ground far ahead. Tall weeds and shadows from nearby pines concealed the area.

"You can see that from here?"

"Yep," he grunted as he tossed Lassiter his reins to dismount. "Comes from hunting men for a living."

He made his way to the spot and knelt. Fingering the turned earth and running a palm over matted grass, he spotted similar tracks all around. "Gors," he shouted back to Lassiter. "A large number of them, too." He rose and headed back.

"Paradin - the Gor King - and his army," Lassiter concluded as Draemel swung back into his saddle.

Draemel nodded and turned to a lieutenant. "Alert the men. We may be riding into trouble."

The officer saluted and turned his steed to go fulfill his order.

Lassiter pulled out the map he acquired from one of the new mercenaries and checked their location.

"We're getting close. Dallin should be over the next ridge."

Draemel fingered his scar. "Slow and steady," he advised. "Stay alert."

Lassiter nodded and signaled for the column to advance.

Now that they were close to the Gilden Plain, trees were sparse and they were exposed to ambush. Nerves were on edge.

When they neared the ridgetop, Lassiter ordered them to halt. He dismounted and gestured for Draemel and several officers to follow him to the top. At the apex, they were greeted with the wide expanse of grasslands.

"Where's Dallin," Lassiter asked. "Did I misread the map?"

"No, you read it correctly. Dallin's been destroyed." Draemel pointed out circles of charred grass off in the distance. "The Gor King's attack was some time ago. See the fresh grass growing up from the burnt circles? Note that the scent of death isn't on the wind and there aren't any bodies strewn about? We can thank the scavengers for cleaning up the carnage."

"We need to track him down and destroy him."

"Are you forgetting the powers the Gor King wields?"

"No." Memories of how Newcomb died washed over him and he squirmed in his saddle. He shook off the emotions and regained his composure. "But to do nothing is cowardice."

"You aren't a coward; but charging forward now would be foolish. You are being wise, just as I've instructed you, building your force until the time is ripe for *you* to decide when and where to fight. Right now, Paradin commands those parameters."

Lassiter nodded and let his eyes drift across the grasslands. "Now what do we do?"

Draemel pondered the question and answered with one of his own.

"Have you been listening in on the men's stories?"

Lassiter snorted and took in Draemel's look. "You mean the ones they tell around the campfires, like the one about there being *another* Gor

King?"

"Yes, as well as the stories about dragons coursing the sky."

Lassiter snickered. "Those are tavern tales, spun from dull minds numbed with strong drink."

Draemel didn't flinch.

Lassiter's snide smile faded. "Please tell me you're not putting stock in those myths?"

"At the heart of every story, even those that sound too incredible to believe, is a kernel of truth."

Lassiter put his hand on a hip and stared at Draemel as if he had just sprouted a second head. "Okay, so let me get this straight. You think there's a rogue warrior out there," he gestured at the plains, "who wears a gor skull and commands an army of criminals and madmen?"

Draemel arched an eyebrow.

"Or that dragons, that were killed off during the Dark War, have *mysteriously* reappeared," he swept the sky in an exaggerated arc, "and who now - thank *goodness* - fight for Allsbruth and not Ebon?"

Draemel remained serious. "After what I saw Paradin do as the Gor King, I'd say anything is possible."

"And what about the myth concerning Min Brock?"

Draemel's face darkened. "Of all the tales, I hope it's true."

"Why?"

Draemel swung his gaze around to Lassiter. "Remember the stories I told you about your father, Hornlynn, and the battle at Min Brock?"

Lassiter met his stare. There wasn't a day he didn't ponder his father's command at Min Brock; the siege by the Ebonites; the demise of the storytellers; the traitors, Quinn and Gundin; the suicide charge led by his father.

"Yes," Lassiter finally braved. "I remember."

The wind picked up, whipping Draemel's red locks like battle flags. He squinted and drilled his eyes into Lassiter. "Then you have the answer to your question. If Min Brock has been rebuilt, there's the possibility that the traitors are there."

Lassiter sized up Draemel. His jaw line was rigid and he was fingering his gor weapon, something he did whenever he was about to launch an attack or the subject of the traitors came up.

"But to rebuild a castle of that size," Lassiter countered, "would take an incredible amount of materials and manpower, not to mention that Ebon would snuff out any such attempts."

"Unless dragons assisted in the construction and protected them from attack."

Lassiter, stunned to hear Draemel offer such a ridiculous proposition, checked on the officers. Had they heard? Judging by their bored expressions and the wind making conversation difficult to hear, he assumed not. He gave Draemel a hot look. "Have you lost your mind?"

"In mad times such as these, sometimes the sane thing to do is be mad yourself."

"Even if Min Brock *has* been refortified, the traitors may not even be there or..." He held his thought and drank from Draemel's cold, gray eyes. "They're already dead."

"Then they're lucky." He wrapped fingers about his gor weapon. "But I know they're alive. I can feel it. It's for this reason that I'm alive."

Lassiter leaned back and crossed his arms over his chest.

"So you want us to cross the plains," he said as he freed the hair blown across his face, "risk being attacked, and head to Min Brock so you can settle an old score."

"This *old score* involves you too, or did you forget that part of the story?"

"No, I haven't forgotten. But what if Min Brock is only a mound of rubble?"

Draemel met his gaze. "It won't be."

"You don't know that."

"*Yes I do!*"

Draemel's outburst startled Lassiter who flinched, afraid the gor blade would swipe his face.

Draemel continued. "I can feel it, here." He smacked his chest with a fist. "I *know* it's there and that those traitors are inside. It's time they pay for their crimes."

"If you think I'm going to risk all of our lives so you can get your revenge, which is based upon myths, you're mistaken."

Draemel ground his teeth. "And what about your duty to honor your father?"

Lassiter snapped. He grabbed a handful of Draemel's shirt and looked him square in the face. "Don't *ever* lecture me on my role as his son! I'll honor his sacrifice. I'm just not going to dedicate my life to revenge - like *you*."

"Of course not. You'd rather a cold-blooded killer like me do the dirty work."

Lassiter pushed Draemel away. He mulled over the accusation and shuddered, but not because it was a windy day. He let his gaze, as well as his imagination, drift in the direction of Min Brock. "We'll ride north along the River Arrgient as far as Ebon and check to see if other villages have been destroyed. Perhaps we'll gain new insights into these myths yours."

"Stories," Draemel corrected without taking his eyes off the charred grass.

Lassiter chose not to argue. "If they prove to be tavern yarns, we'll discuss whether to risk riding to Claire. But if they prove to be authentic…"

He glanced out of the corner of his eye to catch Draemel's reaction.

"We'll march for Min Brock."

Draemel fingered his scar and sneered.

Chapter 18

Mad Times

Lassiter's head nodded in time to his horse's plodding and his eyelids drooped from fatigue. Not only had it been a long day in the saddle, but riding out in the open with the sun beating down on him had zapped him of his strength.

He checked on his men. They looked as tired as he was. Except for Draemel. He sat high in his saddle; reins held at the ready should he need to dash off to scout or attack.

"How do you do it," Lassiter asked.

Draemel kept his eyes glued on the horizon. "Do what?"

"Ride all day in this heat and still look…strong."

"Simple. I once fought out here."

"I know, but that was some time ago. Now, well, you're…old."

Draemel stole a peek at him. "Yes, but this *old* warrior has more stamina than his majesty does."

Lassiter smiled, thankful their prior argument was history. He turned his attention to their surroundings. To their left and a good clip away was the River Arrgient. In the waning light, the current shimmered as the dark water curled across the plains.

"Are you sure the Ebonites can't cross the river and attack?"

"Certain. The water's too deep and the current too strong."

Lassiter nodded with understanding, thankful that since leaving Dallin two days ago, their march had been uneventful. But he knew that the closer they got to Ebon's western border, the more likely it was for them to be attacked.

Off to his right, the Gilden Plains was a rolling sea of grass, small trees dotting the expanse here and there. The sunset painted the yellowed grass with lush tones of clay, amber and orange.

"I never would have guessed," Lassiter said as he followed the flight of a bird of prey from a distant tree, "that the Gilden Plains would look so beautiful. Unbearably hot, but beautiful."

Draemel flashed him a disconcerting look. "Where you see beauty, I see blood stains, and Ebonites so thick the plains were black."

Lassiter shrugged off the reference to the Dark War and faced the Allsbruthian Mountains far west of the river. Shielding his eyes, he marveled at the peaks, now violet and indigo in the dusk, which stood like towers against the sky.

"Is it true what they say," he asked.

Draemel huffed, and without taking his eyes off the landscape, fired a reprimand. "Why are you asking so many questions? Just ride and be quiet."

"They say," Lassiter continued, blowing off Draemel's rebuke, "that if you can reach the forever snow - which no one has done since it's so high - and eat some, that you'll live forever."

Draemel shook his head and snorted.

Lassiter snapped his gaze to his mentor. "What's so funny?"

"*You*," he blurted with another grunt. "The other day you accused me of believing in myths. Now here you are asking me if eating snow will give life immortal."

Lassiter blushed, partially from anger but primarily with humiliation. "Fine," he huffed, "then why is it called *forever snow*?"

"Because no matter the season or how hot a summer gets, it's always present. *Forever* snow. Get it?"

"Well, speaking of forever, are we going to march all night, too?"

Draemel arched an eyebrow. "Tired?"

Lassiter was too exhausted to keep up a strong front. "Yes. So are the men."

Draemel glanced over his shoulder to check on them. "Good. We don't need them up all night drinking and singing around fires. Out here on the plains, even the smallest blaze can spell disaster. A spy could see the glow from a great distance or hear camp songs carried on the wind. And if a soldier is careless or the wind catches some sparks, the grasslands can burst into a raging inferno. Besides, the men need their sleep. We'll be up before dawn to start out again."

Draemel looked forward and pointed out a rise ahead of them. "If memory serves me, on the other side is a tributary that juts off the River Arrgient. Should be plenty of wooded areas and thickets to provide shelter. We'll camp there."

Reaching the summit, Lassiter breathed a sigh of relief. Draemel's memory was sharp and accurate. They started their descent and reached the tree grove at nightfall. Men dismounted, horses were tethered, and camp was set up. Nightfall brought much cooler temperatures, so a few fires were allowed, and these Draemel insisted be kept small.

Lassiter unrolled his blanket in front of their tiny fire. Draemel sat cross-legged on the other side whittling a dead branch with his gor weapon. River rock circled the fire and Draemel had purposefully laid the burning wood apart so as not to flame.

Lassiter curled up on his blanket, the warmth of the embers radiating into his sore muscles.

He closed his eyes and the soft *whick, whick, whick* of Draemel whittling ushered him into his dreamworld.

A commotion awoke Lassiter. He sprang to his feet, still groggy from sleep, and found Draemel nearby brandishing his gor weapon.

"Ebonites," Lassiter asked as he unsheathed his dagger.

"No. The men would have sounded the alarm. This sounds more like a squabble."

Even in the dim light of the campfires, they could see the men restraining someone and leading him their way.

"We caught him trying to steal a horse," the commander reported as he shoved the accused to the ground.

Lassiter bent down to see who it was. "DeMorley," he gasped, flabbergasted to learn he was the thief. "Why were you stealing a horse?"

The minstrel rose and brushed himself off. "It's not like that."

Draemel pressed his giant frame close to the minstrel, his gor weapon even closer. "Then entertain us with your story," he said between clinched teeth.

"I'm a minstrel, not a warrior," he sniffled as he took a step back from Draemel. "I'm bored with the constant marching and camping and nasty food. I was simply borrowing a horse to ride to the nearest hamlet to indulge in some merriment, perhaps sing a song or two, maybe even find a maiden and..."

Draemel lunged, and in one swift motion, had his gor blade to the minstrel's throat. "You know the orders: No one is permitted to leave camp."

"Your majesty," DeMorley whined to Lassiter, "if you'll order this madman to lower his weapon, perhaps I can better explain."

Lassiter put a hand on Draemel's weapon and lowered the gor bone.

"As I was saying," DeMorley said while massaging his throat, "I wasn't running away and was going to return by morning. Now does that sound like an act of treason?"

Lassiter sized up DeMorley, measuring his smile against the cunning that glistened in his eyes. How he wished Newcomb were still alive, for he had amazing discernment in matters such as these. Surely he would spy something out of the ordinary that would reveal DeMorley's true intent.

Lassiter let his gaze run up and down DeMorley, and when he spotted bulging pockets in his long jacket, his heart jumped.

"Empty your pockets," Lassiter commanded.

"What," DeMorley asked as he fidgeted in place.

Lassiter met DeMorley's smile. "You heard me: Empty your pockets."

DeMorley's smile fell. His eyes hardened. Without looking away, he removed the contents of his pockets and dropped them to the ground.

Draemel retrieved them while Lassiter and DeMorley continued to lock eyes.

"What did you find," Lassiter asked, hoping it was nothing but evidence he was a lovesick fool and not a traitor.

"Food; wrapped in cloth."

"Explain yourself." Lassiter's voice was on the edge of anger.

"You know how I am," DeMorley quipped. "My appetite soars when the ale flows. I'm simply going prepared, that's all."

"Was that all you found," Lassiter asked Draemel.

Draemel unfolded a parchment buried beneath the dried meats and fruits. He held it up to study in the firelight. Draemel's eyes became slits. He shook the parchment in DeMorley's face. "*This* is a crude map revealing our location, the number of men, horses…"

Lassiter, stunned by the news and betrayal, backed away from DeMorley. "How could you," he lamented while shaking his head, the treachery cutting him like a blade. "We've been through so much together."

Draemel grabbed the minstrel and jammed his gor blade tight against his throat. "Allow me to spill first blood!"

DeMorley swallowed hard, the sharp edge cutting his skin. He thought about begging or pleading or lying in order to survive. But the evidence revealed his true nature: he was a liar and a traitor.

And yet, despite his love of self and his lust for a fast coin, for the first time in his life, he felt shame.

Lassiter turned his back on them all and shook his head over and over. The fire crackled and popped as he pondered what to do with the man that used to be his friend. Lassiter stopped wagging his head and turned on his heel. He marched up to DeMorley who expected to see his eyes pulse with rage. Instead, he was greeted by raw pain and mistrust. Dishonor enveloped DeMorley and he looked away.

"Give him a horse," Lassiter ordered.

A gasp erupted from the men.

DeMorley's face clouded with confusion.

"A *horse?*" Draemel barked, his chest billowing from rage.

"Yes, a horse. And give him back his food, but search him for any other parchments or stolen goods, then send him away from here."

Draemel ground his teeth and palmed his blade. "Your *majesty*," there was ridicule in his voice. "Treason is deserving of death."

Lassiter squatted and with his back to them, poked the fire. "I can't order a decree on a man who once was my friend."

"This is madness," Draemel fired.

"*In mad times such as these,*" Lassiter quoted as he jabbed the coals, "*sometimes the sane thing to do is be mad yourself.*"

Draemel glowered at Lassiter and then grabbed DeMorley. He pulled him close and pressed his nose into his face. "Once again, luck guards your destiny, minstrel." With that, he threw him to the ground along with the satchel of food. "Prepare the traitor a horse."

DeMorley snatched up the bag of food and pushed himself up from the ground. He took in the men shaking their heads at him and cursing beneath their breath. The commander that had caught him stealing the horse stepped close and spat in his face before turning to fulfill his order.

DeMorley wiped off the spittle and studied Lassiter who continued prodding the embers with the stick. Despite his seasons of cunning and manipulation, he felt something stirring in his gut, something he remembered from his childhood when, for a brief summer, he had been loved and had, in return, loved. He jammed the emotions back down and smothered them with his pride.

A horse was led forward and the reins dropped at DeMorley's feet.

Draemel strutted up to DeMorley and leaned into his ear. "Mark my words, minstrel," he whispered, "when good fortune abandons you, look for me in the shadows. On that day, I won't honor the wishes of our king."

He pushed DeMorley away.

DeMorley scooped up the reins and mounted. Riding to the edge of the camp, he took one last look at Lassiter. He hoped the boy would turn and watch him ride off or wave. In fact, he would have preferred a curse over silence, for it would have at least verified that they had a relationship. Instead, Lassiter kept his back turned and stabbed the embers.

DeMorley's pride returned and with a sharp heel to the flanks of his steed, galloped off into the dark.

Chapter 19

Burdens

Linwith scooped up the last bite of his dinner and dropped his utensil onto the pewter plate. Had he been dining alone, the metallic report would have rung like a dull bell, but the Great Hall was filled with families sitting shoulder-to-shoulder, the cathedral ceiling amplifying the dinner noise to a roar.

Linwith, who preferred dining in solitude and quiet, winced at children laughing and whining, plates being scraped, brash banter from men, shrill squeals from women and shouts for more of this or some of that.

In an effort to escape the hoopla, Linwith turned his attention overhead and followed the long timber beams supporting the high, arching roof. At the zenith, small birds flitted about nests built in the nooks and joints of the crossbeams.

"Isn't this great," Gundin boasted, interrupting Linwith's thoughts.

Linwith let his gaze drop to Gundin who sat across from him popping grape-sized sweets into his mouth; chocolate oozed from the corner of his lips.

"The food, yes," Linwith shouted, "but I could do without all the noise."

"You call this noise?" Quinn added with an elbow jab in his brother's left side. "I've been in taverns louder than this."

"*That* I don't doubt," Linwith snubbed with a counter jab.

Feeling a headache coming over him, Linwith scooted back from the table to leave.

"Is it time to feed your dragons," Gundin chided as another treat sailed into his mouth.

Linwith shook his head and refused to correct Gundin, who felt it was his responsibility to torment him about his worms. He even wondered if Gundin, through some mystical act of the Cauldron, was aware of the vision he'd seen of his son and was taking his frustration out on him. He shook off the thought as being too suspicious. Turning on his heel, Linwith made his way through the crowded hall toward the exit. His status as the Worm Master may have won him great popularity, but it earned him no friends. Quinn's assessment of him earlier was correct: he was a loner.

Linwith pressed toward the door, returning a wave here, a head nod there, but along with the accolades came those that glowered, or turned away, or cursed or spat. At first, such rejection troubled him, but as he analyzed his situation, he realized there were explanations for the varied responses.

Most refugees were frightened of the Worms of Bal-Malin and projected their fears onto Linwith, avoiding him at all cost. Others, like Gundin, disliked the worms and were put off by Linwith's success, convinced his fame made him cocky. The women he didn't understand at all. They either showered him with trite praises along with fluttering eyelashes, or scowled at him with arms crossed, convinced he cavorted with a host of lovers.

But the biggest reason he was alone was tougher for him to swallow.

Me, he deduced.

It was not in Linwith's nature to embrace the popularity that came with his position, yet it was a role he was born to fill. He accepted the tug of war that wreaked havoc on his psyche. He preferred the quiet moments of a day to the grandiose communal meals, a solitary walk to a group hunt, deep conversation to small talk. As a warrior, he knew that such activities were necessary to build camaraderie, but whenever Quinn or Gundin engaged the men in light conversation, he became reserved, tossing a chuckle in here and there to feign interest.

Linwith reached the huge double doors and marched out of the Great Hall. When the doors closed, and the din faded, Linwith breathed a sigh of relief. He arched his head back to drink in the twilight. The sky blazed with color from the sunset - reminiscent of his worms' glowing tales - the wide strokes, as if brushed, fanning across the sky. He basked in the beauty, the simplicity of the moment and became almost giddy at how quiet it was.

As the colors faded, he became increasingly aware of a sharp pain. This ache wasn't from sore muscles or bruised flesh but radiated from deep within. As much as he coveted his isolation, he longed for a woman's touch, her soft refrain of "I love you," a friend to share life with. Such pain struck Linwith at dusk when families settled in for the night or lovers embraced to kiss goodnight.

Such is the price to be the Worm Master.

Linwith shuffled across the courtyard as if another controlled his body, drawn to the central turret like a ghoul to its haunt. He was not surprised by the journey or his destination, for this was as much a part of his nightly ritual as was his melancholic gaze at the sunset.

Once inside, he watched his feet mount the stone steps and he felt himself climb up the circular staircase in a detached manner, as if walking a dream.

Or stumbling through a nightmare.

At the top he exited and headed to the western opening. There, he leaned on the ledge and soaked up the purple hues of nightfall. When the first star appeared, a sign he interpreted to move on, he turned and climbed the wooden ladder to the tiled roof. He unlatched the trap door and flung it open. It clattered on the tiles and Linwith stared through the opening.

Tonight, as with all the other nights, he came to seek fellowship with the most unlikely of participants - the sapphire worm.

The worm, who had anticipated Linwith's arrival, sat near the edge to allow room for him to climb onto the roof. Linwith made his way out, careful to not let the windblast knock him to his death, and rose to his full height, thankful the roof's pitch was gentle.

"So another day ends," he offered as he patted the worm's underbelly, "and war creeps toward us like a fog."

The Worm King arched his head around to peer into Linwith's face.

"Yes, so it seems, but I sense a dread within you that has nothing to do with such battles."

Linwith chuckled.

The fire within the worm's eyes flickered. "What is so funny?"

"I doubt you'd understand; it's Allsbruthian humor."

"Please tell me. Although your humor is a difficult matter to ascertain, I still long to learn."

"Well, you see," Linwith crossed his arms and leaned against the worm's massive frame. "I laughed because you discerned my true feelings, my hidden emotions, like you always do."

The Worm King twisted his head. "I'm still confused. Why is that so funny?"

"Because here I am, sad that I'm alone without a wife or a family, yet feeling connected to you, a worm, while standing high atop Min Brock, taking in the families and lovers below who are connected with each other. To me, the situation is ironic, comical."

The worm, perplexed by his master's logic, shook his head. "For four summers I have tried to comprehend such reason, such philosophy, such an outlook on life. And yet, I am just as confused in the matter as the day I began. I am at a loss to grasp such yearnings, such emotions."

Linwith ran his hand along the worm's plated side. "Don't regret what you can't change or control. It simply makes our relationship all that more complex."

"So you regret becoming the Worm Master?"

Linwith chewed on the question like a horse would grass. He pondered the complexities and mysteries of his role as the Worm Master.

"No," he finally answered, "I don't regret it, but I had no idea the weight it would bear upon me either. Especially the visions of the future conjured by the mandarin worm or the gold worm's ability to peer into another's soul. At first, the notion to do so was exciting, even rewarding, for such gifts gave us a great advantage in preparing for war and getting Min Brock rebuilt."

"But such visions are short and ambiguous," the sapphire worm replied. "How is it possible for you to accurately know how events would unfold? And in regards to the thoughts of others, is this not what storytellers also carry as a burden?"

"Yes, the visions are brief and open to many interpretations. And yes, the gift of mind reading - although from what I can ascertain is different from that of a storyteller - is just as burdensome, I suppose."

"In fact," the worm counseled, "you have the option to *not* gaze into such visions. Correct?"

Linwith sighed in agreement. "True, but once I witness such scenes, they are mine and mine alone to carry. I can't tell a soul. No one in Min Brock must know I possess such abilities. If they did, I'd be harassed and tormented from sunup to sundown with requests, most of which would be trite."

He gazed down into the courtyard. The night cloaked it with blackness. Orange glows glimmered from communal fires where soldiers and craftsmen gathered for warmth. Dotting the interior of the keep were dim spots of yellow marking the dwellings of the refugee families. "The thought of knowing who may live or who might die is a burden I don't wish to carry, nor do I wish to be all-knowing, either. I never sought such abilities."

"Correct. That is why you, and you alone, can be the Worm Master: you possess the disposition to wield and manage our gifts."

"Then why do I feel so burdened?"

"If you did not, then my brothers and I would truly be worried, for you would not possess the character to manage such power for the good of Allsbruth or Claire. Instead, you would become consumed with your own mortality, your own comfort and your own glory. Such appetites lead only to destruction."

"I understand. But why must I feel so…alone?"

"Such are the sacrifices of war." The sapphire worm stopped to ponder and a fresh idea came to mind. "Perhaps it is time to let Quinn in on our secrets. After all, aside from being your brother, he is the leader of Min Brock. Maybe it is time he helped shoulder some of the responsibility."

Linwith let his eyes wander across the darkened courtyard to Quinn's dwelling. "I considered telling him the first time I discovered these gifts, but the more I thought about it, the more I concluded to hold off. If I told him, he would naturally ask me to disclose the visions I saw of Elabea, who is now Ela Claire. And Galadin, who has a new name as well, Romlin. As his brother, I didn't want to give him false hope or be the one that made him lose optimism altogether. After all, the visions are open to interpretation."

"Then you need to heed your own counsel: 'Don't regret what you cannot change or control.' Let Quinn bear that burden, too. After all, he is her father."

"True, but although I know Quinn would never tell a soul, he is married, and wives have ways of finding things out. In time, Areall would counsel Daryess and I'd be stuck telling them what I saw when looking into Romlin's life. At least Elabea, or should I say Ela Claire, had visions of tomorrow, or what I perceived to be tomorrow. But Romlin..."

Linwith let his voice trail off and shuddered at the memory of the revelation. He tossed it from his thoughts but knew it cowered in the recesses of his mind, ready to leap back in like a wild beast.

The Worm King thought long and hard before replying. "Again, should they not be allowed a glimpse into the truth of tomorrow? Are you not prolonging their pain? Besides, maybe the vision is not as it appears to be. Perhaps it's a mystery that, with more time and disclosure, will become apparent."

"I suppose you're correct," Linwith replied with a heavy sigh. "For now, I'll tell my brother. It's time he knew."

Their conversation lulled, and the Worm King raised his head and let his gaze sweep the Gilden Plains. As was par for their nightly routine, they stared without another word into the sky and would do so well past the time Min Brock's fires dimmed or candles were snuffed for sleep.

Linwith reflected on his bond with the Worm King. It was as strong as his relationship with Quinn. In many ways the sapphire worm was becoming more like a brother, while Linwith felt he was becoming...

...more like a worm.

Chapter 20

A Gift

The fire in Linwith's cottage etched the walls with crimson hues. He sat near the coals, not so much for warmth but to reflect on the conversation he was about to have with his brother. He had been up most of the night rehearsing what he would say, anticipating Quinn's responses to his revelation about the worm's visions, but no matter how he scripted it, the ending was always the same.

Disaster. Anger. Mistrust.

Knock. Knock. Knock.

"Come in," he replied.

The door swung open and Quinn entered. "I received your note yesterday," he replied after he closed the door with barely a sound, "but why the secrecy, and why such urgency?"

"I didn't want all of Min Brock to see you here. There are already too many whispers swirling around about me and the worms without adding any more."

Linwith rose and sauntered over to a table where he lit a candle. Golden light embraced the fire's red glow. He turned and retrieved a pot off the coals and poured Allsbruthian tea into two mugs sitting on the table. He motioned for his brother to sit in the chair opposite his.

"When was the last time we enjoyed tea together," Linwith asked as sat and he sniffed the aromatic scent.

"Many, many summers ago." Quinn sat across from his brother and studied him. "But I doubt you invited me here in the wee hours of the morning to reminisce."

Linwith met his gaze. "No, you're right, I didn't." He pulled away from Quinn's piercing eyes and focused on the tea's golden water. "I need to tell you about the gifts and powers of the worms."

Quinn lifted his mug for a sip. "I already know about the crimson's ability with fire, the emerald's capabilities to emit gas, the pearl's gift of invisibility, and sapphire's means to freeze time and motion. The remaining worms, according to what you told me, don't have any gifts or powers."

Linwith braced himself to share the truth and took in Quinn's face. "I lied."

Quinn's eyes narrowed and his brow furrowed. He set his mug down on the table. "What do you mean?"

"The intent was never to hurt you. In fact, my reasoning was to protect you and Areall from pain as well as to do what was best for Min Brock."

Quinn drilled his eyes into Linwith. "Pain? What pain? What are you talking about?"

Linwith leaned back in his chair to put as much distance between himself and his brother as he could. "The amber worm is able to shrink."

Quinn gave a nod to confirm, his face still twisted with confusion as Linwith continued.

"The mandarin can see the future…"

Quinn's eyes widened with understanding.

"…and the gold can read the thoughts of another."

Quinn's face became as red as the fireplace coals. "And you've known this now for over four summers?"

Linwith nodded.

Quinn pushed back from the table and stood so quick that his chair toppled over. He paced about the room, shaking his head and muttering.

Linwith remained seated and simply watched. He knew it was best to let Quinn blow some steam before explaining anything further.

"This is bad, Linwith, very bad. Not only did you not trust me, your brother, but your secrecy reflects a mistrust in my leadership of Min Brock. If this gets out, you could be tried for treason."

Linwith pulled the mug close and kept his eyes focused on the brew. "Don't you think I know all of that?"

Quinn slammed his palms down on the table and glared at Linwith. "Then tell me why? Why would you keep such insights from me?"

Linwith glanced into his brother's eyes. Although his gaze cut to the quick and was filled with anger and betrayal, Linwith steadied himself. "Because these are weighty gifts and powers that I oversee, and the visions and mind-reading are not as clear and simple as you imagine."

Quinn pushed up from the table and crossed his arms over his chest. "That doesn't explain a thing."

"Doesn't it? Then answer me this," Linwith rose and stood face to face with Quinn. "Let's say I told you about these visions from the start. Would you have asked about Elabea?"

Quinn sucked in a quick gasp. He wet his lips with his tongue, but instead of answering, he voiced a question most pressing. "You've seen a vision of her?"

Linwith nodded.

Quinn abandoned reason and grabbed Linwith's shoulders. "Is she alive? Tell me." He shook him as if to free the answer from his mouth. "Tell me!"

Linwith stared at Quinn's grip and then into his face. Linwith arched an eyebrow, and Quinn, realizing he was guilty of what his brother accused him of, let go and backed away.

"That is why I didn't tell you," Linwith explained. "You would have hounded me day and night. And despite your best efforts to keep such information to yourself, Areall would have sensed you knew something about Elabea and she too would have pressed me daily. Soon, Daryess and Gundin would come, as would the others in Min Brock, and my life would be transformed into that of a fortune teller, and not the Worm Master of Bal-Malin."

Quinn nodded and staggered to his chair where he plopped down, his thoughts and feelings consumed with Elabea. After a period of silence, Quinn looked up at Linwith. "Aside from what Digri shared, can you offer me any hope about Elabea?"

Linwith took in his brother's countenance. Although the conversation had gone as he had expected, he was not ready for his brother's needy look. Quinn was no longer talking to him as his brother or the leader of Min Brock. This was the face of a tortured father longing for his child's return.

It was for this very reason that Linwith did not like being the emissary of hope or defeat, and wished at that moment that he could be anyone but the Worm Master. In the case of his brother and Ela Claire, the worm's images did offer hope. Even if it was modest, it was still hope.

Linwith sat back down and leaned across the table to deliver the news. "The visions are but snippets of time, Quinn, so they can be confusing at best."

Quinn nodded. "I want to know."

Linwith swallowed down his emotions and proceeded. "Elabea's alive. She wears a beautiful white dress, no doubt given to her by the King of Claire, and rides a great white bird." He braved a glance at Quinn. His lips trembled with emotion. "And she has a new name."

Tears rolled down Quinn's cheeks. "A new name?"

"Ela Claire."

Quinn sucked in a deep breath, as if in some mystical fashion he could catch his daughter's scent. He closed his eyes and imagined what she looked like, relishing her new name, letting if flit across his troubled heart on a carefree, whimsical flight of fancy. He held his breath, as well as the conjured scene, as long as possible and then let it escape with a soft rush of wind as he whispered her name.

"Ela Claire."

Quinn searched his brother's eyes. "Where is she now?"

"I don't know, but from what I can sense, feel, from the worms, she is alive."

"But the worms; surely they know, or can find her, or can search the regions..."

"Stop right there! It's for this very reason I didn't share such insights with you. You would have been consumed with finding Ela

Claire rather than securing Min Brock or preparing us for war."

Quinn pulled away from his gaze and gave a reluctant nod. "So all along, you've known that the Martyr's Moon wasn't for her."

"Yes, but you also assumed as much."

"No, brother, I merely was *hoping* as much. Digri's news - that they had made it as far as MerriNoon - was comforting but stirred up more questions. One of which was that there was the possibility that the Martyr's Moon was for her, unless..."

Quinn pondered the worms' gifts and came to another conclusion. "The moon was for Il-Lilliad. He's the only storyteller we know of."

"The visions are short and often confusing, so sometimes it is impossible to ascertain..."

"The truth, Linwith. What did you see for him?"

"Blackness. An empty void."

Quinn sank deeper into his chair and ran fingers through his hair.

"But remember," Linwith added in an attempt to give them both hope, "I'm still learning to decipher such visions. For what it's worth, when I tried to read Il-Lilliad's thoughts, or passions, I did sense a purpose and peace in him."

"So we don't know if his trip to the Onderling was successful or not."

Linwith rose and sauntered to his window. "No, we don't."

Quinn perked up as another name popped into his inquisitive mind. "What about Galadin?"

"Like I've said," Linwith replied as he watched the early-risers mill past his cottage, "the visions are but mere glimpses, void of time or exact locations..."

"I understand, but is he with Ela Claire?"

Linwith stalled. "He too has a new name: Romlin."

"And what else?"

Linwith fell silent and shook his head.

Quinn rose and spun his brother around. "I need to know. Gundin and Daryess need to know."

Linwith's face reddened with anger. "And why's that, Quinn? Simply because they're our friends? What about the other refugees of Min Brock? Don't they deserve to know about missing family members, or what will become of their tomorrows?"

"This is different! Gundin is like a brother to me; Galadin like a son."

Linwith ground his teeth. "And I'm *your* brother so don't belittle me. You have *no* idea what it's like to marshal such revelations. They eat at me like flies do a corpse. Not a moment passes when I don't think about Ela Claire and Romlin!" And with an index finger to Quinn's chest: "*Not one moment.*"

Quinn's eyes narrowed. "Tell me your vision of Romlin."

Linwith pressed his nose up to Quinn's. "His was black, just like Il-Lilliad's."

He pushed past Quinn and kept his back to his brother. "Listen, I will use my worms' gifting to serve Min Brock in the ensuing war. And for what it's worth, I've *never* kept any military secrets from you." Linwith faced Quinn. "But I will *not* become some odd commodity sought out by you or others to answer questions about the future. Do you understand?"

Quinn was about to lash out at him again when he noted Linwith's slumped shoulders and the dark circles around his eyes.

"Linwith," he said as he draped a consoling arm over his brother's shoulder, "I didn't understand at first, but now I do. You did what you thought best for Min Brock as well as for Areall and me. Knowing that Elabea, I mean Ela Claire, is alive is indeed a blessing, but I also see that your secrecy was a gift. You're right: Areall and I would have nagged you for updates, and I would have fretted about her night and day instead of getting us ready for war. You took this weight upon yourself, and I thank you."

Linwith flashed a smile. "That's what big brothers do."

"But why tell me now?"

Linwith made his way to the window and watched a mother and daughter walk past. "Because war knocks on our door. And I've had visions of others, one in particular that I don't recognize, whose vision haunts me through and through."

"And judging by your tone of voice, you're not ready to share this with me yet, are you?"

Linwith remained silent, his features a mask to hide whatever torturous vision he'd seen locked up inside.

Quinn let the matter drop and joined Linwith in looking out the window as more and more refugees milled past. "You've given me hope, my brother, great hope. Thank you."

Linwith smiled and his burdened shoulders arched up with pride.

"But you know I can't keep secrets from Areall. She's very curious and persistent."

"Sounds like someone else I know." Linwith elbowed Quinn.

Quinn laughed. "True, and unfortunately, it's only a matter of time before she and Daryess knock on your door."

"I know." Linwith sighed as children skipped past. "The gold worm has already showed me as much."

Chapter 21

The Tracker

Woren spied Mälque's firestick moving through the undergrowth surrounding Ela Claire's cave. "Find anything?"

Mälque pushed out of the bushes, firestick in one hand, book clutched in other. He noted their silhouettes and turned to address them. "Just this." He held the light over the book so Woren and the Gor King could see it better.

"That's all," Woren asked.

Mälque thought about sharing his experience with the whisper and the vision as well as finding the strand of hair, but his gut instinct told him otherwise.

"Yep," he answered as he made his way to his horse. "Unless you wanted me to drag out her bed and books ta show ya. But guessin' ya knew all that stuff was there anyway."

"A book and the feather. Not much to go on, now is it?"

"For an old Ebonite like you, nothin.' But for a Wurmlin tracker like me, lots."

As soon as the last word flew off his tongue, Mälque wished he could retract every syllable. He never meant to sound offensive; he was simply making an observation. Woren snickered which Mälque interpreted as being a good sign. Mälque offered Woren the book as a gesture of good will.

He waved him off. "You carry it. You're the tracker, not me."

Mälque shrugged and before stashing it in his saddlebag, glanced at the Gor King. His skulled helmet glowed in the dim moonlight and the black eyesockets were staring straight at him. Mälque froze and sucked in cool night air. Could the Gor King see through his ruse? Mälque bit his lower lip.

Best secrets are those keepin' me alive.

He gathered his courage to play his role and shoved the book into the saddlebag. The Gor King looked away. Mälque swung up into the saddle with the firestick in one hand and grabbed the reins with the other. The glow from the firestick made Woren and the Gor King look all the more sinister.

"Since you have *so* many clues," Woren huffed, "what's your plan?"

Mälque met his glaring eyes and twitching smile. "The book had a drawing. Showed an island with a castle. Had the letters R-H-Y-T-H-E."

"Rhythe," Woren pronounced. "The Isle of Rhythe. Are you certain?"

"I can show you," he turned to retrieve the book.

"That won't be necessary," Woren said as he waved him off. "I'm familiar with the island, but what does it have to do with finding this girl?"

"I'm guessin' that eagle - or whatever it is - flew her to..." He scrunched his lips, trying to remember the name.

"Rhythe," Woren provided.

"Yeah, the Isle of Rhythe."

"And how do you know?"

"Don't. Just a hunch."

"Anything else?"

"I think she's..." He held the answer and took in their shadowed faces. Once shared, would they swoop into his thoughts, something his superstitions deemed possible, and discover the vision and his dialogue with the whisper? He gulped down his fear and finished, "...a storyteller."

The Gor King shifted in his saddle and his horse snorted.

Mälque flinched, expecting to see the dark skull sockets burn crimson and the blue sword coursing through the air.

Nothing happened.

"What makes you say this?" Woren pressed.

Mälque, still fearing the worst, flicked his long locks to act brave. "'Cause of all the books in her cave. She had lots of herbs and spices, too. But I'm guessin' you all knew that already."

Woren leaned into the light of the firestick. "Yes, we knew. But don't think you're outsmarting us. This isn't a game. If you're holding something back from us, or you can't find the girl, you'll forfeit your life, is that clear?"

Mälque met his gaze with chin held high. "I ain't holdin' back, and even if I was, I ain't afraid no more. There ain't nothin' but dyin' out here anyway."

Woren retreated back into the shadows. "Time will tell." He retrieved his reins. "Your answer was either brave or prophetic." He gestured to the hill that led back to camp. "After you."

"Ain't we gonna start now?"

"No," Woren fired over his shoulder as he and the Gor King made their way toward the incline.

"But the scents, the clues," he eyed the area. "They're strong here. They'll only get weaker the longer we wait."

"But I thought you were a great tracker?" Sarcasm coursed his words.

"I am," Mälque fired with a flick of his head, "but I ain't no fool, neither!"

Woren turned his steed around and rode up to Mälque. Woren stared him down and then with no warning, backhanded him across the face. Mälque recoiled from the blow, cheek on fire, and a metallic, salty taste in his mouth.

"Insolence," Woren hissed as his finger jabbed Mälque's chest, "will *not* be tolerated."

"I don't even know what that word means!" Mälque shoved Woren's arm away and wiped the blood from his lips.

"Oh, you know what it means." Woren sized up Mälque and then snorted. "It's in your stinking, Wurmlin blood! Now come along, unless you'd like some more."

Chapter 22

Wind of Hope

The next morning, Mälque led the Gor King and his army north toward the Gilden Sea. He hoped the clue he was given in Ela Claire's cave - that they were headed for the Isle of Rhythe - was true.

He was betting his life on it.

Along the way, he searched for her trail but all he found were bear droppings, a ravaged deer carcass and a cave inhabited by spitting lizards. With each false alarm, Woren's scowl darkened while the Gor King maintained his stoic appearance.

Olke was like that, actin' like there was nothin' buggin' him. Then he'd snap, get meaner than a cornered boar, and hit ya with no warnin'.

Mälque rubbed his chin, the memories of Olke's abuse still fresh and raw.

By afternoon, Mälque became more desperate to find the trail and cold sweat rolled down his back. He stole a glance at the Gor King. He sat tall in the saddle and as far as Mälque could tell, seemed unfazed by him being unable to find her trail. Mälque feared the worst; his stomach gurgled with worry.

He's gonna snap, I just know it. All I need is one clue, just one.

An idea came to mind. He eyed his saddlebag containing Ela Claire's book. Mälque pulled back on the reins and turned to address Woren.

"I need to go."

"Go where?"

"Ya know, squat in the woods...go."

"Do you think I'm that gullible?"

"Here." He handed Woren the reins. "Take my horse. I'll go on foot. I ain't gonna run, but if I did, I wouldn't get far, now would I?"

Woren's eyes narrowed.

Mälque pressed the issue. "I'll be nearby, in that thicket..." He searched for a suitable spot. "There."

Woren sized up the grove of saplings Mälque pointed to. Mälque, sensing Woren was giving in, fished out the book. "And I need to go alone."

"That I understand, but why the book?"

Mälque snickered. "'Cause I'd rather wipe with parchments than with leaves."

Woren looked to the Gor King for an answer. The Gor King didn't move a muscle and stared at Mälque for the longest time. Mälque was about to drop the matter when the Gor King gave him a subtle nod.

Mälque seized the moment and slid to the ground.

"Just hurry, yung-er!" Woren shouted as Mälque entered the thicket.

When Mälque was certain they couldn't see him, he set the book on the ground and stepped back. He eyed it with suspicion, still not sure he could trust it or the whisper, and remembered another of his mother's warnings...

"Storytellers from Claire are on the prowl."

Mälque shivered at the thought that Ela Claire, his prey, was such a person. If he found her, what would his fate be? He shook off the thought and glanced over his shoulder to make sure he was still alone. He sighed in relief, grateful that Woren hadn't sent a soldier in after him.

Mälque turned his attention back to the book. It sat on a tuft of green moss and dead oak leaves. A sunbeam lit the cover, accentuating the grandeur of the etchings.

Drawn by its beauty, Mälque reached for it but when he remembered more of his mother's warnings, he jumped back as if the book would rise to life and attack him.

But I gotta ask. I gotta know for sure.

Mälque found a long stick and stretched for the book. He flicked open the cover as if turning a stone that concealed a snake and then dropped to the ground and covered his head. He stole a peek, half expecting to see light burst out of the parchments or some vision or beast coming to life.

Nothing.

C'mon. Talk to me. Help me find 'em.

He stared up through the branches for any sign of the whisper from Claire although he had no idea what he was looking for. Mälque, more determined than ever to get an answer, got to his knees and using the stick, turned the pages to the white feather and strand of hair.

Just give me a clue. Am I on the right trail or not?

He sat still and trained his senses on the woods. A light breeze stirred leaves high overhead. A squirrel chattered somewhere behind him. He sniffed in hope of catching the scents of Ela Claire's cave - a warm sea breeze, the dried herbs, her aroma - but all he smelled were the leaves and moss.

Beyond his thicket, a horse whinnied followed by Woren's voice. "Don't make me come in there, yung-er!"

"I'm almost done," Mälque thundered as he rose and glared at the book. And to himself with jaw set: "I'm *done!*"

He snapped the stick across his knee and threw it away.

"My mom was right about you," Mälque half-whispered at the book. "You can't be trusted. Ain't gonna listen to no more whispers. Only gonna follow what I know is true in here." He tapped the side of his head. "I'm done with you; done believin' in magic."

He brought his foot back to kick the book, but stopped.

I'll keep ya for now. If nothin' else, I can use the pages when I really have to go.

He knelt, and the open pages changed from white to black.

Spooked by the transformation, he jumped back. A dark sea materialized on the pages; a crescent moon lit the curling waves with silver. On a distant crag of rocks sat an ominous castle. A warm breeze caressed his cheek. Mälque squatted for a better look. A white bird glided over the water. He leaned closer, hoping to spy Ela Claire, when he heard someone coming.

The vision ended and Mälque slammed the book shut. He scooped it up and turned to spy Woren coming his way.

"Who were you talking to," Woren demanded.

"Just myself." Mälque made his way for Woren while fumbling with his breeches to make it look like he had finished relieving himself.

Woren stopped and scowled. "I'm no fool. You were angry with someone. I heard you, now tell me who you were talking to!"

Mälque finished messing with his pants and met Woren's glare with a smirk. "Look around." Mälque swept a hand about the thicket. "Ain't no one here unless ya think I was talkin' to ghosts or whispers. But if ya wanna *really* wanna know, sometimes I talk to myself when I go."

Mälque pushed past but Woren grabbed his arm and spun him around. Woren eyed the book under Mälque's armpit.

"Open it."

"Why?"

"Show me the pages you ripped out to wipe your butt."

Mälque's eyes widened. Before he could fabricate a lie, Woren released his hold and yanked the book free. He flipped through the pages while keeping one eye on Mälque.

Woren's greasy smile appeared. "You look scared, yung-er."

Mälque tried to swallow but his throat was too dry. "Ain't. Just don't want ya' to loose the feather, that's all."

Woren found what he was looking for and stopped flicking the pages. He turned the book around so Mälque could see.

The pages have been torn out! But how? They were there before!

Woren slapped the book shut and slammed it into Mälque's gut.

"Let's go. You're running out of time."

Woren spun on his heel and Mälque followed at a safe distance. He opened the book and searched for the ripped out pages but found the book was in perfect condition. Even the feather and hair were in the same spot. He closed the book and clutched it to his chest with both hands.

The warm breeze brushed past his face and he heard what sounded like a lark's song. A dormant emotion, one he hadn't felt since his parents were alive, was stirred to life and flowed into his marrow. Like his father's homemade whisky, it warmed him through and through and offered him something he hadn't felt since death robbed him of his family.

Hope.

Chapter 23

The Cost of Mercy

DeMorley galloped at a mad pace away from Lassiter's camp. Expletives, along with spittle, flew from his mouth as he navigated the dark woods and the ominous mood settling over him. He chastised Lassiter for holding on to the ideological notion that as the King of Allsbruth, he would bring peace and prosperity to the lands once more. He blamed Draemel for brainwashing the boy with grand stories about his father, Hornlynn, that he concluded were blown out of proportion. He justified the map he had drawn that revealed the army's location and numbers, as well as the supplies he had stolen, as a minstrel's means of survival. After all, his life was littered with similar betrayals, deceptions and cons. What was one more?

As the woods grew thicker, he paid for his brash pace. Limbs smacked his head and prodded him in the side, giant trees blocked his path, thick brambles made his steed whinny. When a pine bough swatted his face, he cursed, spit out the blood and pulled hard on the reins. Furious, he came to a stop, rose out of his saddle and yelled at the top of his lungs to voice his frustration.

As his voice echoed about the forest, reason returned, if but briefly, and he realized the mess he was in and sat back down. It was the middle of the night, he was alone, unarmed, and had no idea where he was or where he was going.

His imagination, which was so accustomed to self-preservation, kicked into high gear. There was no wind and he relished the silence that enabled him to hear anyone or anything creeping up on him. As he strained to listen, the night sounds conjured horrible images and his joy was short-lived: the distant call of a night bird he interpreted as Wurmlins whistling an attack; the clicking, percussive reports of an animal racing up a tree he perceived to be hordes of vul jens; the paw of a harmless nocturnal beast snapping a twig meant Ebonite scouts were on his trail.

Frightened and unable to decide how to flee or battle such foes, he slumped down in his saddle and further blamed Lassiter and Draemel for his ill-fated trip. Throughout the night he sat in this uncomfortable position and remained slouched for so long that his muscles started to cramp. To relieve the pain, he stretched until another noise made him crouch and he had to grimace, wriggle and moan through the spasms.

When dawn's gray light chased away night's blackness, he was thankful his tortuous ordeal was coming to an end. But as he scanned the woods, his vision became his own worst enemy. He misconstrued a bump on a high bough as a vul jen and was convinced a boulder was a crouching gor. Fortunately, as the sun rose into the sky and the woods brightened, he realized how foolish he had been. Disgusted that his misinterpretation of a tree bump had cost him valuable time, he cursed beneath his breath and prodded his horse onward.

The woods thinned and he breathed a sigh of relief that he was alive and, as best he could tell, not being followed by Wurmlins, Ebonites or beasts. Worn out from sitting all night in a saddle while his imagination was at war with the entire nation of Ebon, he made his way to a thicket of wildeberry bushes to eat and rest. As he rose to dismount, his legs buckled from non-use and he nearly toppled to the ground. When the tingly sensations were over, he dismounted, albeit with the speed of a man twice his age.

He retrieved the provisions from his saddlebag and plopped down. No sooner had he sat than a growl echoed from a distant valley. His horse, spooked by the predator, snorted and pranced about. DeMorley realizing he had forgotten to secure the reins to a tree, hopped to his feet as the steed galloped off. He screamed at the top of his lungs but the horse ignored his call and disappeared into the woods.

DeMorley kicked pine needles in rage and cursed Lassiter and Draemel for his bad luck. His rumbling belly snapped him from his name-calling and he plopped back down to eat. He was so hungry, and so undisciplined, that he devoured all his rations. With a loud belch, he wiped his mouth and rose to his feet. He stared up through the trees in an effort to spot the sun's position to determine which direction to go. And this was when the reality of his betrayal of Lassiter hit him the hardest.

There's no place I can go, he mused.

With war imminent, villages were no longer vestiges of sanctuary where he could sing for a giln, pull a girl into his arms and bask in the warmth of another's fire. If the reports from Lassiter's scouts were accurate, most villages were abandoned, or worse, burned to the ground. Another consideration was the scouting reports about Min Brock. Based upon what he could glean from eavesdropping, there was the possibility that Min Brock had been rebuilt and was attracting refugees from the surrounding lands. But he was shrewd enough to know that if such campfire tales were true, Min Brock would be the focal point of Ebon and the Cauldron's attack and he wanted no part of such bloodshed.

Then a thought, like an epiphany, lit him with hope. He reached inside his tunic and fingered the invitation. True, it was not his, and yes, he had indeed stolen it, but at the same time, he was the one who possessed it. Therefore, he concluded in his typical self-absorbed manner, the King of Claire *must* grant him passage into Claire.

If it even exists.

He noted the sun's position one more time and set out north - for Claire.

Despite being without horse and food, his mood was upbeat and his imagination worked overtime creating scenarios of what it would be like to meet the Only - that he quickly noted may not even be alive - as well as the throngs of storytellers cheering his arrival and pressing him to tell his tales of adventure.

His pace quickened as he daydreamed about the treasure that awaited him for being the sole proprietor of the invitation, even if it bore another's name. And when he pictured himself being named "royal minstrel to the King of Claire," he smiled and added: "But only if he's still alive, of course."

Energized by these fantasies, he trudged throughout the day lost in thought, consumed with the notion that he would finally get what he had always longed for and deserved: a life of ease, comfort and glory.

By dusk, he was famished and instinctively reached into a pocket for a slab of venison. All he fingered was lint and then he remembered his gluttonous meal. He pouted, jettisoned his joy-filled thoughts of Claire, and with a glum sigh, plopped to the ground and buried his head in his hands.

I'm doomed, he moped. *And it's all their fault!*

In an effort to cheer himself up, he pulled his prized lute from around his back and strummed the open strings. He was about to finger a chord when he stopped. As a seasoned thief and con artist, he had conditioned himself to never feel remorse for his thefts or betrayals. After all, it was as much a part of who he was as a minstrel as tuning his Bellini.

So why can't I stop thinking about Lassiter, Newcomb and Draemel?

He ground his teeth and tried to push past the emotions and the memories that blocked his way. Typically, this was an easy process, like trying to skirt around a drunk in a tavern, but this time, the memories towered like stones of life, friendship and purpose. Unaccustomed to experiencing guilt and remorse, he let the Bellini fall to his lap.

But his lapse into honest reflection was short-lived. He bit his lower lip, brushed aside the emotions with a flippant wave of the hand and stood back up to continue on.

Fools, he concluded to try and alleviate the shame percolating through his blood. *Serves them right.*

When he came to a creek, he knelt for a cool drink, but before he scooped up handfuls of water, he took in his reflection. Enamored with himself, he turned his head and posed to see which angle made him the handsomest. With each reflection, he put more and more blame for his dire predicament on Lassiter and Draemel.

He smiled back at himself and threw off his troubling thoughts before diving his hands into the icy water. Lost in his melancholic state of self-preservation, he slurped the sweet water from cupped hands, unaware of a foe sneaking up behind him.

"You are deserving of so much more," a whisper declared.

DeMorley, spooked by the murmur, gagged on the water and he fell backward on his rump.

"Who said that," he gasped as he searched high and low for any sign of man or beast.

"The one who can give you the glory you deserve."

DeMorley scrambled to his feet and ran for cover behind a tree. He peeked around the bark for the source of the whisper.

"Why do you journey to Claire?"

Absentmindedly, DeMorley slid his hand inside his tunic and groped the invitation. "Who says I'm going there?" he fired while his beady eyes swept the shadows for the visitor.

"Your invitation gave you away. You're fingering it now within your breast pocket."

DeMorley jerked his hand out. "Who are you?"

"I've already told you, the one who can give you glory."

"Show yourself!"

"I am a whisper, void of shape and form."

DeMorley gasped and pressed closer to the tree in fear. "You're the Only!"

The whisper snickered. *"Guess again."*

Spooked to realize he was dealing with the Cauldron's whisper, DeMorley panicked and dashed from his hiding place. His Bellini bounced off his back and chimed eerie notes as he raced through the dark woods. Wild-eyed, he stole a glance over his shoulder to see if he was being followed.

"Looking for me? I'm over here."

DeMorley felt a cold wind brush his left cheek.

"Now I'm on this side."

A brisk breeze hit him from the right.

"But wait, now I'm over here."

The arctic wind struck DeMorley's back with such force that he flew face-first to the ground.

He pushed himself to his knees and spit leaves and twigs from his mouth. "I've never put stock in the stories of Claire..." He sputtered out more debris. "Or the Oracles of the Cauldron for that matter, so leave me be."

"So brash you are! A rebel who fights his own wars. I like that. I need that; which is why I am here to offer you what you want."

"What *I* want," he asked, his interest piqued as he rose and brushed himself off.

"Naturally. A man of your quality must want more from life than just food and shelter."

"Isn't it obvious? I want what *this*," he whipped out the parchment and waved it in the air, "promises. Treasures!"

Had DeMorley been more alert and less consumed with himself, he would have heard the whisper hiss when he held up the invitation.

"Yes, you should be rewarded, but put that... thing away."

DeMorley complied and added more to his wish list.

"I deserve a life of leisure along with a title of nobility, or at least the commission to be the royal minstrel."

"Ambitious you are, but why risk your life for the promises of a parchment with shiny letters; from a land that is now a desert?"

DeMorley's shoulders slumped at the news. Although he had his doubts, the whisper now confirmed his worst fears. "Simple: I have no other avenues to pursue."

"Then how lucky it is that I found you."

"What do you mean?"

"Follow me to Ebon where you'll be given title, rank and fortune."

"Ebon," he gasped as his face scrunched up with confusion. "I'll be killed if I go there."

"Alone, yes, but not as my emissary. Not with my blessing."

DeMorley shivered at the thought of serving the Dark Flame. Although a man of no faith or scruples, he nonetheless shuddered with dread at the notion of serving the Cauldron and Ebon.

"I appreciate the offer," DeMorley stammered, "but I'll find another way. I always have and I always will."

"There is no other way. Only I can offer you hope and freedom. War breathes down your neck like a pack of wild dogs."

DeMorley shook his head at the offer. "I may not be a man of integrity, but I'm not a traitor."

The whisper chortled. *"Really? Then do explain the secret map stashed in your pocket and the guilt oozing from your pores that stinks like death?"*

"I wasn't going to betray them," he fired with fists clinched. "I was simply looking out for my own interests."

"Ah! Just like you were with the Lord-Counselor of Ingloid?"

"That was different!"

"Or with taking his prized Bellini and his parchment?"

"He was dead."

"So you did *murder him."*

"No! I happened upon his corpse and figured a dead man wouldn't need them anyway."

"So you're not *a thief or a traitor. You are simply a man who is…misunderstood."*

"Yes," DeMorley shouted in relief that someone, even if it was the Cauldron, finally understood who he was.

"You are definitely misunderstood; not by others, but by yourself."

DeMorley cocked his head bird-like in confusion.

"When you gazed at your reflection in the stream, you were blind."

"I'm not blind," he huffed with arms crossed. "I saw myself."

"I'm not talking about skin and bone but the attributes of your being. Like most men, you are blind to such vision, and like most…"

The whisper enveloped DeMorley in what felt like a cold mist. *"…you are unable to rise to your true worth…your true calling."*

DeMorley staggered backwards as if punched in the gut. The whisper continued.

"You blame others for your misfortune or claim innocence when in fact you are guilty; unwilling to embrace your nature as a thief and a traitor."

DeMorley cupped hands over his ears and shook his head. The Cauldron snickered at his childlike attempts to silence its voice. He entered his thoughts.

"Let me open your eyes and show you who you truly are."

Panic stricken to hear the Dark Flame in his mind, DeMorley broke into a sprint. The whisper laughed, its dark tones accompanying the Bellini as it chimed against his back.

"You can't run away from me, nor can you escape who you are. Join me! Make a name for yourself! Seek revenge on those who robbed you of all you deserved."

DeMorley, too exhausted to run any further, stopped and doubled over to catch his breath. As he panted and sweat dripped from his forehead, the invitation fell out of his tunic and landed near his boot. The whisper hissed at the parchment, and this time, DeMorley heard it.

Scooping up the invitation, he stood upright and wiped the sweat from his face with his sleeve. He tapped the parchment in his hand as a troubling question came to mind.

"I just heard you hiss."

"Your ears are playing tricks on you."

DeMorley shook his head. "No, my hearing is very acute as a minstrel. I know what I heard."

The whisper did not reply or counter which made DeMorley even more curious.

"If Claire is a desert, and the Only is dead, then why murmur at the sight of this?"

He held the invitation high overhead.

"I don't owe you an explanation." The whisper's tone was no longer alluring but dark and foreboding.

DeMorley lowered the invitation and fingered the gold letters. The whisper groaned as if agitated by his motions. DeMorley sniffed the parchment, which made the whisper huff and cough.

"There is more to this invitation than you're telling me."

"Ignore it. It only offers death. I offer life, purpose and greatness."

"But if it is from a dead world and a dead king, then how can it offer anything, even death? All this is," he waved the invitation, "is a worthless parchment. But your reactions tell me otherwise."

"I did not come to discuss logic."

DeMorley ignored the subtle threat and pressed on with his reasoning. "Claire is at least worth exploring before I make any rash decision."

The whisper pressed close, and although it was invisible, DeMorley felt a dread and coldness shroud him. He backed away, but there was nowhere to hide or flee from the invisible threat.

"You are more cunning than I gave you credit for," the whisper spat. *"More cunning indeed. Very well, I will acknowledge that the impotent one lives, but it still does not render my question void: would you, or would you not, like revenge, greatness and glory?"*

"I...I...I suppose."

"Good. Then we are of a like mind. Now throw that thing away and follow me to Ebon. Join our glorious campaign."

DeMorley shivered as he pondered the offer that would give him everything he dreamed of, and yet, he could not shake off the mysteries surrounding the parchment and the King of Claire, nor the memories of the friends he betrayed.

As he fingered the parchment, memories of Newcomb and Lassiter popped into his mind like sunbeams cutting through dark clouds. Although he was not ready to take responsibility for his own mistakes, he was beginning to see life in a new light. Newcomb's selfless love for Lassiter, who was not his own blood, defied logic and explanation, while his sacrificial death was beyond the scope of what DeMorley defined - or knew - as love. The memories gripped him like talons of steel and his curiosity was piqued. Despite his fear of the Cauldron's whisper, he made his decision.

"No," he mumbled as he wagged his head and steeled himself for the whisper's attack. "I will never join you."

A violent wind sucked him up into the air. He screamed and flailed his limbs as he hovered amidst the tree branches, captured by the violent storm. With no warning, he was hurled to the ground. He struck with a loud thud and lost his grip on the parchment. The winds snatched it and DeMorley, dazed from the fall, watched it flit and dance across the leaves.

"No," he shouted as strength returned to him as well as a reason to live. "It's mine."

He lunged for the parchment but it escaped his capture.

"*Yours?*" the whisper taunted from the swirling zephyr. "*It bears another's name.*"

"But it's my only hope."

"*Do you really believe a traitor and a scoundrel like you would be welcome anywhere but Ebon?*"

"I have to believe."

"*Such childish assurance. Like a waif putting stock into bedtime tales. Let me give you something to believe in. Me!*"

The winds stirred up clouds of leaves and dirt that engulfed DeMorley. He gagged, coughed and covered his face with his forearm to ward off the slicing debris.

"*You are nothing. I am everything. Your future is filled with pain and darkness. I offer peace and purpose.*"

DeMorley shook his head and squinted through the cyclone to locate the parchment. "Not until I at least see for myself." He caught a glimpse of the invitation beyond the twirling wind and debris. With all his might, he dove through the storm for the white parchment.

"*Tisk, tisk, tisk.*" The wind jerked the invitation away from his fingers. "*You missed, missed, missed. Now feel this, this, this.*"

The drone's monotone pitch rose above the roar of the hurricane and dropped like a millstone on his prone body. DeMorley's strength weakened and feelings of despair consumed him. But as he imagined the possibilities the parchment offered, his will to live overpowered such debilitating emotions. He grit his teeth and pushed himself up off the ground.

"*No,*" he shouted in desperation more to himself than to the whisper. "I want to find out the truth about Claire for myself; once and for all."

"'*Blind eyes behold what was becomes no more.*'"

The cyclonic winds died and DeMorley lowered his arm.

The parchment danced atop the leaves as if daring him to catch it.

DeMorley reached for it but it hopped away. DeMorley stepped closer but the invitation darted like a rabbit further down the trail. Desperate, DeMorley charged it but the winds yanked it backward and away from his grip.

The whisper chortled.

"How long will you chase a dream? When will you embrace the dark days of your future, manufactured by your own craftiness and cunning?"

DeMorley dove for the white parchment, but just as his fingers closed in around it, the winds yanked it clear.

"I tire of this game of chase. It is time for you to bask in the mire of your misery, the conclusion of your fatal choice. May your death be as painful as your life was."

The winds dashed away and the parchment floated down to the leaves. DeMorley pounced on the invitation, afraid the lull was another trick, and drew it close. He was relieved that the wind was gone, but then gagged on a pungent aroma. Nauseated, he covered his nose and mouth and took in his surroundings. Large forms that looked like boulders were scattered about the woods.

The whisper snickered. *"Death begets death."*

DeMorley's eyes adjusted to the fading light and he recognized the shapes.

An army of gors surrounded him.

DeMorley tiptoed to his right, careful not crack a stick or rustle the leaves. As he took more cautious steps, he recalled Newcomb's demise and Draemel's tale about Paradin being the Gor King and leading an army of gors.

Could this be them?

Snap!

DeMorley glanced down at his boot. A twig - crushed by his heel - stuck up out of the leaves.

"Tisk, tisk, tisk," a voice challenged from the shades. "What's this, this this?"

DeMorley spun around to discover a man rising up from the shadowed ground. Although it was too dark to see who it was, his musically trained ears recognized Paradin's voice. Spooked, DeMorley backed up a step or two until he remembered the sleeping gors. Afraid he would step on one, he froze.

He sounds more ominous than I remember!

Paradin stepped out of the shadows and into a shaft of gray light. DeMorley gasped, shocked by his grotesque features.

He's sheared off his hair and there's a scar on his forehead that looks like a gor!

"So we meet again, do we," Paradin snarled. "I see you are in awe of my new look. Stunning, isn't it?" Paradin posed as if modeling before royalty.

DeMorley gulped down the bile rising from his gut and tried to wet his lips, but his tongue was too dry. Try as he might, he could not stop staring at Paradin's eyes. One swept independently this way and that while the other blinked like a bird's.

The wind shifted and the Gor King sniffed the air as he continued to showcase his appearance. "Ah, yes! I *do* remember your sweet, sweet scent of fear." He stopped clowning and glowered at DeMorley. "And you *should* be afraid, for I vowed vengeance when you and Draemel left me for dead."

"I didn't have a choice," DeMorley squeaked.

"You *always* have a choice."

DeMorley looked for an avenue of escape amongst the sleeping gors.

"Yes," the Gor King crooned. "You're surrounded."

DeMorley snapped his gaze backed to the Gor King.

"Don't look so surprised that I can read your mind. I'm not the same man you left to die like a dog." He puffed out his chest and raised his chin with pride. "I'm the Gor King, a storyteller for the Cauldron." A wicked grin coursed his face as he crept toward the quivering minstrel. "And as a teller of tales, I've glanced into your story. What a diseased half-wit you are."

The Gor King threw a hand toward the trees as if tossing aside trash. A puff of purplish light, clouded by swirling smoke, created a living scene from DeMorley's past. DeMorley's mouth dropped as he watched translucent images from his childhood.

"She never loved you, did she?" the Gor King hissed with another step.

DeMorley stared at the image of his mother. She was wrapped in the arms of a lover, oblivious to him sitting on the dirt floor.

Another flick of the wrist created a new vignette.

"Which one of these fine fellows is your daddy?"

Men's faces, pale and distorted in the lavender cloud, flashed past like pages of a book being flipped. With a brisk wave of his hand, the images flared and splintered into purple sparks that fell like snow to the ground.

"But the quandary I have now is this: do I rend you to bits with a tale, or use you for sport for my faithful gors?"

They locked stares. The Gor King's smirk fell and his twitching eyes widened with a decision. He charged DeMorley.

DeMorley, caught off guard by the attack, reacted. When the Gor King lunged, he swung his lute with all his might.

Crack!

The Bellini splintered into a thousand shards and the Gor King, who had underestimated DeMorley, fell dazed. The gors, awakened by the noise, stirred from their sleep.

DeMorley sprinted through the throng.

"Get him," the Gor King ordered his gors. "First blood to all!"

DeMorley, horrified at the prospect of being eaten alive, ran with wild abandon. Despite the fading light, he was able to navigate around trees and thickets and for a moment, thought he had escaped. His assumption was crushed by the gors terrifying roar followed by the sound of them crashing through the woods, hot on his trail. He increased his speed but in the darkening woods, his footing was often uncertain. Roots grabbed his boots. Branches slashed his face. Thorn bushes snagged his clothing.

He dared a glance back. Shadowed beasts loomed. Shocked at their closeness, he sprinted even faster but underestimated the terrain. He cleared a ridge at full speed and feared he had leapt off a cliff. Before he could scream, he crash-landed and tumbled head-over-heels down the hill like a rag doll. He bounced and rolled, moaning from the impacts, miraculously missing boulders and trees. When he rolled to a stop, he stole a look back uphill. Despite being dizzy, he spotted dark silhouettes racing over the top.

DeMorley pushed himself up and continued his mad dash down the grade. He slid and hopped and crashed through undergrowth with arms flailing. Above the ruckus he was making, he heard barks, grunts and cracking tree limbs made by the gors.

He glanced over his shoulder. *The steep hill…it's working in my favor. They can't run full speed and control their descent. I may be able to outrun them!*

He hurled himself off a small overhang and just as he was landing, heard a whisper.

"DeMorley!"

"Away," he shouted as he raced along, convinced he was dialoguing with the Cauldron. "I'm done talking with you."

"I call your name to offer you hope…life."

"Life," he fired as the sounds of the gor army became louder. "Have you seen what's chasing me?"

Another whisper entered his mind and he at once recognized Paradin's accent.

"You're not deserving of mercy," the Gor King chided. *"Your life is stained with deceit, theft and manipulation. The only hope you have is that my army will end your life quickly."*

The gor army emitted a unison bark to accent their master's last point.

DeMorley increased his speed, slipping and sometimes stumbling down the hill. Death loomed and he was at his wits end. He was desperate.

"Mercy," he cried to the new whisper. "Please, I beg you. Save me!"

The only answer he heard were the short, sharp barks of the gors.

The Gor King laughed within DeMorley's mind. *"Why should you be given mercy when you have never given such luxury to others?"*

DeMorley dodged a tree then leapt over another ledge. His legs were numb from exhaustion, his lungs burned for want of air. The only thing keeping him going was the thought of massive jaws crushing bone and teeth ripping flesh; *his* flesh.

Another ledge. A quick jump and a swift glance back. They were close enough to lunge. The end was near, and yet, he found the courage to call again, only this time he did with meekness.

"I'm a liar and a thief, and I deserve death. All I ask is that when I die, that you call my name with the same passion you did just moments ago."

The Gor King snickered. *"Asking the impotent one for respite and comfort? Pathetic. You can't even die like a man."*

An ominous tone, deep and low, slammed into DeMorley like a broad sword. As the drone from the Cauldron attacked, his body became lethargic, breathing became frantic and his descent more desperate. He tried to call out to the whisper, but the drone dulled his thoughts.

His paced slowed. He was lost.

"I'm the only one who can save you," the Gor King roared so his army could hear as well. "I am the king of life and death!"

A gor swiped at him and ripped off some of his tunic. He screamed in pain and fear. The gor swatted again and this time just missed his head.

DeMorley saw a flash of light.

Lightning?

He braved a glance up through the trees and caught a glimpse of a ghostly figure. A loud explosion in front of him made him look to investigate.

A dead tree splintered and toppled over. The whisper spoke within his mind.

"Lead them to the tree. Do not stop or look within the lair."

The minstrel, putting all his hope in an unfamiliar whisper, battled against the effects of the drone and headed for the fallen tree.

He cleared it and heard another explosion from behind.

He started to look but instead, heeded the whisper's warning and focused on his downhill race.

Gors shrieked in pain and the drone's power weakened.

Something is attacking the gors, but what…or who?

He dismissed the horrific cries and the high-pitched cries he assumed came from whatever was fighting the gors.

DeMorley spotted a stream at the base of the hill. Beyond it was a clearing.

"You can't escape," the Gor King taunted as he and his army continued their attack. "Death begets death!"

As if to retaliate to the Gor King's threat, another flash of lightning lit the sky followed by another explosion. High-pitched barks echoed from behind him followed by gors' pain-filled screams.

"Pitiful," the Gor King exclaimed. "Two swarms of fea dracas can't destroy us."

"*Ignore him,*" the whisper encouraged. "*Run to the meadow.*"

"Yes, DeMorley, race to the meadow." the Gor King chastised. "Let my gors have the open plain in which to capture and devour you."

"*He's right,*" DeMorley worried. "*I can't outrun them in the open.*"

"*True,*" the whisper replied.

"*Is this the only way?*"

"*Yes.*"

Despite his doubts and fears, DeMorley focused his remaining strength on reaching the meadow. He jumped over the stream and pushed himself up the small embankment to the open field.

A giant oak stood in the middle.

"*Run to the tree,*" the whisper ordered.

The gor army exploded into the clearing and gained ground.

"Fool," the Gor King shouted. "The Only has deceived you as he does *all* who listen."

DeMorley propelled himself onward. Arms pumped, legs sliced thick grasses and yet despite his heroic measures, the snorts and yelps grew louder. They were upon him.

"*First blood,*" the Gor King barked.

DeMorley was struck from behind and in an instant, all went black.

DeMorley blinked open his eyes like one awakening from a nightmare: disoriented yet desperate to embrace reality. His head hung on his chest - too weak to lift - and he stared at the ground between his spread legs. Shafts of sunlight dotted the matted grass around his shins.

Daylight...

Despite this revelation, he was at a loss as to where he was or how he got there.

Feeling returned to his body and he felt something against his back. It was hard and didn't budge. His mind continued to clear and he remembered a snippet from his ordeal.

The meadow...I must be leaning against the tree. But why?

Something was digging into his palm. He opened his clinched fist to discover the splintered neck of his Bellini. He fingered it, and as his thoughts sharpened, he remembered smashing the lute on the head of the Gor King, the chase and the whisper.

But where are they now?

Steeling himself for the worst, he lifted his throbbing head. Instead of finding the Gor King, he discovered a broadsword tip poised near his chin.

In his haggard state, he took in the sword with an unusual calmness, as if discovering a weapon near his head was commonplace. He noted that it had an unusual hue - like that of the moon - and as his eyes wandered up the blade, he made an even more startling discovery: the sword's master also glowed and his face burned like fire. Horrified, DeMorley pressed back against the tree trunk.

"I saw you in the twilight, high above the trees," DeMorley noted through parched lips. "Are you the King of Claire?"

Manno Vox's face of shifting lights - blues, reds, greens, yellows - remained fixated on the minstrel.

DeMorley glanced about the meadow for any sign of the Gor King and his army. Plumes of smoke snaked skyward from carcasses he assumed were dead gors. Jutting out of them were crystal bolts the size of arrows with bright orange feathers.

"You destroyed them all," DeMorley asked as his foggy head cleared all the more.

Manno Vox did not answer. He simply cocked his head to the side and studied the man sitting before him.

"What is to become of me?"

The blade's tip pressed into his neck. DeMorley swallowed hard and froze.

"Death," Manno Vox answered, his voice reverberating all about the meadow.

DeMorley blinked his eyes like a frightened bird. In the past when he encountered a situation like this, he would resort to his weapons of choice: his cunning and manipulation. This time, he spoke with candor and meekness. "I've always survived whatever life threw at me by shifting words to mean this or that; a promise derived as a lie or a lie promised as the truth. No more."

He paused to reflect on the ordeal. "Maybe facing my own mortality has shown me how wrong I've been." The memory of Lassiter sitting by the fire, jabbing the coals in anger, cut DeMorley to the quick. "I suppose it really doesn't matter the reason why. What matters is this: I tire of such games, so do with me as you wish, my avenger from the sky."

DeMorley closed his eyes in anticipation of being beheaded, but when nothing happened, he braved a peek.

Manno Vox spoke. "Death stands at your threshold and requires only one answer from you: Do you possess an invitation?"

"Yes."

"Is it yours?"

DeMorley's answer sat precariously upon his tongue. How quick the lie returned. Had he not just claimed to no longer want to live in such a manner? Yet, here he was, contemplating how to manipulate the situation, a situation he could not undo; a fate he could not reverse. He steeled himself and offered the truth. "No."

DeMorley took in the warrior's face in an effort to learn what he would do next. *His face is glowing brighter, like a fire stoked to greater flame. But is it anger, wrath or something entirely different?*

As if reading his thoughts, Manno Vox declared, "DeMorley, the minstrel of lies and deceit must die. Death begets life!"

DeMorley flinched just as the sword shifted from his throat and pierced his heart. He gasped, but not for air, for his lungs felt as if they would explode they were so full. He moaned, but not out of pain, for the blade's tip radiated warmth like a winter's fire throughout his cold body. He opened his mouth to talk, but could not formulate one word to express all the new thoughts, hopes and ideas swimming in his mind.

He closed his eyes, not to slip beyond the land of the living, but to experience all that was happening within him - a whisper, a song sung by many men and women, and a word that flitted within his heart like so many sparks from a bonfire.

Delight.

Manno Vox yanked the blade out, sheathed it and marched toward his fiery steed. DeMorley examined the wound.

Bloodless. And there's already a purple scar.

Dumbfounded, he tried to find his legs and rise from the ground. "I don't understand," he stammered as he rose. "You said I was to die."

"Death waits for you every morning. Touch your scar to remind you of this moment so you can step beyond your failures. Let the stench of your past propel you into the sweet aroma of your future."

"My...future?" He fell back against the tree; his head was spinning and he felt woozy.

"Stay here. Wait for the one whom you will serve."

"Wait? Serve? There is so much I don't understand! Where's the Gor King? Will they return?"

"Yes, but not today."

"Very well. I can wait, but who am I waiting for?" He winced as the back of his head throbbed from the gor's blow.

"You will soon find out," he boomed as he gathered in his steed's reins.

Manno Vox was about to spur his stallion to flight when DeMorley staggered forward. "Wait! Please don't go. At least answer me the question that troubles me most."

Manno Vox turned his surreal face toward the minstrel. DeMorley seized the opportunity and spoke. "Why are you giving me a second chance?"

"Does it matter?"

"Yes, it matters. I don't deserve it. I'm a scoundrel, a liar and a thief. Your mercy troubles me."

"And may you forever be troubled by such truth. Then, and only then, will you be able to abandon your past and discover your future."

With that, Manno Vox zipped up into the sky like a sunbeam retracing its descent.

DeMorley shielded his eyes and followed his rapid flight. Conflicting thoughts, emotions and desires flooded him, but towering above them all was a hunger to begin anew, to right what he had done wrong, and to live as a new man.

Chapter 24

Meadow of Death

As they soared toward the Isle of Rhythe, Ela Claire shook her braid free to the wind and turned her face to the sun. Basking in its warmth, she daydreamed about her former life in Hetherlinn. The memories were like distant dreams, the tenor of once familiar voices - like those of her parents - were but a buzz or not even recognizable. So much had transpired in her life that her childhood felt like it should belong to someone else.

Remembering she was on a mission of war and not a sightseeing flight, she paused to check on her surroundings. Satisfied they were still safe, she closed her eyes and resumed her sunbathing.

A distant explosion, like thunder, startled her out of her lull.

She sat up and studied the cloudless sky.

"Lightning," she asked.

"No. Lightning doesn't look like that."

She followed Previn's line of sight. "It's a streak, not a flash, and it's soaring up to the clouds..."

"Just like..."

"Manno Vox!" they chimed in unison.

At that very instant, the whisper from Claire spoke.

"Go to the meadow and rescue DeMorley."

"What meadow," Ela Claire asked, "and who is DeMorley?"

But the whisper was gone.

"Look," Previn hailed, eyes riveted on plumes of black smoke on the distant horizon. "I detect the scent of burning gors and that of a man. Perhaps DeMorley is this person."

"But is he alive or charred like the beasts?"

"I don't know."

Previn sped toward the battleground. They searched the woods for their enemy or refugees needing their help, but found no one. Satisfied the area was safe, Previn tucked his wings and dove for the clearing. Swooping over the meadow, they surveyed the battle scene.

"There," she pointed to the lone oak. "Someone's leaning against the tree."

Previn banked and spotted him. "If this is DeMorley, there is deceit oozing from his pores. Be on your guard."

The man spotted them and cowered behind the trunk.

"Against him?" She snickered and peered through the tree's foliage for a better look. "He's skinny, weaponless and is hiding from us. He's anything but a threat."

"True," Previn glided down for a landing, "but you of all people should know that appearances can be deceptive."

"I know," Ela Claire replied as she slid off his back. "I'm a storyteller. If he tries something it'll be the last thing he does."

She marched toward the tree. Previn hopped along after her.

"Stop right there," DeMorley challenged from his hiding place.

Ela Claire and Previn complied, not out of fear of being attacked by the wiry man, but because they sensed he was terrified of them.

"We're not here to harm you," Ela Claire offered with a smile.

DeMorley poked his head around the trunk for a better look. "Are you the Only?"

Ela Claire's brow furrowed. "Are you trying to be funny?"

"No, I'm very serious." DeMorley glanced over his shoulder as if expecting an ambush and then eyed the smoking gor bodies. He clung to the bark with white knuckles.

Ela Claire noted his nervousness and spoke in a calm voice to help him relax. "The Only is a king and since I'm a girl..."

"Oh," DeMorley interrupted as his gaze jumped from the corpses to her face. "So, who are you?"

"The real question," Previn asked, "Is who are you?"

DeMorley's eyes bulged. "You're huge - *and* you talk!"

"Naturally. I'm from Claire, so why is this..."

"You're from Claire?"

Previn blinked his eyes in frustration. "That's what I just said, isn't it?"

Ela Claire, although inexperienced as a storyteller, was skilled enough to discover another's identity. She pressed her thoughts toward DeMorley and was in and out of his mind before he blinked.

"He's DeMorley," she announced to Previn.

"He's not what we were expecting, is he?"

She giggled.

DeMorley stepped closer. "How'd you know my name?"

She ignored his question and pressed him for more answers. "Judging by the crystal bolts sticking out of the gors," she jerked a thumb toward a carcass, "you've met Manno Vox."

"Who?"

"Manno Vox," Previn snapped, perturbed not only by DeMorley's lack of insight but his scent that smelled of trickery. "The great warrior whose face looked like a wintery sky on fire and who *obviously* saved your life." He rustled his wings and flipped his head in the direction of the smoldering beasts.

"So that's his name."

"What did he say to you?" Ela Claire pressed.

"It all happened so fast. The gors. Their king."

"You met the Gor King," she inquired with a step closer.

DeMorley, still spooked by her magical abilities to discover his name, retreated a step.

Ela Claire stopped and faced Previn. "Remember the story I shared with you, the one I found in Il-Lilliad's cave?"

"Yes," he answered before reciting the stanzas from memory.

> *Mothers, guard babes; fathers, draw steel,*
> *Thunder approaches, soon blood on the fields.*
> *Tempest of war, so black and so vile,*
> *Spreads o'er Allsbruth; lament suckling child.*

> *Orphaned stories, treasures from Claire,*
> *Like buried embers, burst forth and flare.*
> *Hear not a whisper, sweet lark on the wing?*
> *Tales shall crush steel when gors have a king.*

She looked back at the charred gor remains. "Why would a story from Claire foretell of a Gor King that is not noble and good?"

"But the tale does not say anything about his character," Previn countered. "Besides, you forgot the last stanza."

> *Wisps of white, forever snow doth swirl,*
> *Rays of crimson protect pallid girl,*
> *Waltz of Claire lilting like lace,*
> *Breathe delight o'er sweet child's face.*

> *What was is now past, what loss no more,*
> *As phantom rides winds that mourn for the gor.*
> *Tulips shall bloom despite ice so deep,*
> *Fair daughter do dance, for we no longer weep.*

"I didn't forget," she stammered. "I left it off because that segment doesn't make any sense, nor does it help illuminate the prior section. Besides, we're all witnesses to this Gor King's evil. From his actions we can deduce his character."

She spun to face DeMorley. "So what happened next?"

"The Gor King chased me and then your friend - what was his name?"

"Manno Vox."

"Yes, well I suppose he rescued me."

"You *suppose*," Previn asked, as he continued to sniff and examine DeMorley's true nature.

"Yes, well you see, I was struck in the head." He turned to show them the welt rising through his hair. "I passed out, so I'm not sure what all happened. When I awoke, this is what I found." He gestured at the dead gors.

"So if the Gor King is still on the loose, why were you resting beneath this tree?"

"Manno Vox told me to wait."

"Wait? For what?"

"He said someone would be coming and I was to serve them. Since you are here," he took in her perplexed expression, "I'm assuming you're whom I'm to serve."

"Me?" Ela Claire chuckled as she looked to Previn for insight. He merely fluttered his wings. She shook her head and looked into DeMorley's eyes. "With all due respect, I'm not sure how. You're obviously not a warrior, and since you thought I might be the Only, you're *definitely* not a storyteller."

"Correct. I'm a minstrel."

Ela Claire's smile fell as her mouth went agape. "A...minstrel?" Brow furrowed. "Then I'm confused all the more. We were instructed to rescue you, that was all."

Previn pressed his head close to DeMorley's. "That explains your scent. Minstrels are men of cunning and deceit. Your pores ooze with such stench!"

DeMorley did not blink an eye or become flustered. Instead of countering with a manipulative argument, he swallowed and admitted the truth. "You're correct. I'm a liar and a cheat, but something has happened to me that I can't explain."

Loosening his tunic, he showed them his scar.

Ela Claire gasped and placed her hand over her mouth. "A tulip!" Her thoughts flashed back to the time Romlin was pierced by Manno Vox and received a similar scar.

DeMorley gave the scar a quick glance. "Huh. You're right, I suppose it does resemble a tulip."

"And we are to believe that Manno Vox gave you such a wound," Previn fired, still not convinced DeMorley was telling the truth.

DeMorley met Previn's piercing eyes. "*Yes.*" His voice was impassioned. "Does any of this make sense to you? It still boggles my mind." He shook his head and once more took in the dead gors. "I'm a traitor. I don't deserve mercy. I should be dead, but I'm not, and I need to know why. And *this*," he gestured at the scar, "is filling my head with thoughts that, well to be honest, I've never had before."

Previn moved closer which made DeMorley cower.

"Don't worry," Previn offered, "I'm not going to hurt you."

DeMorley relaxed and Previn arched his head down and sniffed DeMorley. "Amazing," he said as he backed away and looked into Ela Claire's face clouded with confusion. "Amidst his deceit and lies is the scent of a flower. Although faint and new, nonetheless, it's there."

"Flower?" DeMorley scrunched his face up in confusion and sniffed his arm. "I don't smell a..."

"Were you given a new name," Ela Claire interrupted.

DeMorley dropped his arm and shook his head. "A new name? A flower?" His mind flooded with questions, theories and conjectures. "I'm afraid you really have me confused now. All he told me was that I was to serve someone and my guess is it's you."

"I don't mean to insult you," she said as she studied his features, "but as a storyteller, I'm perplexed as to how you're to help me."

DeMorley's eyes widened. "You're a storyteller," he half-whispered with a step back from her. And then to himself: "Why is it that storytellers always seem to cross my path?"

"You've met another storyteller," Ela Claire asked as she flashed a bamboozled look to Previn.

DeMorley nodded. "His name was Newcomb. He was the mentor to Lassiter, the future king of Allsbruth. I met them," he eyed Ela Claire, and knowing she could read his story, opted to tell the truth. "No, I actually manipulated my way into their lives."

Previn hopped closer. "Your tale reeks of lies! There was only one storyteller that survived the March of Reeds, and his name was Il-Lilliad, and the royal lineage of King Culdean was severed by the Cauldron."

"Look," DeMorley countered with hands raised as if to press them back. "I'm not lying." He focused on Ela Claire. "Go ahead. Read my story. You'll find everything I've told you is the truth."

Ela Claire flashed a quick look to Previn for counsel. *"You know I'm new to this."*

"True, but we need to know if he's telling the truth. Focus on what we practiced during our flight."

Ela Claire turned her attention back to DeMorley. "I'll need your help."

"Anything."

"Since I don't know what Newcomb and Lassiter look like, I need you to close your eyes and focus on them. Can you do that for me?"

DeMorley bit his lower lip and nodded. Eyelids closed.

Ela Claire drew in a deep breath to calm her nerves and reflected on her lesson with Previn just days ago.

"Although I am not a storyteller," Previn instructed, "I nonetheless served Il-Lilliad for many a summer as his rusk and listened to his experiences of reading another's story.

"First, you must let go of all prejudice or suspicion you may hold pertaining to the person and yield your heart and mind to the Only's whisper. What a person projects to others in either his personality or his appearance may not be their genuine story. Il-Lilliad said he was always surprised at what he encountered: the shrewd man could be found gullible; the fool could be in possession of great wisdom; the pious follower of the Only reeking of doubt, lust and greed.

"Second, you must contemplate on the stories of Claire as you walk their inner sanctum, for such a journey is perilous. Even in the most innocent you will find morose streams of thought that could stifle your process like muck, or you could round a corner only to step into a current of ambition that, like roaring rapids, could sweep you away to your doom. And never, *never* uncover a dark thought! They will glow like a black pearl and woo you near only to snag you like a wildeberry bur. Leave them be, for deep at their core burns the Dark Flame from the Cauldron.

"Lastly, you must never plant a tale or even the tiniest of words from a Clairian rhyme into their story. As you know from your readings, this is a breach of your vow as a storyteller and is viewed as coercion by the Only. A tale of Claire may only be shared in the outer world and it is the whisper that wills it to do its bidding, not you."

Ela Claire focused back on the job at hand: reading DeMorley's tale. She let her gaze run up and down the minstrel, but try as she might, she found that to free her mind of any preconceived notion of who he was was next to impossible.

I'll have to risk it. We need to know.

She bit her lower lip to help her focus and pressed her thoughts close to his private world. Here, she waited. She had only done this sort of thing once before and her subject was Previn. Her jump into his thoughts was easy and the journey within as sweet as walking a budded garden.

But DeMorley had a seedy past and was a complete stranger.

She steeled herself for what secrets he had tucked inside his veiled world, and with a Clairian story clutched in her thoughts like a sword, leapt into his story.

She was greeted by darkness, shocked to see row upon row of what looked like abnormally large black pearls. She had assumed Previn's description of the dark thoughts had simply been poetic, but seeing the orbs glow and pulse with black light made her squeamish. She recited the Clairian tale to herself and felt her resolve strengthen.

As she tiptoed through the dark maze, she found herself drawn to one pearl in particular, and became curious and even sympathetic to DeMorley's story. She leaned close for a better look when a woman's tormented face, trapped behind the jewel's shiny surface, pressed against the barrier and stared at her with feral eyes. Spooked and remembering Previn's warning, she backed away and pulled the Clairian story around her like armor.

Leaving the field of dark secrets, she climbed a knoll that concealed a glow. At the top, she discovered the light's source: a miniscule radiance pulsed at ground level like a star. But what made her gasp in awe and fear was the warrior that guarded it. He was silver with two sets of wings and leaned on a double-handed red sword whose tip was buried beside the white glow.

Examine the light, the whisper instructed her.

Shielding her eyes for a better look, and squinting as if looking into the sun, she made out the faint outline of a flower.

A tulip, she concluded.

In that moment, she realized that his story about Manno Vox and the whisper from Claire was true, which made her feel more comfortable about their new alliance.

But what about Newcomb and Lassiter?

She left the knoll and rounded another portion of his story only to find herself in a sea of people pushing and shoving as if going to a fair. Their pace was frantic, chaotic, and although their mouths were moving in dialogue she didn't hear a thing.

She searched the crowd, hoping that with DeMorley focusing on Newcomb and Lassiter, she would be given some sort of sign as to their identity.

But what will that be?

She was about to give up when she spotted a faint flame hovering over the mob. Pushing her way through the crowd, she came face to face with a man with snow-white hair walking beside a handsome young man. Clutched in the boy's hands was an invitation, the gold letters pulsing with light, and even in the pushing and pulling of the crowd, could make out the inscription: *Lassiter.*

Excited to not only learn the truth but to successfully complete her first storytelling feat, she pushed off the bottom of his experiences and exploded from DeMorley's private world like a diver from a deep pool.

Back in reality, she beamed Previn a smile. "He's telling the truth."

"Then we have another dilemma," Previn replied. "If Newcomb was indeed killed by the Gor King, then the Martyr's Moon was his portent and not Il-Lilliad's."

Ela Claire's face lightened with the news. "Then that means Il-Lilliad's alive!"

"Yes, but Newcomb, whose identity was kept secret from even us, is not."

Ela Claire closed her eyes and gave a solemn nod. "You're right. I didn't mean any disrespect."

She turned her attention to DeMorley. "Did anything else happen between you and Manno Vox?"

"Nothing of significance."

"The smallest of details may help unravel this mystery."

"He did ask if I carried an invitation."

Ela Claire's interest was piqued all the more. "And do you?"

"Yes, but I stole it."

"You stole an invitation," Previn asked in a hushed voice.

DeMorley nodded. "It's a long story, one that I'm not proud of. I told Manno Vox as much when he was here."

"May I see it," Ela Claire asked with an outstretched hand.

"Sure." DeMorley fished it from his inside pocket and handed her the parchment. "It doesn't bear my name."

Ela Claire read the golden letters over and over, as if to convince herself the Cauldron was not bewitching her eyes. She gave Previn a somber nod and turned to address the minstrel. "But it does, see?"

She held it up for him to inspect. His mouth dropped open. Although he was not an educated man, he knew how to read and write his name.

"When did *that* happen?" He snatched it back and stared, mesmerized by the gold letters glittering on the parchment. "Before the attack, it had another's name, not *mine!*"

"This changes everything," she said to Previn. He nodded.

"What? What does it change?" DeMorley asked as he flipped the invitation over to examine it from all angles.

"It seems you're to join us to the Isle of Rhythe."

DeMorley stared at them both. "The Isle of *Wrath?*"

"No, the Isle of Rhythe. We're to rescue great treasure and return it to Claire."

"Did you say…great treasure?"

"Yes."

"Then Newcomb's stories are true," he half-whispered in awe.

"And we are to *return* it to Claire. Did you hear that part, too?"

DeMorley fingered the golden letters of his invitation. "But I've done nothing to warrant such honors." He tossed a glance at Ela Claire. "I'm sure you saw that much in my story."

She thought about the field of black pearls and answered with a subtle nod.

"And without my lute," he sighed as he retrieved the piece from his pocket, "I can't even offer my skills as a minstrel."

Previn eyed the shattered fingerboard, and catching a dormant scent of the instrument maker as well as the wood's distinct aroma, blinked in amazement. "That isn't just a lute. *That* is a Bellini."

"Was," DeMorley corrected as he tossed the broken neck up and down. "I smashed it over the head of the Gor King."

Ela Claire burst out laughing.

"What's so funny," DeMorley asked as he clutched the Bellini.

"Forgive me," she answered with a hand to her mouth to conceal her smile. "But it's hard for me to picture you getting close to the Gor King and then slamming him over the head…with a lute!"

"A Bellini," Previn corrected, impressed DeMorley possessed such a rare instrument.

"Well, it wasn't because I'm brave. It was simply survival instincts."

"There's more to your story than even what I read," she said, and then to Previn: "Are you capable of carrying both of us to Rhythe?"

He ruffled his feathers. "He's not *that* big of a man."

DeMorley stared at both the invitation and the Bellini. "But how am I to help? This is worthless," he held up the splintered neck, "and this was stolen."

"I know, but for reasons neither of us can explain, the invitation was altered and now bears your name. It's a gift, one which you don't deserve. How your story unfurls from this day forth will be interesting indeed."

She mounted Previn's back and offered DeMorley her hand. He pocketed the Bellini and invitation before taking her hand.

"Better hold on tight," she instructed as he climbed up behind her. "Previn is not one for slow ascents and descents."

He wrapped an arm around her waist and with his free hand gripped a handful of feathers. Previn beat his wings, and true to Ela Claire's warning, shot up into the air.

As they circled the meadow, and with the putrid odor of dead gors heavy on the wind, DeMorley stared down at the hill where his ordeal began. Although the canopy blocked his view, he knew that somewhere on the ground lay the splintered remains of his Bellini. He drew in a deep breath, noting that like the smashed lute, his former life was shattered, destroyed, vanquished. Before him was a new pathway, one he had not reasoned or even dreamed possible. To start anew! But would he be able to rise to such high expectations? Would he shake free of his old habits and manners? He shuddered at the thought, overwhelmed at his new mission, and turned his face into the wind.

Chapter 25

A Great Adventure

Phinnton shut his cottage door, careful not to make a sound. The sun would be rising soon and the last thing he needed was to alert anyone to his mission, especially his father.

A thick fog shrouded Min Brock, which Phinnton took as a good omen, and the cool air put a spring in his already energized step. He slipped from shadow to shadow like a cat, making sure no one was watching or following.

His heart raced with the excitement of being sneaky as well as the thought of executing his quest. Up ahead, barely noticeable in the gray light, was his destination.

The armory.

When he reached the door, he stole a look up at the keep's walkway. The fog shrouded the guards and had they not been lumbering to and fro, they would have been unnoticeable. Based upon their relaxed pace, the fog hid him from their eyes as well.

Phinnton breathed a sigh of relief and turned his attention to the old door hinges. He knew they would squeak when opened, alerting guards to his whereabouts, but he had a plan.

He fished out a wad of cloth from his pocket and unfolded it to retrieve a hunk of pig fat. He rubbed the hinges with the greasy meat and even spit on them for added measure. He tossed the fat away and wiped his slippery fingers on his breeches. He grabbed the door handle and gave one last look up at the shadowed guards.

Hope this works.

The door opened without a noise. Excited his mission was going as planned, he slid inside the dark room and shut the door. Despite the room being as black as a moonless night, he was not frightened or disoriented. As Linwith's page, he knew every nuance and angle of the room and in preparation for his mission, had even practiced walking it during daylight with eyes closed.

With confidence soaring, he sucked in a breath and walked forward ten steps, as rehearsed, and stopped. He could feel the edge of the table pressing into his thigh. He smiled. His plan was going better than he had expected. Although he could not see the table's contents, he knew that sitting in the middle was the stand holding Linwith's saddle. As he had practiced many a time prior with eyes shut, Phinnton leaned out over the table with his fingers extended. The saddle's smooth leather was cold to the touch. Although he had expected as much, he jerked his hands free as the gravity of his actions smacked hard against his resolve.

Perhaps I should ask Linwith first. Maybe I should retreat before my curiosity gets me in trouble.

But he could no more restrain his inquisitiveness than the River Arrgient could alter its course.

Within his mind, he imagined the worms poised like statues upon their respective turrets, asleep but with senses alert. This scene dissolved to the memory of the day Linwith ushered him into the armory to discuss the history and traits of the Worms of Bal-Malin.

"Phinnton, the worms, like people, have habits and even personality traits that you'll notice as you spend more and more time with them."

Phinnton followed Linwith's gaze out the window to the keep's eastern turrets. Perched on top and almost invisible in the fog, were the amber and silver worms.

Linwith continued his lesson. "They've been teaching me their history and I'm amazed at how unique and special they are. Did you know that their mother, some one thousand summers ago, laid seven eggs near their armory's knoll, and that it was the creatures of Bal-Malin - insect-sized wonders - that guarded them until they hatched?"

Phinnton shook his head and strained his neck to try and see the other turrets. "What color were they?"

"The creatures of Bal-Malin?"

"No, the eggs."

"Guess."

Phinnton scrunched his lips together as he continued to try and catch a glimpse of the other worms, which from his angle was an impossible task. "The same color as their tale."

"No, guess again."

"White."

"Nope."

Phinnton, who was now more interested in the answer than in seeing the other worms, turned his attention to Linwith and shrugged.

"Black. And they glowed like polished armor, but the most unique feature were miniscule veins of fire that encircled each egg. They pulsed as if someone blew on them or the wind was stirring them to life."

Phinnton's eyes lit up. "Fires! Just like their eyes."

Linwith nodded. "Once the mother had departed, the creatures of Bal-Malin carried each egg to one of the white oaks and nestled it in the nook of a high branch, guarding it day and night.”

“Where did their mother go?”

Linwith was stumped by the question and furrowed his brow. “Well, now that you mention it, I don’t know; I never bothered to ask, but that’s indeed a good question; a good question indeed.”

Before continuing his lesson, Linwith made a mental note to ask the worms about their mother’s whereabouts.

“As I reflected on my first trip to their island, I realized that at the time, I didn’t notice how many oaks there were. Care to guess?”

“Seven,” Phinnton blurted with confidence.

Linwith smiled and patted the boy’s shoulder to confirm his answer.

“When the time came for the worms to hatch, the eggs became hot and the fire-veins burned bright orange. The worms tossed and turned, as if awakening from a dream, and pushed against the shell that now had a rubbery consistency. Had I been present, I’m sure I would have seen a snout or a wing push the egg outward. But the most notable change would have been the eggs new color. It would have matched the hue of...”

“Their tales,” Phinnton eagerly interrupted.

Linwith again smiled and gave an affirming nod. “And the first to split open its stretchy shell was the sapphire worm.”

“The Worm King,” Linwith cooed as he imagined the colossus perched atop the Great Hall’s turret. “So he’s the first-born; the oldest.”

“Correct. Next was pearl followed simultaneously by ruby and emerald. Mandarin and gold came soon after, and the last to emerge was...”

“Amber, the baby.”

“Now that I’ve spent considerable time with them, I’ve learned their subtle personalities as well as their names.”

Phinnton’s eyes widened with intrigue. “They have *names?*”

“Yes, but you will never call them by such titles. In fact, I don’t myself. These are names they use only when conversing as brothers.

“But the point I’m trying to make is that each worm is unique. For example, take the emerald and ruby worms. When not perched on their respective turrets, they hover near the children whenever they play games. I’ve concluded that the reasoning behind this behavior is that since their gifts bring destruction and are often only used in combat situations, the children renew their resolve to protect and serve those that were weaker. As I’m sure you know, at first, the children were frightened to see them so close, but overtime they’ve learned to trust the beasts and even enjoy their close proximity.

“Pearl has an insatiable appetite and will take extra dives into the Gilden Sea to scoop up fish. Next time we venture to the sea, watch and see for yourself. I have to scold him like a wayward calf and summon him back into rank. He's quieter than his brothers, due in part to his strategy of not giving away his position when invisible, but he's also shy, if such a human attribute can be associated with so formidable a beast.

"Gold and mandarin possess a sense of humor and often play practical jokes - a head push here, a verbal tease there - that I've equated with efforts to relieve the weighty responsibility of their gifts. They are jokesters and once they even tricked me."

Phinnton smiled at the thought of Linwith, the powerful Worm Master, being the subject of a joke. "What happened?"

"Well, they summoned me in the silent tongue; urgency was in their call. I raced around the corner and stepped into a hay-covered hole filled with worm dung."

Phinnton laughed.

"It wasn't funny," Linwith countered. "It took all day to clean off my boots!"

Phinnton did everything he could to stop laughing, but he couldn't get the image of Linwith standing in dung out of his mind. "Did they laugh at you?"

"Like you're doing right now?" Linwith smirked. "Worms can't laugh, but they did bark quite a bit, which I suppose is how they laugh."

"Thanks for the warning," Phinnton said between chuckles. "I'll be sure to watch out for dung holes."

"I'm glad you find my misfortune comforting." He rustled Phinnton's hair before continuing.

"Last but not least is the sapphire worm. As you've probably noticed, his mood is always serious. This is in part because he's the older brother as well as the fact that he's the Worm King, a title that bears more weight than his brothers' titles. If you watch him closely, you'll see his eyes flare whenever he's watching their antics. He lets them have their fun although he has confided to me that such tolerance on his part is difficult to endure. And when he feels they've strayed too far from the decorum of being the Worms of Bal-Malin, his tale glows and he reprimands them in the silent tongue. It should also be no surprise that he spends a lot of time with me because of his role as the Worm King and because we're both the oldest in our respective families.

Linwith gave a sigh. "And then there's the amber worm..."

"He shrinks."

"Yes, and he reminds me a lot of you."

Phinnton cocked his head to the side.

Linwith took in the page's gaze. "He's inquisitive."

Phinnton, who did not understand the word's meaning, shrugged.

"You know, curious, probing. *Nosy*."

Phinnton smiled and took the jab as a subtle compliment.

"In the early days, I was doing everything possible to accelerate my education with the worms. So I experimented with the amber and had him shrink to the size of a small bird."

Phinnton's eyes popped as he tried to imagine such a physical transformation.

"But," Linwith added with a finger in the air, "I did so within the armory to avoid curious eyes." He shook his head. "*That* was a mistake."

"Why?"

"Well, that's when I learned how *nosy* he was," Linwith answered with a playful finger jab into Phinnton's shoulder. "He flitted off my shoulder and perched on the saddle stand. Spying something else of interest, he sprung off and sent the stand toppling. He landed with talons wide and ripped a hole in one of my tunics. But did this stop him? No! He tried to land on a pewter mug only to spill wine everywhere. He was worse than a cat! I honestly don't see much use for him."

Phinnton left the memory behind and instead, pictured the eastern wall's turret, the one closest to the Addoli Ridge, where the amber worm awaited first light. Maybe Linwith did not see much use for the amber worm, but Phinnton knew exactly how his gifting could serve his secret mission.

"*Are you ready for our great adventure?*" Phinnton whispered toward the amber worm, knowing full well he could not hear him. "*We're both so similar: full of gifts that no one can place a value upon. It's as if we're brothers.*"

Phinnton opened his eyes. The room was no longer black but dark gray, a signal that dawn was nearing. Rising up before him was the saddle horn. Even in the gloom, the jewels sparkled.

"I've never practiced this part of the plan. I sure hope it works."

He bit on his tongue as he lowered his thumb to the amber crystal. "I must not touch any of the other jewels. Your brothers must not know of our journey." When his flesh touched the jewel's cool surface, he felt a stirring within his mind.

"*Wake up,*" he ordered the worm. "*We must make haste!*"

Phinnton magically entered the worm's thoughts, and when the colossus opened his eyes, Phinnton could see everything the worm saw despite the fact that he was in the armory.

He gasped with awe at the view from high atop the turret. As the worm arched his neck upward and then downward toward the armory, Phinnton's stomach did cartwheels and he became giddy as he stared at the armory from the worm's perspective. He giggled.

The worm spoke into Phinnton's mind. *"So you are going to pursue this quest that you shared with me days before?"*

"Yes."

"May I presume that Linwith has given you permission, and Bruun, your father, has also blessed us?"

Phinnton hesitated. He hated to lie to the worm, but it was the only way to accomplish his mission. *"Yes, and he has granted me permission to exercise your gift."*

"So be it."

The amber worm extended his wings and glided off the tower. As Phinnton experienced the flight through the worm's vision, he became so excited that he almost lifted his thumb off the jewel. He was amazed to feel the cold wind whistling past and his tummy flipped when the worm banked hard to his right. When the amber worm landed just outside the armory, Phinnton even felt the coolness of the dirt as the worm's talons dug into the ground.

Phinnton lifted his thumb from the gem and the vision ended. Excited by the prospect of their quest, as well as the fact that the sun would soon be rising and reveal their secret flight, Phinnton dashed to another table. He groped amongst the items strewn on the tabletop until he felt the familiar smooth leather. His heart jumped as he recalled the moment Linwith surprised him with the gift.

"Keep your hands over your eyes," Linwith ordered as he led Phinnton toward the armory.

"What is it," Phinnton asked as peeked between his fingers.

"No looking," Linwith scolded with a smile. "You'll find out soon enough."

Phinnton moaned and squeezed his fingers tight to block the view. Linwith led him through a doorway and stopped in front of a table.

"Open your eyes."

Phinnton dropped his hands and gasped in wonder. Resting atop a wooden stand was a saddle, helmet and bridle.

"What do you think," Linwith asked, equally excited to present the presents to his page. "I had the craftsmen of Min Brock fashion replicas of mine."

"These…are for me," Phinnton asked, shocked not only to receive such gifts, but that Linwith had taken the time to have them crafted for him.

"Yes, just for you." Linwith lifted the saddle off the stand. "It's large enough for you to ride the amber worm's back, but small and light enough for you to carry yourself. Here, see for yourself."

He dropped the saddle into the boy's open arms. "Wow," Phinnton cooed. "It's light...and beautiful."

"True, but you won't find any jewels on the saddle horn. We don't need any more accidents, now do we?"

Phinnton smiled as he recalled his fireball incident not too long ago.

"Try on your helmet." Linwith grabbed the replica and dropped it over Phinnton's head. "Look! A perfect fit. You even have alabaster to protect your eyes." Linwith tapped the lenses.

"Can we go try them out," Phinnton asked, his voice sounding metallic as it echoed out from his helmet.

"I thought you'd never ask."

Phinnton shook off the joyous moment, grabbed his gear and headed for the door. Once he had everything staged outside, the amber worm lowered himself and Phinnton dragged the mounting stairs close. He positioned the saddle on the worm's back and then jumped to the ground, retrieved the bridle and darted for his head. The beast opened his mouth and Phinnton slipped the bit between dagger-like teeth. Tongue flickered about as the worm settled it into place.

Phinnton darted to his side as the colossus rose to allow Phinnton access to his cinch straps. In a flash, the saddle was secured. Not only was the craftsmanship impeccable, but the artisans had shortened the stirrups and lengthened the harness used to climb into the saddle to account for his size.

Next, Phinnton put on his helmet as he climbed the stairs. With a firm jerk on the straps, he tightened it and stood on his tiptoes and stretched for the saddle's leather harness. He grabbed it and shinnied up the worm's side until he could reach the saddle horn. With hands wrapped about the horn, he pulled himself high enough to reach the stirrup with his foot. With a great push upward, he swung his right leg up and over the saddle. Once seated, he retrieved the reins draped over the worm's neck and took in the remaining worms as well as the guards of Min Brock.

"They haven't seen us yet," Phinnton whispered.

"But if our mission has been approved by Linwith," the worm replied, "then they should be expecting our departure, so why such secrecy?"

"Uggh..." Phinnton wiggled in the saddle as he struggled to find an explanation to his blunder. "Well, your brothers know, of course, but not the guards."

The worm spun his head around to take in Phinnton. "You had better not be lying."

Phinnton's stomach gurgled. He thought about telling the truth but his desire to complete his objective overpowered his conscience.

"Linwith said our mission is so secret that not even the guards can know."

The fire in the worm's black eyes flared.

Phinnton held his breath, hoping the worm took the bait. Phinnton reasoned that the amber worm would overlook the lies once they successfully completed the quest.

The worm's fiery eyes faded back to normal. "I will trust your word, but remember, lying does not become a page."

Phinnton breathed a sigh of relief. "You'll need to time our flight with the guards' patrol. Look."

The amber worm studied the keep's massive walls masked with fog and noted the slow, methodical gait of the guards nearest them.

"When they reach the end of their walk," Phinnton instructed, "they'll come face-to-face, stop and then turn to retrace their steps. That's when you fly away."

The amber worm watched and waited, and when the sentries met and stopped, he beat his wings with slow, strong strokes rather than the quick repetitions typically used to ascend. The worm lurched and rose into the air.

Phinnton lowered himself to avoid detection as well as to warm himself in the heat emanating from the worm. He cast a look over the worm's side to witness the wall of Min Brock pass beneath. This was the moment he knew was critical to the success of their mission. He sat upright and waited for the alarm to be sounded or the remaining worms to bark or pursue. But the worms continued to sleep and the guards lumbered back and forth along the wall like mules, oblivious to their plan.

Phinnton breathed a sigh of relief and hunkered down for the cold flight. The amber worm set course for the Pillar of Addoli and kept their altitude lower than usual, using the ground's darkened features to camouflage their flight. He sniffed the wind in search of their enemy and was relieved to catch only the scent of lions and the sea.

Although Phinnton had logged time flying, he had always done so with Linwith and the other worms. Flying solo gave him a new sense of freedom; everything seemed fresh, alive and larger than life. When they crossed the Addoli Ridge, he gushed with wonder at the sunrise: the fog was lifting and orange light danced atop the Gilden Sea making the black water shimmer like a pearl.

The worm banked and followed the foggy shoreline. Far ahead stood an ominous monolith.

The Pillar of Addoli.

The tower rose out of the fog and looked as if it floated on a cloud. A sheaf of sunlight made the water trickling down its sides look like molten ore. Somewhere waves broke; gulls sang; wind whistled through crags on the cliffs. All of this tinted orange by the alabaster lenses of Phinnton's helmet.

Phinnton wriggled in the saddle and wondered if his quest was such a good idea.

The amber worm glanced back at him. "I do not detect any of our foes; it is safe to land. Yet I sense apprehension in your sweat."

Phinnton sat up as straight as he could and swallowed down his apprehensions. "I'm fine. Just cold, that's all. Let's land."

"Hold on. The top doesn't have much room for a landing."

Phinnton wrapped the reins around his hands and gripped the saddle horn.

Wings were extended and the worm glided down for the pillar. The top of the tower grew bigger and bigger. At their current speed, Phinnton worried they would slide off the side or into the pool.

At the last possible moment, the worm cupped his wings and caught the wind, which decreased their speed considerably. The tower loomed and the worm pulled up from his descent and dropped his appendages. Talons scraped across the rocky surface and the worm beat his wings in the opposite direction bringing them to a stop near the pool.

"Wow," Phinnton exclaimed as he dismounted. "That was amazing!"

The worm gave a nod to the compliment.

Phinnton jumped down and removed his helmet, setting it on the ground.

"By now Linwith is awake and has noticed our disappearance."

The worm lowered his colossal head toward Phinnton. "But if he knows of our plan, then this should not be of surprise, correct?"

Phinnton bit his lower lip and continued to lie. "Obviously Linwith knows our whereabouts. I was referring to the guards."

The amber worm pressed his head to that of the boy. Phinnton stared into the worm's black eyes that searched and probed him for the truth. The fires in the worm's eyes shimmered with light. His tongue flickered and Phinnton was overwhelmed by the scent of fish and sea.

On more than one occasion as a page, Phinnton had experienced the worms searching his thoughts. Even with eyes closed he knew which worm was investigating his inner world simply by matching personality with methodology. Since the amber worm was curious by nature, Phinnton recognized his probing mind by how he would flit, hop and dig amongst his thoughts until a new idea or precept stole his attention and he went to explore.

Phinnton stood at attention like a soldier and tried to focus on his fabricated story, hoping to throw the investigative worm off the trail of truth. But the more he thought about his deceitful story, the bigger and brighter it grew.

Phinnton stole a glance into the worm's eyes, hoping he would overlook or miss seeing the lie altogether. But his normally calm, yellowish fires sparked and flamed bright orange.

Phinnton knew the game was over. He stepped back from the beast.

The amber worm shot his head skyward. "You lied to me, young Phinnton. Linwith and Bruun know *nothing* of our journey!"

Phinnton waved his hands up at the worm as if such antics would reverse the worm's conclusions or better yet, protect him should the worm attack. "Yes, I'm sorry! I never planned on deceiving you, but it was the only way to get…"

"Enough!"

Phinnton gasped and dropped his arms to his side. He prepared himself for the worst.

The worm's black orbs fired with red light. "Deception and fabrication are *not* the marks of a page for the Worm Master!"

"I know. I have no excuse."

"Grab your helmet and climb back into your saddle. We shall return at *once*."

Phinnton glanced over his shoulder at the pool. The fog was dissipating and the morning light made the water radiant. "Since we're here, please let me retrieve the Singing Stones of Addoli. Then we can return to Min Brock where you can have me punished."

"No. I will no longer participate in this ruse."

"I'm not trying to manipulate you or get you into any more trouble," Phinnton replied as he followed the waterfall's plummet from the high overhang down into the nearby pool. "But aren't you the least bit curious about the stones?"

"What I want or what I *feel* at this moment is of no consequence."

"I understand, but I'm already in trouble, so what's wrong with taking just a little more time to retrieve the stones? I promise to tell Linwith this was all my fault and that I tricked you into coming."

The worm turned his attention to the pool. Since his view was higher than Phinnton's, he had the advantage of seeing the stones lying in the shallow waters. He flicked his tongue with interest. Next, he focused on Phinnton and studied him for a long time. Convinced he was telling the truth and curious himself about the Singing Stones of Addoli, he addressed the page. "Very well, I will comply. But be advised, young Phinnton, that I will be alert to any more of your trickery."

"I promise," Phinnton said with a hand over his heart. "But I have one more thing to ask of you."

The worm stepped closer. "Yes?"

"We agreed that part of the plan was that you would shrink in size so we won't be spotted by demoliths or vul jens. No offense, but you're huge and can be seen from far away."

The worm, who had already been investigating Phinnton's thoughts and motives, scanned the skies before turning back to address the page. "I don't detect any of our enemy in the area. I don't see the need."

"You know as well as I do what Linwith believes about our enemy."

The amber worm did know, but still not trusting the boy, he feigned ignorance. "And what might that be?"

"Demoliths and vul jens have exceptional eyesight. Possibly better than yours."

"Your point being?"

"They could spot us before you caught their scent or saw them approaching. And if they attacked from downwind, we could get caught in a trap."

"Be that as it may, your lie has jeopardized any right you claim to order me to alter my form. I shall stay my normal size."

Phinnton started to argue but knew that it would be a waste of time. Instead, he wandered to the pool and stared at the water. "Now that I'm here, it seems much larger and deeper."

He followed the shoreline toward the waterfall. "It's like a giant bowl. The outer rim with all the rocks is shallow and doesn't look too deep, perhaps only up to my knees." He stopped walking and imagined wading through the shelf's water and estimated that five strides would bring him to the edge where it dropped off into the black waters of the pool. Spooked, he took a step backward as if the water could magically suck him down into its depths. "It goes straight down. How deep is it?"

"I do not know for certain, however, there is a story that the Pillar of Addoli is a water portal to another world."

"Another world? Where?"

"Your world calls it, the Onderling. The bottom of this well is connected by a series of caves and passages to an underground lake known as Karajan in the nation of SriBrune."

Phinnton, whose curiosity overrode his common sense, knelt and stretched his hand out over the water.

"Do *not* touch it!" the worm warned.

Phinnton froze, his palm poised above the surface. "Why not?"

"Your ripples will awaken the dansel lors, underground water dragons that will rise from the depths to devour you. They are the protectors of SriBrune as well as the Singing Stones of Addoli."

"But it's already covered with ripples from the waterfall."

"Yes, but they fan out in a pattern; a constant rhythm like that of a heartbeat, coursing the surface in time to the waterfall's pulse. A mere hiccup or breach in this watery meter would be detected by the dansel lors."

Phinnton scooted back and stared at the pool's edge and the stones shimmering beneath the rippling surface. He shook his head. "So how am I to get them out?"

The worm did not answer.

"There must be *hundreds* of stones. Are all of them the Singing Stones?"

"No. According to the tales, only a few are the actually Singing Stones. As far as how to remove them without alerting the dansel lors, you must slip your hand beneath the water in time with the water's pulse. In essence, you must mimic the waves; you must become like water."

Phinnton stared at the stones. "But which ones do I take?"

"I do not know."

"There's not enough time to examine them all."

"Correct. But if you are indeed the one to discover and retrieve these stones, then I have to believe that they will assist, although I am puzzled as to how."

Before Phinnton penetrated the surface, he glanced at the ominous pool and imagined what a dansel lor looked like, since he had never seen one before, and wondered if his mission was such a good idea after all. Nervous at the beast he created in his imagination, his hand shivered from fear.

"Steady," the worm encouraged. "Do not concern yourself with the dansel lors. I shall keep watch should they attack. You focus on matching the waterfall's meter perfectly and capturing a stone."

Phinnton nodded to the plan, held his breath and slid his fingers into the water.

Ice-cold.

Stunned by the drastic temperature and the pain it caused his hand, he exhaled his held breath with a loud huff.

"Steady," the worm once more encouraged. "You must stay the course."

"I know," Phinnton spat through clinched teeth. His fingers were already numb and his head ached from the frigid temperature. "I just didn't expect it to be so *cold!*"

He grimaced and pushed through the pain. He thought about

speeding up his pace in order to end his torturous ordeal. After all, should he stir the water and a dansel lor attack, the worm would protect him.

But even so, the worm would insist we leave. And what if I didn't grab a Singing Stone?

The thought of failing his self-made quest made him shiver more than the frigid water. He threw off his worry and pressed his fingers toward the stone he had his sights set on.

He closed his grip around it and even with numb fingers, sensed the stone was slimy. As he pulled his hand out of the water with the same turtle-like speed, he groaned in agony from the frigidness.

Once free of the water, he sat up and dropped the stone into his free hand before sticking his frozen fingers under his armpit for warmth. Despite his trial, he stared in awe at the wet stone cradled in his palm. "It's so smooth and round, like an egg."

The ivory colored stone glistened.

"Are you a Singing Stone," he asked as he rolled it about in his hand.

He held it to his ear. "Nothing."

He shook it as if to awaken it and listened again. Frustrated and convinced it was not a Singing Stone, he tossed it over his shoulder and it clattered across the pillar's top.

The water stirred.

"Did you see that?" Phinnton scooted back in fear that the dansel lors were attacking.

"Yes, but it is not the dansel lors. Some of the stones moved."

"Really," Phinnton asked as he stood up and studied the submerged rocks. "Do you remember which ones? Maybe those are the Singing Stones."

"You may be correct, but I cannot pinpoint which ones moved; I was too focused on the pool."

"But they broke the water's pulse," he said with backward strides to put as much distance between himself and the black well as possible. "Won't the dansel lors attack?"

The worm scoured the water looking for any sign of an attack, but when nothing happened, they both relaxed.

"Although the shimmering stones beat at a different meter," the worm concluded, "the dansel lors must be accustomed to such activity."

"Okay," Phinnton said as he braved himself and neared the pool, "but I still don't know which stones shivered. If only we saw them when I dropped the... Wait! I've got an idea."

Phinnton spun around and retrieved the stone he had tossed aside. Returning to the water's edge, he raised it overhead and far away from the water. With his eyes riveted on the underwater stones, he let the rock fall.

Clack!

"There," Phinnton exclaimed as he pointed to one of the stones that quivered.

He collected the dropped stone and raced to where he had seen the movement.

Kneeling by the pool's edge, he focused on the underwater stones and struck the pillar with his rock.

Click! Clack!

Movement.

Phinnton slid his free hand into the water. This time, the freezing waters did not seem as cold. Perhaps he was better prepared for the experience, or the zeal of fulfilling his mission made the ache tolerable.

"Aha! Got you."

He retrieved the stone and compared the two rocks. "Identical, except this one's black."

He brought it near his ear. Silence. He shook it. Nothing. He tossed it up and down. Again nothing.

"Why isn't it singing? Did I catch the wrong one?"

"No, I watched you carefully. You caught the one that moved."

"Maybe this isn't a singing stone but a moving stone."

"Or perhaps it is awaiting words from its master, a story to awaken it from slumber."

Phinnton chuckled and flashed the worm a smirk. "You want me to tell this rock a story?"

"Do you have any other suggestions?"

Phinnton stared back at the submerged stones. There were too many to examine individually, and he knew that the worm would grow impatient and would want to whisk him back to Min Brock before more trouble occurred.

With a shrug of his shoulders, he said, "Very well, I'll tell it a tale, if I can think of one."

He set the ivory stone down and cupped the black rock in his palms.

As he stared at the egg-like stone, he was surprised to hear his mother's voice, albeit in his memory. She was telling him a story, and up until now, he had forgotten all about it. Flashes of recall told him she had done so at night, out past the marker of Hetherlinn, back when he was just a toddler. Now, her story pushed its way past the other tales cluttering his mind and stood as tall as the Pillar of Addoli itself.

> *Sing aloud, Oh one so still, sing aloud, Oh one I hold.*
> *Let sleeping heart burst into flame, sing aloud, Oh one so cold.*

> *Sing aloud, Oh one so still, sing aloud, Oh one I hold.*
> *Song of life and sweet refrain, sing aloud, Oh one so cold.*

Phinnton finished reciting the tale and turned his ear toward the stone. Silence. He was about to heave it off the pillar when he felt it move. "It's vibrating. See?" He held it up for the worm to inspect. It quivered as if deathly chilled.

"And it's getting warmer," Phinnton added, "as if a fire has been lit within."

"That is what your story implied: *Let sleeping heart burst into flame.*"

Phinnton brought the stone to his ear. Above the sounds of the waterfall, the wind, the gulls and the drone, he heard a new sound. It was subtle, soft and gentle - like a child singing a high note - never falling in pitch, tone or volume.

Phinnton held it up to the worm. "It's singing! Can you hear it?"

"Yes," the worm exclaimed, overjoyed by the pure musical note. "And what a soothing sound it is; I have never heard such wondrous music. And look at the pool!"

Phinnton walked to the edge. The surface rippled as if a school of fish were spawning.

"The Singing Stones are moving as if coming alive; or waking up."

Phinnton placed the black singing stone in his pocket and knelt to retrieve more. In no time he had retrieved two more stones.

Diving for the fourth, the worm called out a warning.

"Phinnton, danger is near."

Phinnton ignored him and stuck his tongue out of his mouth as he zeroed in on the shivering stone

"Leave it!" The worm had turned his attention away from the pool and to the sky behind them.

The slimy rock slipped from his grasp. He tried again.

"Phinnton!"

"No, I almost have it!"

As he wrapped his fingers around the stone, long shadows fell over him. He clutched the stone and glanced over his shoulder.

Five large creatures were flying his way.

He pocketed the stone and checked on the amber worm.

He was gone.

Chapter 26

Rescued

Phinnton gawked at the beasts hovering a stone's thrown away. He was certain, based upon Linwith's descriptions, that these were demoliths: faces were a mish-mash of human flesh and reptilian scales; featherless wings arched above broad shoulders; feral eyes pulsed with yellow light and radiated heat.

But it was one thing to learn about demoliths in the safety of the armory and a whole other thing facing them alone.

Phinnton wanted to run but his legs wouldn't budge, and even if they did, where would he go? Without the worm, he was trapped on the stone tower. And why did the worm leave? Cowardice? No! Worms were the epitome of courage. Perhaps the abandonment was punishment for lying, but Phinnton knew the protocol of the worms, and although he deserved reprimand, the amber worm couldn't hand out a sentence without first consulting Linwith or his brothers. Nevertheless, his reasoning still fell short of explaining where the amber worm had gone.

Phinnton tried to remain calm, tried to keep his wit about him, but his heart raced and his mind flooded with scenarios, most of which ended in his death.

The horde pressed forward.

"What's this?" The demolith commander's voice was a rumbling deep bass, sinister, and rose above the noise of the waterfall. The demolith continued his taunt; voice rumbling up through stone, into Phinnton's boots, coiling around his bones like a giant snake. "Why it's a boy. But how did one so puny scale the slippery slopes of the Pillar of Addoli?"

Phinnton found his courage, what little there was, and backpedaled. His heel entered the water and he froze in place, realizing his mistake, trying not to stir the water and summon a dansel lor, or loose his balance and fall in. He regained his composure, his balance, and stepped back onto the stone.

"And his scent," another demolith added. "Do you smell it, my brothers? The putrid odor of a young storyteller."

"So it is," the leader noted. "Why would a storyteller be upon the Pillar of Addoli? Are you by chance gathering singing stones?"

Without thinking, Phinnton placed a hand over his bulging pocket.

The demoliths hissed. "How innocent and faithful are the young, risking life for the gathering of such mystic rocks. What loyalty you have - yet all for naught! For just like all the tales of the lost one, this one is also a lie."

The heinous beast mocked as he recited the tale.

> *Pillar of rock so grand you stand,*
> *with flattened top and pool of blue,*
> *Beneath your water's glistening depths,*
> *are stones with voices true.*
>
> *No man may hold these precious rocks;*
> *pure tones no man may own,*
> *For the Singing Stones of Addoli*
> *hum songs from distant throne.*

The demoliths intensified their heat, forcing Phinnton to his knees and shielding his head with his arms.

Where are you, worm? When will you attack?

But nothing happened and Phinnton knew if he wanted to live, it was all up to him. A plan came to mind, albeit risky, and he peeked under an arm in search of the first stone he retrieved from the pool.

There…not too far away.

He drew in a deep breath, gathered his nerve, and eyed the rock. *I hope this works…*

Like a cat, he lunged for the stone, and lying on his back, hurled it for the pool.

Plop!

The Demoliths intensified their heat-gaze and Phinnton curled up into a ball. He sucked in blistering hot air and coughed; sweat streamed off his body. He lifted an elbow and eyed the pool: waves from his stone lapped the edge.

Come on! Where are you?

The pillar answered with a rumble. Tremors rose into his body. He checked on the demoliths. They were moving in for the kill.

"Phinnton, lie flat on your belly!"

Phinnton didn't recognize the voice ordering him in the silent tongue so he remained coiled up in a ball.

"Trust me. Lie flat or die."

Phinnton didn't see the point but knew he was out of options. So he risked it all, trusted the voice, and sprawled out with his hands over the back of his head.

There was a great splash followed by a wave of icy water dousing him from head to toe. Startled, he sat up.

Three huge snake-like creatures, that Phinnton assumed were dansel lors, looked black against the backdrop of the sky. Clutched in each of their long snouts was a demolith. The dansel lors shook their prey with the viciousness of lions. Bones snapped; flesh ripped; cries and squeals deafening. And as fast as the dansel lors had appeared, they disappeared into the pool, dragging their victims back to Karajan.

The two remaining demoliths retreated to counterattack.

"Worm of Bal-Malin: Return to size!"

Phinnton cupped his eyes and searched the sky for Linwith. Instead, he witnessed the amber worm popping back to his normal proportions near the demoliths.

The worm grabbed the nearest demolith, crushed him in his talons and dropped him into the sea.

The remaining demolith seized the opportunity and dove for Phinnton. Phinnton stared in horror.

The amber worm won't get here in time!

The demolith's invisible fire blasted Phinnton who dropped to his knees and shielded his head. The temperature went from a hot summer to a raging bonfire. Phinnton dropped and tucked himself into a ball, preparing for the worst.

A loud explosion ended his fiery ordeal.

Phinnton sat up in time to see the demolith being hurled off the pillar by a fireball. Phinnton spun and discovered the ruby worm hovering off the pillar, lingering smoke from the blast spiraling out of his mouth.

Phinnton searched the sky for Linwith and the worms and discovered their silhouettes high overhead. As Linwith glided down for a landing, Phinnton's exuberant feelings of being alive gave way to those of guilt and shame. The sapphire worm landed and Linwith slid off and stormed for Phinnton.

"Thank goodness you came," Phinnton exclaimed, hoping against hope that his master was not angry, but his gait and clinched fists told another story.

Linwith stopped just short of knocking Phinnton into the well and put his hands on his hips. Linwith's eyes looked yellow through the alabaster lenses and seemed to burn as hot like those of the demoliths.

"You've caused quite an alarm back in Min Brock," Linwith exclaimed with an arm thrust in the direction of the keep. "Your father is worried sick and Quinn is ready to throw you to the lions of the Gilden Plains!"

Phinnton gulped. He knew he'd be punished but did not consider the possibility of capital punishment. "Execution? Lions? Really?"

Linwith let his arms fall to his side and smirked. "No, I made that part up, but now that I think about it, it's not a bad idea."

"But I can explain!"

"Your actions tell me all I need to know. You betrayed me *and* the worms."

"Yes, I know, but it was your idea that I should retrieve the Singing Stones of Addoli. And I did, see?"

He retrieved a stone and held it up for Linwith to inspect. Phinnton hoped his victory treasure, as well as his pleasant demeanor, would extinguish Linwith's anger.

Linwith released a dramatic sigh. "Yes, so I see, but commandeering a worm and flying off on some childhood adventure was *not* what I had in mind."

"But how else was I to do it?"

"You could have asked me for help."

"Well, I assumed you'd say..."

"See," he interrupted with a stiff finger near the boy's face. "That's your problem. You assumed and didn't bother asking."

Phinnton, unable to bear Linwith's disappointed expression, stared down at his feet.

Linwith grabbed his shoulders and shook him. "You nearly died!"

Phinnton took in Linwith's yellowy eyes. The anger was gone. In its place was concern and worry.

"I know, but the dansel lors defended me as did the amber worm."

"And what would have happened if the worm had been wounded or killed?"

Phinnton glanced at the worms flying in formation overhead and sighed. "I never thought about that."

"And what do you think Ebon will do when that demolith patrol doesn't return?"

Phinnton looked in the direction of Min Brock. "I guess I didn't think about that, either."

"Of course not!" Linwith released his grip and stepped away. "You're lucky we got here in time."

"Yes, but someone else helped me before you arrived."

"Who," Linwith asked with a puzzled look.

"A voice I didn't recognize spoke in the silent tongue and told me to lie down when the dansel lors attacked the demoliths."

Linwith leaned his head back as if he wanted to sun his face and let out a rueful sigh. "Just wonderful."

"What's wrong? This whisper saved me from being snatched by the dansel lors."

"That whisper was the Only. Now *he* knows about your little mishap and lie."

"That was the King of Claire?"

"And what's worse is that I'll be held accountable."

Linwith shook his head and turned for his worm. Over his shoulder he fired, "We'll discuss your punishment when we get back to Min Brock."

Phinnton could only nod. There were too many emotions rising into his throat for him to talk.

"You know," Linwith said when he reached the sapphire worm, "You and the amber worm are a perfect pair: too curious for your own good."

"I know. I'm sorry. I didn't mean to cause so much trouble, honest. I just wanted to help in the war, and I will with this, see?"

He held the Singing Stone up higher and flashed a weak smile, hoping to restore Linwith's trust in him. Instead, Linwith turned to mount his worm.

"We'll discuss this back at the keep," he said as he climbed up into his saddle.

"I promise it won't happen again," Phinnton pleaded.

Linwith settled into his saddle and eyed the page. "Phinnton, you almost died." And then in a softer, reflective tone: "You almost died."

Phinnton's head dropped and he pocketed the stone. He shuffled over to retrieve his helmet and while putting it on, headed for the sapphire worm.

"What will be my punishment," he asked.

"For starters," Linwith answered as he set his thumb on the amber jewel, "you're grounded."

Summoned by Linwith's command, the amber worm glided in for a landing.

"When he lands," Linwith added, "hop on. I'll control his flight."

Linwith covered the sapphire gem and the worm took off to make room for the amber worm to land. The amber worm touched down and Phinnton avoided eye contact, certain that his black orbs blazed red with anger and disappointment. Phinnton, overwhelmed at the trouble he was in, stared at his feet as he shuffled for the worm.

"Right your shoulders, young Phinnton," the worm urged, "and prepare yourself as a page, with dignity, for whatever punishment Linwith has in store for us."

Phinnton dared a look at the worm's face. His eyes weren't red but yellow, like that of a sunrise or perhaps, with his future as a page hanging in the balance, more like a sunset.

"You're in trouble, too?"

The worm gave a nod.

"I never meant to get you in trouble."

"That I know, young Phinnton. That I know. But I have no one to blame but myself. Now hurry. We do not need to get into any more trouble."

Phinnton jumped, albeit half-heartedly, and grabbed the leather harness. With some kicks and grunts, he shinnied into the saddle. Before he could take hold of the reins, the worm took off. Phinnton was startled by the sudden takeoff until he remembered Linwith said he'd be the pilot.

But how long will I be grounded?

The thought of enduring one minute, let alone days or seasons of punishment, made him squirm in his saddle. To take his mind off the matter, he glanced back at the Pillar of Addoli. Ripples from the waterfall fanned across the pool as if the dansel lors had never appeared. The only proof that a battle had taken place was the smoke rising from the charred demolith on the beach and his comrade floating face down in the sea. And then it hit him. Linwith's words echoed through his thoughts like a warning gong.

"Phinnton, you almost died."

Realizing how close he'd come to death, Phinnton became queasy, dizzy and couldn't catch his breath. He eyed Linwith up ahead and considered calling for help in the silent tongue. Before he could make a peep, a whisper, that he assumed was the same one that helped him on the tower, posed a notion.

"Don't bother. He won't answer. Why should he? You lied and betrayed his trust."

Phinnton accepted the whisper's indictment without so much as a whimper. Shame, like the heat from the demoliths, smothered him.

He turned from Linwith and yearned for the one person who had loved him unconditionally: his mother. He longed for her touch, her voice, her gaze of adoration.

The whisper presented a question; one it knew Phinnton had pondered time after time. *"Why was your mother taken from you at so early an age?"*

The question ravished the remnants of his hope; emotions lodged in his throat and his breathing became more erratic. Desperate for relief from the ordeal, he slid a hand into his pocket and fingered the Stones of Addoli. They shimmered and warmed to his touch.

The whisper snickered but Phinnton focused on recreating his mother's face. How many times had he done this? Countless. But each time took longer and he feared one day he wouldn't imagine her at all. But today would not be that day! Dark hair, fine and shiny as spun silk, graced her shoulders; petite smile arced to moon-like dimples; eyes so dark, so captivating, that not even the deepest midnight could match their intensity. And there she was; as vivid and real in his mind's eye as when she was alive.

She whispered in his ear...

"Lift your chin, my love. Trust the true whisper. Trust the songs from distant throne. Be strong."

As if on cue, the stones hummed a bell-like tone that calmed his panic attack and chased away the foreign whisper. Phinnton pulled out the black stone; tone so pure, so alive. He palmed the rock, liked its weight and how the surface caught the sunlight making it glimmer like an egg.

The Singing Stones of Addoli lifted their voices, their music protecting Phinnton in a cocoon of bliss. With shame no longer nipping at his heels, Phinnton sat up in his saddle and lifted his chin into the wind.

Chapter 27

Reversal of Skies

Quinn, on his way to man the wall, navigated his way through the people milling about the Great Hall for lunch. He was so preoccupied that he didn't notice two old women pushing their way through the crowd to intersect his path.

They blocked his way with arms crossed, but Quinn, still deep in thought, ran into them at a good clip. Despite being rotund women, he sent them sprawling to the ground.

"I'm *so* sorry," he stammered, as they lay sprawled at his feet. "I wasn't paying attention."

"Obviously," the woman wearing a red scarf snapped. Strands of gray hair jutted out from beneath the scarf like straw, and a white smock, smudged with soot, was tied about her tattered gray tunic. But her most distinguishable feature was her left eye. Black and blue bruises encircled it.

"How could you not see us?" the other fired, her face bulging and dotted with age spots. "We're not exactly tiny, you know."

"Again," he helped them to their feet, "my deepest apologies."

"No matter," the red-scarfed woman huffed as she brushed herself off. She caught his eye and motioned for him to lean close.

"We need to have a word with you. In private," she whispered into his ear, her breath reeking of onions. "It's a matter of grave importance."

"Yes," the other added in a half-whisper as she glanced about to see if anyone was listening. Thankful that the onlookers were no longer concerned about their collision, she whispered into his other ear: "It's of great urgency."

Quinn was about to brush off their request with a polite rebuttal when he sized them up. Something in their eyes told him this was not about a family squabble or dissatisfaction with a vendor's goods, issues that he was bombarded with daily as the leader of Min Brock.

"Very well, but I only have…"

Before he could finish, they dragged him behind the corner of the hall, and when they were certain no one had followed or was listening, delivered their news.

The red-scarfed woman grabbed his lapels and stared up into his face. "Something's wrong with the sun."

"There is," Quinn asked, overcome by her foul breath and turning aside to find fresh air.

"And the night sky," the other woman added, as she checked left then right for spies, her plump jowls flopping back and forth. "It's not right either, as if it's broken."

Quinn nodded, not in comprehension but in an attempt to collect his thoughts. "I'm sorry," he finally offered with an amiable smile, "but I'm not sure what you're talking about."

"The sun," the red-scarfed woman pressed, pulling hard on his tunic, urgency in her voice. "It doesn't rise as high anymore and it's not as bright."

"Well," Quinn offered with a condescending tone as he worked to release her fingers from his lapel, "that *does* happen during the different seasons."

Her brow furrowed and she overcame his prying fingers and yanked him even closer. "I *know* that! I'm not some *tart* from Torrens Bay."

"No, of course not." He coughed to clear his sinuses of her onion breath. "All I'm saying is that..."

"All you're saying," the other woman pressed with a finger to his chest, her breath rivaling that of her friend's in stench, "is that you think we're just two old crazy women drunk on wildeberry wine."

Quinn shook his head, wishing he smelled alcohol instead of onions and rot on their breath. "Not at all, ladies, but with all due respect, as the leader of Min Brock, I've been preoccupied with more important matters."

"Oh, I see," the scarfed woman nodded with an elbow poke to her friend's ribs, "now our issues are *trite*...even trivial and bothersome."

Quinn closed his eyes and sighed. "Ladies, please." He pried off her fingers and stepped back to drink in clean, smelling air. "All I'm saying is that I need more information. Your report isn't making any sense."

The woman with the spotted face crossed her arms over her bosomy chest. "Very well, take the night sky. The stars and moon are draining away."

"Draining away?"

"Yes," her friend chimed, energized by his interest. "And when it's well past midnight, the western sky glows as if the sun is rising, but how could that be?"

"Not to mention," her friend added, her voice rising in pitch to match her zeal, "that the morning light is dimmer, and no..." She glowered at Quinn. "It's *not* because I'm going blind, either."

Quinn was about to brush them off with his usual, "I'll look into this," rhetoric when his memory sharpened. He reflected on his recent watches and tapped his chin.

"You know," he offered as his face lined with thought, "I've been so consumed with looking for our enemy that I didn't notice the sky, but now that you mention it, there *have* been some strange phenomena."

The women beamed.

"Ladies," he said with a huge smile, "this *is* of great importance." He flung his arms open to express his enthusiasm. They misconstrued his open stance and threw themselves into his arms. Quinn, caught off-guard by their affection, returned the hug, albeit restrained, and then pulled away.

"Funny, isn't it," he added as he savored their smiling faces. "It took a pair of old eyes to see what younger eyes had missed."

He held his breath, so as to not catch a whiff of their stench, and kissed them both on the forehead. They blushed and giggled.

"Now if you'll excuse me," he said as he gave them a polite bow, "I need to deliver this news to the other leaders."

Turning on his heel, he made his way for the central turret.

There, he mounted the stairs and raced up, bumping against passers-by in his haste. Nearing the top, he slowed and stepped out onto the platform.

Linwith stood alone, which was customary, and stared at the Gilden Sea that was but a glint of light on the far horizon.

"Linwith," Quinn fired as his brisk pace carried him to his brother's side, "I just learned the most interesting news."

"Was it from the two old women who witnessed the reversal of the skies?"

Quinn let his exuberant expression fall. "You mean to tell me you knew about this?"

Linwith patted the wall with his palms and shifted his weight to a more comfortable position. "Of course. The mandarin worm showed me."

"Ah, I forgot," Quinn nodded with a sigh. "Your visions. Do I have *any* secrets?"

Linwith eyed his brother with a mischievous grin. "Do you really want to know?"

Quinn arched an eyebrow. "No, I suppose not. But why haven't you told me about the reversing skies?"

"Because like you, I missed seeing it and just learned of it from the worms this morning."

"So what do you make of it all?"

Linwith's smile melted like wax to the flame. "It's not good, Quinn, not good at all."

"Go on," Quinn coaxed.

Linwith wet his lips. "A while back, I focused on Ebon, and the mandarin worm showed me a vision of Kise. Men, women and children were amassed around a monstrous bonfire. Some danced about as if drunk or crazy while others bowed prostrate before the flames. A few stuck their hands into the fire that licked their flesh like ravenous beasts. With scorched hands raised to the Cauldron, they shouted *First blood!* and *Death begets death!*"

Quinn scrunched his face up in confusion. "But what does that have to do with the skies?"

"Nothing, until another vision revealed more. I heard what sounded like soldiers singing a song. Although I could not make out all of the words, one key phrase emerged."

> *Dawn! Alter course and rise up from Ebon,*
> *Light! Flee the stars and mar darkest heaven.*
> *Hope! Wither off like grapes on the vine,*
> *Anguish rule and conquer their minds,*
> *Usher in the days of deception.*

Quinn stared north to Ebon. "So the reversal of skies is a result of the Cauldron and not a sign of Claire entering the war."

"So it seems," Linwith sighed.

"And what of Claire?"

Linwith sighed. "I've had just one vision; that of a single star shining in a black sky high above the Addoli Ridge."

Quinn turned to take in Linwith's face. "What does *that* mean?"

Linwith shrugged. "Well, it at least means that the Only isn't dead, so there's hope. Other than that, I don't know."

They leaned on the wall and searched the sky for a solitary star but it was still too early in the day.

"Do you have *any* good news," Quinn asked.

"Not much," Linwith offered in a sleepy voice. "I did see a large army - not Ebonite, by the way - marching for Min Brock."

Quinn perked up. "Really?"

Linwith nodded. "Well armed, too, but the vision was too cloudy for me to decipher anything else."

"That *is* good news!"

"Indeed," Linwith said in a dull tone. "Indeed it is."

They continued to search the sky and Linwith refrained from sharing his other visions with Quinn, particularly the one that made him toss in his sleep and awake in a cold sweat. When he had gathered enough factual evidence instead of vague conjecture, which was all he had to date, he would tell Quinn about the vision.

In fact, he longed to be free of the ghoul who tormented his thoughts day and night, a rogue warrior who wore a skull for a helmet and was hailed as…The Gor King.

Chapter 28

Vision Quest

Two dark figures slipped from shadow to shadow. When the guards of Min Brock weren't looking, they darted across the parade grounds. Sliding into deep shadows, they pressed their bodies close against the keep's cold stones. Breaths were caught as they looked for any guards or midnight strollers that might spy them and ruin their undertaking. Convinced they were alone and unrecognized, they crept along the wall toward the dwelling. Reaching the door, they hesitated before opening the latch.

"Are you certain of this?" one woman whispered.

"Yes. What have we to lose?" her friend whispered back.

They opened the door and slipped in like a breeze.

Blue-silver moonbeams crisscrossed the floor, revealing a bed where the occupant slept with his back to the door.

They tiptoed closer, his breathing deep, unlabored, signs that he was adrift in his dreamworld. Nearing his side, the women launched their well-rehearsed plan.

One woman's firm hands pinned him down while the other woman covered his mouth.

Linwith's eyes blinked open.

"Shh!" the women coaxed, but unable to see his captors and fearing the worst, Linwith thrashed and kicked and screamed, although muffled. The women had anticipated as much, and the one holding his arms sat on his legs to hold him down.

"It's Areall," said the woman nearest him, "and sitting on you is Daryess."

Linwith's eyes darted from one woman's silhouette to the other, trying to see their faces, but it was too dark. Overcome with panic and mistrust, he thrashed all the more.

"If you can't see us," Areall offered as she restrained him, "surely you recognize our voices."

Linwith stopped wrestling. His breathing was fast, a result of his effort and fright. "If you promise to stay quiet," Areall continued, "we'll release you. Nod if you agree to this."

Linwith gave a decisive nod.

The women released him and Linwith sprung out of bed.

"What *are* you doing?" he rasped as he pulled his night garments close to hide his flimsy clothing.

"Please be quiet! We can't alert the others."

"Quiet? Alert?" he fumed, now irritated at their presence and tactics. "You scare me to death and *now* you're worried about the others?"

"Shh!" both women hushed.

Linwith shook his head and marched to a nearby table. He lit a candle and poured a goblet of water. Slurping it down, he wiped his mouth with his sleeve and sized up the two mothers.

"I know why you're here," he informed them.

"You do," Areall asked.

"I saw this event long before tonight, in a vision," and then to himself, "I only wish it had shown me *how* you'd awaken me." Shaking off his frustration, he set the goblet down and approached them.

"You have questions about the worm's visions of your children."

They clasped hands and nodded.

"Wasn't Quinn's account sufficient?"

Areall flashed Daryess a glance before answering his question. "No. We need to see the visions first hand."

"More specifically," Daryess added after flicking a nod at Areall, "we wish to see where they are today."

Linwith put his hands on his hips. "No," he replied in a curt tone. "All you need to know I shared with Quinn."

"But the MerriNoons have confirmed that they journeyed to Claire. All we're asking is that you show us where they are now."

"I've given my answer. Now please, leave before someone sees you in here and rumors begin to swirl."

"Linwith," Areall said, her voice soft and pleasing to his ears, "in all the years I've been married to your brother, have I ever asked a favor of you?"

Linwith crossed his arms and pondered the question, but before he could answer, she continued.

"Have I ever sought your counsel or shared my problems with you or said a bad thing about you or your brother?"

"No," he stammered. "You are like a sister to me."

"And Elabea. Has she ever been a burden or a nuisance to you - her uncle?"

He sighed at the uncle reference, dreading the conclusion she was leading him toward. "Of course not. I love her as if she were my own daughter."

"Then why will you not allow us this one request?"

"Because if I do, then it'll lead to another question or riddle you'll want me to decipher. It'll never end, Areall. And despite your best efforts, the refugees will find out what I did for you two and will want me to do the same for them. I don't have time for that!"

"That is why we came in secret tonight. We won't tell a soul."

"I know, but words slip out or conversations are overheard, or the Cauldron's whisper aids in spreading this gossip."

"We promise that no matter what the visions, whether good or bad, we will not trouble you any more."

Daryess nodded her head to accentuate Areall's promise.

Linwith rubbed his chin as he contemplated their request. He stalled knowing that the visions could shatter their hope and he didn't want to feel the weight of that burdening him with guilt.

"If you *promise* to tell no one about this," he offered, "and promise to *never* ask me again, I will do as you wish." He stuck a finger in the air. "Just this once."

The women smiled, hugged and nodded to the agreement.

"But I must warn you," he continued, his hushed tone robbing the joy coursing their veins, "that the visions are incomplete, dream-like, obscure."

They steeled themselves and gave a firm nod.

"As you wish," Linwith sighed as he donned a heavier tunic to ward off the night's chill and blew out the candle. Escorting them to the door, he led them from his dwelling.

They tiptoed through the shadows to avoid detection and in no time reached the armory where they slid unnoticed inside. Despite the dull light spilling through the windows, the seven gems sparkled and glowed as if light dwelt deep within their facets.

Linwith turned and took in their shadowed faces. "Are you certain you wish to see?"

Two heads nodded.

He took Areall's hand in his and looked into her eyes. "When I touch the jewel, place your finger atop mine. Close your eyes and focus on her new name, Ela Claire. The worm will do the rest."

Areall nodded.

Linwith turned and rested his index finger on the mandarin gem. Areall placed her finger on his, closed her eyes, and focused on Ela Claire. The mandarin worm whisked her thoughts into a world tinted with orange. Areall smiled as she beheld the vision of her daughter - now with the body of a woman - soaring across the sky on a white harrier.

"She's beautiful," Areall gushed. "And so, so regal!" The vision faded and Areall panted. "No," she begged, "Please let me see more."

Linwith lifted their hands off the saddle horn. "I'm sorry, but the worm controls the visions, not you or I."

Areall nodded and beamed a smile at Daryess. "Oh, Daryess, you are going to be amazed!"

Daryess stepped forward.

Linwith eyed her, and knowing what the vision held for her, took her hand into his. "Are you sure you wish to see?"

She gave a solemn nod.

Linwith sighed and positioned his finger over the mandarin gem. "Do exactly what Areall did except focus on Romlin. Remember, the visions can be difficult to decipher."

She steeled herself and wet her lips before giving a nod.

Linwith touched the gem and she lowered her finger to his. She found her thoughts beyond her own time and comprehension. Her hopeful expression fell and lines stretched across her forehead as she tried to comprehend what she was witnessing.

She sucked short gulps of air, as if startled, and gasped as if seeing something - or someone - beyond her worst nightmare. When the vision ended, she spun around, and unable to find her voice, stared wide-eyed into Areall's face.

"What's wrong," Areall asked, alarmed by Daryess' pale face and quivering lips.

Daryess did not answer. Instead, she crumpled into Areall's arms and wept. Areall stroked her back and flicked a concerned look to Linwith.

"What did she see," she asked.

Linwith pulled away from her pain-filled eyes. "I tried to warn you. I tried."

Areall rested her head against Daryess and rocked back and forth with her sobbing friend.

Linwith, unable to bear the scene and the guilt he now felt, made his way to the door and slipped out into the night. Shuffling back to his dwelling, he tried to shake off Romlin's vision that he knew Daryess had experienced.

It was black, silent and cold. Like a tomb.

Chapter 29

The Living Dead

Previn and his passengers, Ela Claire and DeMorley, arrived at the Gilden Sea well into the evening. Blue moonbeams made the white caps crashing against the rocky shoreline all the more mystical.

As they zoomed over the beach Ela Claire tapped DeMorley's leg and pointed at the sea's horizon.

Rising out of the ominous waters, like a dragon from the deep, was a dark island of rock with towering cliffs. Perched on top was a castle. Although not large, it appeared foreboding and menacing. Five large walls were constructed close to the island's cliffs, while five towers, spaced at equal distances along the walls, rose well above the walls' zenith.

"The Isle of Rhythe," Ela Claire shouted over her shoulder to DeMorley.

"It looks dangerous."

She nodded.

DeMorley reflected on his vow to repay the mercy he had been given. He never fathomed it might cost his life. "Are you going to destroy it with a story?"

She shook her head. "If I do, the Cauldron will know our exact whereabouts and could thwart our mission."

DeMorley eyed the citadel. They were closer. He could see the waves pounding the isle's windward side and then skirting around the craggy isle in glimmer of silver. He scanned the walls and towers for any sign of their enemy, but they were still too far away to tell for certain.

He gulped down his fears and tossed a look at the sea. For a moment, he contemplated jumping until he realized this would be suicide. "So if you can't tell a story without alerting the Cauldron, and I'm not a warrior, and Previn - although strong and brave - is but one harrier, what's the plan?"

"First, we fly over it to see what we're up against."

Previn began a steep climb. Ela Claire leaned forward and pulled DeMorley into a similar position as they flew higher and higher. After what DeMorley thought was an interminably long time, Previn leveled his flight and slowed his pace. Ela Claire and DeMorley sat upright and scanned the sea far below. Rhythe was directly below them.

"It's shrouded in darkness," Ela Claire noted as Previn circled high overhead. "There's not even the glimmer from a torch or a fire anywhere. It's as if no one lives there."

"Yes; my keen senses," Previn added, "confirm that there are no Ebonites on the walls, towers or in the courtyard."

"Or," DeMorley interjected with his habitual pessimism, "they know we're here and await inside to ambush us."

"Maybe it's deserted," Ela Claire added with a note of joy in her voice.

"Deserted," DeMorley chortled. "I may not be the *bravest* of men, but I'm not a *fool!* The Ebonites would *never* leave a castle full of Clairian treasure unprotected."

"DeMorley's correct," Previn said. "This could be a trap. I'll descend for a better look."

Previn adjusted his wings and tail and glided downward in a circular path. He stopped when they were just beyond the flight of an arrow yet close enough to make out shapes and shadows within the keep.

"There," DeMorley pointed to a corner of the courtyard. "Look within the darker shade. I saw something glowing."

All eyes focused on the corner in question. Ela Claire was about to chastise him for scaring them when she too saw it. Purplish light, that was only a faint glow, pulsed as if breathing. At its brightest point, they could make out its features: fog-like in appearance, the purple light clung to the ground and rolled out into the courtyard.

"Is it a lair for vul jens," Ela Claire asked as she remembered her encounters with the dreamhunters back when Previn was her rusk.

"No," he reassured her. "I would have caught their scent long before now. This creature has a musk I haven't encountered before."

Within the mist, diffused by the purple fog, a great mass shifted about.

"Did you see *that?*" DeMorley gasped as Previn instinctively gained altitude. "Something huge lives in that fog! We're no match for it. We need to retreat."

Neither Previn nor Ela Claire answered him. Instead, they were preoccupied with the creature. It continued to move as if adjusting its weight while asleep, and yet its mannerisms were mesmerizing and unlike anything they had seen before. As best they could tell from their vantage point, the creature's body was long, wingless and looked to be coiled.

A high-pitched wail rose from Rhythe, its eeriness making even Previn shudder.

"Maybe DeMorley is right," Ela Claire said as she associated the forlorn cry with the beast, "without a story, we can't defeat this thing, whatever it is."

An enormous snake-like head emerged from the mist. Ela Claire clasped a hand over her mouth to muffle a scream. DeMorley, on the other hand, squealed at the top of his lungs.

Hearing his voice, the beast looked their way and tasted the night air with its long, thin tongue.

"He's about to strike," DeMorley shouted, releasing his hold and pointing out the coils slinking around in the purple mist. "We're no match for…"

The wingless dragon lunged and although Previn was far enough away, he nonetheless banked. DeMorley, who still hadn't grabbed a hold of Ela Claire, lost his balance and toppled head over heels toward the dragon.

"Fool!" Previn barked after DeMorley. And to Ela Claire: "Hold on."

Previn dove to rescue the falling minstrel and Ela Claire clung tight and pressed close to be as streamlined as possible.

"What's your plan," she asked him in the silent tongue.

"Plan?" Previn snapped. *"Any plan we had was dashed when that lunatic fell."*

DeMorley, who had somehow managed to right himself, fell feet first flapping his arms like a goose and screaming like a gutted sow.

"You attack the dragon," she advised. *"Hopefully that will give us time before the Cauldron is alerted. I'll rescue DeMorley with a story."*

With a deep breath, as if diving into the sea, she launched herself head first off Previn's back and began her tale.

> *Into the dark we plunge, into death's pool we dive,*
> *Song of Claire echo loud and keep us both alive.*
> *Cloak us with lights from thousands of stars,*
> *And guard us from even the slightest of scars.*

When she caught up with DeMorley and grabbed his flapping tunic, countless miniature stars enveloped them and stopped their fall. Safe within the glittering sphere, they floated on the wind like a thistle away from the dragon.

A white blur whistled past them.

Previn! she acknowledged.

When their sparkling sphere touched down inside Rhythe, they pressed against the lighted ball to watch the battle unfold.

Previn landed on the dragon's head and latched his talons deep into its flesh. The dragon threw its great coils into the air in an attempt to lasso Previn, but he released his grip just as the black spirals came near and soared out of range. Before the beast could react, Previn circled back for another attack.

His dive was a blur of white and his razor sharp talons sliced the dragon's head like a sword, tearing and ripping reptilian flesh that he dropped to the ground. The dragon whipped more coils into the air and shrieked. Previn spiraled through them and struck blow after blow on the dragon's snake-like body. The fight became so intense that the sky was a blur of white and twisting black as they battled for the right to be Lord of the Isle of Rhythe.

The dragon, weakened from Previn's many blows, slowed its attacks. Previn landed on the beast's crown to deliver his deathblows. With talons dug deep, he pecked its eyes like a woodpecker. The beast thrashed about, its barks shrill and deep, and tried to throw the harrier off, but Previn had exceptional strength. Despite the rocketing ride, he maintained his balance and more importantly, his attacks.

Blind and desperate for victory, the dragon swirled his head toward the nearest wall. Previn, who realized the dragon's strategy was to crush him against the stones, shot up at the last possible moment. The dragon slammed into the wall with such force that Ela Claire and DeMorley felt the impact inside their cocoon. Without a groan or shriek, the dragon plopped dead to the ground.

With the battle over, Ela Claire released her tale and the glittering lights faded away.

Previn landed beside them and together, they studied the purple fog. The mist twirled over the ground and then retreated at a slow pace as if being inhaled by a giant. When it disappeared from view, they could see the crack in the wall that aided its escape.

"It's gone back to the sea," DeMorley theorized, "to hail another dragon."

"We don't know where it's going," Ela Claire countered. "But my gut tells me it's joined my story and is now racing to alert the Cauldron. Either way, we don't have much time."

As if to confirm her concern, the same horrific cries they had heard while circling Rhythe sounded again, only now, they emanated from all around them.

Ela Claire gasped. "I thought the dragon made those sounds."

"As did I," Previn concurred as he sniffed the wind and scanned the crags in search of their enemy.

DeMorley and Ela Claire stood back-to-back and scanned the keep for whomever or whatever had made the forlorn moans.

"Now we know why Rhythe is void of Ebonites," DeMorley whispered as he pressed against her back. "The *living dead* protect this keep!"

Chapter 30

Cell Number 17

The clouds above the Isle of Rhythe parted. Silver moonbeams slashed across the castle's walls and towers. Visible for the first time were wooden doors leading into the five towers. Archer slits, black and foreboding, snaked up the tower in a deadly spiral.

"This castle is deserted," Ela Claire noted while taking in the towers.

"But we heard those fiendish cries," DeMorley countered. "And what about those?" He motioned to the large entrance behind them. "That purple fog disappeared underneath to who knows where, while this one..." he spun around, "probably leads to the lair of that beast we heard baying."

The cries started up once more; spurts of darkest pain followed by horrifying silence.

"See," DeMorley exclaimed as he scooted closer to Previn. "Maybe there aren't warriors in this castle, but *that* proves this place is haunted."

His eyes darted this way and that, scrutinizing every shadow for form or figure. Spying the dead dragon lying near the wall, he jumped and accidentally ruffled Previn's feathers. "What if the dragon isn't dead?" he half-whispered more to himself than to his colleagues. "What if we turn our backs and it comes alive and..."

"Shhh!" Ela Claire scolded as the howls began again. Turning her head to the side, she crept toward the distant entrance, straining to discern the author, or authors, of such noises. "The sounds are familiar."

"You are correct," Previn agreed as he followed. "And yet the walls muffle the cries so that it is difficult to identify."

"Here's an idea," DeMorley blurted as he ran to catch up. "Let's fly back to the beach and wait until morning to..."

"There," Ela Claire pointed to the dark entryway. "The sounds are definitely coming from inside." She flashed Previn a beaming smile. "We must be near the treasure."

"Treasure?" DeMorley challenged as he cowered behind Previn. "It could also be the dwelling place of the damned! Can't you hear how horrific they sound? And there is more than one down there. More than we three can battle."

"Then you why don't you stay here and guard the entrance," Previn snapped.

DeMorley looked over his shoulder at the other opening. "Stay here when that purple fog could return at any moment, or," he eyed the dead dragon, "that *thing* comes back to life to end mine?" He jerked his head back and stared into the black entry way.

"Not much of a choice, now is it," he huffed. "But it's dark inside and we don't have any torches or..."

Ela Claire, who had been whispering her story while he fretted, glowed a soft, orange light.

Previn took in DeMorley's stunned expression. "You were saying?"

"Oh. Wonderful," DeMorley sighed as his shoulders drooped. "We can see several steps in front of us while those creatures can see us from afar."

With no further ado, Ela Claire and Previn entered the darkness. DeMorley hesitated. He took in the distant portal and the dead dragon and considered taking his chances waiting, but his imagination got the better of him and he raced to catch up.

Ela Claire increased her light's strength. Orange beams cast long shadows to reveal a large room with a low ceiling. At the furthest wall was another entryway that spiraled down into the depths. She tiptoed toward the entrance and stopped to examine it further. Damp stone composed the walkway and a pungent, stale odor hung thick in the air. From far below came the rhythmic sound of water dripping onto the stone.

"It is wide enough for a wagon to traverse," Previn noted.

"Or a legion of warriors," DeMorley whispered.

The cries sounded again, only this time they were much louder.

"It's down there," Ela Claire half-whispered as she descended the walkway.

"And much clearer," Previn added.

"Yes, yes, yes," DeMorley noted as he kept pace. "But you don't have to go so fast. What if it's a trap?"

"Because," she said over her shoulder as she jogged, "I recognize the sounds."

"As do I," Previn exclaimed.

"Well I don't! I think Previn should investigate while we provide protection from the rear."

"Protection?" Previn challenged as he kept pace. "For who?"

Ela Claire and Previn raced on and DeMorley slowed down. They dashed around a bend and Ela Claire's glow made the wet stone glisten orange. DeMorley sucked in air and noticed it was colder.

"Fools," he concluded. *"They're racing to what could be their tomb. I'll*

follow when it's safe. And who knows, if they happen to perish, I could have all the treasure to myself."

Ela Claire's orange hue disappeared and he was shrouded in darkness.

"But then again," he glanced over his shoulder. *"That purple fog could be slinking up behind me."*

He picked up his pace only to run into the wall. His hand slid over the slimy stone and he panicked. Feeling his way down the corridor, he started to trot. The sounds of dripping water ignited his imagination and spurred him to a run, all the while dragging fingers along the slippery wall to keep his bearings. When her orange glow came into sight, he sprinted to catch up.

He was running so fast that when he rounded the bend, which happened to be the last turn, he ran into Previn.

"Careful," Previn chastised.

DeMorley caught his breath and peered around to see what had made them stop. The corridor emptied into a wide hallway. Wooden doors, spaced symmetrically apart, were on either side.

"The dungeon," Ela Claire whispered.

Hanging beside each door was a large metal key. Two torches were mounted on each wall and their flames lapped the musty air like wild hounds.

"Torches?" DeMorley whispered. "Then that means…"

"We're not alone." Ela Claire finished.

"No doubt lit by Ebonites," Previn concluded. "But how long ago and when will they return?"

Above each door was a crudely painted number.

Ela Claire reminisced. *They look like the numbers on our cottages back in Hetherlinn, back when Romlin was still…* She shook off the memory of his death as if it were a bad dream and focused on her mission.

"They must be within one of these cells."

"Who," DeMorley asked, still oblivious to whom or what made the horrific sounds.

"But which one," Previn asked. "Even my keen senses cannot find any trace of them in this dank place, and we dare not open them all. We may release a beast or fiend that should have remained encaged forever."

They continued to listen, hoping the sounds would come again. Aside for the rhythmic drip of water and the torches hungry flames, the dungeon was quiet.

"This is an ambush," DeMorley whispered as he cowered behind Previn.

"Stay here," Previn ordered. "I'll investigate."

He stepped to door Number 1, placed his head close and listened.

Nothing. On he went to cell Number 2. A sniff and a quick listen. Once again: nothing. He proceeded down the hall, repeating the process until he reached the last door. He was about to shake his head and turn around when a faint scent accompanied with a muffled sound caught his attention. He ruffled his feathers and signaled for them to approach.

Confident strides carried Ela Claire down the hall while DeMorley cowered behind her, eyeing each door they passed with suspicion. When she reached Previn, she stood on her toes to retrieve the key and eyed the cell number. She gasped and flashed Previn a concerned look.

"Rather fitting, wouldn't you say," he asked her.

She gave a solemn nod. "It gives some insight as to why the King of Claire sent me on this mission."

DeMorley, unable to make the connection, pushed his way forward. "What are you two talking about?"

"Ela Claire has the distinct honor of rescuing treasure from a cell bearing the same number as her cottage: 17."

Ela Claire became overwhelmed with memories of Hetherlinn: her parents, the meadow, her oak. When Romlin's handsome face appeared, she swallowed hard to regain control over her emotions. She shook her head to rid the sorrowful memories and inserted the key into the rusty catch.

DeMorley stopped her hand from turning it.

"Are you sure about this," he whispered. "Previn is too large to enter with us, and once open, we may not be able to shut it again."

She took in his face lined with worry and looked deep into his eyes glazed with fear. She patted his hand and smiled.

"I'm certain."

Something about her radiant face, which he was unable to fully comprehend, convinced him to trust her. He released his grip.

She turned the key and the cries erupted within.

Chapter 31

When Kings Clash

Lassiter sat cross-legged by his fire nibbling on his breakfast of smoked venison and fresh berries. The dawn was cool but he knew that by mid-morning it would be blistering hot, just like it had been the days prior. Such was life on the Gilden Plains.

He ripped off another bite and noted the men waking up. Flint and steel sparked fires, tea was prepared, meals were shared and chatter was minimal.

Lassiter turned his attention to Draemel sitting across from him. He was raking a stick through the embers and his red hair, typically well groomed, was disheveled and littered with debris.

Lassiter smirked and couldn't pass up the opportunity to tease his general. "You look tired this morning. I mean *really* tired."

Draemel shot him a hot look. "I'm not."

Lassiter popped a berry into his mouth. "I see." He gestured at Draemel's locks. "So you've woven grass, leaves and twigs in your hair to make yourself more attractive, or to camouflage yourself?"

Draemel was about to give him a tongue lashing when a commotion brought them to their feet. Officers and soldiers were gesturing at a rider who had crested a ridge and was galloping their way.

"It's our scout," Lassiter noted.

"Yes," Draemel answered as he cleaned his hair of the trash, "but his breakneck speed tells me there's trouble."

The horse galloped into camp and the scout slid off before his steed came to a complete stop. He saluted his commanding officer and delivered the news. Alarmed by the report, the captain escorted the scout to Lassiter and waved the other commanders over to join them.

"Sir," the captain said after saluting, "you need to hear his report."

Lassiter eyed the scout who looked to be no more than twenty summers of age. "What's the news?"

"A column of Ebonites, sir."

"How many?"

"I'm not sure; they were too far away."

"Too far away?" Draemel crossed his arms over his chest and delivered his next words to both the captain and the scout. "You mean to tell me that you didn't get close enough to verify?"

Both men stiffened.

Draemel fingered his gor blade and eyed the scout. "I'm waiting."

The scout kept one eye on Draemel and the other on the fingers drumming the weapon. "My orders were to scout the area but under no circumstance was I to give away my location. Had I moved closer for confirmation, I would have compromised my position to the villagers as well as our enemy."

Draemel stopped his tapping and fingered his scar. "I'm a veteran of the Dark War. Did you know that?"

"Yes, sir," the scout answered, not quite sure where the conversation was going. "You're reputation is outstanding."

"And did you know when we fought on the Gilden Plains, that we were able to do reconnaissance without compromising our location?"

"Yes, sir."

Draemel leaned close, and in a half-whisper said, "So please explain yourself. What exactly did you see?"

"A dust cloud east of Gilden."

"A dust cloud?"

"Yes, sir, but more like a line of smoke."

"A line of smoke."

The scout missed the sarcasm in Draemel's tone and nodded.

Draemel's face became as red as his hair. "So without any verification, you charge into camp, tell your captain that you've spotted a column of Ebonite cavalry, when in reality all you witnessed was a dust cloud?"

"More like a line of smoke, sir."

"Which could have been nothing more than a stampede or a *shirado*."

"A what, sir?"

Draemel threw his arms into the air and turned to deliver his fury to the captain. "Unbelievable! You send this boy out as a scout and he doesn't even know what a *shirado* is?"

The captain kept his mouth shut and remained at attention. Draemel continued to drill him. "So what made you pick him to be a scout?"

"The men from his village say he's the best hunter and tracker."

"But he doesn't even know what a *shirado* is!"

Lassiter rested a hand on Draemel's shoulder in an effort to calm him down. "Our soldiers are doing the best they can. At least he didn't give away our position."

"Yes, he maintained secrecy, but for all we know he may have just seen a herd of deer, not Ebonites."

The scout cleared his throat. "Permission to speak, sir?"

Lassiter gave a consenting nod.

"Tell me what a *shirado* is and I'll tell you if that's what I saw or not."

Lassiter glanced at Draemel out of the corner of his eye and could tell he was too upset to bother with an answer. "It's my understanding," Lassiter replied, "that a *shirado* is what the people of the Gilden Plains call a dust storm."

"Can you describe it?"

Lassiter felt Draemel's shoulder tense under his hand. "Since this is my first time on the plains," Lassiter said as he patted Draemel's back, "I'll defer to my general."

Draemel exploded. "It's a dust cloud! What more is there to explain? A massive wall of dust!"

"Perhaps," Lassiter said with more reassuring pats, "if you share some of your vast knowledge and a *wee* bit more detail, it will help our scout give us a more accurate report."

Draemel thought the matter over, and when he spoke, there was still an edge to his tone. "*Shirados* vary in size and only occur in the dry season."

"Which is now," the scout offered, eager to prove his knowledge and worth.

Draemel gave a subtle nod to confirm. "During my campaigns, I saw one small *shirado*. It twisted and hopped like a sprite and was harmless. But then there was the giant..." He leaned closer to intimidate the soldier. "It looked like a tidal wave of brown dust. Winds so strong, that had I not been in Min Brock, I would have been seriously injured...or worse."

The scout didn't flinch and mulled over the information. "No sir, that's not what I saw."

Draemel leaned back and gave him a condescending look. "Really? Only a moment ago you weren't able to tell me much of anything and now you're certain the dust cloud isn't a *shirado?*

"Sir, I may have failed in getting closer, and I won't let that happen again, but with all due respect, I know the difference between a dust cloud made by cavalry from that of a *shirado.*"

"And that being?"

"Like I've said, it was more like a thin ribbon of smoke."

"That could have been stampeding animals."

"No sir, not in this season and not in so orderly a line."

"My, aren't we bubbling with confidence."

"Sir, my confidence comes from what I've learned from hunters and veterans of these plains, and none of what they've told me lines up with what I saw."

"And what have they told you?"

"As you know, gors travel in small packs and are therefore incapable of making as much dust as I witnessed. Lions never stampede, and since I saw a line of dust and not a cloud indicating a hunting or killing frenzy, they're out of the equation. Which leaves only wild horses, most of which, as I'm sure you're aware of, were destroyed in the Dark War. And since the remaining herds migrate this time of year to cooler temperatures and more abundant water supplies, I've ruled them out as well."

Draemel crossed his arms. "You're forgetting deer and jit-jit and the horned ra-ez."

The scout didn't bat an eye. "Deer, if attacked or spooked, retreat for the Addoli Ridge. They prefer height as a defense. They don't march single-file through the plains to be picked off by predators. Plus, they stay in smaller herds, not large ones like the horses, and the dust cloud I saw was too big for this.

"Jit-jits are much too small to stir up that much dust and prefer burrowing over stampeding, while the horned ra-ez defend themselves by circling with tusks outward. When they do stampede, which is rare, they do so in a horizontal formation, not in a line."

The scout let the moment hang and then straight-faced added, "Of course, it could have been stampeding field mice or crazed jackrabbits, sir."

Lassiter bit his lip to keep from laughing while several officers smirked and turned away before being spotted by their general.

Draemel glared at the scout who refused to blink or smile or give any indication that his comment had been snide. Draemel sized him up, liked the fire he saw in his eyes despite his sarcasm, and ended the stare down with a question. "What's your nationality and name, soldier?"

"I'm Karshe from Ingloid, sir."

Draemel stepped back and planted his hands on his hips. "I should have guessed. Only an Ingloid would be so brash before his general."

The scout kept his poker face. "Brash, sir?"

"Yes, brash! Even your name oozes contempt. Who would name their son after the sea dragons Ingloids hunt?"

"It's not my birth name, sir. When my father didn't return from a karshe hunting trip, my mother changed my name. She said it was to remind me of his sacrifice, as well as my future."

Draemel looked him over. "You can't be more than seventeen summers of age."

"I just turned eighteen, sir, and I know what you're implying: that I'm too young to have hunted the dragons."

"Indeed. Only boys of eighteen summers are permitted. It's their *Rite of Bourge*."

Karshe didn't flinch. "True, sir, but I passed the training and proved myself worthy of the *Rite of Bourge* at an earlier age."

Draemel reflected on his *Rite of Bourge* with a crew of seasoned hunters. He could still hear the waves lapping the narrow hull of their craft; the glare from the water making it impossible to spy any sign of the silver colossus in the deep blue. Sweat and fear, from even the bravest of warrior, thick on the wind as they waited for beast to rise from the depths.

"You're either very brave or very foolish."

"Or very motivated, sir."

Draemel arched an eyebrow and gave him a nod of respect.

"You have potential, soldier." And in a softer voice, "but watch the mockery, and on your next scouting mission, get closer."

Karshe saluted and Draemel turned the matter back to Lassiter. Lassiter searched the faces of his commanders. "You heard Karshe's report. I'm open to suggestions. Speak freely."

A leader from Ferra, tall and dark skinned, spoke up. "Sir, I suggest we continue north to Claire. We can investigate what he spotted, and with the advantage of surprise on our side, determine a course of action."

"Good," Lassiter said, "but we'll be exposed crossing the Gilden Plains and there's the chance their scouts will spot us first, unless the column isn't Ebonites but jackrabbits."

Lassiter swatted Draemel on the back and the men chuckled.

An Allsbruthian officer chimed in. "There's been talk of heading to Min Brock. I say we march to the keep and avoid whatever is north of us."

"Min Brock," the warrior from Ferra jested. "You actually believe those tales? How could it be rebuilt and in so short amount of time?"

"Because there are too many stories confirming such a marvel has happened."

"And who is telling such tales? Who among us has first hand evidence of such a thing happening?"

The officers mumbled and debated the topic until Draemel raised his arms to settle them down. "Ultimately," Draemel said as he made eye contact with each commander, "the decision is your future king's."

He swept his arm to Lassiter.

Lassiter mulled over the options, took in his commander's faces, sized up his men sitting about fires who were watching his every move, knowing his decision determined their fate.

"True, no one knows for certain if Min Brock has been rebuilt, and to journey across the Gilden Plains this far south of the Addoli Ridge is dangerous. It's nothing but a wasteland of grass with little water. The journey is at least a five day march from here, am I correct?"

He eyed Draemel who gave a consenting nod. "Another option,"

Draemel offered, "is we retreat to Ingloid and then head north. It's much longer but is safer."

Lassiter was dumbfounded. Retreat? Go another direction to Min Brock? Was Draemel that desperate for revenge to risk journeying to a castle that may not exist? Lassiter caught Draemel's smirk and realized he was discreetly helping him make a tactical decision. Lassiter delivered his next words loud enough to be heard by the soldiers huddled around their fires.

"I don't know what lies north of us but I do know this: you didn't leave your families to march all this way to retreat or cower from our enemy in a keep, if it even exists."

Heads nodded. He continued.

"You've proven your devotion, your commitment, your bravery against our enemy. But even if we defeat the Ebonites, whether that be north of us or at Min Brock, how do we destroy the Cauldron? By sword? Lance? Arrow?"

Lassiter let the reality of what they faced sink in before continuing.

"Our future, one not controlled by Ebon or the Cauldron, is anchored to one truth." He shot a finger up to accent his next point. "Without the Only's whisper or stories, we are doomed."

More nods.

"That is why we'll march north, to Claire. And if the column that's been spotted is indeed Ebonite cavalry," he smiled at Karshe, "then we'll engage the enemy." He unsheathed his blade and thrust it into the air. "And avenge those that have fallen by their blade!"

Loud cheers erupted from his men.

Draemel slapped him on the back and leaned close to his ear. "Nice speech. You are definitely your father's son."

Lassiter drank in the compliment and led them to their horses.

Lassiter raised a clinched fist and the army stopped. Karshe and Draemel, returning from their scouting, stopped in front of Lassiter.

"He was correct," Draemel said with a head nod to the scout. "It's an Ebonite patrol. Looks to be forty or fifty, and yet…"

"What?"

"They're stirring up more dust than I would have anticipated."

"Maybe the wind is playing tricks on your old eyes," Lassiter jested.

"Perhaps." And then after a moment of thought and missing the joke, "Doubtful."

"So what's our plan?"

"The rear of the formation has passed our location so we have the element of surprise, especially with the stiff winds concealing the noise of our advance and our scent."

"Scent?" Lassiter smirked. "They can smell us?"

Draemel ignored his question and continued.

"Once we reach the top of this ridge," he shot a thumb over his shoulder at the summit, "order the men to fan out into a single line. We'll descend en masse, swords drawn, and when we reach the valley, we'll gallop to attack. Got it?"

Lassiter nodded, passed the command on to his captains, and signaled for them to advance. At the ridgetop, Lassiter and Draemel drew their weapons; the army followed suit. Lassiter gestured with his sword to his right, and the line directly behind him spread out atop the ridge. Draemel pointed to his left and his line fanned out in the opposite direction.

Lassiter gestured with a sword thrust into the air and they advanced down the slope. When they reached the bottom, Lassiter signaled the attack and they stormed toward the Ebonites.

When they were within an arrow shot, the Ebonite cavalry increased their speed as if they had been alerted to the attack, but not a single rider had turned to spy them. Lassiter looked to Draemel for an explanation and was stunned to see his face clouded with worry. And when the Ebonites divided and one half turned to charge Lassiter's force head on while the other tried to outflank them, Draemel shook his head in disbelief.

"It's a trap," Draemel shouted over the noise of their horses. "Order a retreat!"

Before Lassiter could react, hundreds of gors materialized out of thin air behind the wave of charging warhorses. And leading them was a fiend they both recognized.

"Paradin," Lassiter exclaimed as he pulled back on his reins and signaled his forces to slow down. "And his army!"

Draemel came to a stop beside Lassiter and checked on the other Ebonite force. "It's a pincher maneuver: They'll attack us on both flanks. How could I have been so blind?"

He took in Lassiter's frightened expression, Hornlynn's face flashed in his memory.

"*Tisk, tisk, tisk, what's this, this this,*" Paradin taunted from afar in the silent tongue. "*You witnessed Hornlynn's death and now you'll be privy to his son's.*"

Draemel glared in the direction of the Gor King. "Unless I kill you first!"

"Vows, vows, vows. Did you keep your promise to Hornlynn, your bride, your son, Farron?"

Draemel ignored the insult and addressed his closest commander.

"Have the men circle up. Order archers to fire at will. Go!"

The officer turned to carry out the orders.

"Fun, fun, fun. But you can't stop me, me, me. Do you remember when I did this to Newcomb?"

Lassiter groaned and slumped in his saddle.

Draemel shouted at Lassiter in an attempt to snap him out of the spell but his eyes remained glazed over and his head wobbled as if he were drunk.

Paradin snickered and sang DeMorley's song of praise in a singsong manner.

Newcomb, your sacrifice,
Shall crush the drone, shall crush the drone.
Allsbruth, your king awaits,
To claim his throne, to claim his throne.

"Enough," Draemel muttered between clinched teeth. "This ends *now!*"

He sheathed his sword and charged the attacking gors and Ebonites. At best, he knew it was a suicide mission, but if he succeeded, it might be the turning point not only in the battle but in the ensuing war. Without taking his eyes off the Gor King, he fished out his sling and a spiked ball. He whirled the orb overhead and urged his horse to a faster clip.

"Death begets life," he shouted, more as an encouragement to himself than as a prayer to the Only. He grit his teeth, gave the sling one great whirl, and sent his shot sailing.

Mälque spurred his horse through the dismounted cavalry, ignored their off-color comments and hot looks, and focused on the two mounted warriors in front of him: Woren and the Gor King.

This wasn't his first scouting report and yet his stomach flipped with excitement and dread. He told himself not to stare at the Gor King, but the more he tried to look away, the stronger the desire to gaze became.

Mälque pulled back on the reins and stopped before them. He gawked at the Gor King, unable to find his tongue.

"And," Woren asked in an effort to break Mälque's bug-eyed spell. "What did you see?"

Mälque snapped out of it and gestured over his shoulder. "Beyond that ridge are two forces. One's an Ebonite cavalry that's headin' home. The other's a force I've never seen before. They're headin' east at a fast clip. I'm thinkin' they're gonna ambush the Ebonites."

Woren leaned back in his saddle. "How many in each?"

Mälque eyed the Gor King, afraid that any misinformation would forfeit his life. The Gor King repositioned himself in his saddle; warhorse whinnied; leather groaned. He met Mälque's gaze.

Mälque steeled himself and gulped down his fears as if swallowing bad medicine.

"About three, maybe four hundred in that mystery army, but I ain't sure about the Ebonites."

Woren leaned toward Mälque. "And why not?"

Mälque scrunched up his face and wrestled with not only how to describe what he saw, but worried the Gor King wouldn't accept his answer as the truth. "Well, my eyes only seen 'bout a hundred, but..." He let his voice trail off and checked the Gor King. Would his tomb-like sockets flare red? Would the blue sword be drawn?

"Mälque," Woren barked to break the boy's trance. "Finish your report. Nothing is going to happen to you."

"*Yeah, right,*" Mälque thought to himself. "*Just like nothin' happened to Olke...Vonn.*"

The Gor King flinched, albeit unnoticeable to the others.

Mälque scrunched up his face. "*Did you just read my mind,*" he wondered.

Mälque thought he saw the Gor King grin. And if he did, was it a sinister smile or more in line of what he used to give Vonn whenever they were up to no good?

Mälque shook off his conjectures and finished the report. "Reason bein' is that the dust cloud was big."

Woren cocked his head to the side. "Explain."

Mälque shrugged. "What's to explain? Like I said, my eyes only seen a hundred, but that cloud of dust looked like somethin' made by over four hundred riders."

Woren nodded and whispered something to the Gor King.

In one swift motion, The Gor King drew his sword and thrust it into the air. His men fell silent, eager to hear his command.

"Advance." His voice was as dark as night. "Prepare for battle."

The army of riff-raff, criminals and bounty hunters, that Mälque noted lacked the precision and decorum he had witnessed in the Ebonite units, became disciplined when given an order by the Gor King. In no time, they had mounted horses and formed into two columns.

Mälque followed Woren and the Gor King to the front, and with a signal from Woren, the army advanced at a slow trot.

Up ahead was a ridge, and when they reached the apex, the army fanned out into a single line with the Gor King positioned in the middle. In the valley below, the mystery army was attacking the rear flank of the Ebonite cavalry.

"I had my doubts about your report," Woren said, "but I agree with you: the dust cloud is much too large to be made by that unit alone."

As if on cue, the Ebonites increased their speed and split their forces. Gors, hundreds of them, materialized out of thin air. Leading them was a bald-headed man riding a bull.

"It's *him*," Mälque exclaimed as he rubbed his eyes to make sure they weren't playing tricks on him.

"So it is," Woren said nonchalantly. "The other Gor King."

The mystery army halted, and after what appeared to be commands being exchanged, formed into a half-circle to defend against the two fronts. With no warning, a rider with long, red hair, dashed away from the formation and straight for the gors.

"What's he doin'?"

Mälque's question was rhetorical. He could see the warrior whirling a sling and noted that he was on a collision course for the other Gor King. It was a suicide mission.

Out of the corner of his eye, Mälque saw the blue sword of their Gor King rise into the air.

Woren noted the signal and shouted the command down the line. "Archers!"

Long bows were pulled off backs and arrows nocked.

"Aim for the gors," Woren instructed.

Bowstrings groaned as they were drawn to cheeks. Arrow tips were raised skyward.

"Fire!"

Lassiter rolled his head, saw Draemel gallop off, tried to order him back, but couldn't move his tongue or make a sound.

"*Ah, yes,*" Paradin taunted from his charge, "*you do see, say I! When my gors have ravaged Draemel's body, you'll be next to die.*"

Lassiter felt detached from reality, unable to distinguish pain from euphoria, hope from loss. Everything looked too bright, and a low-pitched drone was all he could hear. He checked on his commanders. Their eyes bulged with urgency; spittle flew, no doubt requesting orders, but the drone drowned them out.

He checked on Draemel, saw him twirling the sling, caught the ball's release and followed the flight straight for the Gor King's head. The Gor King snatched it out of the air barehanded and held it up for him to behold.

"'*Tales shall crush steel when gors have a king.*'"

He pulverized the spiked ball as if it were clay.

"*And now, my forces shall crush you!*"

The Gor King used his power to make Lassiter look to his left. Charging in for the kill was the other flank of Ebonite cavalry. Lassiter had enough whereabouts to know that unless he ordered a counterattack or a retreat, they would be destroyed. But he was too light-headed to do anything but stare.

Something glinted from the hill behind the Ebonites. Lassiter sensed another presence, one that wrestled his attention away from Paradin's control and directed it to the ridge. Cavalry lined the summit, and at the center was a warrior donning a skull helmet and brandishing a blue sword.

As a Wurmlin, Mälque had seen his share of bloodshed, he had Olke to thank for that, as well as his share of the bizarre, he had his mother to thank for that. But none of those experiences prepared him for the carnage unfolding in the valley below.

Mälque held his breath as the lone rider galloped toward the gor army. He caught the sling's orbit, the release, and hoped the shot would split the Gor King's head wide open. But when the Gor King caught it barehanded, Mälque let his breath out and feared the worst for the redheaded assassin. The rider beat a hasty retreat, the gors hot on his trail, and Mälque found hope restored and cheered the warrior on.

Arrows whizzed from Mälque's left and right, twisting up, black missiles against blue sky. He watched them arc over the gors then rain down piercing heads, flanks, necks, backs, jowls. Gors shrieked, dropped, thrashed, broke rank and slammed into other gors. Blood spurted, ran; brown grass and fur were stained red. Thuds rumbled as gors collided or fell and plowed up sod.

An arrow slammed into the shoulder of the baldheaded Gor King and Mälque, along with the archers, shouted a loud hooray. The Gor King eyed the shaft as if it was a bothersome thorn then yanked it out. He tossed it aside and gestured to his gors to continue their attack.

Mälque noted something glowing out of the corner of his eye. He turned to discover the Gor King's sword emitting an ethereal blue light. A hum, which Mälque associated with the sword, became so loud that he covered his ears.

Mälque checked on Woren and the other men, wondering if they were equally impressed by the sword's mystical energy. They remained poised; proof that this wasn't their first time witnessing such power.

The Gor King pointed the sword at the valley and a line of blue fire shot out of the tip like an arrow. Blue-white fire exploded at the base of the hill and raced across the plain, cutting off the advancing gors and

Ebonites. The baldheaded Gor King ordered his army to halt and stared at the wall of flames then shook a fist at those on the ridge. With a gesture to his gors and the Ebonites, he led them away from the fray.

Mälque turned and stared in awe at the Gor King. The blade no longer emitted fire but continued to blaze while steam swirled out of the tip. His arm muscles bulged as if he'd been in hand-to-hand combat. Sweat glistened, rolled. Lips quivered from either the exertion or because he enjoyed the moment. But what sent a chill coursing Mälque's spine were his eye sockets.

They pulsed with crimson light.

Lassiter tried to blink, tried to look away from the warrior on the ridge but was unable to break the spell he was under. He sensed a presence, something dark and enigmatic that could not only dominate his will, but thwart Paradin's taunts and the Cauldron's drone. He associated the presence with the warrior and deduced, based upon the campfire tales he'd heard his men tell, that this was the other Gor King.

Out of the corner of his eye, Lassiter saw a flash of blue light and heard the crackle of dried grass bursting into flame. He tried to turn for a look but the Gor King held his head in place. Lassiter could feel a great heat from the flames, smelled the burning grass, and saw enough from his peripheral vision to conclude the fire had stopped the advancing gors and Ebonites.

"You saved our lives," Lassiter thought.

"I like to think of it as delaying your death."

Lassiter, spooked to hear the Gor King's reply in his head, stared at the sword flaring with blue light. Lassiter braved a challenge. *"So join us. Together we can defeat the Ebonites and the Cauldron."*

"Herein lies our dilemma: there can only be one king."

"Yes, which is why you will bow to me since I'm heir to the throne."

"No, it is you who will submit to my command. I've earned it today by saving your lives."

"Yes, for which I'll be forever in your debt, but I will not abdicate the throne."

Dark laughter rumbled.

"Time will tell about that. Just remember this: A time will come when I'll return to collect what you owe me."

The blue sword dimmed, was sheathed, and the Gor King signaled his men to retreat off the ridgeline. As they disappeared from view, Lassiter felt the spell weaken. He had the sensation of floating up from the bottom of a dark well, and the higher he rose, the more his senses and abilities returned to normal. When he broke the surface, he found himself staring into the concerned eyes of Draemel.

"I'm glad to see you're back with us," he said.

Lassiter nodded. "I was under the spell of both Gor Kings."

"That much I deduced." He looked over his shoulder at the wall of blue fire. "He saved our lives yet retreated. Why?"

"Like the tales allude to, he serves no man, king or entity, just his blade of blue." Lassiter turned his attention to the vacated ridge. "But he made it clear that one day he'll call on us to ante up."

Draemel followed Lassiter's line of sight. "Well, now's not the time to discuss such things. There's no telling how long these flames will burn to keep Paradin at bay or if the new Gor King," he flicked his head back at the summit, "will return to attack."

"Agreed, but the fire is blocking our advance to Claire."

They cupped their eyes and looked east. The blaze stretched into what looked like forever.

"Although it's not what we planned," Lassiter said, "I think it's time we head east to Min Brock."

Draemel snapped his gaze back to Lassiter. "But you don't believe it's been rebuilt, not to mention that it's a perilous journey."

"I know, but now that we've confirmed there's a second Gor King, maybe the tales about Min Brock and the Worms of Bal-Malin are accurate as well."

Draemel flashed him a wry smile and repeated Lassiter's challenge from the other day. "Please tell me you're not putting stock in these myths being true."

"In mad times such as these," Lassiter offered with one last look at the ridgeline, "sometimes the sane thing to do is be mad yourself."

Chapter 32

Treasure

Ela Claire tried to open cell Number 17's heavy door.

It didn't budge.

"I don't hear them anymore," she whispered to Previn as she motioned for DeMorley to help her.

"True," Previn concurred with a sniff, "but I'm certain they are within."

DeMorley wagged his head. "Your secrecy is making me more nervous."

"You'll be fine," she comforted, "just help pull."

They strained, grunted and dug boot heels into the muck to get better leverage. Rusty hinges groaned as the door creaked open, releasing a cloud of stench - rot, musk and human waste - that enveloped them.

DeMorley and Ela Claire gagged and covered their mouths and noses with their hands while Previn, unaffected by the stench, stuck his head in and peered about the darkness.

DeMorley and Ela Claire, with hands still over their mouths and noses, looked inside as well. A torch, secured well out of reach from the ground, cast an eerie glow. The cell was as large as Rhythe's courtyard and was constructed of tall walls oozing moisture.

As their eyes adjusted to the dim light, they spotted movement in a far corner.

Cowering within the shadows, as far away from the intruders as possible, were the occupants of cell Number 17.

DeMorley blinked his eyes to make sure he was not seeing things. "Children," he blurted through fingers covering his mouth. "I was frightened by *children?*"

He dropped his hand and spun to face Previn. "And you knew it, too. Did you enjoy watching me cringe the entire way here?"

Previn didn't reply. Although he had savored DeMorley's fright-filled journey, the suffering children had Previn's full attention now.

DeMorley huffed and eyed the cell. "But where is the treasure?"

Ela Claire ignored his question and stepped into the cell. Her orange glow filled the gloom with warm light.

Witnessing her body pulsing like fire, the children gasped or cried or threatened her with loud shouts.

Ela Claire stopped and raised her arms to show them she was

without a weapon. "I won't hurt you."

They quieted but eyed her with suspicion.

She battled the nausea caused by the foul air and tiptoed closer. A quick head count told her there were thirty. They huddled like a pack of wild animals: some shook with fright, others stood motionless and eyed the muck, a few threatened her with raised long fingernails to claw and bared teeth to bite.

Ela Claire ignored their threatening gestures and saw them for what they really were: tortured children with grimy faces, gaunt cheeks and hollow eyes.

She glanced back at DeMorley and Previn. "They've been starved."

Turning back to eye the children, compassion brought a tear to her eye while anger for their plight formed her hands into fists. Previn, unable to fit through the doorway, voiced a warning.

"Do not be rash, Ela Claire. I know you want to run and cuddle them, but remember: this is a prison cell, and although they are children, there has to be a reason they are incarcerated."

She nodded as she took in their bare feet, ratty tunics, and disheveled, greasy hair. "Maybe so," she fired over her shoulder, "but children, even those that deserve punishment, should not be tortured."

Ela Claire crept forward. "Please, don't be afraid. We're here to help."

The pack pressed back into the wall, and those bearing their claws and snapping teeth, howled, hissed and spat at her.

Ela Claire stopped and bit her lip to keep from weeping. She glanced back at DeMorley. "That's what we heard on the beach and in the courtyard. Do you still think this castle is haunted?"

DeMorley, who typically was so self-absorbed that nothing beyond his own condition ever concerned him, became overwhelmed with emotion. He closed his eyes and turned away.

Ela Claire realized she could not get any closer without either frightening them or getting hurt herself. She stopped and thought about telling a story to demonstrate that she was their champion but felt it would be too much like manipulation. She needed to gain their trust first, then she would reveal her wondrous tales.

But why are you here, she wondered.

Needing to learn more about their story, she searched their minds, being careful not to alert them to her activity. She eyed a girl who was glaring and slashing at her like a feral wolf.

"Denli, a Wurmlin girl of seven summers; torn from her parents by raiding Ebonites; brought to the Isle of Rhythe because one leg was shorter than the other; incarcerated for two summers."

She eyed a boy whose face looked as if an invisible palm had stretched one half out of place. He shivered and stared glassy-eyed at her.

"Akking of Tristan; five summers of age; abducted by warriors because of his deformed features; imprisoned now for three summers."

Another story.

"Lolling. An Ingloid of no more than four summers; ripped from her cottage by Ebonites; flown to the Isle of Rhythe by vul jens; her mind never to mature past that of a child."

Ela Claire, sensing something unusual, stopped her search and stepped back from the children.

"Previn," she called out over her shoulder, "did you sense that?"

"Yes. Miniscule whispers probing our thoughts."

"What does that mean," DeMorley asked. When Previn didn't answer, he shouted into the cell, "What does that *mean*?"

Ela Claire also ignored him and squinted as she studied the children's faces. "Subtle pushes of thought," she said loud enough for even Previn to hear, "coming from within this room." She crept forward, her instincts and muscles ready to spring into action should they attack.

"Yes," Previn concurred. "And there is more than one."

Ela Claire stopped. "There you are," she half-whispered to herself.

Hiding away from the others, in the deepest shadows of the cell, was a band of children. They too varied in age, gender and nationality, but unlike the others, they did not have any birth defects.

"Please," she said with hands extended to show them she was unarmed. "I promise not to hurt you." She slid her feet over the mucky floor and they backed away.

"I know how you feel. You are different from the other children and no one can tell you why...until now."

Another step and this time the children did not move.

"And when I entered the thoughts of your friends, you tried to do the same thing with us, but you lack the experience and skill."

They flinched in fear. She stopped.

"Don't worry, I'm not angry with you. You simply long to know your true nature; to escape this horrid place; desperate to understand why you were sent to Rhythe since your bodies and minds are not deformed."

They stared at her with curious expressions.

"Do not be frightened," she said in the silent tongue. *"I know who you all are."*

Their eyes bulged wide open, stunned that she was within their minds. They chatted amongst themselves in the silent tongue and cast suspicious glances her way.

"Yes," Ela Claire continued. *"I can read your thoughts and speak the silent tongue...just like you."*

Several children flashed expressions of joy, excited that Ela Claire was just like them, while the others crossed arms and scowled.

"Has anyone told you why this is so, or who you are," Ela Claire asked.

Their collective voices probed her mind, and although timid and weak in ability, voiced a resounding, *"No."*

"Look." She lowered her head and began to part her hair all the while making her orange glow brighter. *"Do you see my birthmark? It looks like a purple tulip. My guess is that you have one too."*

Curiosity brought them close to her light but they made sure to stay clear of her reach. When they spied her birthmark, they scampered back to a safer distance.

"See for yourselves. I'll stay here. No tricks. I promise."

They looked at each other with great wonder, and as if on cue, several bowed their heads for examination. Dirty fingers dug and parted hair, being ever so gentle, in search of the tinge of purple.

"I found it!" one boy boomed for all to hear.

The others swarmed around and stared at the girl's scalp.

"You've got to look close," he instructed, "but the outline of the tulip is there. See?"

"Yes," they shouted.

Excited by the discovery, and their fears of Ela Claire diminishing, they intensified their efforts, moving closer to have better light.

"Here, in the back," a girl exclaimed with a proud smile.

Like miners knowing where to dig for buried treasure, their search quickened and reaped faster results.

"Her's is right here," a boy of ten summers shouted as he pointed to a spot behind the girl's ear.

"His is above his forehead!"

"Found it. On the very top!"

When every birthmark had been discovered, a boy of eleven summers asked Ela Claire the question plaguing them all. "So we're prisoners simply because we have purple tulips on our heads?"

"There's more to it than that," Ela Claire answered with a broad smile. "Your birthmarks are signs, or proof, that you are all…storytellers."

"A storyteller," one girl asked with her head cocked to the side. "What can they do?"

Ela Claire's face beamed. "Everything. Watch."

Spinning around, she took broad strides to the center of the cell and closed her eyes.

Curious, yet still apprehensive, the young storytellers gathered around her. This enticed the other children of cell Number 17 to trust as well, and they hid behind the storytellers.

When Ela Claire's orange glow shimmered with bright colors, the children *oohed* and *ahhed*. Balls of multi-colored lights sparked to the dirt floor and bounced across their bare feet, but instead of burning, they tickled toes and the children giggled and danced.

Ela Claire rose off the floor with eyes closed, and the new storytellers applauded her efforts, giddy with the thought that in time, they too could perform such feats.

Hovering above their heads, Ela Claire focused on her story.

A sudden burst of air - fresh, clean, and smelling of the sea - burst through the cell doorway. Hair was tossed and the tunics flapped and fluttered in the winds. The breeze sailed about the cell, herding the stench into one invisible mass and whisking it out of Rhythe.

The ceiling throbbed and pulsed as if trying to draw in a deep breath. The children, fearing its collapse, gathered beneath Ela Claire's waterfall of light. Then, with a loud *bang*, the ceiling exploded with a bright flash of light.

The children screamed and covered their heads. Surprised that no debris had fallen, they emerged from the rainbow of light to investigate.

Overhead was a clear blue sky with the sun burning low on the horizon.

The walls started to tremble and quake as if invisible giants shook them, and just as they had done when the roof exploded, the children sought shelter beneath Ela Claire.

Four loud explosions, one following the other, came from each wall. When the rumbles stopped, the children peered through the dust to discover they were in a meadow. Nearby was a massive oak with long branches that were low and wide like steps. Tall green grass swayed in the breeze and soothed their calloused feet with cool dew. Birds of all shapes and colors chirped and flitted about. Far on the horizon was a snow-capped mountain that in the waning light was lilac in hue.

"Look," one child exclaimed. "Up on top of that mountain. Do you see it?"

"Yes," a boy answered as he pointed out the discovery to the others.

"A castle!"

"Who lives there?"

Before they discovered the answer, a whisper as gentle as a lark's song emanated from the palace and hovered above the tattered, deformed, filthy children like a butterfly.

"*Behold*," the Only whispered. "*My treasure! My delights!*"

Ela Claire opened one eye to witness the children's reactions to hearing the King of Claire. Some basked in the warm sunlight and let the sea breeze revive their lost innocence as the whisper soothed forlorn hearts. A few closed their eyes and swayed as if being cuddled by their mothers or fathers. Others spun around and around, arms spread wide with smiles even wider. Some crumpled to the grass and cried, but not out of fear or pain or even anger; their tears expressed feelings of gratitude words could never convey.

Ela Claire eyed the young storytellers. They stood with mouths agape, mesmerized by the wonder and beauty of Claire. And just like her experience in the mystic land, she knew they were absorbing every essence of the encounter.

She had no doubt that they dined upon the landscape's rich colors, longing to examine every hue, every shadow, every reflection and refraction of light, to glean eternal tales of this grand kingdom. She was certain that their hearing was acutely sensitive to the whooshing grass, the rustling leaves of the oak and the whisper that hailed them as his own. *Now,* she reasoned, *delight danced with delight, joy embraced darkest demise, and hope championed despair.*

When she spied some children racing for the great oak, Ela Claire ended her story. Her colorful lights faded to orange and she floated back down. When she landed, the landscape of Claire dissolved and cell Number 17 became their reality once more.

The storyteller of eleven summers stared at her with a smirk and crossed arms. "Just magic tricks. They can't really help."

She searched his face being careful to not let him read her thoughts. *"His eyes...they're so dark in color, like lumps of coal on fresh snow, and yet so hardened, so troubled. Within, I sense you are a protector of your friends, and I shudder to think what horrors you've witnessed."*

"Not magic," she counseled. "But stories that unfold beyond our darkest conditions."

"Our," he repeated. "What do *you* know of our suffering?"

She answered with a smile, which infuriated him.

He ground his teeth. "Look at you," he yelled. "Wearing a pretty dress and cape; your face all clean and your hair so nice! How could *you* know what *this* is like?"

Ela Claire did not respond. In fact, she had hoped he would continue his tirade.

As he took the bait and argued his point, Ela Claire seized the moment. She knew that in his argumentative state, he was vulnerable to her entering his inner world unaware. As he bantered on and on, she slipped into his thoughts and read his story.

"Ballin. An Ebonite. From birth, your mother knew your destiny as a storyteller. She kept it secret for many summers and serenaded you with Clairian songs as you slept. To hide your birthmark, she never cut your hair

and it grew thick like a lion's mane. And her plans and clandestine efforts would have kept you safe had it not been for one suspicious man. Your father."

Ela Claire gasped in the horror at where the story was heading but pressed deeper anyway.

"Cries from your mother as he yanked you from her arms. Gloved fist striking her face. Warriors crashing through the doorway. Your mother singing to you as they carried you off. Her song silenced by a blade. You, tossed into a wagon full of dung. Slashes of the whip. Gagged mouth. Bonds around tiny wrists, cutting deep into your flesh."

Unable to endure any more of his pain, she exited his tale just as he reached his conclusion.

"…and *that's* why being a storyteller doesn't change *anything!*"

Ela Claire reached for his arm but stopped short to see if he would comply.

Ballin studied her with his hardened eyes. Tears rolled off her cheeks. Unfazed by her show of emotion, he gave a flippant nod. She held his hand and rolled up his sleeve. Purple scars circled his wrist.

"You're right," she said as a tear trickled from her eye. She rolled his sleeve back down, "Being a storyteller won't change the story of your past."

Ballin blinked, stunned by her honest answer.

"But," she continued, "in time, the stories will right the wrong in your heart, and although the scars will always remain, there will be a purpose to the pain."

He stared at her and bit his lip to maintain his tough demeanor. "How do you know?"

She knelt in the muck to take in his face. "Because I've known my share of pain too."

He swallowed, and unable to maintain eye contact, glanced back at his peers. "Well, it still doesn't help us now, does it?"

Ela Claire stood back up. "That depends."

Ballin eyed her and set his hands on his hips. "Depends on *what?*"

"Well," she offered as she took in the faces of the other children, "if you choose to stay here, then you're correct: nothing changes. But…"

She held her words to study their eyes and hopped from story to story to find out what the others were thinking and feeling. "If you choose to believe and follow us out of Rhythe," she pointed to DeMorley and Previn, "then your future, as well as hope, will be an adventure of unforeseeable beauty."

Denli, the Wurmlin girl, stepped forward. "So we won't get hurt anymore?"

Ela Claire reached for her hands. Denli extended them to her. Ela

Claire gripped her dirty fingers and squeezed warmth into her cold hands. "No, I can't promise you that. But I do promise that you'll never be alone again. *Ever*. Besides, some of you can't even remember life before being locked up, can you?"

Many heads nodded.

"So you see," Ela Claire said to Ballin as she let go of Denli's hands, "there is so much more to gain than lose. Hope can conquer loss."

Ballin's stoic expression softened. "But what you're saying is still hard to believe."

"I know," she answered with a genuine smile. "Everyday, I too have my doubts and wonder if I have the strength to continue. But had I quit, then I wouldn't have discovered the most wonderful of treasures..."

She drank in their expressions, savoring the glimpses of hope glowing in their faces. "You," she finished.

Lolling, the forever child, made her way to Ela Claire and threw her arms around Ela Claire's leg. "You're nice," she cooed. "Just like him."

Ela Claire's face crinkled with confusion. "Just like who?"

Denli draped a consoling arm over Lolling's shoulder. "She's confused. She says an old man visits her when we're all asleep."

Lolling pushed away from Denli. "He does!"

"An Ebonite?" Previn inquired from the doorway.

Ballin shook his head. "No. She says he has white hair and wears a simple tunic. He tells her stories."

"Was he a storyteller," Ela Claire asked as she glanced at Previn. He was equally surprised and had his head cocked to one side.

Ballin snickered. "Are you serious? You actually believe her?"

Ela Claire knelt and turned Lolling her way. "Tell me more."

Lolling smiled and tried her best to explain all she had experienced, but her words clogged in her thoughts and she could only voice a few at a time. "Nice face...magic stories...boy...king...and *him.*"

She pointed to DeMorley.

All eyes turned to stare at the minstrel.

"Me?" he thumbed his chest. "Impossible." He wagged his head and waved off Lolling's tale.

Ballin shrugged. "Doesn't make any sense, now does it?"

Ela Claire focused back on Lolling. "This nice man, did he tell you his name?"

Lolling nodded, her smile wrapping from one ear to the other. She squinted to try and find his name that was jumbled up in her clogged memory. Her eyes opened wide at the discovery. "Newcomb."

DeMorley huffed and aimed an accusing finger at her. "That's utter nonsense!"

The children, sensing DeMorley's hostility, gathered around Lolling.

Ballin stood between Lolling and DeMorley with chin raised.

DeMorley stormed forward. "Newcomb is *dead!*"

Lolling peered around Ballin, and although DeMorley scowled, she was unaffected by his demeanor and gave him her biggest grin. "He said you'd be grumpy."

"Really," DeMorley asked as he planted his hands on his hips. He shook his head at her and turned his attention to Ela Claire. "Tell me you're not putting stock into this simpleton's tale."

Ela Claire glared at him and ground her teeth. "Don't *ever* call her that again, do you understand?"

DeMorley blushed with embarrassment and looked away. "Fine," he huffed. "But Newcomb is dead. I know that for a fact."

"No," Lolling answered with a wag of her head. "Look."

She pushed her way out of the circle of children and ran to a far corner. There, she knelt and pulled out several loose stones from the wall. Sticking her hand inside, she pulled out something covered in a filthy blanket and cradled it in her arms like a doll. She walked back, careful not to drop it, all the while smiling at DeMorley.

When she reached the group, the children stared in awe, stunned that she had kept a secret from them and wondering if perhaps her story was true after all.

Without a word, they parted to let her enter.

"What's *this?*" DeMorley scowled as he eyed the moldy blanket and the bulge underneath.

"Newcomb's gift. For you."

DeMorley leaned down and raised a corner of the blanket as if it covered a box of snakes. He stared underneath and became pale. Dropping the shroud, he backed away in such haste that he stumbled and fell to the damp floor.

"No. That's impossible!" His eyes bugged out as he gasped for air and scooted across the muck. "You've bewitched me or used a storyteller trick."

Ela Claire, curious to what frightened him so, removed the blanket. Nestled in the crook of her arm was a lute.

"Here." Lolling presented DeMorley with the lute, but he only squealed as if the instrument was charmed and pressed up against the cell wall.

The children gathered around Lolling and bombarded her with hundreds of questions.

Ela Claire intervened and quieted them all down. She turned her attention to DeMorley who was trembling and had his knees pulled up to his chest.

"It seems," she pressed, "that the lute and Newcomb's mysterious appearance validate why the King of Claire summoned you on this mission."

DeMorley could only shake his head and gasp for air as if he was suffocating.

"This can't *be*," he muttered more to himself than in reply to Ela Claire. "I'd recognize a Bellini lute anywhere. The master only crafted two. I smashed mine over Paradin's head." His voice trailed off as he stared at Lolling's lute. "And no one knows where the other one is."

"Until now," Previn added from the doorway.

"Unless," DeMorley said with a glint in his eye, and his voice no longer shaking "this is a fake to trick us."

He pushed himself up from the mud and stumbled forward.

Snatching the lute from Lolling, he searched its interior for Bellini's signature.

DeMorley froze and lowered the lute.

"It's...genuine," he half-whispered in shock.

He glanced into Lolling's friendly smile and spoke in a kinder tone. "I still have many questions about your story, especially the part about Newcomb, but for now, I'll accept your gift."

He cradled the instrument in the crook of his arm and fingered a string. A bell-like *ping* echoed through the dank cell.

Lolling clapped. DeMorley smiled at her. "Finally," he said in jest to Previn, "a true admirer of my art."

Ela Claire pulled Lolling close. "Did Newcomb say anything else?"

She nodded and pointed to DeMorley. "Teacher. Warrior."

DeMorley's face paled and he almost dropped the lute. "Teacher? Warrior?" He stared into the faces looking back at him. "But...but...I'm not qualified...for *either!*"

"For once," Previn snapped, "you've spoken the truth."

Ela Claire shot Previn a hot look before taking in DeMorley's stunned expression. "Well," she chimed, "it appears that just like the children, you also have an adventurous journey before you. But the King of Claire never forces a decision of the will. The choice, DeMorley, is yours to make."

DeMorley, lost in thought, positioned his fingers on the fingerboard. He strummed the chord and the notes rang off the walls of cell Number 17. "It's in tune, as if in anticipation of my arrival."

DeMorley took in the huddled children and bit his lip as he realized there was no gold or jewels to make him rich. According to the whisper, *they* were the treasure.

But how? he mused.

He sighed and thought about walking away, which he felt was his right as he was convinced Lolling's account of Newcomb was trickery or at best, a ghost story. But when the whisper from Claire stirred his dormant memories, like a finger swirling a drink, he found himself adrift in a sea of emotions from his childhood.

Forgotten. Hurt. Angry. Alone.

DeMorley, who had spent a lifetime trying to forget such feelings, winced with each pain-filled remembrance as if being slugged by a brawler. When the last vignette faded, he eyed the children with renewed vision. He realized another reason he had been led to their cell.

He was just like them.

Chapter 33

Escape

"Fifty-two," **Previn** announced as the last child left cell Number 17.

"There used to be so many more," Ela Claire lamented as she recalled Ballin's stories that swirled like dark smoke in her mind.

"DeMorley is leading them out of the dungeon," Previn added. "Have you thought of how we're to get so many safely across the sea?"

She didn't answer. She was engrossed on the corridor that led deeper into the keep's dungeon. Based upon Ballin's story, somewhere in the blackness was a large hole that plummeted to the sea. Ebonite boats would anchor below, secure ropes within the gaping opening, and climb into the castle. This was also how supplies were hauled up or prisoners brought in and out. Ballin's tale told of something even more sinister; a heinous task they had him perform since Ebonite blood flowed through his veins.

Ela Claire shivered as she envisioned the scene.

"Did you hear me," Previn asked again, jerking her thoughts from the memory. "How do you plan..."

"I heard," she interrupted in a soft voice, her eyes fixated once more on the corridor's blackness. "The only way into the castle is through the opening down this corridor. But it drops into the sea and we are without boats."

"Surely that is something your stories could change."

She nodded. "Yes, I suppose. But Ballin's stories, which were nightmares, tell me we need to find another way."

Once more, her thoughts drifted to the young Ebonite's story, and she began to relive every aspect. She watched him being forced by the warriors to haul the dead children out of cell Number 17. Through his nostrils, she smelled the stench of death, and within his ears she heard stiff limbs drag along the wet corridor. She felt their cold, lifeless flesh when he rolled them into the abyss, and she shuddered - just as he had - when the *splash* echoed up from the sea. But what horrified her the most was Ballin being forced to cart the sick - still alive - to the same fate time...after time...after time...

"Ebon will pay for this," she vowed between clinched teeth as she pushed past Previn.

They marched up the circular ramp and walked out onto the parade ground. The children were huddled around DeMorley's tall frame, the moon bathing them in argent light.

The three adults looked toward the opening where the purple fog had retreated.

"Nothing," Ela Claire said relieved.

"Nothing yet," DeMorley added, "but we must hurry and get the children out of here."

Previn eyed the minstrel. "I do believe that was the first selfless thing I've heard you say."

DeMorley, who was equally stunned by his voiced bravery, swallowed down his fears. "Well, I'm still scared as ever! How will we get out of here?"

"With a story," Ela Claire answered.

"But the Cauldron," DeMorley blurted as he took in the children's frightened faces. "Won't it hear, and find us and..." He was unable to finish his thought, the notion of anyone or anything harming the children filling him with worry.

"By now," Ela Claire said, "that purple fog has alerted the Cauldron. Besides," she said with a grin, "I'm sure the story I used to save you from your fall was discovered long before anyway."

Even in the pale moonlight, they could see him blush. "Oh, yeah," he mumbled beneath his breath. "I forgot about that."

"We'll be fine," she offered with a gentle pat to his shoulder.

She faced the children and squatted to take in their faces. She expected to see eyes full of fear and panic. Instead, she was greeted with expressions of hope and excitement.

"Are you ready for a great adventure," she asked.

They all nodded.

"It will be very dangerous."

"No worse than what we've already lived through," Ballin replied.

Ela Claire remembered the corridor, the opening to the sea, the splash...

She brushed the memories aside. "You're right," she answered, "but nevertheless, I need you to promise that if we tell you to do something that you obey. You can't question us. A moment of hesitation could spell death."

Taking the truth to heart they nodded.

"So be it," she confirmed as she stood back up.

"So how will you get us out of here," Ballin asked.

"I'm not. You all are."

Ela Claire strutted out to the middle of the parade ground, her dark cape swooshing with her gait, and summoned the young storytellers to her side.

"Tonight," she instructed with a broad smile, "you're going to witness the greatness of the tales of Claire. Tonight, you will be embracing the role prepared for you long before you were born. But," she stuck her index finger up to accent her point, "the Cauldron will also witness our powers as well as discover your secrets, and will hunt you for the rest of your lives. Do you understand?"

They nodded and she continued.

"Once we begin this story, we cannot stop until it is finished, no matter what. This may mean days, perhaps even years of standing true to our tale. Do you still wish to continue with me?"

"We've already suffered great losses," one boy replied. "We're ready to experience great triumph."

Ela Claire smiled. "Well said." She patted his head. "I'm going to teach you how your stories can be used for good. Now close your eyes."

They obeyed.

"Listen to my words. Do not question; do not resist them. Let them fly within your heart, let them carry you beyond this place of horrors to the land of true tales. Then repeat them aloud, speaking as one, but let them hail from your deepest emotions and your strongest delights. Are you ready?"

With eyes shut tight, they nodded.

Ela Claire closed hers and hovered off the ground. Her story unfurled.

> *Young pyres of anguish, lost hearts black as night,*
> *Shall bloom like a tulip, shall stand tall and strong.*

The children repeated her refrain. Ela Claire continued.

> *Justice we call forth, ride moon's bluest light,*
> *And rescue such treasure who sing their lost song.*

Again, they repeated. Once more Ela Claire instructed.

> *So fly shattered hearts, upon the winds of Claire,*
> *Gird loin and arms amidst the Cauldron's gales.*
> *Castaways of darkness, young hearts don't despair,*
> *For whispers birth stories, and lore begets tales.*

When their last word was spoken, the winds shifted and brought the scent of spring to their nostrils. Young eyes blinked open in anticipation of something spectacular coming their way. They scanned the skies but only saw the clouds being chased away by the fresh wind. They looked about Rhythe, but all they witnessed were shadows. And when they were about to question their convictions and ask Ela Claire to explain, the ground shook. Overhead, thunder cracked. They cowered together but no lightning was seen sparking the darkness.

Ela Claire descended to the ground and faced the wall closest to the distant shoreline. With another boom of thunder, the wall exploded outward. Chunks careened high into the air, flying end over end through moonbeams before crashing into the dark sea. When the dust settled, there was a massive gap where the wall had been while the scattered stones provided a manageable access down to the sea.

"Very impressive," DeMorley said as he came alongside them. "But we still need to cross the Gilden Sea."

"For now, let's help them descend," Ela Claire said as she grabbed tiny hands and led them to the descent.

DeMorley followed and helped them all climb down the stony embankment.

Once at the water's edge, they studied the wind swept waves and the distant shoreline.

"It's too far to swim and the sea is too strong," Ballin shouted above the wild winds. "How will we get off Rhythe?"

Ela Claire freed strands of hair from her face and took in his concerned look. "Simple. We walk."

Stunned, Ballin's mouth dropped open.

Ela Claire waved for the other storytellers to gather around and spoke in the silent talk.

"*You did so well awhile ago. Now let's do it again, only this time in the silent tongue since the winds are so strong. We'll focus on the water. Ready?*"

They answered, "*Yes,*" in her thoughts.

She faced the waves lapping the shoreline and started another story. The children didn't miss a beat and matched her every word.

> *"From ancient of days we call forth a tale,*
> *Buried within summers, awaiting our hail.*
> *Rumbles of greatness within fathomed depths,*
> *Arise into moonlight and provide us stoned steps."*

The churning surf calmed to became a smooth, black pathway. The moonlight paved it with silver and it stretched straight to the other shore. An invisible barrier on either side of the passageway kept the wind-swept waters from crashing across.

Ela Claire stepped onto the path and the children gasped.

"She's standing on water!" One child gushed.

"Yes, but we need to hurry." She gestured for them to join her. "The Cauldron and all of Ebon will be hunting us now."

The children closest to the water held hands and set timid toes on the path. When their feet didn't sink, they let their fears fly and joined her. The remaining children followed suit with DeMorley helping those in the rear.

"Hold hands," Ela Claire ordered. She turned to the boy and girl beside her and clasped their outstretched hands. "And let's stay together. Here we go!"

She led them across the waterway at a good clip. When they were far from shore, she glanced over her shoulder to check on their progress. Previn flew overhead to protect them from an aerial attack. DeMorley held Lolling and took up the rear, helping any stragglers.

What impressed her most were the children. They ignored the waves smashing against the invisible walls on either side of them, constant reminders that they traversed what could be a watery tomb. Within the wind, she heard them singing. Their melody was infectious and was sung in perfect harmony, carrying them far away from cell Number 17.

Chapter 34

Back From the Grave

Linwith made his way across Min Brock, focusing on keeping his pace slow, a task he found difficult to perform after viewing a new vision. The latest was alarming, to say the least, and he wanted to run to Quinn and deliver the news, but to do so would draw too much attention to himself.

I only have myself to blame. He eyed the worms perched on their turrets as he reflected on that fateful night.

I weakened and let Areall and Daryess witness the visions of their children.

They honored their word and didn't ask for another vision or tell anyone else. Daryess even kept the secret from Gundin...

Linwith let his gaze fall to the courtyard.

...I should have known that wouldn't last.

He stopped and took in the refugees milling about. Some waved and smiled at him. Others turned and eyed him with mistrust.

Romlin's vision was too disturbing, even for a woman as strong as Daryess.

He began to make his way through the crowd.

She kept Gundin at bay for some time, but he's a persistent brute. She gave in to his nagging but made him vow to keep the vision and the worm's abilities a secret.

Linwith waved to an elderly man leaning against his threshold smoking a pipe. The man shook his head and entered his home.

Linwith shook off the rejection.

Gundin is a man of his word; a warrior who knows that gossip and speculation are poison to an army's resolve. What he didn't factor in was his disdain for the worms overpowering such tenets. After a long day patrolling Min Brock's wall, he joined his men around a fire in the courtyard. Stories and drink were passed and by the sixth round, the tales were of epic proportion. Gundin, not wanting to be outdone, let the secrets slip out...

Linwith gave a nod to some soldiers sharpening their blades with a honing stone. They returned the gesture but glowered at him as he passed.

Gundin's account spread like wildfire through Min Brock. I was bombarded with requests for a vision. Some offered grain, fresh meat, even gold for a glimpse into their future. One went so far as to offer his daughter in marriage. A tempting offer, until he showed me his beauty...

He shuddered as he remembered her face being unveiled.

After some time, the refugees tired of my refusals and stopped pestering me. Now...

His eyes swept the faces staring at him.

...they look at me with discontent, mistrust and jealousy.

He brushed past a woman who cursed him beneath her breath.

A pack of children spotted Linwith and surrounded him as he walked. They pulled at his flight jacket and peppered him with demands and questions.

"Did you see me in a vision," a cute girl asked. "What's going to happen to *me?* Will I grow up to be pretty?"

A large boy yanked her aside to take his turn. "My parents say it isn't fair you get to see into the future. They hope you see your own vision and *die!*"

Linwith donned a broad smile - phony at best - and waved to their parents. No one returned the gesture.

Linwith stopped and eyed the gang of children.

"You want to know your future?" An impish grin fanned out across his face.

The children pushed and jumped up and down to be picked first. Linwith held up a hand and they stopped fidgeting. "You." He pointed to the pretty girl. "Your future is this: You will grow up to be fat and ugly, but primarily ugly. And you," he turned to address the tattler who wished him dead, "must hurry home to say good-bye. Tonight is when *you* die."

Only Linwith never said those things; he simply had imagined it. And as he took in their curious faces, he mulled over his role as the Worm Master.

They think seeing into the future is a blessing. At first, so did I. After all, the visions are puzzling, somewhat charming and mystical. But now?

He eyed one of the fathers.

How would you react if you knew that tomorrow, your son would choke to death in the Great Hall?

Linwith waved and the man answered with a scowl and crossed arms. He turned his attention to the mother of the pretty girl.

Or you, how would you handle the news that you'll die before seeing her wed?

His eyes wandered over the gaping faces of Min Brock staring back at him.

Would you change for the better or for the worse? Would your last breath draw a curse or a thankful whisper? Would you embrace your mortality or waste time trying to reverse the inevitable?

He took in the children again. *I didn't ask for this role as Worm Master, and yet, it's mine to bear. And despite your constant barrage and even your hurtful comments...*

He eyed the boy who had made the cruel statement.

No matter what, I'll protect you to the fullest.

"Your futures are this," he offered with a genuine smile. "You will experience a wonderful day."

"Really," one boy asked. "How come?"

"Because you are alive, have each other and," he looked up overhead, "there's not a cloud in the sky, so be thankful; it's going to be a beautiful day."

"That's not a vision," the bratty-boy drummed.

"No," Linwith answered as he gave him a stern look, "and for that, you can also be thankful."

Linwith pushed past them and continued to the stairs leading to Quinn's residence, He wanted to race up to give his brother the news.

Instead, he paused and made light conversation with some soldiers gathered nearby. He tossed in a joke and the men laughed. Linwith let the moment hang, said goodbye and mounted the steps.

When he reached the landing, he made his way to Quinn's home and delivered three firm knocks to the door. After a brief moment, Quinn opened the door. Linwith hugged him and whispered in his ear: *"Invite me in. I must speak with you in private."*

Quinn released his brother, and with a beaming smile, motioned for Linwith to come inside.

Linwith sauntered into the home, and when the door had closed, let his true emotions out.

"Is Areall here," he asked as he pulled back the tapestry covering the window and peered out.

"No. She's walking the wall with Daryess. Why? What's wrong?"

"I've seen another vision and she doesn't need to know about it." He dropped the curtain and faced his brother.

"Was it of Ela Claire?" Fear coursed his veins.

Linwith shook his head. "No. Someone we both presumed to be dead."

Quinn's brow furrowed. "Who?"

"Il-Lilliad."

Quinn's eyes widened with bewilderment. "But the Martyr's Moon," he rebutted. "Your worms confirmed it wasn't for Ela Claire so we assumed it had to be for Il-Lilliad."

"Well, we were wrong."

"Then I'm perplexed. The Martyr's Moon only appears when a storyteller is slain."

"Correct, which means that another storyteller perished."

"But when Il-Lilliad met us in Hetherlinn, he said he was the only surviving storyteller."

"Then he too was in the dark about this other person."

"Do you know their name?"

Linwith shrugged. "No, and to be honest, it's not important. What *is* important is the vision I saw of Il-Lilliad."

Linwith made his way to a table where a pitcher of water sat. He poured himself a goblet and downed the water with slurpy gulps. Wiping his mouth with a sleeve, he eyed Quinn's face lined with worry.

"The vision showed Il-Lilliad alive but held captive by hundreds of Ebonite cavalry on the Gilden Plains, not too far from Min Brock."

"I don't understand. Il-Lilliad's a storyteller, so why doesn't he summon a tale and destroy them?"

"No idea."

"Why only several hundred Ebonites? Surely they'll attack us with all of their forces."

"Again, I don't know."

"And why didn't your patrol spot them..."

"Quinn," Linwith interrupted as he slammed the goblet down on the table. "Don't you think I've already wrestled with such questions? All I know is what *I saw*."

Quinn paced. "We need more proof."

"Agreed, which is why before coming to seek your counsel, I dispatched the pearl worm cloaked in invisibility to search the Gilden Plains."

Quinn paused by his window and took his turn peeking out. "Good; very good. Once your worm has found them, and we learn more about their numbers," he let the drape fall, "we'll assemble a force and ride to Il-Lilliad's rescue. The last thing we need is to fall into an Ebonite trap."

"Agreed."

Quinn made his way to Linwith's side and poured himself some water. "When will the pearl worm return with his report?"

"I'm not sure, but it really doesn't matter."

"It does if we need to form a strike force."

Linwith smirked. "What I mean is that if you go with me to the armory, I can let you witness everything the worm is seeing and experiencing on his scouting mission."

"How," he asked as gulped down a few swallows.

Linwith motioned with his head for Quinn to follow and headed for the door. Quinn drained his goblet and caught up.

Once outside, they strode side by side down the stairs, but Quinn -

excited about Il-Lilliad being alive - raced ahead only to be snagged by Linwith.

"Nice and easy," Linwith whispered into Quinn's ear. "We don't need to alert anyone else."

"Who else knows about this," Quinn asked as struggled to match Linwith stride-for-stride.

"Phinnton," Linwith replied. "I've learned, from trial and error, that he's better at keeping secrets if I disclose them to him instead of him stumbling across them on one of his storytelling exercises."

"But I thought that was part of his punishment, that aside from being grounded from flight, he couldn't use these gifts?"

Linwith gave a confirming nod. "True, but at the same time, I have allowed him brief moments in which to practice. After all, he's an active boy with an even more active imagination. The short excursions have been a blessed relief for him and for me."

"How's that?"

"You'll see."

When they reached ground level, they kept their walk slow so as to not arouse too much curiosity from the onlookers. To those who did stare at them, Linwith made certain to smile and wave. A subtle elbow into Quinn's frame urged him to do the same. They rounded a corner and made their way to the armory.

Linwith ushered Quinn in and closed the door behind them.

Phinnton, who was busy polishing Linwith's saddle, turned and saluted them with a humble nod. "I've finished with the saddle and your armor and I've fed and watered the worms."

Linwith acknowledged as much with a trite wave of his hand as he and Quinn made their way to where he stood.

Phinnton bit his lower lip and fidgeted back and forth, yearning to ask more questions, especially with Quinn present, but knew to do so would add more time to his punishment.

Linwith eyed him and snickered. And to Quinn: "See what I mean?"

"Is he always like this," Quinn asked as Phinnton wobbled from foot-to-foot and crossed his legs as if he needed to race to the latrine.

"Yep," Linwith answered with smacking lips. He turned his attention to the fidgeting page. "The suspense is killing you, isn't it?"

"*Yes,*" Phinnton exploded with arms gesticulating his exasperation. "I'm not allowed to ask questions and I can't use my storytelling skills unless you ask me to."

"And yet standing before you is a quandary, isn't it?"

Phinnton nodded and twisted and turned as more and more questions popped into his brain.

Linwith patted his head and flicked Quinn a whimsical look. "It's been the best punishment. And to think, tomorrow marks the end of his sentence."

Phinnton stopped prancing and let his eager eyes dance across the men's faces. More questions surged inside him, but not wanting to jeopardize the end to his sentence, he clasped a hand over his mouth and settled down.

Linwith set his thoughts on the issues at hand and looked into his brother's eyes. "When I position my hand over the saddle horn, rest yours on top of mine. I'll touch the pearl with my finger and you'll join me on this visionquest."

Linwith positioned his right hand over the saddle horn, and when Quinn grabbed hold, he lowered a finger to the pearl gem located on the bottom left side.

Quinn gasped when he found himself soaring high above the Gilden Plains, feeling and witnessing everything the pearl worm was experiencing. A milky, translucent luster of white and silver - that reminded Quinn of the worm's glossy tale - tinted their view.

Although Quinn could not see his own body or that of Linwith's, he nonetheless knew he was present in the moment as was Linwith. He could feel the wind brushing past his face and caught the scent of the plains: grass and earth and sea.

The worm flew at an altitude well above the Addoli Ridge not for concealment, since he was already invisible, but in order to get a better view of the Gilden Plains. Pearlesque tones colored the vast grasses and landscapes with a glimmering sheen.

"Search left and right," Linwith ordered the worm in the silent tongue. Quinn sucked in air since this was the first time he had heard the magical conversation between master and worm. His brother's voice resonated with power yet was rooted in humility, and sounded different than when he conversed normally.

The worm swept his head left then right, looking for any sign of the Ebonite cavalry, and more importantly, Il-Lilliad. The worm zeroed his hearing in on certain spots on the plain, and Quinn, aghast at being able to hear a field mouse scurry or a distant lion purr, almost jerked his hand off Linwith's.

A black smudge appeared on the southwest horizon. Linwith gave a command and the worm altered his course toward the dark object. Zipping along at a faster speed, the worm cut the distance in half. The dark splotch became more defined while sounds, churning hooves, animal snorts, and the occasional grunt from men, alerted them its identity.

"Ebonites," Quinn noted.

Linwith ordered the worm to slow and glide down for a closer inspection. The Ebonite company consisted of cavalry, foot soldiers and archers. In the middle of the army and standing out in stark contrast to the black armor, was a man wearing peasant attire with his hands tied behind his back.

Il-Lilliad.

At that very moment, Il-Lilliad raised his head and looked into their faces.

"How does he know we're here," Linwith pondered. *"Worms fly as quiet as a moth and we're invisible! He must be staring at something else, but what?"*

Linwith, fearing demoliths were near, ordered the worm to climb higher even though they were transparent. The worm beat a path upward in a circular fashion in order to look this way and that for their foe, but the sky and plain were void of their enemy.

Linwith, now more perplexed than ever at who or what Il-Lilliad had stared at, ordered the worm to return to Min Brock. Satisfied the worm was on course, Linwith lifted his thumb and he and Quinn were once more back in the armory.

Quinn, who was overwhelmed by the experience, stared wide-eyed at Linwith.

"Well, that *looked* like Il-Lilliad," Linwith said.

"Looked like," Quinn questioned as he tottered and stumbled from the dizzying flight. He braced himself on the table. "That *was* him; I'm certain."

"Quinn, nothing in this war is certain."

"Then who else could it be?"

"It could have been the Gor King."

Quinn, with the room no longer spinning, pushed up from the table and took in his brother. "The Gor King," he repeated.

Linwith squeezed Quinn's shoulder. "Remember when I summoned you to my chambers and told you about the visions?"

Quinn nodded. "Yes, and you also mentioned seeing others. Is the Gor King one of these?"

Linwith let go and sighed. "Yes. All I know is that the Gor King, whoever he is, has aligned himself with the Cauldron, commands an army of gors, and has the ability to alter his form."

Quinn scrunched his face with concern. "So he's capable of looking like...Il-Lilliad?"

Linwith paced, finger drumming his chin. "Possibly. I think so." He stopped and eyed his brother. "The visions I've had pertaining the Gor King have been inconclusive and the gold worm is incapable of reading his thoughts. As to why this is, I can only speculate. But if that *was* him, then where were his gors, and for that matter, why disguise yourself as Il-Lilliad and act like a prisoner?"

"Simple," Quinn answered. "To bait us into a trap."

Linwith fingered his chin. "Could be, but did you see him look at us?"

"Yes, but it could've been coincidence, or he was just checking on the weather."

Linwith stopped rubbing his jaw and smirked. "Really? That's what your gut instinct tells you?"

Quinn snickered as he realized the absurdity of his statement. "No, not at all."

"Then what *do* you think?"

"That whoever *that* was, he was watching us…even though we were invisible."

Linwith sighed and paced once more. "Exactly, and what's even more alarming is that he didn't look surprised to see us. It was as if he expected us, or at least the worm, to be there. But how?"

An idea came to Phinnton, but honoring his punishment, he clapped a hand over his mouth while waving the other to get their attention.

Linwith caught his gesture and turned his attention to the page. "Go ahead, what are you thinking?"

Phinnton dropped both hands. "Is it possible that as a storyteller, he's able to see the pearl worm when invisible?"

"Or," Quinn added, "that the Gor King can as well."

"We can at least experiment with Phinnton's first proposition," Linwith said as he eyed his page. "But to do so would require the Supreme Commander of Min Brock," he rested a hand on Quinn's shoulder, "to grant you an immediate pardon so you can use your skills."

Phinnton's eyes bulged.

Quinn caught his brother's eye, and sensing that this was indeed a necessary step in securing Min Brock's safety, walked up to Phinnton.

"By the power vested in me by the King of Claire, I hereby revoke your punishment."

Phinnton smiled and Quinn patted him on the shoulder as Linwith knelt to look the page square in the face. "Now, here's what I want you to do…"

Phinnton slipped out of the armory, and per his instructions from Linwith, made a beeline for the central tower.

Although he was spotted running, no one gave him much mind; they knew Phinnton was an energetic boy with a vivid imagination. They were accustomed to him racing up a staircase just to watch a sunset or sprinting across the courtyard trying to catch a butterfly.

Phinnton eyed the tall turret, and more specifically, the sapphire worm perched on the tile roof. The worm was eyeing his approach.

"*I'm almost there,*" he informed Linwith in the silent tongue.

"*I know. I'm watching you through the eyes of the Worm King.*"

Phinnton threw open the door and dashed into the tower. He brushed past guards meandering down the circular stairs, and when he ran into a leader from Tristan and sent papers he was carrying flying, he gave a quick apology and continued up the stairs.

Like Linwith, Phinnton counted the steps even when skipping several at a time, which was what he was doing today.

"*99...*"

"*You're almost there.*"

He cleared the last step and ran out onto the platform. He made his way to the turret wall and focused on the western sky; the winds from the plains whistled past his ears.

"*I'm here,*" he informed Linwith as he caught his breath. "*Nothing yet. Is he close?*"

"*Yes. I'm now viewing everything through the eyes of the pearl worm. Min Brock is looming. You should be able to see him soon.*"

"*If storytellers can see him when invisible, you mean.*"

"*Correct, but we need to eliminate any possibilities and uncertainties.*"

Phinnton strained, willing himself to see the pearl worm, hoping his efforts would not only aid the war but would help rescue the storyteller known as Il-Lilliad.

"*I'm within range,*" Linwith told him. "*You should be able to see him.*"

"*But where,*" Phinnton asked as he squinted and shielded his eyes. "*You could be anywhere.*"

"*That's part of the test: to ensure you are capable of such spotting.*"

Phinnton was about to protest when a dot above the Adolli Ridge caught his attention. He waited, which was not his strong suit, and patted the ledge while muttering, "Come on, come on, come on."

The dot, that was now the size of a pea, was taking shape and in a few moments would have the telltale signs of the worm: distinct wing pattern and the pearly glow from its tale.

Phinnton hopped up and down, urging the flying object closer with his activity, hoping he was witnessing the flight of the invisible worm and not something else.

When the dot was the size of his fist, he stopped fidgeting and blinked to make sure he was not seeing things, or worse, conjuring the image of his desire with his imagination or storytelling skills.

A proud smile flashed over his face. "*I see him; the pearl worm. You're approaching Min Brock from the Addoli Ridge.*"

"You're certain?"

"Yes."

"What's happening now?"

The flying anomaly changed course.

"He banked and turned…toward the east."

"And now?"

Phinnton locked his gaze on the worm to note any flight change. *"Now he's hovering, and staring at the tower I'm in."*

"Good! So you've proved one theory: storytellers can see him when invisible."

"Yes, but we still don't know if the Gor King can or not."

"Correct, so we'll have to proceed with caution to rescue Il-Lilliad."

"You could take the worms, destroy the Ebonites, and bring him safely to Min Brock."

"True, but if that isn't Il-Lilliad, then the worms could be in danger. Plus, Min Brock would be defenseless from an aerial attack which would be exactly what the Cauldron would want."

"I could stay here with several of the worms," Phinnton suggested. *"Even though you'd be far away, you could still order the worms from your saddle horn and speak to me in the silent tongue."*

The sapphire worm lowered his head past the tiled roof and looked the page over in his upside down position. *"Are you ready for such an important mission like that,"* Linwith asked as he studied Phinnton's countenance through the eyes of the Worm King.

Phinnton gave an energetic nod. *"Yes. I'm ready."*

Linwith liked what he saw in the boy. His impish grin was gone and he stood still, something that was rare for his temperament. Standing before Linwith was a page ready for combat.

"So be it," Linwith answered. *"I'll have Quinn alert Gundin to amass a small force to join me. Meanwhile, make your way to the amber worm's tower and stay there until further instructed. Understood?"*

Phinnton nodded, and although not sharp by military standards, saluted the sapphire worm.

Chapter 35

To Battle

Three worms soared away from Min Brock. On either side of the sapphire worm was the pearl and emerald worm. Down below, and well ahead of their flight, were Quinn and Gundin leading a hand picked group of warriors. Settling into his flight, Linwith gave Phinnton some final instructions in the silent tongue.

"Remember: stay in the amber worm's turret at all times. Should I need you to mount and fly, you'll need to do so right away."

"I will."

"As curious as you'll be, you must not read my story or anyone else's during this mission. Understood?"

"Yes," he answered halfhearted.

"Lastly, keep your eyes on the sky and the Gilden Plains all around Min Brock. Should you see any warriors, vul jens or demoliths, alert me. Do not fly off on your own to attack. You're too young for combat."

Silence.

"Phinnton, did you hear me?"

"Yes," he whined. *"But when will I be old enough?"*

"All too soon. All too soon."

Satisfied his page would obey, Linwith focused on the attack plan devised with Gundin and Quinn prior to leaving Min Brock. Linwith would maintain a high altitude to keep from being spotted while Quinn's forces would approach the Ebonites in as loud and as obvious a manner as possible. If they took the bait, and based upon prior combat experience with their enemy, they knew that the Ebonites would rally around their prisoner while an attack force would be sent to deal with Quinn's men. When that happened, Linwith would dive from overhead and strike. The pearl worm - who would be invisible - would snatch Il-Lilliad prior to the sapphire worm encasing the Ebonites within his translucent blue sphere. With Il-Lilliad clear of danger, the emerald worm would spray his poisonous gas on the frozen enemy to destroy them. And if Il-Lilliad proved to be the Gor King in disguise, then it was better to have him in the talons of the worm than in Quinn's unit.

Linwith noted a black spot far off on the plain and shook off his introspection.

"The Ebonite army. Time to alert Quinn."

His thumb found the pearl on his saddle horn and he ordered the worm into action. Becoming invisible, the worm dove for Quinn and Gundin's forces. Linwith observed through the eyes of the pearl worm, and when he was soaring beside them, he ordered the worm to reappear. Spotting the sign, Quinn and Gundin waved and shouted orders to their men. Linwith ordered the pearl worm back into being invisible before having him join their formation.

He was about to check on the advancing Ebonites when something beyond Quinn's position caught his attention. With countless scouting missions under his belt, Linwith was adept at identifying their enemy, even from great distances. What he saw took his breath away.

"Demoliths!"

He checked on Quinn's force.

"There's not enough time to warn them."

With his mind scrambling for a plan, he studied the demoliths.

"Twenty or so. Flying at tree top level. They'll intersect the Ebonite cavalry and not Quinn. But why?"

Another thought made cold sweat bead on his back. He shielded his eyes and glanced over his shoulder into the sun. Diving out of the blinding light was another patrol of demoliths. Instinct took over.

His hand smothered the gems and the three worms banked and ascended to attack head on.

"They're diving too fast; no time to freeze and gas. But they can't see the pearl worm either."

The two forces soared at each other, neither veering off course. At the last possible moment, Linwith ordered the sapphire and emerald worm to bank right while the invisible pearl he sent left. Demoliths zoomed past and turned to pursue the sapphire and emerald. Hot on the tails of the demoliths, and cloaked in invisibility, was the pearl worm.

Linwith, with his thumb smothering the pearl of his saddle horn, watched the aerial combat from the pearl worm's perspective. Cloaked in a milky hue were fifteen demoliths who matched every turn his worms made. The demoliths cawed as their bodies - a mesh of man-flesh and reptilian scales - flew within the slipstream created by the much larger sapphire and emerald worm.

"They're using us to block the wind so they can match our faster speed!"

Linwith felt a great heat hit him and he turned his attention to the rider atop the sapphire worm - himself. And had he not been in a fight for their lives, he would have savored the fantastic viewpoint: silver chest armor and helmet glistening in the sunlight; the Gilden Plains stretching toward the sea; his upper body streamlined against the worm's long neck. Instead, his gaze hopped off his flight back to the demoliths.

"Heat; invisible flames…coming from the beasts. The worms won't be fazed; their plating is too thick. But as for me…"

He eyed his metal encased head and torso. Despite the brisk flight, sweat pooled on his back and the temperature within his helmet was so hot that aside from sweat rolling down his face, he found it difficult to breathe.

"I'm in an oven!"

Panic set in. He verified Quinn's location.

"Safe...for now. But I won't let him down...not again...not like in the Dark War."

While still viewing the flight from the pearl, he willed his body to get as close to the sapphire's neck as possible to avoid the heat. He simultaneously touched the sapphire, emerald and pearl jewels. He sensed the worms in his thoughts, awaiting his next command, their resolve strong, their desire to fight greater than he had imagined. He voiced his orders to them in quick bursts, his mind melded with theirs as man and worm, synchronized as one, engaged in the first aerial combat of the war.

Linwith led the demoliths on a frantic chase across the sky away from Quinn's forces. The worms dove and corkscrewed through the air, but despite such tactics, the demoliths were still in pursuit and looked to be closer. Time was running out.

Between labored breaths, he studied the demoliths, looking for a weakness that would enable him to turn the battle in their favor. He focused on their wings and an idea came to mind.

"I hope this works."

He tightened his grip on the saddle horn, pressed his knees hard into the sides of the sapphire worm and gave the order.

"Dive!"

The worms tucked their wings and plummeted head first for the Gilden Plains.

The demoliths pulled their wings close and followed, cawing for *First Blood*.

"Faster," Linwith urged as he took in the view from the pearl yet felt wind whip inside his armor and cool his overheated body while perched on the Worm King.

"Hope my assessment of them is correct," he fretted as he focused on the demoliths closing the gap.

"Too late to worry now. It's kill or be killed."

The ground loomed. Heat baked Linwith's torso and skull but he remained poised, focused on the dive, knowing he needed to time their next move perfectly.

They had performed such a stunt countless times over the Gilden Sea. But that was for sport. This was for life or death.

The scattering of trees on the plains, once dots, grew in size and dimension. Plateaus and hillocks took shape. It was now or never.

"Climb!"

The worms extended their wings like sails, and with incredible strength coupled with their extraordinary flying skill, went from a crashing dive into a sharp climb.

Not to be outdone and lose their prey, the demoliths followed suit, and just as Linwith had hoped, their wings could not handle the drastic change of direction and windblast.

Wing bones snapped like dry wood, membraned wings ripped as if cut by steel, and agonizing screams filled the air until the Gilden Plains silenced them once and for all.

Chapter 36

Truth About Il-Lilliad

Quinn led the small force from Min Brock up a hillock at a canter. On the other side and still a good ways off was the Ebonite cavalry.

Quinn and Gundin drew their swords.

The warriors of Min Brock followed suit.

Before shouting an order, Quinn checked the sky for his brother. Without the Worms of Bal-Malin providing air support, they didn't stand a chance against the larger Ebonite force.

"Halt!" Quinn shouted as he pulled hard on his reins.

Hooves ripped open the plain and armor rattled as the thundering cavalry came to a quick stop.

"What's wrong," Gundin asked as he followed Quinn's line of sight.

"Where's Linwith? He was there just moments ago."

Gundin eyed the sky and like Quinn, could not spot the worms. He ground his teeth and muttered beneath his breath: "Worthless skymules."

"There they are," a nearby general shouted. "Look."

They looked in the direction he pointed in hope of spotting the worms. Instead, they spied a formation of beasts - part man, part dragon - flying straight for them at ground level.

Impact was imminent. They only had moments to react. Quinn reasoned that a retreat, without Linwith's aid against the horde, would be catastrophic, and to advance would put them closer to the Ebonite cavalry and certain death.

"Dismount," Quinn ordered his troops as he jumped from his steed. "Take cover."

Men dove off just as the demoliths flew over, talons just missing the last man to dismount.

As the men scampered to regain footing as well as to steady their prancing steeds, Quinn followed the flight of the demoliths that zoomed toward the Ebonite force.

Gundin stared in disbelief at the dark cavalry. "They stopped when the demoliths were close, but why?"

"I don't know," Quinn replied as the demoliths circled back for another attack. "Perhaps it has something to do with their prisoner: Il-Lilliad. Right now, we have other issues at hand."

He turned to address his men. "Stay dismounted but steady your stallions. We don't want them to dash off and leave us on foot." He took in the men's faces: white with fright. This was their first taste of combat and what a taste it was: outnumbered and hemmed in from the sky and ground. Even as a seasoned veteran, Quinn found his nerves strained and frazzled.

"We must hold them off," he instructed with as much confidence as he could muster, "until Linwith arrives."

The men nodded but Quinn knew they too must have been wrestling with the same concern he had: what if Linwith didn't arrive in time?

He shook off the fear and eyed the archers. "Make every shot count. Fire at will."

The archers nocked arrows and took aim at the flying horde. Before they could release their missiles, a heat wave, like that from a stoked fire, slammed into the force. Surprised by the blow, the men screamed from the stinging heat and coughed for want of a cool breath. Others moaned from the pain, while one unlucky warrior screamed in hysteria when his tunic started to smoke. The archers, overcome by the heat, struggled to aim an accurate shot. Bowstrings zinged and arrows sailed away, but only a few were on target and those were incinerated before striking a demolith.

"Steady," Quinn ordered as he strained against the heat blast as well as his bucking horse. "Use your shields and steeds to block the heat!"

The men cowered behind steel and horse to find comfort, but as the demoliths got closer their heat increased, and this last refuge was rendered useless. Warhorses, unwilling to yield any longer, jerked free and bolted across the plains.

Men shouted for mercy while others buckled to the ground and prepared for the worst.

"Where are those blasted sky-mules," Gundin seethed as pockets of dried grass burst into flame around several men.

Quinn scanned the sky for any sign of his brother. Empty.

He ground his teeth and wiped the sweat pouring off his face. Infuriated that he had fallen into a trap, as well as his brother's abandonment, Quinn became desperate. He ripped off a chunk of his tunic and dove for his weapon. Wrapping the cloth around the hilt to ward off the heat, he stood and brandished the weapon toward the diving demoliths.

Gundin, energized by Quinn's desperate last stand, did the same. "Men," Gundin boomed to the remaining warriors, "find your weapons. Prepare to fight!"

Tunics were ripped and swords regathered to make a final stand against the demoliths. The men huddled together, shoulder-to-shoulder, with swords raised toward their nemesis.

The demoliths dove. Talons loomed and their heat wave smothered the men.

Quinn turned his face away from the blast but stood his ground with weapon poised for combat. He strained against the fiery attack, overcome with the scent of burnt grass, tunics, flesh and sweat. Like his men, he drank desperate gulps of air and groaned in pain. He took in Gundin's face. His friend's eyes told him that the end was near.

Men screamed and collapsed.

"Stand strong," he heard himself shout, but his voice sounded impotent against the horrible sounds he heard his men crying.

The last thing Quinn remembered was Gundin swinging his great weapon at the beasts and then his world went black.

Quinn awoke on the ground, and although still dazed from the attack, strained to get his footing. He pushed himself up from the charred grass, could feel one side of his face throbbing from being burned, and took in what was left of his unit. Most had survived, and judging by their reddened faces, were experiencing the same pain he was feeling. Others, however, were not so lucky. Torched bodies lay about the blackened area; some still engulfed with fire while others were nothing but smoldering ash.

Quinn turned away from the gruesome site.

Gundin labored to stand. "Where did Linwith go," he shouted as he got his footing. "And what about his blasted skymules? A lot of good *they* were!"

Quinn, still stunned, watched his men stagger toward him, looking like something from a nightmare. Faces were blackened with soot and red from the demolith heat. Eyes were white with shock and limbs dangled to their sides dragging weapons and comrades back into formation.

Quinn battled the dazed feeling, knowing he needed to get his thoughts centered and focused on their survival. He sensed Gundin beside him as he took in their position.

Surrounding them in a large circle were the demoliths and the Ebonite cavalry.

Gundin mumbled the question plaguing Quinn. "Why aren't we dead?"

The answer came from an unlikely source.

"Well done," the Ebonite commander praised the demolith squadron leader. "We now have even more Allsbruthian prisoners."

"Commander," the demolith leader snapped, "You know as well as I do that Ebon never takes prisoners. We merely stopped so that your men could enjoy First Blood with us."

"Of course, but Brairtok has issued a new decree," the commander replied while fingering his long beard and eyeing Quinn and Gundin from his mount. "He wants as many prisoners as possible." He motioned over his shoulder toward their prisoner. "See for yourself."

The demolith eyed Il-Lilliad and chuckled. "And look how many warriors it took to capture one, old man. No wonder Brairtok wishes to increase the ranks of the demoliths."

His squadron joined his cackles.

The Ebonite commander stopped playing with his beard and maneuvered his warhorse toward the squadron leader. "Do I need to remind you that I outrank you?" The Ebonite's eyes were slits of rage. He pulled up short from plowing the demolith into the ground. "Your humor has breeched Ebonite protocol. I could have you executed."

The demolith raised a deformed hand mottled with scales and flesh. His snickering horde fell silent.

"Please forgive us," the demolith mocked with an equally contemptuous bow, "we did not mean to *insult* the commander."

The two leaders' eyes locked.

Quinn braved the stalemate as an opportunity to whisper into Gundin's ear. "Prisoners? Open bickering between units? What's going on?"

"I don't know," Gundin replied as he checked on their men. "I only wish we weren't in such disarray. This is our chance to attack."

Quinn shook his head. "Even if we were strong, it would be suicide."

Quinn and Gundin focused back on their enemy wondering what would happen next.

The Ebonite commander and squadron leader continued their stare-down, and finally, in order to avoid court martial, the demolith pulled away but flicked the air with his reptilian tongue.

The Ebonite commander shifted in his saddle to address his men. "By the order of Brairtok, and for the greater good of Ebon and the Cauldron, we shall relieve the demoliths of their prisoners."

The cavalry commander led a few of his riders to where Quinn and Gundin stood.

Leaning out over the men, he glared down at them.

"Have your men bow before us," he ordered.

"Never," Quinn fired as he stiffened his back.

The commander motioned to a portion of his foot soldiers. "Assist our stubborn Allsbruthians in showing proper *respect.*"

The warriors stormed forward. Grabbing the men of Min Brock, they pushed and kicked them down to their knees.

"Lower," the commander demanded.

Leathered boots pressed backs down into the blackened field.

"Much better," the commander sniffed as he viewed them lying face down.

He sat upright to address his entire unit. "Warriors of Ebon," he boomed, "let us honor the demoliths for their achievement on the battlefield!"

Quinn and Gundin strained from their precarious position on the ground to watch what would happen next. They were stunned to see the entire Ebonite force bow their heads in homage to the demoliths.

"Before we leave with the prisoners," the commander announced, "I have just one more thing to say. First blood!"

Quinn and Gundin expected their lives to end with a March of Reeds. Instead, they heard the sound of metal slamming into flesh followed by ghoulish squeals.

They pushed up to their elbows in time to see Ebonite warhorses stomping on demoliths struck to the ground. Those that survived the surprise attack flew away to regroup.

"Archers," the Ebonite commander shouted. "Take aim."

Nocked arrows were drawn to cheeks.

"Fire!"

Quinn followed the missiles through the air and was not only amazed at the accuracy of the shots, but the fact that the Ebonite cavalry had attacked the demoliths.

"Get up," the Ebonite commander ordered.

Stunned by the apparent military coup, Quinn and Gundin, along with the other men, rose from the ground. They huddled together with defiant faces and fists clinched. If they were to die by a March of Reeds, they would not go down without a fight.

But instead of ordering his unit in for the kill, the commander motioned for their prisoner to be brought forward.

Il-Lilliad soon appeared, and as he caught Quinn and Gundin's perplexed stares, he brought his arms around from behind his back.

Flabbergasted, Quinn's mouth fell open. "You were untied the entire time?" he noted as more and more unanswered questions plagued him. "But why? What's going on here?"

Il-Lilliad dismounted and made his way to them. "Haven't you figured it out yet, old friend?"

Gundin huffed. "If Quinn had, he wouldn't have asked you!"

Il-Lilliad flicked a jovial glance into Gundin's scowling face. "And it's good to see you again, too."

Il-Lilliad turned his attention back to Quinn. "I am positive," he said with a twinkle in his eye, "that your minds are swimming in a sea of confusion; perhaps even mistrust.”

“Yes,” Quinn snapped as he eyed the Ebonites that encircled them. He tossed a quick glance overhead.

“Don’t worry,” Il-Lilliad said after reading his thoughts and following his line of sight, “Linwith is safe; he and the worms will be here in no time.”

Quinn let his gaze fall back to the storyteller. “Are you an apparition?”

Il-Lilliad thumbed his chest, his jolly features now perplexed. “You think I’m a ghost?”

“Or trick of the Cauldron,” he muttered as he set his jaw.

Il-Lilliad’s smile returned and blazed like the sun. “If that were the case, why would we attack the demoliths?”

Quinn blinked. He didn’t have a plausible answer.

“Perhaps by viewing the impossible,” Il-Lilliad rested a hand on Quinn’s shoulder, “you’ll see the obvious.”

Il-Lilliad gave a nod to the Ebonite commander.

The commander shouted an order to his men in a tongue Quinn and Gundin weren’t familiar with.

The Ebonite force - cavalrymen, infantry and archers - dissolved away like ripples on a pond. Standing in their place was an army of small men with brown skin whose large eyes danced with light.

“Allow me to introduce,” Il-Lilliad swept his arm at the assembled force, “the Army of SriBrune.”

Quinn and Gundin stared dumbfounded at the transformed army and were speechless.

The SriBrunian that had poised as the Ebonite commander dismounted and strolled up to Il-Lilliad.

“And this is Kinmin,” Il-Lilliad said as he rested a hand on his small back, “the future King of SriBrune.”

Quinn and Gundin blinked and stared at the tiny man.

Il-Lilliad cleared his voice. “The future *King* of SriBrune,” he repeated with emphasis to clear their minds.

Quinn, realizing they needed to acknowledge Kinmin’s title, elbowed Gundin as he bowed at the hip. Gundin, who was too overcome by the day’s events to voice his typical rebuttal, followed suit.

Kinmin returned the salute with a subtle nod of his head and Quinn and Gundin returned to their upright positions.

“As you can see,” Il-Lilliad continued, “the SriBrunians can alter their appearance, reflecting whatever they behold before them, or they can capture an image from another’s thoughts and become this vision as well.”

Quinn studied Kinmin. “You’re amazing. I’m especially impressed that you spoke fluent Ebonite.”

“That is part of the transformation,” Kinmin explained. “We not only take on another's appearance, but their personality and language, too."

Il-Lilliad turned his attention back to the sky. "Ah, here they come, right on time."

All eyes looked overhead to watch Linwith and his worms—the sapphire, emerald and pearl, now visible, glide down from the sky. The worms lowered their back legs and the SriBrunians parted to make room for their landing

"It's about time," Gundin huffed. "While we've been in battle, Sir Dragonboy has been flitting about on his dragons."

"They're worms, Gundin," Quinn corrected in a stern voice, *"worms."*

"Call them what you want," Gundin snapped as he crossed his muscular arms over his burly chest, "as far as I'm concerned, they're foul-breathed mules of the sky, that's what they are."

As the worms touched down, Quinn addressed Il-Lilliad. "So how did you know Linwith was with the Worms of Bal-Malin?"

"Simple: I saw you both earlier today."

Quinn flicked his eyes over to Il-Lilliad's smiling face.

"That's right, I saw you both today. I sensed a presence in the sky and detected the scent of Claire, the Worms of Bal-Malin as well as you and Linwith. I naturally concluded that Linwith had become the Worm Master - a hint of which I discovered in his story when we first met in your cottage - and that the invisible force I detected was no doubt one of his worms. The pearl one, if memory from my studies long ago serves me correctly."

Linwith slid off the sapphire worm, tucked his helmet under his arm and jogged their way. As he ran, he took in the blackened field, the smoking corpses and the decimated demoliths. His brow furrowed with horror as he envisioned the bloody battle the men of Min Brock endured.

When Linwith came alongside of Quinn, Gundin seethed with rage. "A lot of good your magic *dragons* were today!"

The three worms reared their heads and glared at Gundin. Black orbs flamed with fire; long tongues licked the air; tails raked burnt grass.

Linwith fired Gundin a hot look. "We were ambushed, Gundin. We nearly died ourselves."

"Ambushed," Gundin chortled. "I thought your *mules* were invincible?"

Quinn stepped between them with arms raised. "Both of you settle down. It's been a long..."

"I'm sorry about your son," Linwith fired, knowing that Romlin's vision was at the heart of Gundin's dislike for him and the worms. "But it's not the worms fault!"

Gundin's face reddened and he charged.

Quinn grabbed him around the waist. "Stop it," he shouted as he struggled to restrain Gundin's burly frame. "Haven't you both had enough violence for one day?"

Gundin pulled away and glowered at Linwith with clinched fists. "They're wrong about him. Wrong!" And with an index finger aimed at Linwith added: "You'll see! You just wait and see." He turned on his heel and stormed off.

Il-Lilliad turned his attention to Kinmin. The SriBrunians stared at the Allsbruthians, shocked to witness such an open display of contempt. "As you can see," Il-Lilliad offered with an amiable smile, trying to make light of the situation, "Allbruthian relationships are a bit more complex than those of SriBrune."

Kinmin eyed Gundin marching across the grassland, arms pumping to accelerate his speed. "Where is he going?"

Without so much as a glance at his friend, Quinn answered. "Back to Min Brock."

"On foot," Kinmin asked, wondering if this too was some strange Allsbruthian post-battle custom.

"Probably," Quinn added with a sigh. "When he's this upset, it's best to stay clear of him."

"But doesn't he know Min Brock is very far," Kinmin added. "And that he is a very large man who won't make it there without a horse?"

Quinn chuckled. "Kinmin, *that,*" he gestured a thumb over his shoulder at Gundin lumbering up a hill, "is nothing but solid *muscle.*"

The Allbruthians and Il-Lilliad caught the joke and chuckled. Kinmin, however, pursed his lips and scratched his head. "With all due respect, I beg to differ. He looks fat to me."

The men laughed even harder.

As they chuckled, Il-Lilliad noted their reddened skin and blistered hands sustained from the demolith attack. Recalling his time in the Onderling when the vapors of Salu burnt his skin, he brightened with a solution. "Concerning your injuries." He gestured to Quinn's crimson face. "The SriBrunians have *wonderful* salves that will heal those in no time."

Kinmin motioned to some men to bring the necessary supplies while watching Gundin storm up a hill.

Il-Lilliad took in the smoldering bodies. "I'm sorry for your loss," he offered Quinn. "They were brave men."

Quinn followed his line of sight. "Yes they were." His jaw line tightened. "They deserve to be buried with full military honors in Min Brock but..."

His gaze wandered to the cindered remains of a soldier. "...there's nothing left to bury."

"May I make a suggestion," Linwith offered.

"By all means," Quinn replied without taking his eyes off the remains.

"The sapphire worm can encase the charred bodies in his blue sphere and fly them back to Min Brock. The ashes will have to be gathered by hand."

Quinn gave the matter some thought. He turned and dispatched some men to carry out Linwith's orders.

"Before we landed," Linwith added. "I spotted your horses grazing on the other side of that rise." He pointed out the hill. It was in the opposite direction Gundin was walking.

"Allow us to assist," Kinmin offered. "We'll herd the horses back. Maybe by that time your big friend will be ready to ride."

Quinn followed Kinmin's gaze. Gundin had reached the top of the hill. Quinn smirked. "Kinmin, you don't know Gundin like we do."

Chapter 37

No More Secrets

"Get up, *yung-er*."

Mälque, who was curled up on a bed of pine needles, didn't budge.

Woren kicked him in the gut. "Now!"

Mälque groaned and rolled to his other side. "I just went ta bed. It's still night."

"Guess again."

Mälque blinked open an eye. The sky was gray with light.

Morning? Already?

Mälque sat up, stretched sore arms and back, and took in their camp. Here soldiers shuffled about. Here some warmed chilled fingers over yellow flames. Soft conversation meshed with the cracks and pops of morning fires. It had been days since the battle in the valley, and not a moment passed that Mälque didn't think about it, specifically the Gor King's magic sword and of seeing his eye sockets burn red.

"Let's go," Woren urged before spinning on his heel and walking away.

Mälque pushed himself up off the ground and followed. He caught the aroma of oats being stirred in a pot and meat sizzling in a skillet. His stomach gurgled.

"What about breakfast," Mälque asked.

Woren fished something out of his pocket, and without losing a step, tossed it over his shoulder.

Mälque snatched it in midair.

"Dried meat?"

"Take it or leave it."

Mälque thought about throwing it at Woren's head but knew it would get him smacked and his meal confiscated. He opted for survival and ripped off a bite.

When they reached the horses, Woren turned to address Mälque.

"Today is the day."

"What are you talkin' about," Mälque asked between bites.

"It's been fifteen days since we left the cave and you haven't found a single clue. You either find something by nightfall or you'll be answering to *him*."

Woren jerked a thumb over his shoulder.

Mälque looked in the direction Woren gestured. Off in the shadows sat a warrior mounted on a black steed. Even in the dull light, Mälque could make out the heinous gor helmet. He gagged.

Woren leaned close. "I know when I'm being led on a wild goose chase!"

Mälque coughed out the lodged morsel. "Ain't no goose chase! I know she's at the Isle of Rhythe."

"You know? How?"

Mälque stole a glance at his saddlebag holding the book. He nibbled off more jerky. "Just do. That's all."

"You're such a Wurmlin! You're betting your life on a mystic sign you discovered, aren't you? What was it, mushrooms growing side by

side on a wildeberry branch? A white stag?"

"That ain't your concern. I just know."

"It's my concern," Woren drilled a finger into Mälque's chest, "if you're lying."

Mälque stepped back. "I ain't lyin'. Besides, we'll reach the Gilden Sea tonight anyway, won't we?"

"Yes, unless you take us down more rabbit trails."

"Then you're right: today is the day we find her at the Isle of Rhythe."

Mälque pushed past Woren and climbed into his saddle. He stared through the gloom at the soldiers eating their breakfast. "They ain't even ready to march."

"Who said they were coming?"

Mälque scrunched his lips together in confusion.

Woren snorted. "Didn't get a vision for that, now did you?"

Woren mounted and came alongside Mälque.

"After you." He gestured toward the woods.

Mälque whipped his hair and clicked his tongue. As his horse lumbered forward, he had the sensation he was being watched. Mälque glanced over his shoulder: the Gor King followed several horse lengths behind. One hand held the reins, the other rested on his pommel. Mälque shot Woren a troubled look.

"Tonight," Woren answered as he kept his eyes on the trail, "he'll either hail you as a champion or," he took in Mälque's wide-eyed look, "slaughter you like a pig."

Mälque flicked his hair and nudged his horse into a faster gait.

Lunch came and went and they still had not found a single clue. Tensions mounted, and although Mälque was convinced he'd catch her scent at the Gilden Sea, he became doubtful with every glance back at the Gor King.

I'm such a yung-er! Trustin' my life to mumbo-jumbo from a whisper and a vision. Followed by: *But the whisper helped me with the fea dracas and the visions looked so real. This is my only hope."*

Mälque threw off his apprehensions and checked on Woren riding off of his left flank. Something was different about his expression.

Beads of sweat…on your forehead. But why? It's cold out and…

Mälque mulled over the possibilities until he finally put two-and-two together. He smirked; giddy he may have something on Woren to use in his favor.

"Now I get it," Mälque said over his shoulder.

Woren's brow furrowed. "Now you get *what?*"

"For some time now, I've been askin' myself, 'why us?' Only thing I could figure was that the Gor King ordered ya to find the girl and ya suggested roundin' up some Wurmlins to do the trackin'."

Woren spurred his stallion and came alongside Mälque. "What's your point?"

"Well, you're sweatin'."

"So?"

"It's cold out. Never seen you sweatin' like this before, so I figure you're scared."

Woren chuckled. "Ebonite's fear no one."

"Unless that someone's him."

Mälque gestured back to the Gor King. Woren's smug expression fell.

"So I'm guessin' that if I fail, you fail too. Which means whatever he's gonna do to me, he's gonna do to you."

Woren regained his edge and puffed out his chest. "You have quite the imagination, *yung-er!*"

"Ain't imaginin.' Just statin' the facts and tryin' to stay alive. Ain't nothin' but dyin' everywhere." Mälque turned his head and spat to emphasize his point.

Woren, as if bored with the conversation or to get Mälque off the trail, checked the surrounding woods. "And if your conjecture is true, what of it?"

"Nothin'," Mälque shrugged. "Unless you want to live. In which case…we work together."

Woren dropped his act and snapped his head around to face Mälque. Eyes burned. Jaws flinched. "And do what, run away," Woren hissed through clinched teeth. "He'd find us no matter where we go."

"So say you."

"Listen." Woren did another quick check on the Gor King. "He has powers that go beyond reason. You witnessed what his sword can do! Even now, it's possible he could be listening."

"How? We're whisperin'."

Woren shook his head and wet his lips. The anger burning in his eyes faded. Now, his gaze reminded Mälque of his mother's look when she realized an Awakening had killed her husband. Trouble. Peril. Anguish.

"You don't get it, do you? Our *only* hope is to find the girl."

"Which we'll do."

"But how do you know she's on the Isle of Rhythe?"

"Just do."

"Tell me. Now."

Mälque checked on the Gor King to see if he was on to their conversation. Unable to discern one way or the other, Mälque risked the answer.

"Her book. Sometimes it shows me where she's at."

Woren's eyes swelled with comprehension as if he'd discovered the answer to an age-old question. He stuck out a gloved hand. "Let me see it."

"Now?" Mälque checked on the Gor King.

"No more secrets, Mälque."

Mälque, surprised to hear Woren use his birth name, gave Woren a good looking over.

Ya tryin' to soften me?

Woren continued. "Okay, so you're right: you're fate is my fate. Like it or not, we've got to work together. Now hand me the book."

Mälque hesitated. Could he trust Woren? Or was this a ploy? He went with his gut. He finagled the book out of his saddlebag and handed it over.

Woren rested it on his lap, and with the reins in his left hand, flipped the pages with his right but soon stopped. Brow furrowed. "How did you fix the torn out pages?"

"I didn't. They weren't really torn out. The book tricked you."

Woren thumbed through more pages. His face clouded with doubt. "I don't see any vision."

"It doesn't work like that. I can't even make it happen. It just does it when it wants to."

Woren slammed the book shut and nudged his animal forward. "Did you ever stop to think that this vision was a trick, just like the one that tricked me into seeing torn out pages?"

Mälque leaned back. Woren's eyes were slits. Anger had returned.

"Not really."

"And why not? Wurmlins trust no one, so why would you trust this book...this vision?"

"Because I heard somethin' in the cave."

"What?"

"A whisper."

Woren's face paled. He double-checked the Gor King. Satisfied he hadn't heard, or at least hoped as much, Woren leaned closer to Mälque. "Fool! Never listen to or trust a whisper."

"But it's the same one I heard when I was gettin' the fea dracas. It saved my life. Why is this time any different?"

Woren leaned back into an upright position and mumbled to himself. After a brief period of reflection, he focused back on the book and thumbed through more pages. When he reached the section where the feather and hair were stashed, the Gor King's steed whinnied.

Woren and Mälque turned to see what had startled the animal. There was no visible threat and yet the stallion bucked and snorted.

Mälque eyed the hair and came up with a hunch. "Shut the book," he ordered as he pulled back on his reins to halt.

Woren halted his steed and glared at Mälque for giving him an order.

"Her hair." Mälque pointed at the strand. "Don't ya get it? It bewitched the horse!"

Woren sized up Mälque, and although he wanted to give the boy a stiff backhand for insolence, his gut instinct told him the boy was right. Woren closed the book and the warhorse became docile. Woren cocked an eyebrow.

"How'd you know the hair cast the spell?"

"Don't matter. Look" Mälque gestured to the Gor King trotting their way.

"Let me handle this," Woren said under his breath. "Don't say a word and turn to face him. He detests any signs of weakness."

Mälque maneuvered his animal to face the Gor King and checked on his eye sockets. They were as black as coal, which gave him some comfort. Sweat glistened on his arms from the exertion with the warhorse; veins in his biceps and forearms bulged like fat worms. Mälque breathed a sigh of relief until he spotted his gloved hand: fingers were at the ready to unsheathe his blade.

Just one twitch and I'm takin' my chances gallopin' off!

The Gor King pulled up and stared into Woren's face. Woren met his gaze and dared not blink or look away.

Satisfied of Woren's mettle, the Gor King ended the staring match and pointed to the ground. Woren understood the gesture and nodded. He passed the order on to Mälque.

"We're to dismount."

Mälque shook his head and gripped the reins tighter. "Ain't doin' it. Ain't nothin' but dyin' everywhere."

Woren caught Mälque's wild-eyed look, the flick of his greasy hair.

"Don't be a fool," Woren hissed. "You'll never make it. You saw what happened when your brother ran."

Mälque gave the woods a parting glance. "Ya better be right."

He dismounted, but only after Woren started the process first.

The Gor King stretched out a hand for the book. Woren handed it up to him. The Gor King studied it from every angle and even held it to his ear. He shook it, whether in an attempt to break its magic or listen for something rattling inside, Mälque was unable to tell. The Gor King turned to the feather and hair, which made his horse snort and prance. He closed the book and his animal settled back down.

Satisfied he found the source of the spell, he tucked the book under his arm, tossed Woren the reins and dismounted. He made a beeline for Mälque. Mälque retreated and tripped over a root. The Gor King charged, and with his free hand, jerked Mälque off the ground.

Mälque came face-to-face with the warrior and fought for his life. He kicked at his head, beat his arm, spat in his face. The Gor King retaliated by shaking him like a snared rabbit. Mälque increased his efforts and clawed like a wild cat and cussed like he'd heard Vonn do when drunk. The Gor King, ready to end his tirade, spun him and swatted his rump with the book over and over.

"Okay," Mälque shouted as pain shot across his rear. "I'll quit fightin'."

The beating stopped and the Gor King pulled him up, eye-to-eye.

Now will they glow red?

Before Mälque got a good look, he caught a whiff of the Gor King's breath: Sulphur and wildeberry. Water and musk. Hot and cold: A fusion of scents and temperatures that made Mälque turn away.

"Anymore tricks," the Gor King asked, his voice rumbling like an avalanche in a far away valley.

Mälque, who refused to look at him, shook his head.

"No more tricks."

"You're lying."

The accusation, like a blow to the gut, made Mälque gasp with worry. Was the Gor King on to his secrets or was he simply baiting him? Mälque decided to play his part to the very end.

"Lyin'?" He glanced at the Gor King out of the corner of his eye. "About what?"

"Secrets in her cave. A whisper…a vision."

Mälque stared off into space, heart racing, and continued his ploy. "I don't know whatcha talkin' about."

The Gor King pulled him closer. "Confession is good for the soul."

"Ain't nothin' to confess. Besides, ain't nothin' but dyin'…

"Tell me. Now!"

Mälque, who still didn't trust Woren completely, nevertheless looked to him for guidance: tell the truth or lie? After what seemed like an interminably look time, Woren answered with a subtle nod. Mälque flashed him a *you-better-be-right* look before turning his attention back to the Gor King.

"Okay," Mälque half-whispered as he leaned back as far as he could to avoid the foul breath and ominous eye sockets. "I saw strange things in her cave…heard some things too, a whisper, but how'd ya know…"

The Gor King shoved the book into Mälque's gut.

"Show me the vision."

"Don't know if I can."

"Yours is to do, not try."

"Ya don't get it." He held the book up to the Gor King's face. "This does what it wants, *when* it wants. Look." He thumbed through the parchments. "See? Just pages and pages of stuff I can't read and…"

A warm sea breeze brushed Mälque's left cheek and he froze. The book pulsed…

Like a heartbeat!

A vision flashed on the cover.

No…not now…

He clutched the book to his chest in hopes it would protect him from the fire, or whatever else could come out of the Gor King's eye sockets.

"Quit stalling," the Gor King thundered. "Show me the vision!"

You didn't see it?

Mälque checked Woren's expression. *Ya don't look surprised neither, so I'm guessin'…*

The Gor King slapped his head.

Mälque reeled from the blow. Ear buzzed. Face was on fire. He rubbed his throbbing cheek.

Why didn't ya see it? Followed by a more troubling thought: *And how did ya know about the whisper and vision from her cave?*

The Gor King poked the book. "Show me the vision."

"I…I…"

The Gor King threw Mälque to the ground and reached for his sword.

Mälque, stunned from the fall, rolled onto his back. The book lay nearby and the Gor King was closing ground. Mälque stretched for the book, hoping its magic would save him, but he couldn't reach it. He tried to scoot away but the Gor King was on him.

The Gor King straddled Mälque and rested the tip of his blue blade on his throat.

Mälque winced and closed his eyes. *Just make it quick.*

After what felt like forever, he felt the tip leave his neck. Mälque kept his eyes closed and made fists, steeling himself for the deathblow.

When nothing happened, he braved a peek, expecting to see the sword poised over the head of the Gor King, ready to hammer down with swift fury. All he saw was gray sky.

Mälque sat up. The Gor King, who had sheathed his weapon, was making his way to Woren and his warhorse. The book, clutched in one hand, swung like a pendulum.

"Tie him up," The Gor King ordered.

Mälque watched with trepidation as Woren retrieved several ropes from his saddlebag. Instead of heading his way, Woren tied the ends of both to trees straddling the horse's head.

Mälque breathed a sigh of relief and watched as Woren went to work. He took the loose ends and tied them to either side of the bridle. He pulled the ropes tight, which told Mälque he had used slipknots, and secured the warhorse between the two trees.

The Gor King retrieved Ela Claire's hair and his warhorse snorted and bucked; eyes looked like moons, white with fright. The Gor King brought the strand close to his flaring nostrils and the warhorse strained against the ropes but was unable to loosen the bond. The Gor King stroked his snout while waving the strand and blowing into his nostrils.

The Gor King continued his ritual until the spell was broken and the animal quieted.

With a parting pat, the Gor King walked away holding Ela Claire's hair up to the light. He twirled it between his fingers and eyed it as if inspecting a gem.

He sniffed it.

Whether he caught her scent, Mälque could only speculate, but one thing he was certain of: his lips twitched, as if in a smile.

Chapter 38

Ain't Worth Dyin' For

Cloaked in the darkness of night, Mälque led Woren and the Gor King to the top of the bluff without a sound. Near the ridge, they dismounted and tethered their horses to a tree. Mälque gestured at the cliff and tiptoed toward the precipice. Woren followed while the Gor King remained in the background, waiting; watching.

They proceeded hunched over out onto the rocky cliff and when they neared the lip, crawled the rest of the way on their bellies.

"There," Mälque whispered.

At first Woren didn't see what he was pointing to, and then his eyes adjusted to the darkness. Snaking up from the valley was a wisp of smoke, a silver thread against the backdrop of the black woods. Woren followed it to its source and discovered the campfire. A few coals flickered orange, mere dots of light.

"Could be anyone's."

"But it ain't. Can't you see 'em? She's sleepin' on her side near those kids, and that man is over by those little ones, there."

Woren squinted and looked again, but his eyes were too old and the light too dim. "I don't see them."

Mälque nudged his shoulder. "Then look over there." He gestured to a location away from the fire. "Surely ya can see him, can't ya?"

Woren stared at the spot. Nestled on the ground beneath some trees, cloaked in shadows, was a large creature. Woren blinked, squinted, even leaned a bit out over the ledge to better identify the beast. Something white, like a moon shrouded in fog, glowed.

"The bird," Woren cooed. He patted Mälque on the back. "Another good day of tracking."

Tonight was the sixth time they had spied on Ela Claire from the shadows. As with the previous nights, and at his insistence, Mälque tracked her alone by day and returned at dusk to lead them to her location. Initially, Woren objected to such an arrangement, sighting his past experiences trusting Wurmlins as well as the fact that Mälque would bolt for freedom the moment he was out of sight.

Mälque argued that he needed to work alone since he, and only he, could track her without being discovered. This only infuriated Woren who kept insisting he accompany the *yung-er*.

The argument heated, and Mälque resigned himself to defeat until the Gor King cupped his head between gloved hands.

"I know who killed your father."

The news made Mälque's blood boil, and although he had intended to dash to freedom, just as Woren suspected, the Gor King's secret baited him into returning. Avenging his father's death, as well as Vonn's, consumed his thoughts and gave purpose to his life. How the Gor King knew this about him was another matter, but for now, this was the first clue to finding his father's killer.

Mälque and Woren scooted back from the edge of the cliff, and when they were certain they couldn't be seen from the valley, stood up and made their way back.

The Gor King met them with arms crossed.

Mälque rubbed his swollen lip. Tracking Ela Claire had been easier than he expected, he could thank the children for that. Their exodus from Rythe left a swath of footprints, broken branches and turned soil; he could have followed them blindfolded. But instead of reaping praises from the Gor King, Mälque got an occasional backhand. The taste of his own blood reminding him that he was just a dog to be put down once the Gor King had Ela Claire.

He returned his thoughts to the moment, bracing for a blow, but the Gor King brushed past and headed for the horses.

Mälque breathed a sigh of relief and eyed his saddlebag containing Ela Claire's book. He was thankful that the visions and whisper had kept him alive, even aiding him in tracking her, but the whisper's warning back in her cave confounded him...

"Be careful, Mälque. She has a purpose, but not as you are hoping."

Doubts and concerns about her nature, as well as his, swirled like gnats in his mind. He whipped his hair as if to swat them away and mounted his horse.

Mälque expected the Gor King to lead them down the hill, like he had on the previous nights. Instead, he led them out onto the cliff. Mälque caught Woren's look of surprise. The brazen move by the Gor King would expose them, and since previous scoutings were done with the utmost secrecy, Mälque made a quick deduction.

He's plannin' his attack! But will we return to camp for reinforcements or strike now?

Mälque let his gaze wander to Ela Claire. Tracking her had been the easy part. Leaving to report her position was another matter.

His first encounter with her, aside from the visions, was when he was high on a bluff and far downwind. His heart pounded. He'd seen her handiwork at the Isle of Rythe. A whole section of wall obliterated as if a giant had kicked it out to sea. Even Woren was speechless.

As a powerful storyteller, would she sense his presence on the bluff and use a story to destroy him? He imagined the story being like a magic arrow, diving on him, chasing him through the woods, splitting him in half and incinerating him like chaff. But she continued along the path, oblivious to his watching eye.

Encouraged, Mälque sized her up to determine how she would react when cornered, if that were even possible. What he observed made him rub his eyes to make sure he wasn't seeing things. She offered a helping hand to a straggler, ruffled the hair of a boy, tickled the belly of a little girl.

I don't get it. Why risk your life for them kids? I caught their scent. They ain't no better than me, maybe even worse. And that man ain't nothin' but a minstrel. They ain't worth dyin' for. Nobody is.

But it was their collective voice that had him scratching his head.

Whatcha singin' for? Don't ya know creatures from the Awakening are everywhere, and I'm huntin' ya for the Gor King?

He lingered on the bluff, for how long he couldn't remember, but it was well after the last child rounded the bend and the music faded on the wind.

His next spotting was at dawn and he dared to get closer. She awoke before the others and stirred the coals to flame. She set a small pot of water on the fire and stared into the fire, mumbling to herself, rocking back and forth. Was she conjuring tales of destruction? Was she plotting the future? Mourning her past? He could only guess.

When the water boiled, she poured it into a pewter mug. Based upon the dregs she tossed on the ground, that he inspected long after they were gone, he detected tart buckroot, spicy ollusk leaves and the sharp bouquet of jarmeen buds: Allsbruthian tea.

Next, she wrapped her arms around drawn knees, white dress falling around her like fresh snow, and cradled the mug with both hands. She nibbled on wildeberries, sweet roots and smoked fish, deep in thought, vapors from her breath and tea drifting off like tiny clouds.

She pursed her lips and blinked her eyelashes and set hair behind an ear with a graceful finger. He knew these were clues to her personality, insights to the schemes she was hatching, but his thoughts flitted like bees over a flowered meadow, soaring beyond anything he had felt before. Or could control.

On his next scouting mission, getting even closer to her, he noticed the curves of her figure, her determined gait, her dimples. The following day, her giggle: it rained from the sky as she soared on the harrier's back. With each encounter, he stayed longer than before and longer than he needed, explaining such delays to Woren as part of his fact gathering missions.

He brushed off his new emotions with the flick of his hair, telling himself he didn't care what happened to her, that if it came down to it, he would slice her throat or die trying. But he knew it was a lie and even imagined Vonn snickering at him and calling his bluff.

Mälque shook off the memories and eyed the valley. First light was chasing away the shadows. Here trees and shrubs. Here sleeping children. Here Ela Claire. She awoke with a start and sat up, head turning this way and that to get her bearings.

"What spooked her," he whispered more to himself than to Woren or the Gor King.

"A bad dream," Woren suggested in a monotone voice.

"Fate," the Gor King stated.

Mälque, astonished to hear the Gor King speak on the matter, glanced his way and found him closer to the lip of the cliff…

As if ya want her ta see ya.

Mälque turned his attention back to Ela Claire, expecting to find her squatting over the fire making tea like she did every morning. Instead, she was walking toward a clearing with the harrier.

Mälque drew in short breaths, alarmed at her new routine. Sweat pooled between his shoulder blades as he told himself she deserved to be caught. Fingers balled into fists, although he had no idea who he would hit, or why.

Her voice, like a murmur from wind-blown reeds, echoed up to him.

She's calm. Don't even know we're here.

Out of the corner of his eye, Mälque saw the Gor King shift in his saddle. Whether he was drawn to her voice or wanted to give away his position, he could only speculate. Whatever the reason, his warhorse sensed his master's desire, and whinnied.

Mälque spun to take in Ela Claire's reaction: she was pointing out their position to the harrier.

He held his breath, waiting for her to deliver a death story, wondering what it looked like, if anything at all. When nothing happened, he let his breath escape with a great rush and eyed her in a new light. Something in his gut shifted, like the crack of ice on a pond, and he thought about shouting her a warning. But he caught himself for being such a yung-er, and whipped his hair.

She turned to head back to camp when the sunrise crested the ridge and a sheaf of golden light fell across the Gor King.

Mälque saw the fear in her eyes. It was all he could do not to shout, "Run!"

Chapter 39

Quandary

Ela Claire struggled against the currents, trying to remember how she had fallen into the river, trying to spot Previn, DeMorley, the children...

But nothing came to mind and no one was there. She thrashed, she clawed, she screamed but the rapids roared back and dragged her deeper into its lair of shadows. Spears of sunlight crisscrossed the brown water as she descended. Icy temperatures signaled she was nearing the bottom. Lungs burned for want of air; her next breath would be her last.

Panic, colder than the river, cut her to the quick.

I'm going to drown...just like Romlin.

Exhausted from the fight, her vision blurred and darkness, like a wave of endless sleep, washed over her.

A whisper chortled, *Death begets death!*

Ela Claire awoke with a start. She was lying on her back, panting as if she'd actually been drowning. She noted the gray sky through the tree limbs and was relieved it was almost sunrise. She relaxed, chalking it up to another bad dream, when another thought made her sit up.

Where are the children?

She checked the campfire, now just coals, to find them asleep around DeMorley. In the dim light, they reminded her of lambs nestled beside their shepherd.

"Are you all right," Previn asked from the shadows.

"Yes. Just another dream." She shuddered as the sensation of drowning returned. She shook it off and stood up.

"Judging by your tossing about, I'd wager that it wasn't one conjured from Claire."

"No," she snickered. "Definitely not."

Previn made his way to her side. "I admire your bravery."

"I'm not brave."

"You were on the Isle of Rhythe."

"That was different. I couldn't bear to have the children suffer any longer."

"Yes, but you knew a tale would alert the Cauldron to your whereabouts. It's been six days since we escaped. Can you remember a night when you didn't have a nightmare?"

He didn't wait for her answer. "I'd call that bravery."

Ela Claire gestured at the sleeping children. "They're the reason I'm brave."

Previn eyed them and nodded. "Love can do that."

He turned his attention back to Ela Claire. "May I assume that tonight's nightmare was like the others?"

She took in his concerned look, nodded, and stroked his feathers. "I try not to think about Romlin, but it's impossible."

"I'd worry if you stopped."

"But don't you get tired of me talking about him?"

He leaned back to look her in the eyes. "I'm hurt you would even insinuate such a thing."

"But…"

"Ela Claire," he interrupted, his voice as soft as the morning breeze, "you have an inner strength that burns like a tulip on fire. Such vigor has risen from your tears, your pain, your loss. It is the essence of who you are. To suggest I tire of listening to such tales is, well, insulting."

He gave her time to mull over his rebuttal before continuing. "Never forget those that are gone. Never stop telling their story." He rustled his wings to emphasize his next point. "Never!"

She sighed. "But it's been four summers and the pain still cuts like a blade. When will it end?"

"If it did, wouldn't it signal that your love for Romlin has died?"

She turned away and covered her mouth. Her shoulders heaved.

Previn pulled her under his wing.

"Thankfully," he reassured, hoping to get her mind off the past, "the children have not been attacked and have had pleasant dreams."

She wiped her eyes and nodded.

Previn continued. "In fact, I'm most impressed with their courage. It's uncharacteristic of children their age."

She sniffled. "I agree." She stepped out from under his wing to check on them. "They're inspiring."

After a moment of reflection, she led him to a clearing where she gazed up at the sky. Pink hues marked the eastern horizon. She sighed with relief. "This is my favorite time of the day. There's such serenity, as if all my troubles - past and present are beyond the veil of Claire. It's when I can reflect on Clairian stories to find courage and purpose for the coming day."

"And sip Allsbruthian tea."

She flashed him a smile. "Yes, that doesn't hurt. Care to join me for a cup?"

She turned for the fire when a distant whinny made her spin around.

"It came from up there." Previn gestured with a wing at the bluff off to their left.

"Three riders," she pointed out. "But who are they?"

The wind shifted and Previn sniffed for their scents. "A Wurmlin boy, an Ebonite man and a..."

Ela Claire trained her eyes on the unknown figure. Even in the dim light, his physique stood in stark contrast to the others. A chill ran down her spine.

Previn shook his head in frustration. "There are too many scents on the wind now. I'm not sure who he is or what his intent is."

The sun cleared the ridge and a sunbeam lit the mystery rider.

Ela Claire covered her mouth in shock. "His helmet!" Her muffled voice was full of dread. "It's a *gor skull!*"

Before she could close her eyes to read his story or destroy them, the warrior led the others off the cliff, disappearing into the shadows.

"The Oracle," Previn recalled. "It foretold of a Gor King. Remember?"

He recited the first stanza.

> *Mothers, guard babes; Fathers, draw steel,*
> *Thunder approaches, soon blood on the fields.*
> *Tempest of war, so black and so vile,*
> *Spreads o'er Allsbruth; lament suckling child.*

Ela Claire comprehended his logic and added the second stanza.

> *Orphaned stories, treasures from Claire,*
> *Like buried embers, burst forth and flare.*
> *Hear not a whisper, sweet lark on the wing?*
> *Tales shall crush steel when gors have a king.*

Ela Claire checked on the children.

> *"...blood on the fields...*

She imagined what would happen if they fell into the hands of the Gor King.

> *"...lament suckling child..."*

She threw off the gruesome images and they dashed back to camp. DeMorley, awakened by their commotion and urgent voices, pushed himself up on his elbows.

"What's wrong," he asked as he yawned and rubbed sleepy eyes.

"We saw the Gor King." There was urgency in her voice. She continued to stir the children from sleep.

DeMorley, recalling his ordeal with the fiend, sprang to his feet. "Where? Here?" He hopped about as if the Gor King would magically appear out of thin air.

"No," Previn answered while rustling children with his wings. "We spotted him on a cliff overlooking our location. We have time to escape before he can reach us, but we need to hurry."

DeMorley, relieved to be out of danger for the time being, helped rouse the others. "Are you sure it was him?"

"Yes," Ela Claire answered as she rocked Ballin until he opened his eyes. "He wore a gor skull for a helmet."

"A gor skull?" DeMorley repeated. "You must have mistaken his bald head for a helmet."

"No mistake," Previn blurted as he herded the yawning children together. "It was a gor skull; sun-bleached white; ominous eye sockets."

DeMorley shook his head as he tried to make sense of their report. "Eye sockets? Gor skull? I suppose that's possible, but then again…"

"Does it matter," Ela Claire snapped. "We need to hurry and get away from here!"

"Yes, of course," DeMorley concurred as he looked for Lolling. "Except, well…"

Previn glared at DeMorley. "Spit it out, man!"

"My point is this: I smashed my Bellini over the Gor King's *head*, not a helmet, remember? So if this isn't the Gor King, maybe we have nothing to fear. Besides…" He lifted Lolling into the air and she wiggled her toes and giggled. "Didn't you discover all of this when you read my story some time ago?"

"At the time I was only looking for Newcomb and Lassiter, not the Gor King."

"That's right," he recalled as he shifted Lolling into the crook of his arm. Eager to set the matter straight, as well as be the center of attention, he spewed out the story. "You see, Draemel, who was a bounty hunter, had a partner, Paradin, who we left for dead, but didn't die, and instead formed an allegiance with the Cauldron, at least that's what we assumed because one eye twitched like that of a ghoul while the other one…"

"DeMorley!" Previn interrupted, "You're scaring them."

DeMorley, engrossed in his storytelling, was oblivious to the wide eyes and gaping mouths turned his direction. He took in Lolling's round face. Lower lip quivered; tears welled.

"Oh, no," he murmured as he pulled her close and reassured her with a pat. "There, there. I didn't mean to frighten you." And then to Ela Claire, "So with two Gor Kings on the prowl, what are we supposed to do now?"

Ela Claire mulled over the last line of the Oracle with the same scrutiny she had given Il-Lilliad's books during her tenure in his cave.

Tales shall crush steel when gors have a king.

She eyed the young storytellers, and inspired by their fixed gaze brimming with optimism, reexamined the words from a fresh perspective.

She spoke the verse, "*Tales shall crush steel when gors have a king.*"

Previn and DeMorley heard a question in her voice.

She tapped her chin and twisted her lips as she untangled the words, deciphered their meaning, considered their implications. She paced. Cape swooshed. She mumbled the verse. Repeated. Word by word. And then she stopped with her back to them.

"Tales shall crush steel when gors have a king." This time, her tone was emphatic, nor wavering, as if she were making a declaration of emancipation...or war.

She spun around. Her face glowed as if the comprehension she had gleaned was lighting her from within.

She gestured for the children to huddle around. "We don't have much time, so listen up: this is what we're going to do."

Chapter 40

Bull Gor and the Dragon

Mälque swayed in his saddle, eyelids heavy from the monotony and the heat of the day. He shook off the lethargy as if being splashed with ice water and reset his nerve.

Wake up, yung-er. This ain't no pleasure trip!

He eyed the drivers of the wagon he was keeping pace with.

Bull gor and the dragon.

Hoffrader, the Ingloid, was the bull gor: bulbous head atop mountainous shoulders; wide, flat nose; sunken eyes; long arms leading to burly hands, the horse reins like twine in his grip. Ebonite armor wrapped around his barrel chest squeezing his rotund gut outward, a result of too much ale and gorging, that wiggled in time to the wagon's rhythms.

A pewter helmet, more like a bowl, sat atop his sheared crown. Scars and a jaw that never closed properly were proof Hoffrader was a seasoned veteran, a warrior not to be trifled with.

He gnawed on venison jerky, flipping it from one side of his mouth to the other, until he caught Mälque eyeballing him and yanked the meat out to use as a pointer.

"Whatcha lookin' at, *yung-er?*" He jabbed the venison at Mälque like a sword, his voice primal, grating, throaty.

"Nothin'," Mälque rattled as he tried to avoid eye contact. And then to the object strapped into the wagon: "Ain't nothin' but dyin' everywhere."

Hoffrader glanced back at the cargo. For a brief moment, his eyes lit up. Fear? Wonderment? Mälque could only guess.

Hoffrader stuffed the jerky back in his mouth. "You worry about your job." The venison flicked up and down. "I'll worry about mine." He thumped his plated chest with a thick thumb. "Just keep your eyes off me, you hear? I hate Wurmlins! Nothin' but filthy, stealin' vermin." He snapped the reins down hard on the flanks of the two horses.

Mälque turned his attention to the second man.

The dragon...Gruun.

Mälque knew dragons no longer roamed the lands, but the bedtime stories his mother spun, as well as those from Bal-Malin, had captured his fancy. Based upon her description, and fueled by his imagination, Gruun was a perfect match.

Gruun was tall, lean, and unlike the other men in the Gor King's army, had a face void of cuts or facial hair or wrinkles or spots. And with skin as pale as snow, even after longs days in the sun, Mälque wasn't sure if he was twenty or forty summers of age.

Timeless. Like a dragon.

By outward appearances, and in comparison to Hoffrader, Gruun looked unintimidating, but Mälque was no fool and could still hear Vonn's sage advice six summers ago…

"When you're trackin' and stealin', don't let the size of someone fool ya into feelin' safe. Remember: the bear fears the badger; the wolf avoids the snake. Be a Wurmlin. Don't trust nothin' or no one."

Mälque analyzed Gruun with such scrutiny. A loner who could skin a rabbit with teeth and fingers faster than anyone Mälque had ever seen, Gruun had eyes that were green slits, reflecting intelligence, cunning and a cold-blooded nature. Mälque witnessed the later when soldiers discovered a songbird trapped in a briar patch. Bored with the routine of army life, they poked and prodded the bird into chirping and flapping its wings. Gruun pushed his way through, reached into the thorns barehanded and snatched the bird. Before his cronies could chastise him for ruining their sport, he crushed the bird and left it hanging in the brambles. Whether he wanted to deliver a *coup de grace* or lusted for first blood, no one could say. Whatever the reason, rumors and speculations about the warrior grew.

Late at night, when fires burned low and imaginations flamed, Mälque listened in on the men's whispers about Gruun: Tristanite from Draiglore, the birth place of dragons; discovered as a babe in a grotto; kills his first man on his tenth summer; wily as a mage; drinks his victim's blood; grows scales and wings when the moon is blue.

As a Wurmlin, Mälque was savvy to know these tales were the result of too much ale and too little sense, but somewhere in the middle of the yarns was the truth, albeit the size of a grain of sand.

Gruun checked on Mälque out of the corner of his eyes. He swiped his tongue over thin lips and fingered his dagger. Mälque was drawn to the hilt: a dragon's head cut from white stone; polished to burn like silver. Mälque noted Gruun's warning and looked away, reflecting on how he came to be with such a lot.

After Ela Claire spied them on the cliff, the Gor King led them back to their base camp a day's journey away. At dusk, the commanders gathered around the Gor King's fire. Woren handed out mugs of ale but these weren't lifted with bravado or tavern songs like he'd seen them do at previous meetings. The men gave Woren their full attention as he marked the dirt with a stick, his voice but a murmur as he laid out the plans for their next campaign. The men sipped their ale, nodding when they understood the drawings, jabbing an elbow into ribs to commemorate the gold and adventure coming their way. A question was raised, bits and pieces floating on the wind to Mälque:

"Who…handle…girl?"

Woren turned to the Gor King for the answer. He rose to his full height, the firelight making him all the more ghoulish looking, and pointed. All eyes turned to stare at Mälque.

He shook off the memory with a flick of his head.

"I don't like this plan," Mälque mumbled more to himself than to Hoffrader and Gruun.

"And we do?" thundered Hoffrader as he chomped the jerky. "Not only are we stuck with your stench, but we gotta haul *that*." Hoffrader jerked a thumb over his shoulder.

Mälque eyed the log strapped in the back of the wagon. To the untrained eye, it looked like they were hauling firewood or a post for a tall wall. But upon closer inspection one would note daggers buried in either side with leather straps clamping the shields tight over the splintered ends. And if an ear were pressed close, a buzzing sound came from within.

"Just help me get it set," Mälque said.

"Oh, we'll do that," Hoffrader spat. "But you handle the girl and those fea dracas…alone."

"But you're suppose to stay nearby…in case there's trouble. That was the order."

Hoffrader rolled his big head back and barked a laugh. Even Gruun smiled.

"Order?" Hoffrader snorted. "Don't remember no…order."

Mälque ground his teeth and focused on their surroundings.

They were north of the Gilden Plains; the terrain was flatter and trees and brush dotted the landscape. The tall grass thinned, and in some spots, he could see the soil. Gone was the black, pungent dirt of Allsbruth and the brown clay of the mountains. This top soil sparkled, from quartz he presumed, and was sandy like the type found in the gentle bend of a river. But it was the miniscule chips of orange intermingled with quartz that caught his fancy. This was his first clue that they were nearing Claire, and the orange desert he had heard the men discuss over pipes and ale.

Hoffrader pulled back on the reins and the wagon lumbered to a stop.

"Up there," he used the jerky to indicate a location to their right. "That's the clearing Woren described. And there," he eyed a feature to their left, "is the dry creek bed."

Gruun grabbed the bulkhead and stood up. He put his full weight on the wood and surveyed the location. Something caught his eye and he pointed out two trees straddling a grove of bushes.

Gruun sat down and Hoffrader slapped the reins.

When they reached the location, they went to work. Hoffrader flicked away his jerky and untied the ropes securing the trunk while Gruun clambered into the wagon and grabbed the thinner end of the log. With a grunt, he lifted his end and waited.

Hoffrader tossed the ropes to Mälque and grabbed the larger end of the log sticking out of the wagon. He knelt, heaved it up onto his shoulder, face reddening from the effort, and with several strong strides, pulled it forward.

A dark tone reverberated from the hollow tree and sounded to Mälque as if it were groaning a warning. But it was the low rumble, like a distant storm, that made his skin crawl.

"Careful," Mälque warned as he pictured the swarm fluttering their wings, blue eyes in search of prey, claws and teeth poised to rip flesh. Flashes of Olke's white bones glowing in the sun made him squirm in the saddle.

"Shut up," Hoffrader spat. "You're not helping!"

Gruun reached the end of the wagon and shouted for Hoffrader to stop. Gruun set his end down. Gently.

The murmur in the den grew to a hum. The shields shivered but the straps remained taut, keeping them battened down.

"We need to be quick about this," Hoffrader noted.

Gruun hopped down, knelt under his end of the trunk and lifted it with his shoulder. As a team, they marched it toward the trees. Reaching the bushes, Hoffrader lowered his end to the ground first, being careful not to dislodge the shield or daggers. Satisfied they were intact, he made his way to the end Gruun was holding. The hum grew to a buzz and vibrated into their fingers, hands, arms, bodies.

"Hurry up, *yung-er!*"

Mälque wanted to argue the plan, wanted to make them promise not to leave him with the fea dracas, wanted to turn and gallop off. He drifted off in thought.

"Ain't nothin' but dyin'…"

"Now!" Hoffrader screamed over the buzzing, screeching and scraping sounds.

Mälque chose the tree to their right and stood in his stirrups to reach a thick limb. He stretched and wrapped one end of the rope around the trunk and branch and knotted it. He plopped back into his saddle and made his way to the fea dracas den. He looped the rope below the end the men were supporting and went to the tree on the opposite side. He bunched the remaining rope together and threw it over a high, stout limb. It cleared the branch and unfurled as it fell to the ground.

He dismounted, making sure he double-knotted the reins to the bushes, and retrieved the rope. With a boot set on the trunk, he put his back into pulling, and the rope snapped tight. Hoffrader and Gruun pushed the log up, moving hand over hand until it angled into the sky.

"That'll do," Hoffrader ordered between breaths, arms fully extended.

Mälque wrapped the rope several times around the base of the tree, and as he was knotting it, heard the clank of the wagon as it rolled away.

"Good luck, *yung-er!*" Hoffrader shouted over his shoulder followed by a flippant hand gesture. Gruun flashed an insidious grin; fingers tapped his dagger.

Mälque spat on the ground and watched them roll away. A smile crept over his face. This was the moment he had been waiting for. Even though Woren and the Gor King were close, marching the army into position, now was his chance to escape. He untied the reins of his horse and was drawn to the saddlebag containing Ela Claire's book. Swinging into the saddle, he tried not to think about her, but despite his best efforts, memories from his time in her cave flashed.

"Be careful, Mälque. She has a purpose, but not as you are hoping."

And that was his dilemma: he didn't know what he hoped for her. Death? Life? Nothing? Feelings for her ranged from anger to intrigue to something he didn't know how to describe. His gut churned from it all, and he kept telling himself no one was worth dying for, that Wurmlins didn't help anyone, and that it was her own fault if she fell for the Gor King's ploy.

"So why ain't I dashin' off?"

The question riddled him, then it infuriated him. He whipped his hair in an attempt to rid himself of her, the book, the whisper.

"Get a grip! "Ain't nothin' but dyin' everywhere."

He was about to drive his boot heels into the horse's flanks when another flash of recall from her cave stopped him short.

"So you're gonna kill me."

"No. I offer you life, just as I did Vonn."

He imagined her on the white bird, cape flapping like a sail, the children below, a song on the wind.

He shielded his eyes to search the sky.

And waited.

Chapter 41

Chosen Sovereign

Something was astir. Ela Claire could feel it in her bones; smell it on the wind. She clung to Previn's feathers as he circled high above DeMorley and the children, thankful their escape from the Gor King had been uneventful. From what she and Previn could ascertain, he was not on their trail, which made her wonder if the encounter had simply been a fluke.

The hair rising up on her neck told her otherwise.

Claire was a day's journey away, and although this made her spirit soar with optimism, she kept her senses sharp. If they had not caught the scent of the Gor King the other night, was it possible he could sneak up now undetected? And why hadn't the Cauldron attacked? Surely the story she used on the Isle of Rhythe had alerted the Dark Flame to their presence.

She pushed her concerns to the side and focused on the task at hand: looking out for danger. To the north, the terrain flattened and vegetation and trees were sparse. Although they would be exposed to attack, the landscape meant that Claire was close, as was the veil. She pictured it shimmering like an endless waterfall and dreamed of ushering the children through, whisking them up to Marsien Vur where they could dance, sing, laugh. Forever.

She checked her zeal and eyed the horizon to her right. A perfect line of blue atop emerald green marked the intersection of sky and the Gilden Sea. A black dot amidst sparkling silver was the Isle of Rhythe. Had their escape only been a few days prior? It seemed much longer.

To her left, and almost imperceptible, were the Cliffs of Claire. She reminisced when she and Romlin dashed off the top, hand in hand, trusting a whisper to save them from death.

She shook off the memory, and the emotions that came with it, and glanced down at the children's location: the northern edge of the Gilden Plains. Here the land rolled like waves, trees and thickets dotted the vista, dry creek beds meandered off from the River Arrgient.

And somewhere out there was the Gor King.

"I don't see anything," she shouted through the wind to Previn, avoiding the silent tongue in case the Cauldron or the Gor King, if he had such capabilities, was listening in.

"Nor I," he piped back. "Let's check on the children. Hold on."

Ela Claire leaned close to his neck and he tucked his wings and dove.

When he leveled at treetop level, she sat up and looked over his side. DeMorley carried Lolling on his back, the Bellini swinging in time to his gait, and led the children down a dry creek bed. Scouting ahead were three storytellers. Taking up the rear was Ballin and the remaining storytellers.

She reflected on their plan from an earlier night.

"Don't you see what the Oracle is trying to tell us? We are the ones to be feared, not the Gor King! You all," she nodded at the young storytellers, "will be able to defend, even attack, with a story."

Faces clouded with doubt. She scanned their thoughts.

"I know, I know, you lack the experience, but if you trust me, and listen to me, we can act as one to defeat our enemies, just like we did to break out of Rhythe and travel over the Gilden Sea."

They gave a collective nod. She continued.

"I want you and you and you..." she gestured with her head, "to be our point, scouting ahead for any sign of trouble. If you see, hear, smell, or sense *anything*, alert me in the silent tongue. Okay?"

They nodded.

She turned to Ballin. "I want you to protect the column from the rear with the other storytellers. And you," she faced DeMorley, "will be in charge of the remaining children."

DeMorley caressed Lolling's back. After a moment of thought, he nodded to his calling as their tutelage.

Ballin cocked his head to the side. "Where will you be?"

"Flying overhead on Previn. We'll be able to see danger well in advance, which means..." she raised a finger to get their attention and to emphasize her next point, "don't chatter, especially in the silent tongue, unless it's absolutely necessary. I need to know I can get your attention in a flash. Plus, we're not sure who can listen in on us. Does everyone understand?"

Ela Claire let the memory fade and focused back on the task at hand. The sun was high overhead. Maybe with a little luck, they would reach the veil with no altercation with the Gor King, Ebonites or the Cauldron.

But she was no longer Elabea, *Dreamer of Days*, the naïve girl from Hetherlinn. She bore a Clairian title: Ela Claire: *Dreamer of Life*. And like the children, had weathered a crucible of pain and heartbreak that made her wise beyond her summers.

She drew in a deep breath to gather her nerve and imagined Romlin whispering encouragement in her ear.

"Expect the worst but hope for the best. Stay sharp, Ela Claire, stay sharp!"

Something up ahead flashed in the sunlight. Previn spotted it as well and gained altitude, veering toward the clearing north of their position.

Another glint. She zeroed in on two trees straddling a grove of bushes. From her experience observing terrain flying on Previn's back, she learned that flashes often indicated ponds, rivers, waves, or on rare occasions, exposed minerals or gems. But there were no streams or ponds, and the intensity of the light was more in line with something man-made, like abandoned plates, mugs or coins.

"Or armor," she reasoned.

Previn cawed. "There. By the grove. The Wurmlin boy and the Ebonite we saw on the cliff."

She leaned forward and cupped her eyes. "Are you sure? It's still too far away. Do you see the Gor King?"

Before Previn could reply, something that looked like a dark cloud appeared over the grove.

Mälque, with hands shielding his eyes as he searched the sky, heard a horse cantering toward him. Certain it was Woren or one of his men checking up on him, he continued gazing skyward. From the corner of his eye he recognized Woren.

"Where's Hoffrader? Gruun?"

"Ran off." Mälque kept his eyes on the sky. "Guessin' they joined the others at the creek bed."

Woren squirmed in his saddle as he processed the news. Had this been an Ebonite army, both men would have been hunted down and executed in a March of Reeds. But this was the Gor King's army, and although Woren did his utmost to maintain a certain level of military decorum, standards were much more relaxed. He would deal with them later. He stared at Mälque. "You could have galloped off to freedom."

"But I didn't."

"Why?"

Mälque met his look. "Don't go thinkin' it's 'cause I wanna help you...or him."

He gestured at the tree line behind them where, hidden in the shadows, was the Gor King and a portion of his army.

"That much I've already deduced, which has me concerned."

Mälque turned his attention to the sky. "Why's that?"

Woren didn't answer. He let the matter go, not wanting to disclose too much to Mälque in their game of cat and mouse. He cupped his eyes to look for the giant bird and Ela Claire. After a long moment, Mälque broke the silence.

"Ya sure they'll come this way?"

"They have to. This valley is the most direct means to Claire."

"Ya know she can wipe us out with one story. Ya seen what she did at Rhythe...whole wall blown to bits. Never seen anythin' like that before. And neither have you."

"You focus on your orders. The Gor King knows what he's doing."

Mälque reflected on the second half of his mission: climb the log and place her strand of hair where the fea dracas could catch her scent. Loosen the leather straps then flee.

Mälque swept the sky with his gaze and at the same time shook his head. "Ain't gonna work. Fea dracas ain't dogs. They may catch her scent; may not. Either way, she ain't no fool. She ain't gonna fly into a trap."

"We'll see about that."

"And what if the fea dracas do attack, and what if she can't destroy them fast enough like he's hopin', then what?"

Woren digested the question with a tilt of his head, but he never answered.

"Besides, we both know he's got powers so why all the plottin' and schemin'? He could just blast her from the sky with his sword."

"Maybe his intention is not to harm her."

"Still don't make sense unless..."

"Unless what?"

Mälque looked in the direction of where the Gor King hid. "Unless he's scared of her."

"Scared? I doubt that."

Mälque turned his attention back to the sky. "What's he gonna do with them kids and that minstrel? Never heard a plan to catch 'em."

Woren rolled his head and cracked his neck. "This is war." Voice calm, detached, as if discussing children being fatalities of combat was as commonplace as chatting about spring rain. "Don't get soft, Mälque. Just do your duty."

Woren turned his horse and plodded away. "Remember," he shouted over his shoulder, "we can see everything. Everything."

"Aint' gonna do it," he mumbled, more to hear how it sounded out in the open than to alert Woren to his plan.

And then with gusto, "Ain't gonna do it!"

Woren pulled back on the reins. "Mälque." His tone was cold and direct. "Don't push your luck. Just do your duty."

Mälque glanced at the saddlebag holding her book, her strand of hair, and then stared back at Woren. Eyes locked. A distant caw made them both check the sky. A black dot marked Ela Claire's location.

Mälque turned his attention back to Woren. Both set of eyes narrowed. Mälque whipped his hair.

"Don't be a fool, Mälque."

But Mälque had already made up his mind. With a click of his tongue, and boot heels deep into his horse's flanks, he turned away from the tree line and galloped off.

"Stop," Woren shouted as he gave chase. "He'll kill you! Just give me the book and I'll do it."

Mälque urged his horse faster, but they had given him an older animal, and the nag was already frothing at the mouth.

Another glance. Woren was on him.

Mälque whipped the reins against his steed, shouting, pleading for it to go faster. The blow came with no warning and Mälque flew out of the saddle and landed with a thud on the ground. Dazed, he sat up, rubbed the welt rising on the back of his head, felt the blood oozing out, and watched Woren fish out the book. Woren flicked open the cover, one eye on the turning pages, one eye on the bird.

"There you are!"

He grabbed what he had been looking for, threw the book at Mälque's horse, which dashed away, and galloped for the fea dracas den.

Mälque staggered to his feet. His world was a blur of light, sound, motion. A quick glance skyward: the great bird was taking on form: wings beating air, Ela Claire sitting high on his back.

"*Hurry,*" a whisper urged.

Mälque took one step. Two. Three. Four.

"*Faster, little brother, faster!*"

"Vonn," Mälque asked as he managed to work his legs into a jog. And then with sorrow, "Vonn."

Whether the voice was real or something his battered skull conjured, he wasn't sure, but the memory of Vonn dying, and his inability to save him that day stirred Mälque to action. He ignored his throbbing head, blood rolling down his neck, and focused on catching up to Woren. But how does an injured boy catch a horse?

"*Death begets life,*" whispered another voice.

Mälque recognized the whisper: it was the same one that greeted him in Ela Claire's cave; helped with the fea dracas. Was it here to help? Or was it announcing his impending death?

As if to answer, a blast of warm, salty air rushed past Mälque. The wind grew to hurricane force and slapped Woren out of the saddle, causing him to roll head over heals across the ground like a rag doll. When he came to a stop, he staggered to his feet, noted Mälque, checked Ela Claire's flight. Injured and favoring his left leg, Woren half-ran, half-skipped for the den.

Mälque was encouraged. Senses were sharper; muscles stronger. He was closing in. He could make out the *whisk whisk* of Woren's trousers rubbing, noted his labored breaths, caught a whiff of his sweat, his glances back.

Mälque knew it was now or never. He dug deep for more speed, closed the gap and grabbed Woren's right shoulder. Woren, anticipating as much, spun and swept the dagger. Mälque ducked and Woren brought his good knee up. Mälque caught the blow with his right cheek. Something cracked. Something like fire burned across his face. Neck. Shoulder. Bees, or fea dracas he imagined, buzzed his right ear. And something like night swallowed him whole.

When he came to, he was on his back, staring up at Woren straddling the log, head just below the shield. He had loosened the daggers and the shield rattled as if covering a boiling pot, but Mälque knew there wasn't water or stew bubbling inside.

Woren dangled Ela Claire's hair before the groping claws and leering sapphire eyes. Mälque sat up; waves of nausea rolled over him, the taste of blood thick on his tongue. He squinted, trying to squeeze the three images he was seeing into one. Vision sharpened and the sun caught the strand. It shimmered like a golden thread.

The tiny dragons snatched it and Woren went to work sawing one of the leather straps with his dagger. The shield loosened, and it bounced, wobbled, chimed like a crazed gong. Beasts pushed, clawed, gnawed at the steel, the tree. Splinters flew off in every direction. Dust, like vapors from a volcano, billowed out of the den as wings beat with frenzy.

The leather strap stretched, the cut became a V, now wider, now taut as sinew. Woren slithered to the ground and something like thunder exploded out of the tree.

DeMorley carried Lolling on his back. Tiny arms dangled over his shoulder, swaying in time to his steps; head beside his neck, breath soft and warm, coming at easy intervals, a pattern he associated with a ballad: slow and relaxed; tender and sweet.

Sleep, my forever child, sleep.

He checked on the children following him down the creek bed. Limestone and slate littered their path; a maze of stone that wobbled or toppled or rolled when stepped on. The going was slow. Most of the children held hands, tiptoeing from rock to rock, adjusting their balance when a rock slid, flipped, seesawed. The sure-footed ones took broad steps, eyes glued on the rocks, pace matching his. And then there were the four jokesters who, as he had observed since their escape from cell Number 17, made a game out of everything. Today, it was a game of tag. Like field mice, they scampered up the embankment, down, around stragglers; slate chiming, cracking, clanging; dust rolling, billowing.

"Stop it," DeMorley half-shouted. "You're making too much noise!"

The group fell silent, gave each other a parting shove, and fell in line.

Lolling stirred. "Song?"

The Bellini, hanging off one shoulder like a quiver, nudged DeMorley's thigh as if in response to her request. He wanted nothing more than to gather the children, finger the strings; serenade them with music to forget, if only for a moment, that two Gor Kings were on the hunt. He shook off the sentiment and kept on walking. "Not now," he cooed as he shuffled her into a more comfortable positon on his back. "Soon. I promise."

He checked on Previn and Ela Claire overhead. Previn's wings were outstretched: gliding, circling, hunting. Was it a good sign? Yes, yes indeed. Nothing spotted; nothing to fear. Yet.

He focused on the meandering creek bed. It was more like a gorge: wider than two wagons with steep embankments concealing them from view. But the camouflaged ravine came with a price: sunlight reflected off sand and stone, and with no breeze, it felt like they were marching through an oven. Sweat streamed off his brow, pooled beneath Lolling, rolled down legs, arms.

A commotion up ahead took his mind off his parched lips. Rounding the corner, slipping and sliding as they ran, were the three storytellers Ela Claire posted as scouts. Panic made moons out of their eyes; quick glances tossed back at whatever was hot on their heels.

DeMorley checked on Previn. *Gone.* Where? When?

Uproar from behind him took his mind off the questions and made him spin around for a look.

Ballin and the remaining storytellers were running toward them shouting warnings, waving arms, desperation etched across their faces. And then DeMorley felt it, rising through his boots: a shudder. Waves of vibrations, growing in intensity, made the surrounding stones chime warnings. A rumble peeled above the screaming children like a deep drum beat; hundreds of drum beats. His eyes filled with horror, looking like balloons about to pop.

"Get out!" He took Lolling in his hands and shoved her up the embankment. Little feet dug, kicking sand and debris in his face and eyes. She pulled herself up and their gaze locked.

"Catch," he tossed her the Bellini and caught her troubled look. "Don't worry. I'll be there in a flash."

The others had already started climbing, frantic to escape the corridor that, only moments before, offered protection. But why hadn't Ela Claire spied the trouble? Why wasn't she telling a story to save them?

DeMorley pushed aside the nagging questions and helped a boy struggling up the bank. DeMorley pushed and the boy grabbed roots and managed his escape.

Whatever was charging up the creek bed was closer: the ground shook; small avalanches of sand and shale landed on DeMorley's boots. He shook off his fear and focused on pushing the last boy up to the hands reaching down. They pulled him to safety and then gestured, shouted for DeMorley to hurry.

DeMorley grabbed a root, and hand over hand, dug, clawed, pulled his way up. He was almost to the top when a handhold gave way and he slipped back down. He hung on the side of the embankment and stared down the gorge.

Someone grabbed his forearm. Ballin, leaning head first with arms fully extended, had grabbed hold of his arm with both hands.

"Got him," Ballin shouted back to those holding his legs. "Now pull!"

DeMorley inched upward, and when he got his footing, scurried over the top as the flood of hooves, leather and armor rushed around the bends.

"To the tree line," he ordered as he scooped up Lolling who clutched the Bellini to her chest like a doll.

As DeMorley led them across the field, he tossed a quick glance up to find Previn. Nothing.

He shouted encouragement to the children but the cavalry drowned out his voice.

The black haze zoomed upward, dark edges folding inward, rolling like storm clouds, stretching, splitting, now coming together.

Previn recognized the cloud's true identity. "Fea dracas!"

Ela Claire could just make out their flickering blue eyes, like countless stars, that even from afar were mesmerizing, lulling her to dream.

She shook off the spell and was troubled by another quandary: How did they miss catching their scent or that of the boy and the Ebonite?

A sinking feeling came over her, but before she could attack or warn the children, the storytellers flooded her mind in the silent tongue.

"Cavalry? But Ela Claire should have spotted them…"

"Just run!"

"But we're supposed to tell a story, aren't we?"

"There's no time! We have to warn the others!"

Ela Claire leaned out over Previn to investigate. DeMorley and the storytellers were helping the others out of the creek bed. Out of the corner of her eyes she saw dust clouds sweeping up either end of the gorge.

She was about to call to the storytellers when Previn banked right and it was all she could do to hold on.

Fea dracas zipped past, claws just missing her face. She leaned forward and clung to Previn who was taking drastic measures to outrun the attack: corkscrew, now a steep climb, dive, bank left, right, now a barrel roll. Despite his maneuvers, the fea dracas were hot on their tail.

She checked on the children: free of the gorge, they were dashing across the field toward a distant tree line. Clambering up the embankment was the cavalry.

"I can't save us both," she told Previn in the silent tongue as he banked right, left.

"Destroy the fea dracas. Then we can attack the cavalry."

"But…"

"I can't outrun them! Without you, the children are doomed. Now hold on and lean close just like we practiced; we only have one chance at this."

Previn dove, leveled, and increased his speed.

The swarm tightened their formation, zeroing in on Ela Claire's scent with jaws snapping, shrieks louder.

"Now!"

Previn cupped his wings and caught the wind like the main sails of a ship. Ela Claire held on with all her might as they went from full speed to a stop.

The swarm, caught off guard by the tactic, soared past, claws gracing hair, cape, feathers. Ela Claire focused on the bevy and released her tale.

Mälque thought it looked like snow, black snow, spiraling from the sky, landing beside him on the ground.

He caught several flakes in his palm and after a moment to look them over, blew on them. The fea dracas ash disintegrated and flitted into nothingness.

A smile crept over his bloody, swollen face. Ela Claire's aerial battle had been a marvel to behold. The bird was magnificent, flying faster than he imagined and performing maneuvers that, at times, were difficult to follow from where he sat. But the fea dracas were equally quick and nimble and Mälque feared the worst until the bird came to a stop, a remarkable feat to behold, and Ela Claire unleashed a story, at least that's what he concluded since the fea dracas disappeared in a flash of light.

Mälque had expected flames to shoot out of her mouth or billows of blue steam or a flurry of orange sparks zipping like arrows at her prey. But all he witnessed was a blaze of light that enveloped the fea dracas followed by what sounded like dry leaves burning in an inferno. And then the sky was filled with black snow and he got a whiff of charred flesh.

Mälque tried to get up, but the moment he got to his knees, everything started spinning and he toppled over. Somewhere beyond his topsy-turvy world armor rattled, children screamed, horses whinnied, the great bird cawed. But all he could think about was her book.

"Ain't nothin' but dyin' everywhere."

"But ya can change that, little brother. Go get her book."

"Can't. Too beat up."

"Beat up? Ya ain't no worse than when Olke slapped ya around. Now get goin'."

"But I don't know where it is."

"I do. Now quit whinin' and go!"

Mälque, on hands and knees, made his way through the grass, searching for her book, being led by a whisper, wondering if his dead brother's voice was proof he was going mad.

DeMorley clutched Lolling to his chest and ran for the trees.

"Let's stay together," he shouted to those sprinting ahead but either they couldn't hear him above the noise or had seen the cavalry and were running for their lives.

DeMorley kept running and glanced over his shoulder at those falling behind. "Hurry! Faster! You can make it!"

But the thundering hooves and the dust cloud from the cavalry line told him otherwise.

"Look," a girl running beside him said. "They stopped."

DeMorley turned his attention back to the sprinters. They were huddled in a circle and were gesturing at the tree line. One of the boys turned their way and cupped his mouth.

"Cavalry!"

The sprinters turned on their heels and raced back toward DeMorley as a wave of horses emerged from the shadows. At the center of the charge was their leader: a colossus holding a blue sword and wearing a gor skull for a helmet.

Previn soared through the ashen remains of the fea dracas and banked so Ela Claire had a better angle to help the children.

What she saw made her heart sink. The cavalry from the creek bed had surrounded DeMorley's group. Another wave of riders, coming from the tree line, were pressing forward. In their midst was an all too familiar warrior.

The Gor King.

She steeled herself, nocked the syllable of the first word like an arrow, and closed her eyes to tell the tale. Instead of hearing her waltz or getting a vision of Marsien Vur and the Only, she lost focus. The words tumbled end over end from her thoughts as if she had been tripped and they were knocked from her grip.

Startled, she stole a peek at the Gor King. He was wagging a finger at her.

Was he preventing her from telling a story? If so, how?

More determined than ever, she squeezed her eyes shut and focused on the tale, but as before, words blurred, syllables fell into blackness, verses faded away. She glared back at him and he gestured at the children. A handful of boys and girls were being held captive in the back of a wagon. Daggers, held across their throats, glinted in the sunlight. Two faces she recognized: Ballin and Lolling.

"Previn, what should I do?"

He understood her predicament: she couldn't split her story to contend with the various fronts.

If she destroyed the Gor King first, the men in the wagon would slice the children's throats before she could save them.

And if she attacked the men in the wagon, the Gor King would slaughter DeMorley and the others.

The Gor King motioned with his blue sword at the ground.

"He wants us to land," Previn noted.

"And do what, surrender?"

"I don't like it anymore than you do, but at least we'll be together and might be afforded an opportunity to fight or flee. Right now, I don't see any other options. Do you?"

Ela Claire searched the sky for Manno Vox, listened for a lark-like whisper, and waited for the warm winds of Claire to blow.

Nothing happened.

"Previn, where is the Only? Why isn't he helping?"

"I don't know."

"And how did we miss the scent of the Gor King and his army? And why am I unable to tell a story?"

"Mysteries I too long to understand, but we can't lose hope."

"So surrender is our hope? They'll kill us."

"If that were the case, they would have done so already."

"Are you forgetting the fea dracas?"

"No. I think they were a diversionary ploy to get us away from the children and the Gor King's cavalry. And as you can see, the tactic worked. For reasons I can't fathom, he wants you and me."

"Why?"

"Perhaps to join his forces. You are a storyteller and I offer an aerial supremacy he is lacking."

He banked, dropped in altitude, and flew over the army and children to inspect before making their final decision. The children appeared to be unharmed while the warriors, not certain if she was attacking or not, rattled their swords while the men holding the children in the wagon pressed the daggers tighter.

Previn spotted an open area near the wagon and circled back for a landing. He glided down, and the moment he touched ground, four of the Gor King's riders lassoed his talons and neck. He cawed and snapped at the ropes, tossing Ela Claire about as he thrashed, but the horses dug in and the ropes were too strong.

Previn, realizing there was no way to escape, folded his wings and nestled to the ground. Additional ropes were crisscrossed over him, tightened, and staked to the ground.

Ela Claire, who had avoided being snagged by the ropes, eyed her captors that had formed a large circle around them. Two riders were galloping her way. Off to one side was the wagon; nearby, DeMorley and the others.

Her gaze came to rest on the Gor King and an older warrior that she recognized as the Ebonite they had seen by the fea dracas tree. No doubt he was the same one they'd seen on the cliff.

But where's the boy?

The two riders stopped on either side of her and glared at her, their hands resting on their pommels.

"Vow to never tell a story," Woren advised, "and we promise no harm will come to the children."

Previn attempted to lift his head but was too restrained, so he cawed out to her. "Death begets life."

Her brow furrowed. Did he imply she was to use a story, no matter the cost of lives, and win the day? Or was he simply trying to encourage her to press on despite being a prisoner? She wasn't sure.

Before she could question him, the riders gestured for her to dismount. She slid off, but instead of cowering before them or standing at attention, she headed for the wagon. The two riders drew their swords but the Gor King waved them off and the weapons slid back into sheaths.

"You will find," Woren called after her, "that not one hair has been touched."

"I'll make that call."

"Suit yourself." There was ridicule in Woren's voice. "But I must warn you: no trickery."

She kept her gaze focused on DeMorley, the children in the wagon, and ignored the catcalls, the spittle, the curses coming from the army. She reached DeMorley; his hands were bound behind his back and the Bellini dangled from his neck. She met his somber expression. He shook his head and gave a dramatic sigh.

"This isn't your fault," she consoled.

He bit his lower lip and stared at the wagon.

She followed his line of sight.

"It's okay," she consoled the children. "I'm with you now."

The warriors tightened their hold and pressed daggers against young throats. Her gaze hopped to the warrior holding Ballin. He was a barrel chested warrior with a tiny pewter helmet on his sheared crown. He scowled at her and continued flicking the beef jerky he was chewing from one side of his mouth to the other. She met his gaze unwavering before turning her attention to Ballin. There was determination in his eyes.

"*Why'd you land,*" he asked in the silent tongue.

"*We had no choice.*"

"*They're gonna kill us anyway.*"

"*You don't know that. Now that I'm with you, we can work together and...*"

Hoffrader drew the blade across Ballin's throat and he screamed; blood oozed down his neck.

"No," she screamed.

"I warned you," Woren shouted at her. "No trickery."

She fired a hot look at Woren and the Gor King and sucked in big gulps of air, furious, on the edge of unleashing a story to end it all. Reason returned and she released her rage by clenching then unclenching her fists. Her eyes, now slits of fury, settled on the warrior holding Ballin.

"Only a flesh wound," he gloated. "Next time I'll open his throat."

Ballin's expression begged her to tell a story even if it meant they'd die. She reached out a hand to comfort him, which made Hoffrader press the weapon harder. Ballin winced but refused to cry or beg for mercy. She lowered her hand and Hoffrader relaxed.

Next to Hoffrader was Gruun holding Lolling off the ground with one arm. Gruun pressed the knife into her throat and squeezed her. Lolling whimpered, grimaced. Ela Claire glowered at Gruun but he didn't bat a green eye and tightened his hold until Lolling cried.

"That's enough," Ela Claire ordered.

"It'll be enough," Woren fired, "when you vow not to tell a story."

Lolling wriggled, kicked, round face now red, tears rolling. Gruun held fast, eyes like green ice, unmoved by either Lolling's pleas or Ela Claire's presence.

"What more do you want," she shouted over her shoulder to Woren. "Previn and I landed. We surrendered."

"Vow!"

Lolling choked; staccato bursts desperate for air, eyes searching for DeMorley, now Ela Claire.

"Okay! I vow."

Gruun's eyes shifted to take in the Gor King. And although Ela Claire refused to take her eyes off Lolling, she judged by Gruun's relaxed grip that her promise had been accepted.

Satisfied that the children were safe, at least for now, she glanced skyward in hope of seeing Manno Vox racing to their rescue, or catch the soft refrain of her waltz, or feel the warm winds of Claire brush her cheek. But the blue skies were empty and quiet and still.

The tranquility troubled her. It wasn't like her experiences sipping tea beside the fire or reading Il-Lilliad's books. This lull put her senses on edge, made her skin crawl, as if it were the calm before the storm or the precursor to a dark dream.

She turned on her heel, threw caution to the wind, and marched for the one she held responsible for the deceptive serenity.

"What kind of man," she fired at the Gor King, "amasses an army of criminals and madmen? That bullies and threatens children? That let's an old Ebonite talk on his behalf?"

The Gor King slapped the reins across the neck of his warhorse and charged. Ela Claire stopped and eyed the hooves chewing up sod, caught the hoopla from the warriors cheering on their champion, detected the screams and pleas from the children, DeMorley, Previn. But her mind was made up; she was going to end this one way or another. She headed straight for the charging horse.

The Gor King raced for her, and at the last possible moment, pulled up short of running her down.

Ela Claire planted her feet, crossed her arms and glowered at him. Despite her tough demeanor, her heart raced and she felt sick to her stomach from the ordeal.

The Gor King unsheathed his blue sword which incited his men to war shouts.

She took a step back, regained her nerve, and reclaimed the ground. She did her best not to shudder when noting the blade, his ghoulish white helmet, his black eye sockets.

The Gor King brought the blade forward, slowly, and placed the tip beneath her chin and tilted her face upward. He cocked his head and studied her. Then, with one swift motion, swatted her thigh with the flat of his sword.

She winced and bit her lip to suppress her pain and not give him the satisfaction of seeing her cry. She rubbed the welt rising beneath her white dress, and was about to try and tell a story of destruction when a commotion made her turn to investigate.

Two warriors were making their way into the circle dragging a boy by his armpits. His legs trailed through the grass and his head hung limp; greasy hair, matted with blood, swung back and forth.

"We found him crawlin' away."

They heaved Mälque to the ground in front of the Gor King. The boy didn't move a muscle and Ela Claire thought he was dead. Mälque groaned and pushed himself up to his knees, wobbled to and fro, and eyed Ela Claire.

She covered her mouth to conceal her shock. The right side of his face - black and blue and stained with dried blood - was so swollen that he was unable to open his eye. His good eye widened with recognition at seeing her and he worked his lips to talk.

"I tried," he mumbled as fresh blood oozed from the corner of his mouth. Mälque eyed the Gor King, spat out blood, and gave him a hot look. "Ain't nothin' but dyin' everywhere."

The warrior closest to Mälque kicked him to the ground and pressed a boot into his back, blade at the ready should the Gor King give the order.

"Be quick about it," Mälque gurgled, bloody spittle flying from his lips.

"Enough of this!" Ela Claire positioned herself between Mälque and the Gor King. "He's only a boy."

"No," Woren corrected as his horse lumbered to the Gor King's side.

"He's just a Wurmlin, and a superstitious one at that. But he's the best tracker I've ever seen. Even found you, m'lady." He offered her a mock bow.

"Discovered a strand of your hair in your cave and tracked you all the way to the Gilden Sea. Once you got ashore near the Isle of Rhythe, he watched you, studied you, like you were some animal to be hunted...or a girl to woo."

Mälque noted the hurt, the mistrust, welling up in Ela Claire's brown eyes. But didn't she know he tried to save her from the fea dracas? That a whisper, perhaps the same one that called her name, led him to her trail, even offered sage advice when his life depended on it? That tucked inside his tunic, hidden from all, was her book?

Ela Claire shook her head in disgust and spun around to look at Woren. "As true as that may be, I'm certain he was ordered to do so. Am I correct?"

Woren snickered, rubbed his chin, and gave her a shrug. "Semantics. But then again, I'm just an *old* Ebonite and forget the simplest of things." He gave her a smug look.

"And his wounds," she took in Mälque's haggard face. "Are a result of his allegiance to this plan?"

Woren let his smile fall. "Those are the marks of an insolent soldier."

"He's just a boy."

"Not any longer." Then to the warrior with his boot planted on Mälque, "Get him up. We'll deal with him later."

The soldier sheathed his weapon, gestured to his friend, and they yanked Mälque to his feet.

Ela Claire considered reading Mälque's story, intrigued to know what made him join an outfit like the Gor King's. But if the Gor King could listen in, something that seemed more and more feasible, he would discover her tactic and possibly execute them on the spot.

She turned her attention back to Woren. "Now that we've surrendered." She flicked her head at Previn tethered to the ground. "Let the children go, including him." She gestured back at Mälque.

Woren snickered. "My dear storyteller, the children are our incentive to keep you from breaking your vow. Why would we let them go?"

"As an act of mercy."

Woren's eyes narrowed. He quoted an old Ebonite proverb: "Mercy is the bastard child of peaceful men."

She ground her teeth. "But we refuse to help you, your army, or *him*." She glared at the Gor King.

Woren nodded to her terms. "Naturally."

"So what *are* you going to do; kill us?"

Woren burst out laughing. "Kill you? After all we've been through to capture you?"

He let the moment hang.

"You still haven't figured it out yet, have you?"

Her brow furrowed.

Woren took in Mälque. "You know, don't you, yung-er?"

Ela Claire spun to check on Mälque. He was blinking his good eye, whether to clear dust or signal a warning or dredge up the courage to speak, she could only guess.

Woren continued to press Mälque. "We never told you that part of the plan, did we? But you were too smart for your own good and put two and two together, which explains your defiance at the fea dracas den and your *feelings* for her."

Mälque blushed and looked away.

"Well, go on, yung-er, tell her!"

Mälque wanted to explain himself to her, wanted to help her flee, wanted to defend her honor, but knew he had failed at all three. He licked his swollen lips and took in her face.

"The Gor King has chosen his queen."

Her eyes widened. Fear? Longing? Panic?

Crestfallen, he finished.

"You."

GLOSSARY

Characters

Anessatia: Lassiter's mother; grand-daughter of King Culdean.

Areall: Elabea's mother; married to Quinn.

Ballin. An Ebonite boy; Isle of Rhythm; a storyteller.

Brairtok: Lord/king of Ebon.

Bruun: Phinnton's father.

Council: Dark lords of the Cauldron; seers and overseers of Ebon's power.

Culdean: King Simeion's oldest son; heir to the throne.

Daryess: Galadin's mother; married to Gundin.

DeMorley: Minstrel who joins Newcomb and Lassiter to Claire.

Digri: Jolly, short chef of MerriNoon.

Draemel: Bounty hunter in pursuit of DeMorley.

Elabea: Journeys to Claire with Galadin.

Ela Claire: Elabea's new name as a storyteller; given to her by the King of Claire.

Farron: Draemel's son.

Friarlinn: King Simeion's youngest son; murders his brother to become king.

Galadin: Elabea's friend; superb huntsman; assists her on her trek to Claire. Becomes Romlin.

Gor King: Paradin after making an alliance with the Cauldron and a vul jen.

Gruun: Tristanite warrior for the Gor King; nickname: dragon; born in Draiglore-birthplace of dragons.

Gundin: Great warrior; father of Galadin; married to Daryess.

Hinnmith: Ebonite commander.

Hoffrader: Ingloid warrior for the Gor King; nickname: bull gor.

Hornlynn: Lassiter's father; married to Anessatia; died in the Dark War.

Il-Lilliad: One of the last storytellers; survived the March of Reeds massacre.

King Cameare: Sovereign of Sri Brune; Kinmin's father.

King of Claire: Enigmatic ruler of Claire; also known as the Only.

King Simeion: Once great king of Allsbruth.

Kinmin: Tiny, dark skinned SriBrunian; escorts Il-Lilliad to SriBrune.

Kundle: Ebonite Commander; defeated at Thornnblen.

Korvik: Phinnton's mother; Ebonite by birth.

Lassiter: Hornlynn and Anessatia's son; mentored by Newcomb.

Linwith: Quinn's older brother; See "Worm Master."

Lolling. An Ingloid of 4 summers; ripped from her cottage by Ebonites; flown to the Isle of Rhythe by vul jens; her mind never to mature past that of a child.

Mälque: Wurmlin boy of 13 summers; brother to Vonn; acquired by Gor King to find Ela Claire.

Manno Vox: One of the Only's mighty warriors.

Matralene: maiden of the Slaughtered Sow; flirts with Lassiter.

Merriam: Draemel's wife; lives in Hoitt.

Mithe: Old widow of Hetherlinn.

Newcomb: Lassiter's mentor; storyteller.

Olke: Wurmlin cousin/mentor to Mälque and Vonn. 42 summers of age.

Paradin: Draemel's partner.

Phinnton: Hetherlinn boy; mother sang about the Singing Stones of Addoli. Future storyteller.

Queen Riaa: queen of Sri Brune; Kinmin's mother.

Quinn: Great leader of Allsbruth; Elabea's father; married to Areall.

Romlin: Galadin's new name given to him by Manno Vox.

Rittmar: Bee-like creature; chancellor for the nation of Bal-Malin.

TyNorai: Chancellor of Aggellon; former storyteller of the Only.

Vonn: Wurmlin boy of 16 summers; brother to Mälque; killed by Olke.

Woren: commanding general for the Gor King; Ebonite.

Countries, Places & Cities

Addoli Ridge: Mountain separating the Gilden Sea from the Gilden Plains.

Aggellon: A timeless nation in the Onderling.

Allsbruth: Beautiful, tranquil land; home of Elabea/Galadin.

Bal-Malin: Island nation inhabited by insect-like creatures and worms.

Blomseth: Village where Lassiter performs as a minstrel.

Caace: Veil/portal from Sri Brune into the upper world.

Cauldron: Perpetual fires of Ebon; housed in the citadel of Netniath.

Cave of Freers: Lair of the four vul jens; located in mountains of Ebon.

Claire: Nation reportedly destroyed in the Dark War; home to storytellers.

Cor len Bluun: "Pools of tear" in Claire.

Correll: River that flows from Karajan into Sri Brune.

DioBaith: Stone monolith beyond the veil; scene of Romlin's fall into the River Arrgient.

Ebon: Victors of the Dark War.

Ferra: Nation due east of Allsbruth; Torrens Bay is on its southern coast.

Gilden Plains: Enormous grassy plain; home to Min Brock.

Gilden Sea: Northern sea where the island of Bal-Malin is located.

Hetherlinn: Village in Allsbruth; home to Elabea and Galadin.

Hoitt: Fishing village in Ingloid; Draemel's home.

Ingloid: Nation east of the Gilden Plains.

Isle of Lills: Island in the Sea of Illsbruth; Lassiter was mentored by Newcomb.

Isle of Rythe: "Island of the cursed" off the east coast of Ebon; where Ela Claire is to journey to retrieve stolen treasures.

Karajan: Cavernous lake that guards entrance into Sri Brune.

Kiarrey Glen: Meadow in Claire where Romlin meets the King of Claire.

Kise: Capital city of Ebon; home to the Cauldron.

Marsien Vur: Fortress of the King of Claire.

MerriNoons: Digri's country; noted as excellent chefs.

Min Brock: Once great citadel of Allsbruth; turning point in the Dark War.

Netniath: Citadel for the Cauldron; located in the city of Kise.

Norrburn: Village near the Gilden Sea; location Lassiter learns of the Martyr's Moon.

Onderling: Underground world; home to Aggellon and SriBrune.

Pillar of Addoli: Monolith beside the Addoli Ridge.

River Arrgient: Main tributary west of the Gilden Plains.

Torrens Bay: Southern port town of Ferra; exciting yet corrupt.

Thornnblen: Beach where Ela Claire defeats Ebonites.

Tristan: Nation noted for mining ore and forging weapons.

Sea of Illsbruth: Southern sea; home to karshe and the Isle of Lills.

SriBrune: Kinmin's homeland; located within the Onderling.

Valley of Clouds: Near Waelryth; home to ryators.

Vorak: Brairtok's castle in Kise.

Waelryth: Passage created by the Cauldron to invade Allsbruth.

Worm Master: Linwith's new title; rules over the seven worms of Bal-Malin.

Creatures

Bangaleers: Crab-like creatures of Waelryth; latch upon their victim's face.

Bar-Treb: Romlin's steed from Claire.

Fea dracas: "Little dragons" that live in the hollow of trees.

Fingals: Tiny, shiny creatures in the Onderling; noted for not being very intelligent creatures.

Dansel lors: Large predators that live in Karajan.

Demoliths: *Man-dragons* of Ebon. Created by vul jens entering the dreamworlds of Ebonite warriors.

Draiggs: Round, flat creatures that guard Cor len Bluun.

Gors: Large, hairy scavengers.

Karshe: Silver-plated dragons in the Sea of Illsbruth.

Kodars: Massive Ebonite animals used to transport troops.

La-zeer: Predator from the Gilden Sea.

Previn: Ela Claire's harrier; formerly her rusk.

Rusk: Small animal that defends storytellers; very poisonous tail.

Ryators: Giant, translucent dragons that live in the Valley of Clouds.

Sevritt: Large, swift Ebonite tracker.

Vul jen: Large, dark, dreamstalker; favorite prey is storytellers.

Worms: Mysterious creatures that live on Bal-Malin.

Worm King: The sapphire worm from Bal-Malin.